SPINNING

DIXIE

ERIC DEZENHALL

THOMAS DUNNE BOOKS ♏ St. Martin's Press New York

This is a work of fiction. All of the characters, organizations, and events portrayed in this novel are either products of the author's imagination or are used fictitiously.

THOMAS DUNNE BOOKS.
An imprint of St. Martin's Press.

www.thomasdunnebooks.com
www.stmartins.com

Library of Congress Cataloging-in-Publication Data is available upon request.

ISBN-13: 978-0-312-34063-6
ISBN-10: 0-312-34063-X

First Edition: January 2007

10   9   8   7   6   5   4   3   2   1

FOR MY GRANDMOTHER

MARY "GIGI" BYER

(1913–2001)

After telling my grandmother a story when I was young, I overheard her say, "That boy has some peculiar imagination on him." I don't think she meant it as a compliment, because she added, "I just hope there's some common sense in that head."

My grandmother, "Gigi," was onto something. I started writing *Spinning Dixie* in 1980 when I was eighteen. Twenty-seven years of daydreaming later, it's here, so I hope you will take my grandmother's assessment of my credibility into account when reading this tall tale.

For the record, Rattle & Snap is a real plantation in Mt. Pleasant, Tennessee, that is listed in the National Registry of Historical Places. It was once owned by the indomitable Polk family, but none of the "Polks" (or Hilliards) who appear as live characters in this fictional tale are based on their descendants. The Polks have not owned Rattle & Snap since 1867. I was born ninety-five years later in New Jersey, so our paths never crossed.

Nor is this novel a coy attempt to portray any of the families that have owned and cared for the plantation since that time. My storytelling method inserts fictional characters into historical events and places. None of my relatives in New Jersey, for example, can remember the Civil War, but my scholarly research indicates that it totally happened. On occasion, however, I altered recollections of historical events to suit my storytelling.

I owe my discovery of Rattle & Snap to one of the South's stalwart daughters and her fine Tennessee family, who opened my eyes to another America when we were all so much younger.

For a more accurate portrayal of my actual life and heritage, I refer readers to Margaret Mitchell's *Gone with the Wind*. It is widely believed (by a roommate from my "special time away") that Rhett Butler was modeled on me, probably because we have both been known to stand around telling people we don't give a damn.

E.B.D.
Washington, D.C.
2006

It was one of those tragic loves doomed for lack of money, and one day the girl closed it out on the basis of common sense.

—F. SCOTT FITZGERALD, *The Crack-up*

I wonder how many miles I've fallen by this time? . . . I wonder what Lattitude and Longitude I've gone to?

—LEWIS CARROLL, *Alice in Wonderland*

PART ONE

RIPTIDE

APRIL 2005, WASHINGTON, D.C.

Omnia vestigia retrorsum

(All footsteps turn back upon themselves)

People ask me how a boy who was raised by a mobster grew up to become press secretary to the president of the United States. The answer is, when reporters started hammering me with questions about my pedigree, I did something sly that caught the Washington press corps off guard: I admitted everything.

THE TIMES: Jonah, is it true that upon the death of your grandfather, Mickey Price, you attended a Mafia summit?
ME: Who do you think called the meeting?

FOLLOW-UP: Would you say your relationship with Mr. Price was of the conventional see-Grandpop-on-Sunday kind?
ME: It was the opposite of conventional. He and my grandmother virtually raised me after my parents died. They were my best friends.

GLOBAL WIRE SERVICE: Mr. Eastman, it's been rumored that you arranged for the murder of a mob figure who was said to have crossed you?
ME: Absolutely not. I handled it personally.

As Henry Kissinger once said (but did not abide), "What will come out eventually must come out immediately." People were stunned by my answers. Sure, I was using candor as a spin device, but Washington

found it "refreshing." Washington likes to think it finds candor refreshing, but honesty in this town is a novelty mint, not sustenance.

Nevertheless, the same frankness and irreverence that had been the
"Jonah Eastman brand" for the last two years of the Truitt administration had finally become my undoing. I was fired this morning.

Before I took my job as the president's spokesman, I had been a
Republican pollster. I specialized in handling difficult elections, ones
that needed an unconventional boost. And, yes, my grandfather was
the late Moses "Mickey" Price, the Atlantic City gangster known as
"the Wizard of Odds."

Despite its Nixonian whiff, let me be perfectly clear about something: I am not a gangster. My Edie wouldn't have married a gangster,
but she wouldn't have married a choirboy either. She had choices and,
at some level, knew what she was doing. I couldn't have gotten to the
White House being a cherub, and some of the runoff from Mickey's
jungle of shadows had crept into my frequency. While I am tempted
to reinvent myself for the reader, I am no more immune from my environment than the minor prophet with whom I share a name, the
one in the Bible who tried to run from God and was swallowed by a
big fish. Jonah was chosen by God to be in a sea of trouble, and in my
more philosophical moments, I believe I was genetically predisposed
to scandal. Anyhow, spinning at this stage would be a lie that runs
counter to the spirit of my forced retirement from the lying business.

Officially, I wasn't fired. I resigned. I did so after a few unfortunate
catalysts put me in play. It began when the head of the Republican
Party declared the current recession to be a "communications problem." As press secretary, communications strategy fell under my
purview. Then there was The Remark.

I made The Remark two days ago during a press conference after a
suicide bomber—an erstwhile taxi driver from Yemen—blew himself
up at a Phillies game, killing twenty-four people. Even though I was
technically a New Jerseyan, Philadelphia was the provenance of my
"hometown" sports teams. When asked by the White House correspondent for *The Philadelphia Bulletin* how I felt about the attack as a

man who hailed from the region, I said, "It's hard to believe Western civilization is going to be taken down by a bunch of cabdrivers."

To make matters worse, a network correspondent aboard Air Force One claimed to have overheard the president bark, "Aw, hell, we *always* negotiate with terrorists," in a discussion about potential response options. Moments before taking off, the Big Guy had finished giving a speech where he echoed every other recent president with the canard, "We do not negotiate with terrorists." (FIST POUND/CONVEY RESOLVE—PAUSE FOR APPLAUSE)

The president totally said it, too. I was standing right next to him. Like the Secret Service agent who is trained to throw his body into the line of an assassin's bullet, I defused a potential crapstorm by instinctively telling the correspondent that I had made this remark, too. I was known for doing a mean Truitt impersonation—the molasses Mississippi drawl, literary allusions, tractor-seat wisdom. The network, terrified of a White House freeze-out, agreed to make me the lightning rod.

The feelings of having been accused of something you did do and something you didn't do are both terrible, but have different manifestations. When you're wrongly accused, you feel lost in time and space: there's a sensation of motion between dimensions. When you're accused of something you really did, you feel paralyzed and trapped. I was suffering from a hybrid of these symptoms that averaged out at a common state: panic.

The Islamerica League demanded my resignation on the grounds that I had made a racist remark, the implication being that the Truitt administration saw all Muslims as angry cabdrivers. I dug myself in deeper when I attempted to explain that the suicide bomber really *was* a taxi driver. My buddy Dennis Miller rallied to my defense on his talk show by saying I got in trouble "for making comments offensive to terrorists."

Adding to my predicament were the hearings that loomed for the president's nomination to the Supreme Court of R. MacDermott "Mac" Dewey—a conservative, white, Georgia-bred circuit court judge. Some of the same civil liberties people who were hammering me for my insensitive remarks would soon descend upon Washington to protest the Dewey nomination. Canning me wouldn't neutralize this challenge, but it would be a symbolic gesture to Democratic senators who were reluctant to turn a blind eye toward an administration they regarded as being an enemy of the progressive cause.

My assistant, Tigger, came into my office, which is in the West Wing of the White House (Coordinates—longitude −77.03740; latitude 38.89766)* facing Pennsylvania Avenue. She wore a quizzical expression. Her real name was Alison, but she revved in a reckless exuberance like Winnie-the-Pooh's tiger buddy, so I called her Tigger. In an environment where most staffers sought job preservation by taking no risks, Tigger was oblivious to the consequences of anything. She was my figurative sister, aide-de-camp, and personal social worker in one whippet-thin Chanel-suited vortex. What she lacked in subtlety, she made up for in devotion. (In Washington, if given the choice between genius or loyalty, choose loyalty.)

"Hey, Wonderboy, there's an envelope for you at the northwest gate," she said, quizzically. A *Who's Who in the Truitt Administration* fell off my bookshelf onto the floor. Tigger recoiled as if this had never happened before, but every time she came in, something fell.

I glanced up from my computer screen, which was spitting out all of the reporters I had to call back. *Everybody wants the J-man to trash the president for canning him.*

"Tigger, I don't mean to sound like a diva, but since when do I go outside and retrieve envelopes?"

"The thing is, Jonah, I went out to get it myself, and, uh, *she*"— Tigger drew out the *she*—"said she needed to give it to you yourself. It seems personal." Tigger bit her lip suggestively. She knew I was a married straight arrow with kids, but she had worked for politicians long

---

*Ever since my parents died when I was very young, I've been obsessed with knowing precisely where I am.

enough to know that, well, one never knew, façade being the corner-stone on which political reputations are built.

"Did *she* tell you her name?" I asked.

"She said she had a message from Claudine Polk."

Heat shot up my back. I felt dizzy, and my throat tightened. My heart raced. I was supposed to be the Dark Prince of Cool in the face of hostile data. I had shooting pains in my jaw and arms. Heart attack. Dear God, heart attack. But I exercise and eat right, *how*—?

"Claud—," I managed to half-say. I must have looked like an imbecile. I fell into my chair. "I haven't seen Claudine for twenty-five years. 1980. I was eighteen."

"So, who can it be now?" Tigger asked, singing the question, which was a verse from an early 1980s song by an Aussie band.

"Claudine was a weather system. Something that engulfs you. I mean, you're *in* it. This woman outside, is she my age?" I stood and looked out my window.

"No, Wonderboy. Early twenties I'd say, and . . ." Tigger sighed.

"And what?"

"Ruin-your-life/crash-into-a-tree/light-your-hair-on-fire gorgeous . . . It's the only reason why the Secret Service guy at the gate buzzed me instead of telling her to get lost."

"It's reassuring that our national defense is in the hands of a bunch of adolescents."

The White House's northwest gate was about thirty yards from my office. I could see it from my window. The Secret Service gatehouse blocked my view of a section of Pennsylvania Avenue, and I could not see the mystery courier, just people milling about beyond the gates, and a lone rabbit scurrying among the bushes. Freshly scandal-bait, I wanted to avoid the press corps in the briefing room, so I went out-side the West Wing's main door, the one where the Marine honor guard stands.

It was dusk. There's no more enchanting city in the world than Washington in April at dusk—and, yes, I've been to Paris. It is cool, usually in the seventies, and a misty halo floats beneath the street lamps. I'm not sure what causes the mist, but it's not the humidity yet. Hell doesn't arrive in our nation's capital until May. The sky is a clear azure, flecked with stars slipping across the heavens like fugitive beads of mercury. Politics ceases to be about power, and becomes another excuse for falling stupidly in love. Even if we fail, we still sense our lover-shadow awaits us in Georgetown to fill that bagel hole we all drag around with us.

A few of the camped-out camera crews noticed me, and began to stir. I overheard somebody say, "Riptide." This was the Secret Service call name I was given after I started receiving death threats early in the president's term. My politician's ego had hoped the threats would be traced back to a shadowy foreign revolutionary movement, but I was crushed to learn that my typical nemesis was a constipated retiree in Daytona Beach who had also threatened other people who were on TV.

As I approached the gate, I spied my messenger though the iron bars. She was in profile at first. Her auburn hair was shoulder length, her nose gently sloped—a nose you see in *Vogue*. A ruin-your-life nose. She wore a white sundress, which gave her an otherworldly aura beneath the floating vapor of the street lamp. Lips like a bow, which made me wonder where she kept the arrow. When she turned to me, her green panther eyes narrowed in a challenging way, then quickly softened, opening wide. There appeared to be moisture around her thick lashes. When it comes to women and tears, quantity is an important variable: A few tears make men feel strong; a torrent makes us feel powerless, claustrophobic. Then I thought, April in Washington means allergies. That's what it was.

The thing about an outrageous beauty is that when she acknowledges you, you feel as if you've known her forever. It's the incarnation of the overused term *charisma*—God touching you, leaving out the others. The problem is, when you're in your forties, your baser instincts are derailed by a chronological factor that has its anchor in morality: I was an adult when this *kid* was born.

I felt the concrete go wobbly. My breath was short. Second heart attack in three minutes. I had a family history of fake heart attacks.

The uniformed Secret Service agent buzzed me out of the gate.
"Rattle & Snap," she greeted me. *Raddlinsnap*. Bewitching. Melodic.
Southern. I smelled flowers, but didn't see any.

She handed me a small envelope. I took it. It was embossed:

RATTLE & SNAP

MOUNT PLEASANT, TENNESSEE

I felt my hands tremble, but they appeared to be still.

"It's a Passover greeting," she said. That's right, I remembered.
Passover had just begun. I had lost a sense of the calendar.

"Are you here to liberate me from bondage?" I asked.

"I got you to come out from behind those iron bars, didn't I?"

"Yes, but where are the plagues?"

"No plagues," She of the bow lips said. "You look taller on TV."

"Sorry to disappoint you."

"Oh, I didn't mean it that way." *Thay-at whyy*. That voice. Tell me to
impale myself on the White House gate, and I'll do it. No questions.

"Who are you?" I asked.

"A ghost." She said this in a businesslike manner. But then I caught
a quiver at the side of her lips, and a tiny dimple surfaced. I saw a few
teeth. I wanted one of them.

"Ghosts don't usually drop things off at the White House," I said.
"Although there was that time Millard Fillmore brought me hot pas-
trami on pumpernickel. Which was nice."

The ghost suppressed laughter, and dabbed beneath a perfect nos-
tril with a tissue.

"Are you all right?" I asked.

"Hay fever," she said.

"You weren't crying?"

She waited a beat, then nodded in the negative.

"I have it, too," I said. "Where do ghosts get tissues, anyway? Do
they have haunted Piggly Wiggly stores, Halloween items, antigarlic
lotion for vampires?"

"You're borderline funny."

"And unemployed because of it. The clown goes home alone."

"Then who gets the girl?"

"The strongman. The acrobat. Somebody with no self-awareness."

"I'm not sure about that. I read someplace that you wear a St. Jude medallion."

I showed her the chain. "Patron Saint of Lost Causes. How do you know the Polks?"

"I was asked only to deliver that envelope," she said firmly.

"Was it an easy delivery?"

"Eventful," she said, studying my eyes.

"Mine are green, too," I said. "The eyes. Different shade."

She seemed embarrassed. We were about the same height, and Ghosty's sandals had no heels.

"This is so strange," I said. "Would you wait while I read this? Is that what I am supposed to do?"

She shrugged her shoulders. "Rattle & Snap, sir."

"You've got some sass, don't you?"

"Nobody knows where I got it."

"Well, Ghosty, I know Rattle & Snap is a plantation." By plantation, I didn't mean some nouveau riche development of tract mansions riddled with social-climbing orthodontists calling itself The Plantation. I meant the kind of place that God had set aside long ago for the fleeting use of American nobles.

"Look—" Stall her, Jonah. "Would you like to come into the White House? We've got cable." I felt like a child molester. Still, she'd have to show her identification to get in, which might help with the whole Who-Is-She thing. She said no.

Several tourists walked by and recognized me. I heard one of them say my name. The ghost overheard it, and nodded warmly, as if to say, *And I'm with him.* I liked it, and I wished I had this job when I was single.

Ghosty saw my confusion as I studied the envelope, and she appeared to be pained. She began walking away. A few of the network camera guys sidled closer from the other side of the gate. Not good. I took a few steps to follow her, but a disgraced White House press secretary chasing a Victoria's Secret model down Pennsylvania Avenue might not look good.

"You'll have to reckon with Claudine Polk," she said.

"Claudine wasn't much of a reckoner, as I recall." I stood helpless, watching her step toward Lafayette Park. As my instincts turned protective, she turned to me one more time and said, "You don't look like a thief, Mr. Eastman."

"I'm not . . . a thief." This came out sounding like a question, and I wanted to do another take, but this was real-time—unforgiving.

"And those men you saw out in the field that summer, and in the town?" She swallowed, and I thought she said, "They worry, spaz."

"What? I'm sorry? I don't—"

Then she said it again, but with the blaring of a nearby siren, all I caught was something like "They worry, spaz." While I stood perplexed and shivering, the moonlight touched her in a way that reddened her hair. Then she disappeared among the subversives of Lafayette Park.

The president of the United States, Joseph Truitt, stood facing out the window of the Oval Office. The Washington Monument cut the April night sky like a razor, blurring slightly because of the funhouse effect of the thick bulletproof glass. There is a plaque on the wall beside his desk reading OMNIA VESTIGIA RETRORSUM, Latin for "All footsteps turn back on themselves." No one is more amazed that he is president than the president, which is why he contemplates his position so often. He believes that men who can appreciate their smallness make better leaders.

The Oval Office is another thing that is small. Photographers always use the wide-angle lens that conveys greater majesty than the room really possesses. What the Oval Office lacks in grandeur, however, it makes up for in gravity. The biggest egomaniacs on the planet instinctively lower their voices in here.

The president saw me at the threshold of his assistant's post and gestured to his twin sofas by the fireplace. As the Secret Service agent on duty, a mountainous black man named Roscoe, closed the door behind me, I heard him softly say for the last time, "Riptide is in the Egg." The finality sickened me.

The president spread his arms out on the sofa across from me. Like a great bird of prey, his wingspan was immense. I held my hands on my lap, which accentuated the difference in our natural sizes. "Jonah, son, did those eagle eyes of yours ever notice the difference between the presidential seal on the desk and the one on the ceiling?"

"Yes, sir, someone pointed it out to me years ago." I once had a mid-level polling job on President Reagan's staff. My boss at the time had pointed out that the Great Seal carved on the front panel of the president's nineteenth-century desk displayed the eagle facing the arrows, while the version on the newer dome of the Oval Office showed the eagle facing the olive branch.

"Harry Truman changed the direction of the eagle, son. Didn't want us looking warlike."

"Probably a good move, sir. After he sat at that desk and incinerated a few hundred thousand Japanese."

"Yup. When you're at peace, you romance war, but when you're at war you romance peace," he drawled in his prosecutor's baritone.

The strain of the job was showing around his eyes. The muddy circles were a contrast to his pewter hair. I had the impulse to summon a makeup crew to dab out the darkness, but not everything that is born in this room survives the light. "You know, son, there's a lot of true things we're just not allowed to say, and your mistake was that you said it. My mistake was that I said some cuckoo thing, too." The president tapped on an eyetooth. "It's true, of course. We *say* we don't negotiate with terrorists, but we *always* do in some form or another, which is why they do it. Now I have to make your successor fib her tail off while I have lunch with some sheik who'll compliment me on my statesmanship as he plans to hand over a sack of cash at dinner to a psychopath who'll blow himself up at a Starbuck's in Cleveland."

"Well, sir, it was time for me to go anyway. The great lesson of the Clinton years was that in a bull market, the public *wants* the president to have an intern under his desk; in a recession, he's on his own."

The president laughed so hard he started coughing. When he recovered, he said I had been like a son to him. This wasn't a caramelized brush-off. I had seen him tiptoe plenty of folks out of the White House, and he had plenty of less controversial choices for press secretary than yours truly. That a Jewish, Northeastern, Ivy League–educated gangster's grandson could be so close to a Republican president—a Dixie-bred Vietnam veteran, former Oxford, Mississippi, sheriff and prosecutor—had been the source of much K Street gossip over the past few years. In a screeching article in *The New Yorker* entitled "The Consigliere," a columnist alternatively attributed my loyalty to President Truitt to my desperation for a father figure or to an ethnic self-loathing tantrum. She even hinted at a desire to see me shot by a racist cop. The big northeastern urban city newspapers referred to the president by his full three names whenever possible—Joseph Lee Truitt—as they habitually did with Texas death-row inmates (those hair-trigger bubbas). While campaigning in Virginia, I sometimes hinted that Truitt was related to General Robert E. Lee (utterly false; the name derived from his beloved grandmother Lee Anne). I also winked to folks in Manhattan that the name had been shortened from Liebowitz just to frost *The New York Times*. The American Civil War drags on into the toddling millennium.

"You know I appreciate your sacrifices," the president said. He wasn't just referring to the flak I took for him this week. During his tenure, I had relentlessly beat back media interest in his wife's alcoholism and his college-age son's antics with women, some of whom were impressively no longer Brownies. During Truitt's election campaign, I had also cut a deal with my union contacts in New Jersey to endorse him over his Democratic opponent. New Jersey was a notoriously Democratic state, and deeply disinclined to support a conservative Republican. When the union endorsement came through, it dealt a psychological blow to the Democrats, and Truitt won the state on election day.

What the world did not know were the secret terms of the endorsement: If elected, Truitt would have to support certain federal judges. These judges, as it happened, were skeptical of the Racketeering Influenced and Corrupt Organizations (RICO) judicial template that was used to prosecute organized crime. Which apparently flourished in New Jersey. Who knew?

While the president always executed the final meeting like a statesman, I had never seen him talk to anyone quite like he had to me. I believe in *omertà* and other antique laws of loyalty. This belief has served me well with the president, Mickey's gang, and, of course, my wife.

"In a way, Jonah, I envy you leaving," the president said, a fleeting expression of romance dancing across his pupils. *Aaah INvee yew.* "I thought I'd never miss the white skies of the Mississippi summers and hunting jackrabbits, but I do, Jonah. I do."

"If you're not careful, sir, you'll be a gentleman farmer soon enough."

"My spin doc is always the one to tell it to me straight. Why couldn't I have found myself a good liar like all the other boys?"

"Because you're a rebel at heart."

He knew that I meant this and had long been drawn to Southerners. We had discussed my youthful summertime at Rattle & Snap. I knew down deep that my boss was more impressed by Polks than he was by kings. Growing up in Oxford and painting William Faulkner's fence one summer (a favorite campaign story), President Truitt was eminently conscious of the Dixie caste system that had survived Sherman's March.

"I know I am, son. I want you where they can't see you, where you can play possum, dead on the side of the road. You and I know that we're not through and I will be hurt if you don't call upon me. I see myself as being in your debt. What did they call it in your grandpop's day, a stand-up guy?"

"Right. A stand-up guy."

The president's leonine head turned toward the panorama of monuments.

"If I may say, sir, just one more time . . . it's not your imagination. You really are here," I said.

"I am grateful for your reminder of my coordinates, son."

"May I ask if it was all worth it by your calculations? Getting here?"

"Obsession overwhelms reason, son. You're asking me to make a rational calculation about something that cannot be measured by any device man has invented to date. I've fixated on this coordinate my whole life. I don't claim it was healthy, nor will I be so bold to suggest it was even sane. All I can tell you is that this job was—and remains—a star out on the horizon that has come to define me. It may yet be my Lorelei—that siren who lures sailors to her breast until they are crushed upon her rocks. You were always able to spot those rocks for me, son. My prayer for you is that you can always spot them for yourself."

After I left through the Rose Garden door, I sat on the steps that went down to the Rose Garden. I opened the letter from my Lorelei.

> Shalom lost spark
> Flames char the porch
> My rebel summoned
> At midpoint torch
> Hemp's run low—
> From Union's trap
> Pillars falter
> Rattle & Snap
> —*Claudine*

Claudine had written a phone number on the bottom of the stationery. I returned to my lair, and asked Tigger to set me up with a special telephone line, one that played whatever tricks must be played to frustrate the efforts of eavesdroppers.

The first syllable of Claudine's elemental voice on the line (scientists have proven that certain molecules in the tiniest densities can be devastating) drew me back to Rattle & Snap, where I had hidden out from the worst gangland war since Prohibition. When I collapsed into my cracked leather chair trying to collect the events of 1980, I couldn't decide if civil war had broken out in Philly and South Jersey at the moment I met Claudine, or if I had met Claudine at the moment when the civil war broke out. The order mattered somehow.

The truth was that the White House wasn't the first pillared mansion I had been bounced from. My ejection from the Polks' place had long preceded events at the Executive Mansion. I think Ghosty was alluding to this when she said I didn't look like a thief. *Of course not, Love. The best thieves look good on TV.*

Claudine's voice sounded breathy, vulnerable. "I thought my heart would stop when my caller ID said the White House," she said.

"We're very covert and espionage-y here," I said, cursing Tigger, and thinking that the same intelligence agencies that supposedly assassinated President Kennedy and kept it silent for forty years couldn't hook up a blind phone line.

Claudine refused to elaborate upon the ghost. Nor would she speak on the phone about all of the things she had to tell me. When I told her I couldn't just come to Rattle & Snap for the first time in a quarter century without knowing more, she surrendered a few more details, and sighed. "I'm losing."

You'd have to know Claudine to appreciate how much she abhorred victims. That she sounded like one now shook me to my core.

When we hung up, I called in Tigger. "You saw her, too, right?" I asked. "The one outside? I'm not going crazy, am I?"

"I saw her, Wonderboy." Tigger's glasses slipped from her nose onto the floor. She kicked them a few times accidentally before reacquiring them.

I lay back on the sofa in my office and closed my eyes. The lights outside penetrated my drawn window shade, and I could hear activity on the White House driveway. Alas, the nation's welfare had fumbled out of my hands. A deputy press secretary had been named to succeed me, so when the protests began in a few weeks against Judge Dewey's confirmation hearings, it would be her career challenge.

I teared up a bit (or a lot) while lying down, which isn't smart because of the choking. Fluids and faces didn't mix. I hated guys like me. As soon as I patted my face dry, I dreamt about ghosts, specifically, silvery women in great hoop dresses tiptoeing in between great columns, in search of someone they had lost in the mounds of ash that were swelling on the steps. I could actually taste the ashes. The ghosts were not frightening as much as they were desperate.

I dreamt that my children asked me why I was covered in ashes. I told them, "Twenty-five years ago, there was a volcano."

PART TWO

YELLOW RIBBONS

SPRING 1980

The nineteen eighties have been born in turmoil, strife, and change.

—President Jimmy Carter, State of the Union, 1980

SO FAST—
MARCH 21, 1980, 10:20 P.M.,
SOUTH PHILADELPHIA

"Technically, the Shore 'belonged' to Don Bruno."

Pajamas waited in gray shadows on Snyder Avenue, his shotgun cocked and his brain filled with cinematic visions of himself. His jaw fell slack as a meteor dashed across the Philadelphia heavens. Seeing the celestial development as an omen of his destiny, Pajamas curled his upper lip like Brando, or maybe Elvis, and imagined himself pinching the cheek of a neighbor's child who had come to his house to show respect. Pajamas, like others in his Philly crew, loved—and badly misused—the word "respect." The mythical child would not visit out of respect, but out of his parents' raw fear.

Pajamas was no brute, he reasoned. He saw himself as a cultured man, sensitive to the pulse of the community, a pincher of children's cheeks. He wept at weddings, slipped a few bucks to the local homeless, and had been known to remember the names of the men who drove the trucks of his vending company.

What Pajamas was missing was an awe-inspiring trademark. He had earned the nickname "Pajamas" because, my grandfather once told me, "I know a man who puts people to sleep."

I'm not being completely honest here. As Pajamas primed to kill the "Docile Don," Angelo Bruno, I had no reason to know that it was he who waited. Whenever I heard anyone had died violently, I automatically assumed Pajamas had done it, an assumption I made when I heard about what had happened to Don Bruno.

Now there was a moniker: Don. It encompassed both the nobility and terror that Pajamas had been seeking his whole life. The prospects were linked to this title, and had drawn this would-be Don into the March penumbra.

The Docile Don stood in the doorway of Cous's restaurant in Philadelphia's Little Italy, the last of a breed that actually merited respect. Mr. Bruno deserved respect not because of his career choice, but because he actively practiced peace despite blistering pressure to demonstrate the muscle of his hidden fraternity. Years ago, when he caught wind of a plot on his life, Mr. Bruno forgave his would-be killer, who prospered as a bookmaker until his natural death. In a subculture that cherished *la vendetta*, this act of mercy was an aberration.

Pajamas held no admiration for Don Bruno, who was content to celebrate his children, who had made it in mainstream America. Pajamas regarded the success of the Bruno children as evidence of weakness. For Pajamas, being a mobster was what mattered. It had been only eight years since the release of *The Godfather,* and the Mafia was just beginning to get the recognition he felt that it richly deserved.

Angelo Bruno had no interest in recognition. He just wanted to keep his operations in Philadelphia and South Jersey flowing at a steady enough clip to allow him to die at home in bed at a ripe old age, with his shoes off. At sixty-nine he was close, but not close enough. Besides, he knew what business he was in. Public recognition meant only trouble.

Fifty miles to the east of Snyder Avenue, the winking lights of the new Atlantic City casinos were summoning Pajamas. Technically, the Shore "belonged" to Don Bruno. But the Shore and casino gambling were two different things. While the turf indeed belonged to Mr. Bruno, the gambling industry, long the cornerstone of the underworld, belonged to my grandfather, Mickey Price.

Mickey was precisely the same age as the century. An elfin Jew, born Moses Prinzcowicz in Romania, he had fled to America at the age of ten after a pogrom tore through his entire family over one winter weekend. After a youth on the streets of Camden and Atlantic City's Ducktown section, Mickey rose to become the preeminent bootlegger in New Jersey during the 1920s. It wasn't until Prohibition ended, setting off a gangland panic, however, that Mickey had found his calling: casino gambling.

Coast to coast, mobs of every ethnicity frantically tried to get into the gambling business, and it was Mickey who showed them how. Long after the Irish and Jewish gangs withered in the rise of the Italian Cosa Nostra, or Mafia, Mickey was cutting the Italians into his gambling action around the world. The Italians may not have loved Mickey, but he had survived at his base in Atlantic City because no sane Mafioso would recommend killing the man who had been reliably bringing in huge dividends for a half century.

"The old Yid's mooning us," Pajamas told his big-shot patron. "He's cuttin' in everybody. The Shore is ours, and Bruno does nothin'. It's never gonna end," he ranted.

On this nippy evening, as winter surrendered, Angelo Bruno was content. Sure, Atlantic City was "his," but he was making so much money living peacefully with Mickey, the thought of going to war hadn't been seriously entertained. A war with Mickey Price, after all, could mean a war with every other happy Mob family in the country. Not worth it, Mr. Bruno thought as he waited for his driver beneath Cous's awning.

A teenage boy whipped by on his skateboard. Mr. Bruno wiggled his fingers mildly at the boy in a "slow down" gesture. A barrel-chested man standing behind Mr. Bruno stepped forward to reprimand the boy, who had swiftly kicked his skateboard up under his arm in a maneuver that impressed the Don.

"Fancy, fancy," Mr. Bruno told the boy, who laughed nervously. "You should be careful going so fast." His demeanor was calm and avuncular, which caused the barrel-chested man to withdraw his scolding posture.

"Sorry," the boy said, shaken, slipping into the darkness.

"So fast, so fast," Mr. Bruno said to the barrel-chested man who opened the passenger door of a tannish Chevy sedan that had pulled up next to the awning.

At some point during the two-minute drive to his townhouse from Cous's, Don Bruno's window had been cracked about two inches. It had been opened by his driver, a Sicilian immigrant, who had come to Philadelphia at the recommendation of Pajamas' patron. On any other night, the Don would have felt the cool air waltzing across the silver hair at the back of his neck. Tonight, he felt nothing.

While Mr. Bruno made small talk with his driver, Pajamas stepped from the shadows to consummate his metamorphosis into a boss. He pressed the barrel of his Browning twelve-gauge shotgun against the Don's skull behind his right ear. His skin melted within seconds as scores of steel pellets sliced through his brain.

The cliché is that the target "didn't feel a thing." How does anyone know? Maybe Mr. Bruno felt it in a big way. Maybe the pierced brain actually processes the flight of the pellets and reverses the senses so that their penetration is acutely felt.

The concussion left him with his mouth wide open, seemingly in horror, at the cusp of spring and the end of the region's gangland tranquility.

SHE'S HERE

"The main thing I remember about that night in the Spring of 1980 was how an orange moon appeared to blow rings around Claudine Polk's hair."

On the night that Mr. Bruno's death shook the crust of the Delaware Valley, the rest of the planet was crumbling. I read the evening edition of the *Bulletin* before I went to my after-school job at the Atlantic City Racetrack (longitude −74.63883; latitude 39.45770). Snow was falling in Florida. A volcano in Washington State called Mount St. Helens had begun to hack lava. A preppy lady shot up her boyfriend, an old diet doctor up in Scarsdale. A jury in Chicago convicted a lunatic, John Wayne Gacy, of chopping up thirty-three boys—many my age—and burying them beneath his house. Ayatollah Khomeini had just toppled the shah of Iran and taken sixty Americans hostage. Khomeini's rise in the Middle East disrupted oil production, and gasoline prices skyrocketed. The *Bulletin* reported that a couple of guys at a Pennsauken Gulf station stabbed each other while they waited in line to fill up. The prime lending rate of about twenty percent couldn't have lightened their mood much. Meanwhile, the Russians had just invaded Afghanistan and were the length of New Jersey away from the Strait of Hormuz, the spigot through which most of the planet's oil flowed. And President Carter was about to sign a bill reinstating the draft, and at eighteen I was fair game.

The main thing I remember about that night in the spring of 1980 was how an orange moon appeared to blow rings around Claudine Polk's hair. When Claudine's tall boots planted themselves in the soft peat of the stables, I had been kneeling in the indoor center ring, tightening the girth of an edgy thoroughbred. Showing horses had been part of my job working nights at the track. Linda Ronstadt's carnivorous "How Do I Make You" was playing on the stables' eight-track stereo, and I took it very personally.

I had driven to the stables after school as usual. I was a senior at Ventnor High. Mickey had just bought me a used 1975 Ford LTD, which looked more like a refrigerator that had fallen on its side than it did a car. I was always thunderstruck when it actually moved. Buying an eighteen-year-old a car was a very un-Mickey-like thing to do. He was a big make-your-own-way-in-the-world kind of guy, but I think he made the purchase out of guilt. I had been forced to follow Mickey and my grandmother, Deedee, when he had to flee the country in 1975 to dodge an indictment. "No boyhood for you," Mickey barked at me on the flight out of Philadelphia. We had returned to Atlantic City in 1978. Sounding tough was really Mickey's way of apologizing, and I never demanded tenderness from him. At some level, though, he knew that I wanted to kill him.

Mickey didn't help me get my job at the racetrack, although he was well connected there. I pursued it myself. I had learned to ride horses when I was young, something that Mickey had insisted upon. Carvin' Marvin, one of Mickey's top guys, had taught me.

"Your grandfather wants you to learn to ride," Carvin' Marvin told me when I was ten. "He made us all learn. Me. Irv the Curve." Irv the Curve Aronson was Mickey's chief of staff, mind reader, and public voice. "He figures us *shtarkers* are gonna need the skill someday."

I never quite understood why we'd need the skill, but enjoyed the riding nonetheless. When I was accepted to Dartmouth earlier in the year, Mickey made it clear that he'd pay for my college, but not for "summer fun money."

My boss, a former jockey named Swig, had ordered me to prepare a thoroughbred to show a woman from Tennessee who was driving up that evening. I had the dapple gray horse ready—I called her *Shpilkes*, pronounced SHPILL-kiss, after the Yiddish word for anxiety—but the woman didn't show up on time. She had called ahead from a pay phone saying she had been caught in a long gas line near a place she had to stop in Delaware. I rode Shpilkes around the ring to give her some exercise. I completed a series of minor jumps and one prolonged canter. As I bounced, I imagined God shaking the earth and moon like maracas, and we were all rattling around inside like petrified beans.

"She's here," Swig eventually shouted from his pine office that overlooked the ring. I dismounted and crouched down to adjust Shpilkes's girth.

The first thing I saw was the black crop protruding from Claudine's tall boots. It took my pupils forever to scan from Claudine's toes to her waist, which was possessed by tan riding pants. A white logoless polo shirt was tucked in deep, miraculously revealing no line. Jet black hair with a few natural gold highlights fell around her heart-shaped face. Her eyes were a cruel green, not in the sense of deliberate meanness, but because of the havoc they provoked. They were ancient eyes, emeralds stolen from the tomb of an oriental princess. There was an Old Testament wickedness to beauty this extreme. It was as if God had made Claudine in the same spirit that he smote the Egyptians with plagues: to demonstrate that only He *could*.

Linda Ronstadt's pulse beat down on us from above:

> You're so young but your feelings are deep
> And how do I make you, how do I make you
> How do I make you feel for me?

Deus ex machina. I had just learned the phrase in Mr. Hicks's English Honors class. We had been reading Greek tragedies since the New Year. The phrase meant that a God entered the stage via machine. The implication was that this God could work both miracles and disasters. In class, I thought the concept was ridiculous because it had no real-world utility. Claudine's appearance forced me with the sting of a riding crop to recognize that I had been wrong.

Swig's little bowlegs soon wobbled up behind Claudine, offering up tragicomic dissonance.

"Jonah, this is Miss Claudine Polk from Tennessee," Swig said.

I rose slowly from her boots to her forehead, fell backward slightly (or thought I did), and shook her hand. That's when I saw the moonlight framing her hair. It came from a giant opening in the tin roof of the stables.

"Jonah Eastman," I said, only marginally sure. We circled each other. There was something predatory about it.

"Is she yours?" Claudine asked me. Her voice was musical, but antagonistic. She managed to extend the word "yours" into her own little symphony—*yoo*-ahhr-zzz—leading with a crescendo and ending with a nap on a hammock.

"No, I'm hers," I said, familiar, as if I really owned the animal. "She sets the tone, and I do my best to control her."

"You won't win," Claudine said resolutely. "She'll do what she'll do."

I had no response other than an adolescent chuckle that I immediately regretted. She made me feel combative. I wanted to insult her somehow.

"I'll let you two talk this out," Swig said. "Jonah knows all about this girl." He walked off with a smirk.

"Does she have a name?" Claudine asked.

"I call her Shpilkes."

"*Spilled Kiss?*" She strained at the alien word.

"Shpilkes. It's, uh, a foreign word meaning the jitters. She's highstrung."

"Thoroughbreds," she shrugged. "Shpilkes." It still came out Spilled Kiss. *Speeled Kee-us*.

"What do you think of her?"

"Moody, strong. One speed—fast. What are you looking for?"

Claudine began pacing around Spilled Kiss, as I now thought of her, tracing her fingers along the animals nose and back across her side.

"I live on a family farm. We have plenty of horses, but they're getting old. I'm graduating from high school this year and my grandfather said I could bring home a new thoroughbred if I found one I
liked. The description of her in a newsletter caught my eye. I'm looking at a few other horses in the area. Out in Devon, mostly."

My chemical reaction to Claudine's answer was rage. Darwin had
swung into action and converted everything into a sexual threat. I envisioned her over in Devon on Philadelphia's Main Line, having some
rich, wheat-haired, tanned preppie named Chip, Biff, Hoot, or Dirk
taking her on a dual test ride of an assortment of beasts with risky
names. Of course, she said none of this. I felt it, though, like weather.
I wanted a fight.

"A leg up?" Claudine asked me, ordered me.

I linked my fingers together. Claudine braced herself on my shoulder, pressed down with her heel into my palms, and swung her leg
over the top of Spilled Kiss. As she reached with her foot for the stirrup, she accidentally kicked it away, causing it to sway against the
horse's neck. Elusive stirrups are not unusual. No matter how good a
rider you are, it can be awkward to find the stirrups of a new horse
atop an unfamiliar saddle.

Claudine appeared to be embarrassed by her struggle and whispered, "I've only done this a million times." I enjoyed her weakness. I
validated my dominance by grabbing the stirrup on my side and
bringing it to her, bracing her calf until she had balanced herself.

"Thank you." *Thenk yeeew.* I liked the prolonging of the word *you*,
as if she spoke this way just for me. "Would you take my crop?" she
added.

"I don't take any crop from women," I said, hands on my hips cowpoke style.

A lethal tilt of her head and a smirk bearing a dimple. "Will you
take mine?"

"Yes, but this has to be our secret," I said, taking the crop and holding it to my heart.

"Agreed," she said. "Thank you."

"Welcome," I said, in an abbreviated form of stable talk that attempted to address the way Chip, Biff, Hoot, or Dirk might have spoken to her.

Claudine proceeded to ride around the ring, occasionally jumping the moderate posts that had been left out from an earlier ride. The milky blur of a white rabbit shot across the ring, and momentarily spooked the horse, but Claudine's recovery was slick. She moved with a retributive grace that I hoped was designed to impress me, given her earlier stirrup problem. She controlled Spilled Kiss entirely through leg pressure.

As she rode, I watched, trying to make it seem as if my presence were purely business. I nodded clinically the way Swig sometimes did when he saw people ride. Within minutes, I had translated the loose and natural flow of her limbs on Spilled Kiss into yet a new sexual threat: She was a better rider than I was. I was competent, but my riding skills were tied to my athleticism—pure hustle—not my social standing. I never kidded myself; there was a difference. Claudine's riding was a celebration of her caste.

When Claudine rode back to my side of the ring, I didn't know how to address her. I felt outclassed. When I get desperate, I get wise—as in wiseass.

"You didn't check the horse's mouth," I said accusingly.

"Excuse me?"

"You didn't check his teeth. A serious horsewoman would, you know."

Claudine glared down at me with her wide, steel-mounted eyes. "I like horses. Wanna know why?" she asked, dismounting.

"Sure."

"They know they're stupid, not like some species." Pleased with her parry, her dimple grew deeper. Claudine moved to the rear of the horse.

"Be careful back there," I said. "You don't want to get kicked again."

"Again?"

"That grotesque crater in your cheek." I tapped her dimple and felt my finger slip inside it, which she allowed. "It must have been caused by a horrible accident."

Claudine drilled into my own twin-dented cheeks with her pinkies. "Maybe, but I was only kicked once. It looks like you were kicked twice. Are you able to go to school with those deformities, or did your horse kick all the way through to your brains?"

"My brains are good, Miss Polk. I'm going to college next year."

"Where."

"Dartmouth."

"Ooh, Ivy League. Some say it's the Vanderbilt of the North."

"I take it you went to Vanderbilt before you got old and haggard."

"I'm going in the fall. Unless I'm held hostage and tied up by some wretched Yankee."

"What if you meet one you want to be tied to?"

"Never. I already told you, men are dumb. I'll have no part of them."

"You'll find me different."

"How so?"

"I'll admit that I'm dumb, Miss Polk."

"You already said you were smart, Mr. Eastman."

"I *was* smart. Until you came in here and started giving me crop."

Claudine registered the pun, but in a faraway direction.

In the course of Claudine's inspection, I fumbled out a question about how long she would be in South Jersey.

"I'm going back tomorrow morning."

"Are you staying with friends?" I asked.

"No, at a motel."

"In Atlantic City?"

"Heavens, no. Pleasantville or something."

"Have you ever been to Atlantic City?"

"Heavens, no."

"Why all the heavens?"

"Well, I've heard things about Atlantic City."

"I live there."

"Figures, a cruel bully like you."

"Tell me what you've heard and I'll tell you if it's true."

Claudine smiled broadly. She had a crooked eyetooth, which I took to be an embossment of her divinity. She stepped close and whispered to me, "Gambling and gangsters."

"*No!*" I whispered.

"Really," she whispered, arching her eyebrows.

"I can prove to you that there's no gambling and gangsters there."

"How will you prove it?"

"I'll take you there."

"When?"

"Now. I get off work soon."

"I've never known a plain old cowboy to think so much of himself. I can't just up and go to Atlantic City with some strange, dimpled Yankee man. Besides, I have reservations."

"No need to have reservations. You can trust me. You can follow me in your car. I happen to live in a hotel called the Golden Prospect. I know the owner and he'll comp you a room."

"Comp?"

"Complimentary. You don't pay. And I'll wake you, I mean, take you for a walk on the Boardwalk and show you Atlantic City."

"You're going to do horrible things to me, I just know it."

"You deserve it, the vicious way you treat men. You think you're a queen."

"If you try anything, I'm telling you now that you'll never be a sire."

Ooh, the little—

"What's there to see in Atlantic City anyhow?" she added.

I stepped close to her ear and whispered, "Gambling and gangsters."

Claudine inspected Shpilkes for a few more minutes and announced that she wanted to buy her. "How much are you asking?"

I breathed in deep. A lie was called for. If I owned Shpilkes, which I did not, I would have cause to engage Claudine Polk longer. I thought about the prices I had seen posted in sales bulletins. "Ah, thirty-two hundred," I said.

"That's not bad at all for a thoroughbred. Are you sure?"

Damn. I was low. But what could I say? When love is at stake, the truth can only hurt.

"Yes, thirty-two hundred."

I returned Shpilkes to her stall, placed her saddle on a wooden post that was protruding from the wall, and headed back to Swig's office.

"Swig, look," I said. "She's pretty sure she's going to take the horse. Can you hold her? I'm off now, and I'm taking her into A.C."

"You look jumpy, Jonah. And a little retarded."

THE WIZARD OF ODDS

"We live in a casino. How could we be decent?"

In my rearview mirror I could see the neon of Atlantic City glinting in Claudine's eyes. She drove a pale blue Ford van. Her head was swiveling at the spectacle of light. The Golden Prospect Hotel and Casino stood, cute and small, between two mammoth hotels, like a kid cuddling in bed with his parents. I told the parking attendant that Claudine was with me.

I retrieved her suitcase from the back of her van and we took the elevator from the parking lot up to the lobby. When the doors opened, Claudine recoiled at the blitz of bells, lights, buzzers, and purple smoke, all of it multiplied by mirrors.

The Golden Prospect was the smallest of the Boardwalk casinos in Atlantic City. It was the only one that was not owned by a large corporation. Mickey knew that despite his omnipotent legend, it was the last of the gangster-controlled operations, so he probably figured that building it little would make him a less desirable target to the FBI. I didn't think this was impressive logic, but Mickey and his partners were old-school fundamentalists who were opposed to flaunting. Employees were dressed conservatively. The men wore traditional dinner jackets as opposed to glittering vests; the women showed legs and cleavage, but Mickey wouldn't let their rears spill out of their outfits. There was a saltwater taffy store on the ground floor, which had been Mickey's base of operations for decades before he put up the casino.

The Golden Prospect had its share of glitz, though. Once inside the lobby, we passed through giant golden columns with fake marbled cracks. The columns were much too yellow. It was like they were shouting, "See, we're golden—like *Golden* Prospect, *get it?*" They embarrassed me in Claudine's presence. The phony Colosseum-ruins look was a little sad, too. If you're going for the look of ancient Rome, why not pretend that Rome is still young? They weren't *ruins* back then.

"By the ghost of Jefferson Davis, I have never seen such a place," Claudine said, doe-eyed. "This city can't decide whether to push up to heaven or fall into the ocean. I feel like *Alice in Wonderland*."

Claudine ogled the photographic portraits of the casino's Patron Saints in the lobby. Frank Sinatra holding a microphone, early sixties. Dean Martin gripping a wine glass, late fifties. Sammy Davis, Jr., a testament to Mickey's racial liberalism, I suppose, holding a cigarette.

"Who's this one?" she asked pointing to a large painting of a handsome man of about forty. He had jet-black hair and blue gimlet eyes, and appeared to be standing on sand.

"That's Bugsy Siegel," I explained. "He's the Founding Father of casino gambling. "He was one of my grandfather's partners in the old days."

"He's not a partner anymore?"

"No. Ben—that was his real name—he was killed a long time ago."

"That's awful. Did they find out who did it?"

"His partners."

Claudine's eyes went flat.

I approached the concierge, a smooth local named Lex, and handed him Claudine's suitcase. She was frantically scanning the lobby and the casino. It was cute seeing her, this figure of self-assurance, reduced to girlish awe. She made me think of an automatic pool cleaner, the kind that wanders around the surface getting its only direction from the walls it helplessly bumps into.

"Yo, the big J," Lex said with lascivious eyes.

"Lex, I need a little help. This is Miss Polk. She needs a comp. I'll be back in a couple of hours. Can you handle it?"

"I can handle it," he said dragging his eyes all over Claudine. I gave him tombstone eyes, the hard look one of Mickey's enforcers, Fuzzy, taught me when I was getting picked on in school. These are the eyes that nonchalantly promise death. I suspected that I couldn't pull off the affectation.

"Jonah, can you answer something for me?" Claudine asked. "What kind of boy lives in a hotel?"

"A boy without parents."

She covered her mouth. "I'm so sorry."

"Don't be. My grandparents raised me. I live with them."

"I should call my family and let them know that I'm going to buy Spilled Kiss and that I'm staying someplace else."

I nodded.

Claudine followed me through the casino. She stopped at practically every table to take in the games. She shook her head in disbelief at the sight of all of the cash flowing from the gamblers' pockets across the green felt and down into the little black slits that hungrily swallowed the lost wealth of America. A cocktail waitress named Jamie pinched me on the rear and I jumped toward Claudine.

"It's just me, Jonah," Jamie said.

I offered Jamie a plastic grin. "Oh, Jamie! This is my friend Claudine."

Jamie extended her hand and Claudine studied it like a science experiment. Jamie's cleavage was amply displayed, and her fishnet stockings crawled up toward her backside. Jamie sped away, curling her mouth, as if to say, "What's with her?"

"You know that girl?" Claudine asked.

"She works here."

"But she's our age."

"You can't imagine what she'd be if the casinos weren't here."

"What would she be?"

"Probably not a cocktail waitress."

Claudine again covered her mouth.

We entered a private elevator bank. I removed a key and twisted it to open a small gold-bordered elevator.

"Where are we going anyway?" Claudine asked.

"We're off to see the Wizard. We're going to ask him for a phone."

"No, really?"

"Really. People call my grandfather the Wizard of Odds. You know, because he lives in the casino."

"May I ask *why* your grandparents live here?"

"They work here."

"What do they do?"

"Officially, my grandfather's the bell captain."

Claudine's eyes were lost somewhere around my hairline.

"What about unofficially?"

"He's the man."

"The owner?"

"Not officially."

"Who owns it? Officially."

"A company called Lenape Amusements."

Claudine nodded cautiously. "What happens if Mr. Lenape decides to fire your grandfather?" No dummy, she.

"Mr. Lenape can't. It's a lifetime contract. For everyone. Anyway, my grandmother's the hospitality coordinator."

As Claudine and I rode up the elevator, I was conscious that there were other elevators in the building moving in the opposite direction. These were the elevators that went from the gaming floor to the counting room in the basement. A percentage of the casino's winnings would fall through a false tabletop and travel via conveyor belt to another room, where the skimmed cash would be divided into "shares" that would be bound by rubber bands and distributed via multiple couriers to my grandfather's partners in Philadelphia, New York, and New Orleans. Some of the cash would be on a private prop plane the following morning to the Bahamas, where it would be wired into numbered bank accounts in Grand Cayman, Bermuda, and Zurich.

I was mindful of this invisible operation as I opened the door to the apartment of the scheme's mastermind. We were greeted by the rich scent of brisket-based soup. "Pop? Deedee? I have company. Are you decent?"

"We live in a casino. How could we be decent?" Deedee chirped.

"They answer everything with a question," I quietly advised Claudine, who followed me around the corner.

Deedee was standing in a shimmering showgirl's outfit, massive purple peacock feathers fanning out from her back, doing needlepoint. She had on spiked heels, too. Oh. My. God.

Mickey was seated on a wide easy chair behind a cloud of smoke and feathers wearing a twill suit with a perfectly knotted little bow tie. He was reading the *Bulletin* aloud, lost in the front page.

"We've got the Arabs taking over the world with OPEC. They've got holes burned in their pockets from all the cash they've got. Before long, we'll be the United States of Arabia. Meanwhile, these hotshot prosecutors want to put beat-up old gamblers in jail," Mickey ranted. He pronounced the word *prosecutor* as "persecutor." "And now look at this. The shah's running from place to place looking for an apartment. Not a bad guy for a Persian. They should have clipped that towel-headed bastard Khomeini when he was sipping espresso on the Seine!"

I gave Claudine my best teenage I'm-going-to-die-now cringe.

"You sure did a great job with Castro," Deedee barked back at Mickey, looking down at him from her needlepoint. Seeing Claudine, she grabbed her chest, almost stabbing herself with a needle. She smacked Mickey's arm, causing him to drop the paper. "What, what?" he said.

"Your grandson and Ava Gardner are here."

Claudine snickered, and I stood, sticklike, searching for the appropriate facial expression.

Mickey bolted upright. He ran his eyes above his half-glasses and slapped his cheeks with his palms. "*Kenahora!*" he mouthed.

My tiny grandparents approached, Deedee's peacock feathers following her and nearly knocking over a plant. Claudine shook their hands, munchkins welcoming Dorothy to Munchkin Hell.

"Pop, Deedee, this is Claudine Polk. She's from Tennessee. She's buying that horse."

"Pleasure to meet you, Miss Polk," Mickey said. "I'm Moses Price."

"*Moses*. Oh, he's Moses all of a sudden," Deedee said to no one.

"Can I get you anything?" Mickey asked. I had never heard him make anyone such an offer before.

"No, I'm fine," she said.

Deedee took a few steps back. "Look at the legs on Ava!" she said.

"You know, Deedee, that may be embarrassing to Av—Claudine," I said.

"No, no, I'm fine," Claudine said. She was clearly amused by the munchkins. "You . . . you look . . . nice," she said to Deedee.

"Oh, thanks, doll. I'm just testing out these new outfits for the girls in the show downstairs. I think I'll go with it."

Mickey nodded as if this were normal. I did not.

"I knew Ava Gardner," Mickey offered. "She was married to an old friend of mine. You're even prettier."

"Thank you," Claudine said. "I thought she was married to Frank Sinatra."

"They go way back, honey," Deedee said, with a brushing hand motion.

"Listen to that song of his, 'I'm a Fool to Want You,'" Mickey said. "Frank did that one for Ava. He was choked up when he sang it. Just listen."

Claudine's face froze as she studied Mickey and Deedee. It occurred to me that Mickey didn't look like a munchkin; he looked more like an elf. His skin was deeply tanned, his hair was snow-white, his eyes, like mine, were a deep green, and he was perfectly trim. The glasses perched on his triangular nose gave him the aura of a violin teacher.

Deedee was a different concept. With flaming red hair, small features, and a trim little figure packaged in gilded glory, she looked like a cross between a firecracker and an exploding peacock. In the most recent iterations of her life story, she had been a showgirl. This wasn't true: She had been a cigarette girl in Skinny D'Amato's 500 Club. She had once tried to break into show business, but nothing clicked. As

Mickey's casinos expanded in Vegas, Reno, Havana, and a host of far-off places, Deedee had played mother hen to the showgirls, which is probably how she glommed their identities. She still had showgirl legs.

"Claudine needs to call her family," I told everyone.

"And why should we stand in her way?" Mickey asked. "Now, where do we keep the phone?"

Claudine shot me a perplexed look.

"He hasn't used the phone since the Kefauver hearings in the fifties," I whispered.

Deedee, to her delight, found a phone in the kitchen under a towel. "Oh look," she said, "They make 'em with these little buttons now. No more dialing. Who knew?" Deedee handed Claudine the receiver. "While you're in here, sweetheart, grab yourself a knish. You're so skinny!"

"A ken-*ITCH?*" Claudine asked.

"*Knish*, love. They're the little potato dumplings over on that tray."

"Okay," Claudine said, mildly terrified. I didn't envision her calling her folks with a mouthful of Yiddish cuisine.

I purposely avoided listening to Claudine's call although I was desperately curious to hear what she told her family. I envisioned her father to be a Bruce Dern type answering a telephone that he kept behind the neck of a polo pony.

My grandparents stared me down as if we were about to duel. Mickey's eyes shot me an attaboy, while Deedee's sent a very different signal.

"Tennessee, huh?" she asked.

"Don't start, Deedee," Mickey ordered.

"I'll just say it once," she began.

"She'll say it only once, my eye," Mickey mumbled.

"Shush, *Moses*," Deedee said, jabbing Mickey on his newfound use of his given name. "A girl like that doesn't want to be loved. She wants to *want* to be loved."

"What does that mean?" I asked.

"It means you'll understand soon enough," Deedee concluded. "And that's all you'll get outta me." She made a zipping gesture over her lips, gathered her spectacular feathers behind her, and vamped away.

Claudine reemerged. "How's everything back home, sweetheart?" Mickey asked.

"They're all fine," Claudine said. "They were a little nervous I was going to Atlantic City."

"You want I should get them a message that you're in good hands?" Moses, conveyor of divine assurances, asked.

"No," I cut in. "I arranged for her to have a room in the hotel."

"Good thinking," said Mickey. "Now show Miss Polk the Boardwalk. That nice Barry Manilow fellow is in the theater with his rock-and-roll music. He's a bit wild for my taste, but you're young. Make sure she gets saltwater taffy for her family in Tennessee."

Claudine and I retreated into the hallway. I turned around once and saw Mickey and Deedee shrinking behind me, their little hands, not to mention a few feathers, waving me good-bye.

STEEL PIER

"Behind every official history is another history that no one wants you to know."

"If they're not the cutest people I've ever seen," Claudine said as we approached the Boardwalk past the zinging harassment of Donna Summer's menacing disco anthem, "I Feel Love." "I'd just like to wrap 'em up and take 'em home with me."

"I'm sure we can come to an agreement," I said.

Donna Summer's wrath synthesized through the crowd. Mickey never understood why contemporary patrons liked the loud music. "You can't hear anybody!" he said. "This is 1980," Deedee told him: "Look. Like. Leave. Nobody talks anymore."

I took Claudine past several guards near the theater, who admitted us immediately. I had seen many acts from backstage. Claudine and I wound around the rear of the platform. I let her peek around a curtain to watch Barry Manilow sing "Bandstand Boogie."

"They used to film *American Bandstand* near here, in Philly," I told her. "I remember my mom and her friends talking about how they would stand in line for hours and jump in front of the cameras so people would see them on TV. It was a real big deal."

"Uh-huh," she responded. She must have thought Manilow was as corny as I did, but I found it hard not to like the guy. He was like President Carter: no killer, but you knew his heart was good.

Claudine held my shoulder as I opened the door to the Boardwalk. The breeze was strong and it blew her hair back, fanning it upward like rays around her face. Yellow ribbons, which had been placed on every other light pole in honor of the hostages in Iran, blew toward the Atlantic.

I must have looked pained, because she took my wrist and asked me what was wrong. I glanced away without answering, and guided her toward the old Steel Pier.

"They used to have the best rides here," I said, pointing out rusted amusements that sat like gargoyles. "They shut it down around the Bicentennial. They'll probably open it up again someday, but it won't be the same."

"Why not? They may make it even better."

"It'll be new and jazzy like the casinos, not like the way it was."

I stood against the railing that faced the Atlantic.

"Did I say something wrong?" Claudine asked.

The vision of the strand of hair in her mouth knocked me off balance. I wanted to bite her upper lip. I felt in my joints that the planets would never align the same way they did before that strand of hair blew across Claudine's teeth. My earlier hostility toward her had gone away.

"I just think God took a lot of extra time when he made you is what I think." I glanced across the sea.

"That's a sweet thing to say."

"Well, I didn't mean it!"

"Oh, you are a creepy boy! You've learned nothing from your nice grandparents about treating a lady."

I couldn't maintain my attack.

"I actually did mean what I said about God making you."

"I thought you did."

"You don't think it's stupid?"

"No. Not at all."

"You make me hungry," I confessed.

"That's a strange thing to say to a girl."

"It's a strange thing to feel. Do you like saltwater taffy?"

"I've never had it."

For the next two hours, we walked along the Boardwalk, where the disco song "Funkytown" throbbed from every T-shirt shop and amusement pier, and finished a small box of saltwater taffy. When I asked about her family, she said matter-of-factly that her father had been killed in the Khe Sanh Valley in Vietnam. So much for Bruce Dern on a polo pony. I told her about my parents' sicknesses. I mentioned that I had lived abroad for a few years with my grandparents, but left the criminal catalyst unaddressed. I exploited our tragedies by taking hold of her hand, something I never would have had the courage to do absent our misfortunes.

"Atlantic City must have an incredible story behind it. I can sense the bandit's version," Claudine said as she took in the skyline.

"The bandit's version?"

"Yes," she snickered. *Ye-es*. "My grandfather says that behind every official history is another history that no one wants you to know about. He calls it the bandit's version. He says I've been sheltered. He says he was, too, and that we never saw the side of America that the old Polks did."

She had my interest piqued. "I'd like to meet him. I love historical stuff."

"It sounds like your grandfather, Moses, talks about events, too, from the way he went off on the Ayatollah up there."

"Yeah, Claudine, but nobody ever accused Mickey of being sheltered. Sometimes I get jealous of my friends who don't know what it's like to lose parents, or to live away from home."

"It's not their fault, though."

"Still, it gets me ticked."

Claudine and I had talked so much that we lost our bearings and wandered off into the surf, drenching our riding boots. At one point, she yanked me back toward the beach. I was surprised and intimidated by her strength. She was slender, but her grip was supernatural.

When we climbed the four steps back onto the Boardwalk, a sharp voice cut into my ears. "College," the voice cracked. I turned around and saw Carvin' Marvin approaching us. He had called me College for as long as I can remember. His shoes and cuffs were sandy. He was one of Mickey's men. Carvin' Marvin was so named because of his notorious skill with a knife. He avoided guns. "They're dangerous," he had said. I could see in the swell of his ankle, however, that he was carrying today. Claudine's expression upon seeing him was that of the babysitter in horror films when she first sees the psychopath with the goalie's mask.

"I gotta get you outta here, College," Carvin' Marvin said.

My heart dropped. I saw the pistol nosing its way out of his cuff.

"Is it Mickey?" I asked. "Is Mickey all right?"

"He's fine," Marv said. "They just got Ange in Philly. Mickey says we gotta take you to that place, you know, where things'll be safe."

A rotten part of me was disappointed that Mickey was all right. Then I was relieved. Mickey was always extorting me to do what he wanted with feigned heart attacks. I turned my attentions back toward Claudine.

"I need to take you back to the hotel," I said.

"No, College," Carvin' Marvin said. "Mickey wants you at that place."

"Because of Mr. Bruno?"

"No names, kid. Let's go." He put his hand on my shoulder, gripping it. I wanted to kill him.

"Give me one second. Please." I stepped decisively toward Claudine.

"I have to go," I told her.

"Because of this Ange?" she asked, scared, or maybe intrigued.

"Yes, because of this Ange," I said to her thigh.

"What happened to her?"

"Ange is—was—a man. A friend of my grandfather's. He was killed."

"Did they arrest the guy who did it?"

I instinctively laughed. "No, no, they don't arrest these guys."

She tilted her head, as if I had been speaking Samoan.

"Jonah!" Carvin' Marvin bellowed.

"I'll be right there. . . . Claudine, do you want the horse?"

"For that price, of course."

"Good, where will I find you? I can call and we can make arrangements to get the horse to you."

Claudine pulled a card from her pocket and gave it to me. It was rumpled and moist from both the sweat and sea air on her riding pants. The embossing read "Rattle & Snap, Mount Pleasant, Tennessee," along with a telephone number.

I sank my fingers into her hair and kissed her, probably too hard.

As I tracked her disappearance into the casino, my mind whirred. On what cul-de-sac of our galaxy was Mount Pleasant, Tennessee?

MASADA

"Everything in life is in the hands of its enemies."

On the road to "that place," I thought for the first time about the insanity of selling a horse that I didn't own to Claudine. I hadn't the slightest authority from the stables to do so. But I made the deal anyway. In the course of an evening, I had gone from being a smart kid with a great future to a huckster-fugitive.

I sat in the passenger seat of Carvin' Marvin's Caddy holding up Claudine's calling card to the moonlight, as if new information would emerge if I held the card in the precise way intended by Eros. I brought it up to my nose and vaguely detected flowers.

"Do you have a pen and paper?" I asked.

Carvin' Marvin rummaged around the front seat of the Caddy and tossed over a *Racing Form*.

"It's all I got, College. And here's a pen," Marv added, agitated.

I wrote the name Claudine Polk in the margin and tore it off. I was afraid to write on her card, viewing it as an act of romantic defilement.

"This is serious business with Ange, Jonah," Marv said.

"I know it is."

"Listen to that," Marv said. "Jonah knows it's serious." Normally, a quip like this would have upset me, but Darwin had ranked Claudine Polk's life infinitely higher than Angelo Bruno's death.

"Well," he added, "Mickey'll be happy once you're safe at that place."

"That place" was a refuge near Medford, New Jersey, that Mickey had named, in a fit of biblical pique, Masada. I had never been there, but Mickey told me years ago—even before we left the country when I was thirteen—that he "had" the place.

We pulled into the dirt path of Masada shortly before midnight. It took ten minutes to drive up the path before I saw the torches burning outside of the cabins. If the situation hadn't been so serious, it would have been funny watching Marv's head bobble as the Caddy rumbled over the muddy hills.

At the top of the hill, two men on horseback with shotguns waited. One of them held his hand out. Marv stopped the car, rolled down his window, and barked, "We got the kid." The Kid. Like Billy The. We were waved on.

There were about a half-dozen stark wooden cabins with porches. They were built simply and were practically identical. Armed shadows slid across the earth. When the men spoke, puffs of breath escaped and vanished into the moonlight. Everyone appeared to be distorted because of the way the wind and light from torches caught their figures. A quarter horse was bobbing its head frantically by a stone well. The only things that were missing were gallows and a saloon.

On the porch of the smallest cabin, a tiny shadow stood in waiting, shivering. Deedee ran toward me, her red hair appearing to be burning from the reflection of the torches. She hugged me hard, stepping on my feet with alligator boots. She was wearing a sweatsuit with her boots, indicating that they had left the Golden Prospect in a hurry. My peripheral vision picked up a few other men on horses and a dozen or so on foot with shotguns. I recognized none of them, but knew they weren't my familiar Italians.

"Welcome to our *farshtunkiner Gunsmoke.*" *Farshtunkiner* meant "smelly" in Yiddish. "Your grandfather and his cowboy friends, shooting with guns. I could strangle every one of them."

"I'm okay, Deedee."

"*Okay* you are not!" she shouted, glaring at Mickey, who had his hand on the shoulder of a long-haired man I had never seen before. If I had not just been poisoned by Claudine Polk, I would have sworn that Mickey was talking to a hippie. The long-haired man soon slipped into the night. Mickey's silhouette against the cabin gave off the aura of a floating hobbit. As he drew closer, he appeared smaller, but his shadow danced large in the torchlight.

"Grown men playing cowboys and Indians," Deedee said. "That poor Susie Bruno. Did you see the TV yet? "Ange's sitting in the front of the car with his mouth open and blood all over the windshield. Like he's shocked. You play with guns, this is what happens. What's to be shocked?"

"Deedee, it's not like he opened his mouth because he was shocked—"

"If somebody shot your grandfather, I'd tell him not to look so shocked."

Mickey grabbed my face. At first I thought he was dressed entirely in white, but it was khaki. The torches deepened the crevasses of his tanned face and accentuated the cottony whiteness of his hair.

"So," Deedee said, "Welcome your grandson to *Gunsmoke*."

"Shush a minute, Miss Kitty," Mickey barked back, setting down a suitcase. "Like I'm happy about this? We should tie a yellow ribbon around every tree in the Pine Barrens. We're hostages. My crew's in play."

"Do you know who did this, Pop?" I asked. The goal of my inquiry was to get the discussion over with, not learn anything.

"If I knew, Jonah, I wouldn't be here. When I know, I stay home. When I don't know, I hide out."

"Like Jesse James," Deedee added gratuitously.

We stepped into the sparsely decorated cabin. There were two bedrooms, both visible from the central living and dining area that was built around a small stone hearth. The kitchen was wedged into the cabin's corner. Deedee proceeded toward the smaller bedroom and set out some of my clothes on a wooden chair.

Mickey fell back into the chair closest to the fireplace. I sat on the sofa across from him. I couldn't get comfortable, which I attributed to the sound of murderers pacing on the porch.

"Who are these guys, Pop?"

"Some of them are my guys. Some of them are Israelis. The real deal."

"Where are the Italians? Fuzzy? Blue?"

Mickey rubbed his temples.

"There's always a skunk under the sofa with you, huh? Smart question. They're not here."

"Why not?"

"Because we haven't found the skunk."

"What do you mean?"

"We don't know what this is all about with Ange. Nobody saw this coming. Since Prohibition ended, I've seen these things coming. This one I didn't. That worries me."

I felt momentarily nauseous. Mickey was fine when he saw murders coming but was uncomfortable when he *didn't?*

Deedee reemerged.

"It's me, Ma Barker. Are you hungry, Jonah?" she asked.

"No."

"Fine, I'll make you a sandwich. I have some tuna in the pantry. Which is right next to your grandfather, Bat Masterson's, shotgun I might add."

Deedee walked away into the kitchen.

"Honest to God, Jonah, sometimes I think your grandmother's working for the bad guys. She's probably behind the Ayatollah." Mickey sighed. "Everything in life is in the hands of its enemies. So what's with Ava Gardner?"

"Claudine." I removed Claudine's card from my pocket and handed it to Mickey.

"Rattle & Snap," Mickey chuckled as he read it.

"What's so funny?"

"It's a gambling game they used to play in olden times. Goes back to the Revolution."

"How do you know this?"

"How do I know this? Who do you think you're talking to here? That newspaperman calls me the 'Wizard of Odds' and you don't know how I know this?"

"C'mon, do you know how it's played?"

Mickey's eyes widened. Talking about gambling kept him alive, even evangelical. Everything about it excited him. Talking about it. Watching it. Even fighting for it. The hit on Mr. Bruno was probably tied to gambling. I didn't know this because of any inside knowledge; I knew it because Mickey wasn't grabbing his chest or making Shakespearean allusions to his time running out. He was combative, alive. I had long accepted it as gospel that Moses Price was at his best when he was under siege and would do whatever he had to do to avoid tranquillity.

"It was played in the fields with dried beans, or dice made from goat bones. They'd rattle 'em around in their hands"—Mickey made a shaking gesture with his fist—"and snapped them free. They landed where they landed."

"I never figured shooting dice went back that far."

"Are you kidding? It goes back to the Bible. The ancient rabbis carried dice around the temple. Urim and Thummim they were called. Call 'em whatever, they were dice. They glowed, too."

"What did they bet on in the Temple?"

"When the dice rolled a certain way, it showed God's will."

"Is that what you've been doing in Atlantic City, God's will?"

"In a way," Mickey winked. "Gamblers believe God wants them to be rich. My job is to teach them that this is a false belief."

"But casinos are set up to make people think they can get rich, so you just tell them what they want to hear. You don't teach them."

"Don't be an Ivy League smart guy."

"You wanted me to be an Ivy League smart guy. I just don't think you're helping God, that's all."

Mickey shook his head like Yosemite Sam. "Let's not argue about who I'm helping right now."

Despite the tension, Mickey's knowledge of something associated with Claudine momentarily made me love him. Murder, schmurder. He who moved me south was my redeemer.

SMITH, WESSON,
AND A LITTLE MOISTURIZER

"Rhett Butler, we got here."

"Who are you calling there?" Mickey asked me the next morning.

"I'm calling Swig at the stables," I said. I was shaking.

"Just watch what you say. Don't say where we are," Mickey admonished.

I called Swig on the line he had in his little apartment next to the center ring at the stables.

"Hey, Swig. Did you see the paper?"

"Yeah, I did. Nice picture with the mouth open and all the blood."

"I can't talk about it now."

"So, is Miss Canned Heat gonna buy?"

I went cold with his crude summary of Claudine. This justified my swindle, didn't it?

"Yes, I sold her," I said.

"What do you mean, you sold her?"

"I sold the horse."

"You can't sell the horse!"

"Well, I did."

"For how much?"

"Thirty-two hundred," I mumbled.

Silence.

"I was gonna ask five thousand!" Swig said. "I was gonna throw in some training for the horse to impress these people. Now you gotta call and tell her that it's five thous—"

"No!"

"Look, I don't care who your grandfather is, you don't rook the race track out of nearly two grand!"

"I know. I won't. I'll make it up to you."

"You'll cover the eighteen hundred and deliver the horse?"

"Right."

"To Tennessee, I mean."

"Yeah."

"I don't believe you. I'm gonna tell your grandfather straight out. This is crazy. You call that girl and tell her you lied—"

"*No!*"

"Then I'm selling her out from under you."

"No! I'll get the thirty-two hundred from her and cover the rest somehow."

"Did you lose your mind?"

"Yes. I mean, no. No."

"Since when are we horse couriers, Jonah? We're not paying for delivery."

"I'll figure something out."

"You better, Jonah. What are you thinkin' with, pal?"

Fury at Swig. There are few things more deeply resented than an accurate analysis of one's failings.

"I'll call Claudine and coordinate something."

"So," Deedee said, placing scrambled eggs and toast down on the cabin's dining room table. "*What*, may I ask, is with this Clarabelle? Your grandfather said something about a horse farm, and I hear you on the phone talking like you had a lobotomy."

"You mean Claudine, not Clarabell. You make her sound like a cow."

"She's no cow. I'll say that much. You like the thoroughbreds."

"That's code."

"Code? Who am I, Ethel Rosenberg? It's just a fact. At your age, you want the ones that get away. There are *Yiddishe* thoroughbreds, too, you know, but you won't be sweet on them." Deedee placed a little box of salt on the table. "*Boxes* of salt. This is how we live now. Enough already!"

"How do you know that about Jewish girls?"

"They're too familiar," Deedee said. "You're on to them and they're on to you. You don't want each other. The times are different. This Southern one—*hoo-hah*—it's another world with Tennessee. It's an impossibility. That's what you love now." Deedee produced a napkin out of thin air and dabbed at the corner of her eye and sat down across from me. "I just hate to see you go through it."

I stood and walked around to Deedee's side of the table. I knelt by her.

"I'm not going through anything, Deedee. This situation last night—"

"You mean the girl."

"She had an effect on me," I said.

"*Insanity*, that's the effect," she prodded me back to my side of the table. "They should make a pill for it. Like your grandfather with his insanity. *Die kalah es tu schein*," Deedee admonished in Yiddish.

"What does that mean?"

"'The bride is too beautiful.' It means what it means. And what are you all shaky about?"

I confessed to Deedee about what I had done with the horse. She slapped my head with her palm. "Those Ivy League schools don't test for idiocy, do they? Oh, Jonah. Don't tell your grandfather. Think! Think!"

There were three knocks against the front door of the cabin. Mickey instinctively glanced at the shotgun on the counter. It was standing upright next to a plastic tub of kosher cream cheese.

Deedee peered behind the curtain.

"It's just Irv," she said. "Do you want me to shoot him for you?"

Mickey ignored her and opened the door. Standing impeccably in a poplin suit was Irv the Curve, Mickey's top lieutenant. He had the front page of *The Philadelphia Inquirer* plastered across his chest, as if he had been kidnapped by the Red Brigades like Aldo Moro.

"Well, Irv," Mickey said, "We've got ourselves another pogrom."

"We don't know that yet, Mick," Irv the Curve said, not stepping inside. "This thing with Ange is a young man's move. Hi, there, Jonah. Sorry to pull you away from the chickie."

Everybody knew.

"You look tan, Uncle Irv."

"I found a new moisturizer," Irv the Curve said.

"No kidding," said Mickey. "Does it keep the tan in?"

"Like you wouldn't believe. Doris at Ventnor Pharmacy recommended it. I'll pick up some for you," Irv the Curve promised.

"Smith, Wesson, and a little moisturizer," Deedee droned from the kitchen.

"Look at Ange," Irv said, shaking the newspaper. Deedee and I moved toward Irv to inspect the paper.

It was the most ghastly photo I had ever seen, just as Deedee had described it. Mr. Bruno sat in the passenger seat of a car, his mouth wide open and filled with blood so fresh that the light from the flashbulbs made it shimmer. His right eye was closed; his left eye was slightly open for a final peek at springtime in South Philly. Blood flowed from his ear and nostrils and down on his striped shirt and tightly knotted tie.

COUSIN JIMMY

"So kill me."

"Rattle & Snap," a male, teenage voice answered the telephone. The pronunciation came out *Raddlinsnap*. I felt butterflies orbiting several vital organs.

"Yes," I said, trying very hard to sound routine. "I'm trying to reach Claudine Polk."

"May I tell her who's calling, please?"

"Yes. Yes, you may." A little formal, Jonah. "My name is Jonah Eastman. I met her, I mean, I work at the Atlantic City Racetrack."

"Oh, yeah."

This was good. She had discussed me with this person, perhaps her brother. Or maybe it wasn't so good. Maybe the phone answerer was simply aware that Claudine had bought a horse in Atlantic City. I may have been little more than an errand boy.

There was a muffled handoff and then her springtime voice floated through the telephone wires and vacuumed my brains out through my ears.

"I forgot your last name was Eastman." I thought I smelled azaleas. What did azaleas smell like anyway?

"What's wrong with Eastman?"

"Nothing's wrong, your last name hadn't occurred to me lately."

"Wasn't President Polk from Tennessee?"

"Indeed he was."

"Are you related to him?"

"Cousin Jimmy. Are you related to the guy from Eastman Kodak?"

"I'm not even related to Monk Eastman."

"Who's Monk Eastman?"

"He was an old-time New York gangster."

"Like that Ange friend of yours?"

I was silent. Claudine advanced: "I read about that murder in the newspaper."

"Do you still want Spilled Kiss?"

"Of course. Who do I make the check out to?"

"Atlantic City Race Track. We can work out delivery later."

"When do you think you can get her down to the plantation?"

Plantation?

"After Memorial Day. Will that be okay?"

"I guess. You're going to miss Spilled Kiss, I bet."

"Will you let me visit her?"

"Of course." *A-course.*

I could hear Claudine cover up the telephone and tell someone to get lost. This was a good sign.

"Anyway," she said, "I'm going to our school play now with some friends."

"What's the play?"

"This year we're doing *Fiddler on the Roof*. It's about traditions."

I had to catch my breath, Mickey and Deedee played the sound track perpetually, our very own middle-class department store Muzak.

"It's a good play. I think you'll like it."

"Wow, you know a lot about plays, huh?"

"Plays, yes." Oy. "How was your stay at the Golden Prospect?"

"They treated me like a princess. But I was worried about you, so I didn't sleep too well." With distance came tenderness.

"What about me did you think about when you tried to sleep?"

"Jonah!"

"Sorry."

"Call soon. And one more thing: Stay away from those dangerous men."

Her ostensible disapproval masked curiosity.

"I'm not the one that lives on a plantation. The slaves may rise up."

"Don't be silly, Jonah. We don't have slaves here anymore."

"When did you give them their leave?"

"There was this little war in the eighteen sixties. My family played quite a role in this. How about yours?"

"We fight in other wars."

A guy called Tony Bananas drove his Mercedes 450 SEL coupe up the dirt road to Masada. Bananas was the legendary Blue's deputy, a muscle guy to his marrow.

"Here come the Romans," Irv the Curve alerted no one in particular. "Bananas and his fancy car. Thinks he's Sean Connery."

My Uncle Blue climbed out of the car. His real name was Arturo Cocco. He was Mr. Bruno's underboss, and had been Mickey's partner since Prohibition. Blue was wearing a tweed jacket with leather elbow patches and black slacks. His tie was tightly knotted, the way Mr. Bruno's had always been. Even away from the action, these old guys liked to look right.

Tony Bananas was another story. In his forties, he was a bear of a man. He was dressed all in black, not out of respect for Mr. Bruno, but probably because he thought he looked scary that way.

Mickey emerged from the house and regarded Blue, unsmiling. I followed Mickey out and lingered on the porch. Irv the Curve trailed him. Blue shook his head, with a what's-the-world-comin'-to expression. He stepped toward Mickey, who gestured with his hand toward the gazebo beyond the sand pit. The two men did not shake hands or embrace.

At the time I watched the interaction, I thought Mickey's coldness had been a mistake. Blue, after all, had been his chief source of protection. Only later did I come to understand Mickey's position: An embrace would have been a sign of weakness, an outreach for assurances. While Mickey may indeed have felt weak, he wanted to come across angry. He wanted Blue to feel that their half-century partnership was in jeopardy, and for what?

The power in a relationship belongs to whoever needs the relationship less. By gesturing toward the gazebo, Mickey wanted everything Blue could lose to flash before his eyes. Implicit in Mickey's coldness was the mad stance of a zealot. *So kill me,* his movements said. These men would know everything they needed to know about where each other stood before the meeting started.

The two men muttered something to Tony Bananas and Irv. Both men stayed back while Mickey and Blue proceeded toward the gazebo.

Tony Bananas approached me.

"Jonah. How's school?" he asked. *Joner hazkool?* Tony Bananas gave me a friendly attaboy punch on my shoulder. I hesitated for a moment. He had never shown any interest in me before.

"School's fine," I said.

"School's a good thing. I shoulda stayed in school. I like readin'. You like readin'?"

Irv the Curve studied our exchange silently.

"Yes," I answered. "I like reading."

"Good. Read a little-a this. Read a little-a that. Before you know, you got all kindsa friggin' wisdom. Know what I'm sayin'?"

"Yes."

Tony Bananas put his meaty hand around the back of my neck and massaged it a little, the way a friendly uncle would. The skin on his hands was dry and raw.

PLAGUES

"On this holiday, it is said that we are to ask questions."

I left Masada every morning and went to school at the Shore under heavy guard by Carvin' Marvin. The subject in Mr. Hicks's English class was poetry. We had been tasked with writing a romantic poem. My serendipitous encounter with Claudine Polk had left me suspended in a gelatin of longing, so I sat alone on a rock in the sandpit at Masada and wrote a few verses:

> Break South, urgent for Claudine
> Canter heavy toward drums and irises
> Rebel on purple hills of Rattle & Snap

Mr. Hicks read that verse aloud and shook his head slowly, his mouth lolling open. I could see his fillings. I couldn't determine what he was trying to tell me; after all, I didn't think my verse was very good. The words had bled out of my fingertips onto the paper.

Lisa Connors rested her head on her hand and ran an index finger beneath her eye. She was good-looking, something I hadn't really noticed before. Another girl, Deborah, crossed and uncrossed her legs—she was wearing shorts. She looked sleepy, and I pictured what she might look like with her eyes closed. My heart began to race and I heard a roaring in my ears. I closed my own eyes and felt Claudine tackle me on grass that was more than green.

One evening, Deedee prepared a Passover dinner for the boys at Masada. My Uncle Blue's wife, Phyllis, came too. The casual observer would find this to be a good sign. I wasn't so sure.

Deedee emerged from the cabin to our outside setting holding a steaming soup bowl and wearing combat fatigues, an army hat, and an eye patch. And crimson high heels to match her current hair color. Dear Lord.

"Outta my way troops, hot matzoh ball soup on fire coming through!"

"What the hell is this?" Mickey asked.

"We're at *war* in the desert, aren't we?" she said.

"What the hell are you talking about?"

"I'm Moshe Dayan out here. You boys with your guns," Deedee said.

"Where did you get that outfit?" I asked.

"It's not an outfit, Jonah," Deedee corrected. "It's a *uniform*. I got it from the theater director at the hotel. Women in Israel are soldiers, you know."

Mickey gazed skyward for guidance. "What's the point of this non-sense?"

Deedee fiddled with a plate of hard-boiled eggs and put her skinny arms on her hips. "I'm protesting the war. I've had enough of this violence from all of you. I am . . . *whattayacallit* . . . an *actifed*."

"An activist," I corrected.

"That's right. That's what I am. An activist. A peace activist!"

"With the high heels, you're an activist?" Mickey shouted. "You're an activist like I'm Abbie Hoffman!"

My uncle Blue, who had brought red wine—and seeking to put an end to the spectacle—held up a glass and toasted, "Here's to the sexiest little activist this side of Hanoi Jane Fonda!"

Everyone raised their glasses and toasted, even Deedee, who apparently got what she wanted: male attention. She moved her eye patch to her other eye. When the meal concluded, Blue asked for somebody to tell the story of Passover. "I love that story with the plagues and the locusts. C'mon, Mick."

"Irv's the story guy, you know that," Mickey said.

Blue wouldn't have it: "But you're Moses. I want to hear it from the big guy himself."

"It's a simple story, really," Mickey sighed. "The Israelites lived in Egypt. They multiplied, got more power. Pharaoh sees Jews living in the new fancy condo complex he was planning—the Pyramids at Red Sea. Pharaoh got worried, cracked down, and made them slaves. The Jewish slaves built his pyramids. Pharaoh liked this. This coincided with another problem. The guy he treats like his son, Moses, finds out he comes from Jewish slaves. Moses decides to act. He wants his people freed. Moses, he's got a heavy friend: God. God arms Moses with plagues. Blood. Cattle sickness. Vermin. Frogs. Darkness. Pharaoh eventually finds these plagues illuminating. The real deal. He lets Moses take the slaves out of Egypt. Pharaoh realizes this isn't such a good answer either. He gives chase. God helps him out. The Jews are freed, but it's not the victory they think it's going to be. They wander in the desert for forty years. They fight each other like a Fort Lauderdale condo association. (There's nothing in the Book of Exodus that you can't see at a Fort Lauderdale condo meeting.) Moses dies before his people get to the Promised Land. His people make it, though, but have to keep fighting to live there. After all, God had once told Moses, 'Send men that will spy out the land of Canaan, which I give to the children of Israel; of every tribe of their fathers shall you send a man, every one a prince among them.'

"On this holiday, it is said that we are to ask questions. We are to talk about who is wise, who is wicked, who's a moron, and who is unable to ask questions. By the time my Jonah goes off to college, I hope we will know who's who."

Blue pounded his index finger against the table: "Hey, Moses, what kinda plague are you gonna give Nunzi up in New York? I say you mess with his cattle."

Mickey swatted Blue away. He and Deedee were the only ones who could rib him like this. Nunzi was a New York City Mafia boss.

They suspected that New York was behind the hit on Mr. Bruno.

"Frogs are good," I added.

Blue agreed. "Listen to the kid. Can you see Nunzi jumpin' around with frogs in his boxers?"

Everyone clanged wine glasses and drank.

"Now, Jonah, Phyllis, and Moshe Dayan with the red hair," Mickey said, "The boys are going to talk plagues if you don't mind. *Dayanu*," Mickey added. Hebrew for "enough."

I helped Phyllis and Deedee clear the table while Moses and Company determined who would live and who would die.

LIFEGUARD

"I'm not making predictions, I'm making odds."

I'm in English class and I'm not paying attention. Carvin' Marvin is standing outside the school with a stiletto in his pocket, a Ruger revolver in his shoulder holster, and a Beretta strapped to his ankle. I usually love English, and Mr. Hicks is the greatest teacher of all time.

I am trying to extract some reason for this Claudine disease. It doesn't make sense to me why all I can do is think about her. The science that explains it eludes me, but I've never been good at science. I've lost weight and Deedee's beside herself.

I spent three, four hours with the girl and have been walking into things for weeks. Had she said something profound? Not really. She hadn't even been that nice. When we read *The Inferno* in class earlier in the year, I remember Mr. Hicks telling us that Dante had only seen Beatrice once, when she was ten years old. And look how he became consumed by it. It made no sense, but that was precisely the point.

My operating theory was that I must have had a chemical reaction to Claudine. I began to remember a passage from a book I read for extra credit, *Lolita*. The child-molesting professor refers to his obsession as the "hidden tumor of an unspeakable passion." We have these biological forces colliding with the mental, moral part. That I know better means nothing.

Eventually, I made a simple chart of Claudine's pluses and minuses:

CLAUDINE

+	−
Beautiful	Lives far away
Smart	Snappish
Sweet	Got the Ku Klux Klan there
Perfect hands to hold	Deedee thinks she's a witch
Likes horses too	Every guy in the world wants her
Mouth is perfect	Must kill guy who goes to prom w/C
Has sad stuff too	J will go to prison not Dartmouth
	J will be lynched, not be Pres. of U.S.
	C may hold hands or worse with prom guy

No wonder I can't function. Everything cancels everything else out. I cannot pay attention despite every trick, like trying not to blink. I just want to escape from New Jersey. I have developed a bond with our hostages in Iran.

On the days when I worked at the track, Carvin' Marvin drove me there and lingered while I did my work. The moment I entered the stables, Swig was standing there. He held up the check Claudine had mailed him. "Looks a little light, Jonah."

"It is a little light."

"You know you owe it, right?"

"Of course."

"And you know you're on your own getting that horse down there."

"I know."

"Mickey doesn't know, does he?"

"No, Swig. No, he doesn't. . . . Look, you said something about training the horse to impress the Polks. I can do that. That would have cost you something, right?"

"Not eighteen hundred."

"How much?"

"Maybe eight hundred. Tops."

"Can I shave off eight hundred?"

"Do you know how much time it takes to train an animal like that?"

"I got myself into it, right?"

Swig fell into his cheap orange swivel chair. "Jonah, you've been a real good worker here, but you're pretty dumb for a smart guy. Yeah, I'll shave off eight hundred if you train the horse, but you owe a grand, cash. And if Mickey asks me—"

"He won't."

"Fine, you train the horse, you owe a grand cash by midsummer, and you're getting the horse to Tennessee however you can. It's your problem."

In the ensuing weeks, I took special care of Shpilkes. I cleaned the dirt out of her shoes every day I worked, even though it was unnecessary. I worked Shpilkes out in the ring, but not too hard. Trots and canters mostly.

I wrote to Claudine every couple of days and called the Golden Prospect every day to see if she had written to me. The people in the front office were entertained by my desperation. It was not lost on me that part of the reason for their entertainment was that Mickey never got letters. Never. In fact, he always tilted his head quizzically whenever I got mail. "Why the hell does everybody have to hand things off with a stamp from the government?" he wondered. "Talk about a racket."

Claudine sent one letter for every three of mine. She didn't say much in her letters, focusing on her daily activities as opposed to what she was thinking. The best thing about her letters was their smell. The paper had the same springtime scent as her hair had when I kissed her.

I called Claudine once a week. She never called back, but I didn't expect her to. For some reason, it was easier to call a girl who was far away than one who was close by.

One Saturday morning, I returned from Masada to the Golden Prospect with Mickey, Deedee, and a few guards. I looked for my favorite Dartmouth sweatshirt, but couldn't find it.

An argument with the building's maintenance man ensued because the air-conditioning system in Mickey's apartment had never been shut off while we were at Masada and the controls were frozen so that cold air was coming out at full blast.

I threw on a tank top and went for a run on the beach, attempting in vain to retrace where Claudine and I had walked. A local cop named Duffy paralleled my run in a patrol car along the Boardwalk. I ran about three miles to the south through Ventnor (imagining the theme to *Rocky*) and turned around, the cop car following me. As I neared the Golden Prospect, I spotted a strange, dark sack on the lifeguard stand. I stopped running and walked toward it. Duffy ran up behind me on the beach.

As I drew closer, I felt sick. There was a tugging somewhere down low. I felt hollow the way I had when my mother told me that she was sick. Everyone had tried to make me feel better, but I knew she would not be okay. I was smart that way.

My Dartmouth sweatshirt had been smeared with blood and nailed to the lifeguard stand. Pajamas crept into my mind.

"Jonah, get away!" Duffy yelled.

I could not back off. I froze about three feet from the stand.

Duffy radioed his precinct. As soon as another car pulled onto the Boardwalk, Duffy walked me up to the hotel.

"What?" Mickey yelled the minute he saw us in the apartment. He was wearing Deedee's mink stole and fluffy bunny rabbit slippers, shivering, and holding a suitcase. The air conditioner was still blasting. *This* was who the FBI had been hunting for fifty years?

Duffy told Mickey what we found as I walked into my frigid bedroom and fell face forward onto my bed.

There was shouting in the living room. Deedee was going after Mickey big-time. Within minutes, she came into my room and knelt by my bed. She was wearing short pants and a T-shirt that read "Foxy" in giant, shiny letters.

"Listen to me, sweetheart. We've got to get you out of here. I've told your grandfather a few things. I told him that we're getting you out of Jersey no matter what it takes. He said he can deal with the Ventnor schools—Mr. Connections, your grandfather. You can stop with that job, too. And I told him that I'm gonna personally kill whoever did this."

Looking at her tiny, made-up face, her hair multiplying her mien of rage, I began to laugh.

"What?" she scowled. "You don't think I'd do it?"

"I do. You know, I really do. You're sexy when you're murderous."

"Listen to you talking to your grandmother that way, you *bondit!*"

"I know where I want to go."

"*Ach*, enough already with that Ava Gardner!" she announced skyward. "This isn't love you've got, it's malaria. Sucking the life out of you with this obsession! Did you work off all that money at the track?" Seeing Deedee's stricken face, it occurred to me that I might have leverage.

"Eight hundred of it. I still owe a thousand, so I can't just quit work. Anyway, how can you make predictions about how things with Claudine will turn out?"

"I'm not making predictions, I'm making *odds*. You forget who I've been married to for fifty years."

"What, do you think I'm going to pull a Jimmy Hoffa on you and vanish?"

Deedee cupped her hand to her mouth and whispered, "Boy, was your grandfather pissed at *him*."

I thought any further engagement on the Hoffa matter was unwise, so I just said, "I want to go to Rattle & Snap."

"I don't want to argue right now," Deedee said, cupping my face. "But it's fine with me. Better you learn it now than when you have little ones."

APPLICATION

"Who knows what waits for you in the South?"

Zeus answered the telephone. "Rattle & Snap," he thundered.

My heart was pounding. It felt as if it were echoing off the walls in our Masada cabin. I began to stammer. Claudine's grandfather.

"Yes, I, uh, was—"

"Is this about the stable job, boy?"

Stable job?

"Uh, yeah," I deepened my voice to sound more . . . stable-ish.

"Minimum wage, room and board on the plantation."

"That sounds good."

"Where are you from, boy?"

"Just north."

"Nashville?"

"Yes, sir."

"Uh-huh. What's your name?"

"J-John," I said thinking of the closest thing to Jonah. That way I could write the whole thing off as a misunderstanding if I got nailed.

"When can you start, John?"

"Mid-June." School was out by then.

"Not soon enough. How's after Memorial Day?"

"Memorial Day?"

"Yes, boy."

"Okay, I guess."

"We'll be tickled to have you, John."

"Tickled?" Deedee overheard, walking into the cabin. *"Who* anymore says tickled?"

I felt a rush of heat surge through my backbone.

"So what did they say?" Deedee asked.

"The grandfather hired me."

"As what? A ceramic plant?"

"Stable boy."

"I'll have to make arrangements with the school, stable boy," Mickey said. "And we'll have to brush you up on what goes on down in the South," he added, worried. "It's different from Jersey."

"I know. I'll do fine. I'll be happy there."

"Listen to Jonah *Godol*," Deedee said, world-weary.

Me, perplexed: *"What?"*

"Jonah the Grand. You'll change the South. . . . Oh, it's our fault," she cried. "We pounded that in your head so you'd overcome losing parents so young."

My next phone call, a bit later.

"Raddlinsnap."

"Claudine?"

"Jonah?"

"Yes."

"I made arrangements to have the horse delivered right after Memorial Day."

"I'm so excited."

"You promise I can visit her someday?"

"A-course."

Mickey was outside on the Masada gazebo with Irv the Curve. Two imported gunmen paced nearby. Deedee, standing in the cabin's kitchen, motioned me over conspiratorially.

"Get the matzoh," she ordered in a loud whisper.

I reached for the box and handed it to her. She swatted me away. "Open it."

"Open the matzoh?"

"No, open the Olympic Games. Of course, open the matzoh!"

Cash. A grand. Swig's grand.

"Oh, look, you found the *afikoman*," Deedee said, referring to the piece of matzoh that grown-ups hid on Passover. The kid who found it got money.

"Where did you get this?" I asked.

She threw up her arms: "It's a mystery," she said, turning away from me. "Now, if your grandfather asks what I got you for graduation—he will suspect something—don't tell him about the cash. Tell him I got you this." She handed me a small box with some kind of radio contraption illustrated.

"It's a Sony Walking Man or something. It's a radio that you can listen to yourself and not bother anybody else with the noise. It takes batteries but I don't know what kind. I'm not good with all the scientific things."

Mickey called me up to the gazebo. He waved Irv the Curve and the muscle away. I carried my new Sony Walkman, having removed it from its box. "New York Groove" by Ace Frehley was playing.

Mickey gave my face a light, affectionate smack. "What's that nonsense?"

"A gift from Deedee. A new kind of radio."

"How the hell can you hear anything on the outside?"

"You can't. That's the point," I said.

"Give me that," Mickey ordered.

"No! . . . Why?"

"It's not safe. You can't hear footsteps, people coming."

I contemplated this. I liked the radio, but if I resisted Mickey, he might make a scene with Deedee. If he made a scene with Deedee, there was a chance that the money she gave me for the horse would come up. If that happened, my whole trip to Tennessee would be in jeopardy. Don't be greedy, Jonah. I handed Mickey the Walkman.

"Look, kid, you have an advantage over boys your age," Mickey said.

"What's my advantage?" I asked skeptically.

"You have seen in your young life that God created things larger than yourself. But it's good to see that other forces, other people, have useful skills, powers that can be turned against you. You will go down to see this girl. You are smart and you are handsome, but there may be men down there smarter and handsomer."

"I know."

"You *think* you know. It doesn't get better. This fall, you'll go to college. They've got Rockefellers there, you know?"

"I know."

"You'll go up against these fellows who have better weapons to compete—not just for grades, but for position, for girls, for money."

"You make it sound like I'm some kind of loser."

"The opposite. You are a winner. You've got weapons. Who knows what waits for you in the South? Who knows what will happen with this war around here? For these unknowns, there's two weapons. The first weapon is knowing what your skills are *not*. You're scrappy, but God didn't put you on this earth to beat people up. There are other people to do that." He gestured somewhere vague, as if to say, *Not us.* "I don't have a genius with my fists. I found partners like your Uncle Blue. You should have seen him move in his day. And he's as smart as he is tough, though he likes to play the dumb guinea. I also am not, you know, all fancy with the words, with expression. That's what your Uncle Irv can do better."

"The second weapon, Pop?"

Mickey pointed to a small, heavy metal box on the picnic table.

"What's this?"

"A loan. Open it."

Inside was a revolver.

"Smith & Wesson. Thirty-eight. Two-inch barrel. Stainless steel. Takes six bullets. I've had it since Prohibition."

"Is this for me?"

"No, it's for Leo Frank."

Ah. The Jewish pencil factory supervisor lynched in Georgia for the murder of a thirteen-year-old girl, Mary Phagan. 1915. On his deathbed, a witness confessed to seeing a man other than Frank carrying Phagan's body from the crime scene.

Mickey continued. "You're going South in a few days. Before you go, you're gonna get used to this. Just in case."

I had rehearsed this handoff over and over in my head a hundred times. I had even snuck the gun out into the Pine Barrens to practice firing it. Still, I had envisioned I would be older when this ritual occurred.

"Do you think I'll be a good shot, Pop?"

Mickey frowned. "In this business, you don't need to be good. You need to be willing."

FLY LIKE AN IGGLE

"Maybe he's a little God."

Irv the Curve knocked on the cabin door the following morning at an obscenely early hour. It was still dark out. Mickey answered.

"Didja hear?" Irv asked ominously. "Carter sent helicopters into Iran to save the hostages. The copters crashed in the desert."

"Oh, the *putz*," Mickey snapped. "He'd screw up an invasion of Bayonne."

Irv came in and showed us the cover photograph in the *Bulletin*. All I could make out was sand and metal. And a quote from Carter beneath declaring the mission an "incomplete success."

"Do you think they'll ever get the hostages out?" I asked.

"Not at this rate," Irv said. "Khomeini doesn't fear us. Without fear, he sits there and says this is the will of God. It makes him look . . . mystical."

After breakfast, Irv the Curve gave me a few numbers where I could reach him over the summer. A few of the "panic numbers" were in New Orleans, but I didn't ask why. Irv and Mickey told me that I shouldn't be surprised if the Polks weren't happy to see me, especially since Claudine did not know I was personally coming, and had used subterfuge to get there. The Ku Klux Klan, Irv cautioned me, was born in Pulaski, Tennessee, not far south of Rattle & Snap.

"The Polks are not in the Klan."

"Well, they're not singing 'Hava Nagila' either," Irv said.

Yeah, yeah, yeah. Get me down there.

Mickey, Deedee, and I climbed into a van that was attached to a horse trailer bearing Shpilkes. Deedee was dressed all in black. "I'm in mourning because that girl is *killing* you!"

Carvin' Marvin drove the van to the Thirtieth Street train station in Philly. Irv the Curve tapped on the window and handed Mickey his *Bulletin*.

Deedee was sniffling, her head against the window. *"I'm in mourning over here!"*

"Now, Jonah, I took care of things with the school. They know about the special circumstances," Mickey reminded me. "You'll get your diploma."

Deedee: "Your grandfather with all of his magical *connections. Woooo!*"

I started to laugh. I couldn't help it. Carvin' Marvin bit his lip. As America fell deeply in love with the Mafia, Deedee saw the Life as a pathetic joke. I was inclined to agree. If these guys were so powerful, why were they being chased all over the place by cops in polyester suits?

As we drove through the indignities of Camden's Admiral Wilson Boulevard—strip joints, quickie motels, booze shops, and warehouses praying for gentrification—I read on about Secretary of State Cyrus Vance and President Carter. Carter's inability to save these hostages meant that even powerful men could be chained down by their times.

"Do you know who Issac Bashevis Singer is?" I asked Mickey.

"Do I know? Of course I know. Gimpel the Fool," Mickey said. "Why?"

"I read an interview with him. Somebody asked him how he could believe in God when all these awful things happened. You know what he said? He said, 'Maybe he's a little God.' "

"Little is right," Deedee said.

"Carter's a little president," I added.

"Where's this going?" Mickey wondered. "Do you want to be a big president?"

"Yes, I do."

Deedee, rolling her eyes: "Listen again to Jonah *Godol*."

Mickey, flicking his wrist: "Go, fly like an eagle." Mickey pronounced it *iggle*. "And when you're with that girl, you be careful. You know about the condos, right?"

"You're building condos?"

"No—*condos*, in case something happens with that girl. You know, private matters. The things from the drugstore."

Unbelievable. *Condos*.

"Yes, Pop, I know about condos."

"There are consequences," Mickey reminded me.

The train rolled impossibly heavy past the piles of junk strewn beside the tracks of West Philly. These scraps had once been automobiles, I thought—cars that someone had once been proud to drive home and show off to bouncing children. A collective sigh echoed through the car as we passengers who did not know each other mourned our soldiers twisted beneath metal in a desert.

I walked back to the rear of the train and patted Shpilkes's nose as she stood in her vented car. Her eyes bugged out humanly.

Where the hell am I going exactly? Shpilkes's eyes asked, young, smart, and bitchy.

"I'm taking you to a place called Rattle & Snap. To a girl who calls you Spilled Kiss." I turned around, paranoid. No one could see this. But I had a gun—if they saw me talking to the horse, I could shoot them and dump them near Baltimore.

That's not my freakin' name. This from the animal.

"I know, but you should see her."

I did. They're all the same. They're buttocks and legs as far as I'm concerned.

"This one's more than that."

Yeah, yeah, yeah. Pbhpbhpbh. Hruuuhhhh.

I couldn't take much more of this, so I returned to my seat, upset with myself for letting a horse talk to me this way. We were approaching Wilmington.

An old man with a yellow mustache, white beard, and a Western hat looked me up and down. His eyes sparkled like saltwater.

"Saw you back there talking to that horse," the old man said.

Nailed.

"Me? Talking to—no—I mean, I was—"

"T'sall right. I talk to 'em myself."

I threw my arms up. "I felt bad about leaving her back there."

"I understand. Horses is people, too."

I laughed. He didn't.

"Where you headed, son?"

I felt around at my backpack. The cold steel of the gun was in there. Lie here, Jonah. At least be vague.

"Delivering the horse in Nashville and then going to visit friends out west."

The old man winked at me. "You got a crowded head, I'd say. I seen plenty of crowded heads in my day. You're thinkin' thoughts, talkin' to animals like Doctor Dolittle."

"Uh-huh."

"How old are you, eighteen?"

"Yes."

The old man smiled showing a few stringy teeth. "Only one thing at that age can turn a man's head to such chaos. What's she like, son? Tell Easy."

"Tell easy?"

"Easy. That's my name. Easy."

"How'd you get that name?"

"'Cause I just listen. Don't make nobody listen to me. I make it easy. Let people tell their story. Learn more than all the college boys in the world put together."

"Easy, I don't think my life will ever be the same."

"Won't, son."

"Is it stupid to even go?"

Easy hit my knee. "You got to go. T'swhat this whole time-a-life's about. Goin'."

"How will it turn out?"

"The way it's supposed ta."

"That doesn't tell me much."

"I dunno much."

"I thought you knew more than all of the college boys."

"I do. They don't know pumpkins."

I shook my head. "Then what will happen?"

"The beginning will happen. Beginnings always start with some sign or some woman. Right now, you're thinkin' 'bout how you'll be received, how it ends. What you'll know someday when you're my age is this is how it begins."

"Just what do you think is beginning, Easy?"

"Findin' the Promised Land. Makin' your own home."

"You think I'm getting *married?*"

"Sure, someday."

"To Claud—" *Damn.* "To Claudine?"

"To some girl. You leave. You find. You begin. You return. You go home. You go home once you leave, you find, you begin and return. It's easy."

"It sounds hard."

"It is, boy."

"But you said it was easy."

"It's easy for me to understand."

"Why?"

"Because I'm old and I'm Easy." He howled, self-satisfied. I stared at the old man worshipfully throughout the steely roll into Nashville. When we stopped, the workmen unloaded an uncooperative Shpilkes from the rear.

I shook Easy's hand. He rose, strangely tall, angelic.

"Boy," he whispered, "you'll be received different where you're goin', but you'll be all right. There're some folks who ain't exactly happy 'bout how things turned out. You know. Civil War."

"Where are you going?" I asked.

"Everywheres. I go wherever somebody keeps a candle."

As I guided Shpilkes down a ramp toward a huge warehouselike room, I turned back toward the train. Easy stood between cars. He tipped his hat as the train vanished in the direction of the burning Delta.

PART THREE

FUNHOUSE

2005

No more fair play. From now on it's dirty pool and judo in the clinches. The savage nuts have shattered the great myth of American decency. They can count me in. I feel ready for a dirty game.

—Hunter S. Thompson

AT HOME WITH WONDERBOY

"I thought when you were done, you were done."

I called Edie as I drove across the Delaware Memorial Bridge because the kids liked to ambush me upon my arrival home. I could see them bouncing like music notes on the covered porch from a few hundred yards. This was our house on Edie's parents' farm in Cowtown, New Jersey, home of the famous Cowtown Rodeo. That's right, a rodeo in New Jersey. People from other parts of the country (like New York) can't believe it, but it's only minutes after crossing the Delaware River from Philadelphia that a soul will find himself in the middle of the prime farmland that encompasses much of South Jersey.

It was spring break, and Ricky, seven, and Lily, five, were off from school. Edie was thrilled I was leaving the White House. She was the only person I've ever known for whom power held no allure, and it was one of the reasons I was still so fascinated by her. I had the intangible sense I had betrayed her—and my children for that matter—but outside of working too hard, I had not, to my knowledge, committed any of the conventional sins. When I was away from them, it pained me physically, especially behind my eyes.

Edie had to restrain Lily, who, having no sense of a universe outside her own thoughts, would have run right in front of my car. Edie released both of them as soon as I cut the engine, and they draped themselves against the driver's side door, not understanding that they were preventing me from getting out.

"Come out, Daddy! Come out!"

"He can't get out when you're up against the door," Edie explained with characteristic patience, pulling both children back with some difficulty.

I spent the first twenty minutes at home flat on my back because Ricky and Lily felt it was important to sit on me in order to show me the pictures they had drawn. There was a policeman with a huge pumpkin head (Lily shared my fascination with big-headed things) and a psychedelic car with wheels like marbles (Ricky used color to convey speed). The pièce de résistance was a black horse—pooping, of course. Edie shook her head in resignation at this picture, knowing that the joint effort was likely to be validated with a paternal laugh. It was.

No mention had been made of my career implosion.

"They miss you so much, Jonah," Edie said after Ricky and Lily ran into another room.

"How about you? Do you miss me?" I asked.

"Of course. What kind of question is that?"

"You know me. The whole abandonment thing."

"When do you have to go back to Washington?"

"Tomorrow morning. I have to finish out a special project, and then I'm done."

"I thought when you were done, you were done."

"I wish it worked that way."

"It works that way if you want it to work that way."

I had decided in the car that I could not tell Edie yet about Claudine having made contact. She vaguely knew that I had had a Southern girlfriend a long time ago, but we never discussed old romances. I had never inquired about her history, not because I didn't care, but because I cared so much that I felt the slightest detail might destroy me. I had heard stories of people hearing news so traumatic that they would just fall over and die. More likely, I was afraid that any such knowledge would become a thorn of obsession: I am not a progressive man, I do not LET GO, MOVE ON, GET CLOSURE, or PUT THINGS IN PERSPECTIVE. I obsess, I ruminate, I grieve, I overanalyze, and I ache.

For Edie's part, she knew that I had never been one to troll around. I had never drawn that postmodern line dividing sex and love. She intuited that despite the erotic impulses I might feel toward other women, my puritanical superego would beat my id down like a Republican in Malibu.

The success of my grandparents' long marriage (my only model) taught me the limits of communication. In an age when "sharing" was considered the panacea, I believed that thrashing around alone was preferable to forcing Edie to swim around with the livid salamanders in my soul. Deedee dealt with her "issues" through delusions of having had a pedigree in show business. Mickey went for walks. Perhaps they had other ways of managing the is-ness of life, but I'll never know what they were.

"Do you think that whatever it is you have to wrap up will redeem how things ended?" Edie asked.

"You mean losing my job in front of the whole world?"

"What else would I mean?"

Stupid, Jonah.

"There's a part of me, Edie, that's afraid of coming home notorious."

Her great squaw's brown eyes blinked (Edie is one-quarter Lenape Indian). "Like your grandfather."

"Right."

"We don't see it that way, Jonah. Notoriety is your . . . mental fixture."

Mental fixture. It was an apt term—a thing that becomes a permanent part of a person's psyche, the way a landmark cannot be separated from its physical landscape—the Grand Canyon or Devil's Tower. We get these notions lodged in there, and can't shake them loose.

On an intellectual level, I knew Edie was right, but this storm was raging in a different part of my brain. The part postmarked Atlantic City. I felt as though my family saw me as a fugitive, and I couldn't face them just yet. I had to clean things up. But now I've been dealt this gorgeous joker outside the White House gates with some kind of prophesy from Mount Pleasant, Tennessee. *You know you've got to go down there before you can come home, Wonderboy.*

Edie's hands were long and warm. When I ran my fingertips over them, I remembered how I needed to be within her reach.

"I know you don't see it that way. It's why I want to make things perfect. Because that's what you deserve."

I leaned in toward her, but rapid footfalls stopped us. Ricky and Lily, freshly changed into pajamas, dive-bombed onto the sofa pinning me against their mother. It hit me that the scent of a child's hair was Revelation.

ABOUT THAT PROMISE

"It's a queer thing, surveying what you love from outer space."

Tommy Jacomo sat me at my favorite booth at the Palm on Nineteenth Street in Washington, D.C. I figured I'd get here first because the Panamanian worked, well, where he worked.

The Panamanian's real name was Marcus Dalendo. I called Marcus "the Panamanian" because he was born in Panama, and because I thought it sounded cool to call him "the Panamanian." He was from South Jersey, too, and, by cosmic coincidence, also ended up working in Reagan's White House twenty years ago.

Marcus was . . . let's just say, a lawyer who did intelligence work. You may assume this means CIA. Woo, spooky. Whatever. The reality was that in the modern age of terror, the most lethal operatives were independent contractors unfettered by bureaucracy. Since I became press secretary, he occasionally used me to leak disinformation at my noon briefings, which I did because I thought it was cool. The Panamanian arranged for Claudine to be expressed a "black," or untraceable, mobile phone with which we could talk until I could get to Rattle & Snap, which was about an hour south of Nashville.

Marcus did not go to work each day in a squat government building. This was critical to his ability to be effective in the war on terror. A man unfettered by a punch clock is a man who can get lots done. A man who does not exist cannot be guilty of anything; he cannot be quoted in newspaper articles; he cannot be fired; but he can solve problems.

Marcus was a spy in the original sense of the term—he eavesdropped on people to find out their most precious vulnerabilities in order to leverage this information against them.

We had met at a Xerox machine in the White House basement in 1984. He was a twenty-two-year-old punk working in the national security advisor's office. I was a twenty-two-year-old punk working for the president's main pollster. We studied each other for a moment, wondering which genius knew how to unclog a paper tray. I knew I had a friend when Marcus found a letter opener and began hacking away at the thing. "You know, Jonah, violence often *is* the answer," he said.

"Totally agree," I had said.

Ours was a visceral friendship perhaps because of our rogue streaks, which were stifled in a bureaucratic environment where there was no higher achievement than not visibly screwing up. My most recent favor for the Panamanian was stating at a news conference that the president was considering a visit to Milan, where we quietly suspected a terrorist cell was forming. The president had no such intention, but when the terrorists heard he might be visiting, they began scrambling to plan an attack. Their chatter allowed the Panamanian's assets on the ground to track the plotters down to an apartment above a Milanese café, which exploded, killing six terrorists, a few weeks later. "Another senseless tragedy caused by improperly leavened pita bread," the Panamanian remarked at lunch the following week in the White House mess.

The Palm's daily march of the Self-Deluded had begun—lobbyists and operatives trickling in sufficiently after noon so that an audience had assembled to witness them sweep from Tommy's podium down the runway to that lofty altitude of the Ego. There appeared to be an awful lot of bowing for a twenty-first-century crowd. No one bowed to me, but a big-name lobbyist greeted me by my first name as I made my way down the aisle. President Truitt once referred to this as "cross validation"—the rewarding sensation that one gets when one is acknowledged by a person in one's own rarefied league. There was something about that naked desperation to be a player that filled me with a contempt that I could barely contain. Perhaps this was because I was eminently aware of my status: recently disgraced. In addition to their fries, this was the secondary sell of the Palm: the aftertaste of having *been there* when something—or someone—big was going down.

The faces of dead senators and nouveau riche real estate developers beamed down at me (*Mazel tov! You made the wall!*), while a kid in his twenties at the next table kept turning toward me and grinning. I could see his unripe mind working: *I'm sitting next to a guy who sat next to the president, thereby making me . . . what exactly?*

I glanced at a newspaper article in *The Washington Post* that caught my eye. Scientists working to build a more effective roach trap had invented a synthetic chemical that mimicked the pheromone of the female German cockroach. This chemical caused the male of the species to become so obsessed that he would forgo food and oxygen for a frenzied chance to have sex with his lust-scented Object. Of course, once he chased the scent, he would become immobilized in a sweet-tasting substance inside the trap, which he would futilely try to flee, only to spend his remaining hours hyperventilating, severing his own legs from his thorax, and asking himself who was the cockroach who ended up with the elusive and achingly hot cockroachette? Good Lord, I thought, it was all chemicals.

The Panamanian, Marcus Dalendo, looked over his shoulder and slid into the booth. He slid a manila envelope across the table, and studied the miniportrait on the wall beside him. "Who the hell was Roman Hruska?"

"Senator," I replied. "From a million years ago."

"Big nostrils, huh?"

"That's what he was known for. Very progressive on nasal issues."

The Panamanian grabbed a knife and sliced a pickle. "A little green in honor of Passover?" he said, sliding the bowl toward me.

"No thanks, I'm saving myself for a heaping side of bitter herbs."

I opened the envelope, which contained satellite photos of Rattle & Snap. "I forgot how close the airport was," I said.

"Lots of fields, too," Marcus said. "I threw in a shot of your farm in South Jersey just for fun."

I placed aerial photos of the two properties side by side and ex-haled slowly. "God, Marcus, it's a queer thing surveying what you love from outer space."

"How are you holding up after the fall?" he asked after downing a pickle slice.

"Press secretary's a tough job. You use one wrong participle and can set off a war in the Balkans."

"Bummer."

The Panamanian adjusted his wire-rimmed glasses and ask me cryptically, "Did you talk to Scarlett?" Claudine.

I nodded. "I'm a little shaken up."

"What about that ghost that visited you? You got an ID?"

"Not yet."

"What's our mission?"

"She needs my help in a big way."

"Thank you for the specificity. And she thinks you'll help her why exactly?"

"Because she knows me, Marcus."

"She knows you believe in damsels in distress, knights in shining armor?"

"Yes. She knows I believe in those things . . . in some order."

"What's in it for you?"

"My history, I suppose."

"How can I help, Jonah?"

"Can you go down with me?"

"I've got vacation time."

"I can't do this alone."

"What about your former boss?"

"I'm going to see him after lunch."

"Does he know how to return favors?"

"I think so."

"Do you know what kind of help you need?"

"I have a few scenarios in my head. Now we have to make it hap-pen on the street."

"Tell me."

I slid the satellite photos back into the envelope and let him in on an old secret.

Even when the Secret Service knows you, they have to check your driver's license once you leave the White House staff. It had only been two days since my farewell, but the rules are the rules. I was now the worst thing a former political *playa* could be in Washington: a citizen. When you set aside all of the common-man worship nonsense, the whole point of democracy was having the freedom to become better than everybody else.

Tigger greeted me with a big hug in the West Wing lobby.

"Can he see me, or is he in the Bubble?"

"He knows you're coming."

Let me explain the Bubble and its paradox. We are all part of a food chain of desirability, of power. The president of the United States is at the top of that food chain: Everybody wants a piece of him.

Now, take somebody like me. When I was press secretary, I was very high on the food chain. One of Tigger's main functions was protecting me from grasping acquaintances who wanted to trade on their link to me. But to, say, the secretary of state, I was a functionary—someone to be treated civilly, but no one who needed to be reckoned with.

When you are the president, being in the Bubble is necessary. Lots of people walk away frustrated, "dissed," to use the current jargon, when they aren't admitted. But it has to be this way because, without the Bubble, the president would be devoured.

There is a huge risk living in the Bubble, and herein lies the paradox. When you are isolated from life functions, your immune system grows precious. If and when a harsh truth, or another of life's rusty nails, penetrates the Bubble, your defenses have become flabby and you are not equipped to do combat.

President Truitt was sensitive to the existence of rusty nails, especially his endorsement by the New Jersey unions I had delivered a few years ago. I had predicted that there would have been greater scrutiny of that deal, especially since the president had since appointed several anti-RICO federal judges. The scrutiny never happened, which he viewed as a stay of execution. And it gave him incentive to keep a close eye on the guy who engineered the whole thing.

Tigger and I cut through the Roosevelt Room and made the diagonal to the corridor outside the Oval Office. The president's personal assistant was on the telephone, but mouthed "Go on in."

Roscoe opened the Oval Office door, and we glanced around the room. No Big Guy.

"He was with Mr. Cane in there a minute ago," Roscoe said.

Dexter Cane was the national security advisor, and had been the president's closest friend since they served together in Vietnam. Cane was also cheating on his helmet-headed horse-country wife. With Tigger. Tigger told me everything. I had vowed to keep her secret, but I suspect Cane knew that I knew. Eastman: 1, Cane: 0.

"He must be in the study," Roscoe said.

Indeed, we found President Truitt in the small study that adjoined the Oval Office. Dexter Cane wasn't here. Different presidents used this room for different purposes. Reagan used to have lunch in here (there's an adjacent kitchen). Lyndon Johnson used to sit in the bathroom and void his bowels while getting briefed by his staff. Because he could. President Truitt used this room to rest his lanky frame on the sofa with his feet up and go through his papers.

The president got right to the point: "I don't mean to be callous, son, but why would you go out of your way for this Polk woman at this stage in your life? You still bewitched?"

"No, I don't think so. We're middle-aged now."

"Doesn't mean a thing. People try to bring back old memories on a desperate basis inside that funhouse we call middle age—all those misshapen goblins flashing up at us, with nowhere to run. Those things seldom work out. Besides, so much of that intensity is anchored in the moment."

"I agree."

"So, if there's no rekindling, what's the motive? Old times' sake?"

"Sure, sentiment."

The president narrowed his eyes and sighed. "The Secret Service tells me you met a real looker out by the northwest gate a few days ago."

"That's true. Right before I came in to say good-bye to you."

"And you didn't introduce us. I'm hurt, son."

"I invited her in. I told her we had cable."

"Heh-heh. Y'know, I don't get good reception up in the residence," the president said, scrunching his nose. "You'd think I would."

"This is God's way of keeping you in touch with the people."

"Well, I'll thank the Lord for yet another blessing when I hit my knees tonight. Now, son, there's some things I don't need to know, but it always concerns me when a man behaves out of character. A man, a-course, can always trick you, but you never struck me as one to keep a twinkie."

"The girl out at the gate? No, sir. I had never met her before. She brought me a message."

"From Tennessee? That old plantation?" The president scratched his ear with the tip of his glasses.

"Yes, sir."

"When was it you hid out there?"

"Nineteen eighty."

"Any chance you may have left Princess Buttercup with a little knish?"

I laughed despite the subject's gravity. Something about the Southern leader of the Free World saying "knish."

I squirmed in my seat. "She would have told me, wouldn't she?"

I did not want to hear his answer. I welcomed a lie. I thought, *You're the president, lay one on me.* The rasp of the alley cat Clinton tickled my throat: *"I did not have sexual relations with that woman."*

The president leaned forward and stretched his neck. I heard a small pop. He sighed. "Let's think about this for a minute now, shall we? A Jewish boy, raised by a grandfather who ran an illegitimate gambling enterprise and Lord knows what else, falls in love with Confederate royalty, a family that helped create the America we all know. That family, I bet, wasn't too sweet on you. That millionaire's boy you came up against sure as hell didn't want you as his date for cotillion."

"I don't remember telling you all that, sir."

"Then you don't remember that I have an FBI for supplementary purposes. My point is, if the Confederacy had a cannonball for every reason the Polk family would want to keep a half-Dixie, half-Israelite baby quiet, the capital of the United States would be Richmond right now. You folla?"

"I do."

"Did you notice any resemblance?"

"My daughter, Lily, has auburn hair. My grandmother was a redhead. This messenger girl had auburn hair. Green eyes. A dimple."

"Green eyes? A dimple? You look in the mirror lately, son?"

"Claudine has green eyes and a dimple, too. That's not enough to convict, sir."

"Uh-huh."

The president ambled to his bookshelf, and studied the titles with his reading glasses. He paged through Faulkner's *The Reivers* until he came to a highlighted passage. He began to read aloud in his peach-schnapps voice:

"Because there are some things, some hard facts of life, that you don't forget, no matter how old you are. There is a ditch, a chasm; as a boy you crossed it on a footlog. You come creeping and doddering back at thirty-five or forty and the footlog is gone; you may not even remember the footlog but at least you don't step out onto that empty gravity that footlog once spanned."

The president returned Faulkner to the shelf, removed his reading glasses, and awaited my response. Hearing none, he asked me, "And what do we learn from Mr. Faulkner?" he asked.

"You're telling me that this time I may step in a ditch, sir."

"I'm not telling you a thing. I'm shrewd, but I'm not wise. Faulkner was wise, but he wasn't shrewd. Shrewd men don't become writers. You, son, are up against a cunning greater than your own. I don't know if that cunning is a woman or time itself, but don't get yourself into something you can't get out of. What was that Yiddish proverb your grandfather taught you?"

"Entrances are wide, exits are narrow."

"That's the one. Now, you need some assistance, I suppose, and I promised you some. What have you got in mind?"

I handed the president a piece of paper, which he studied. "Now, son, all you want me to do is say these few lines here at a press conference, and we're square?"

"That's all I need for now."

"Will I just blurt these lines out like I have Tourette's syndrome?"

"No, an issue will surface in the news prompting a question."

"An issue?"

"Yes, sir. The rest will take care of itself."

"Heck, boy, the last time you told me that, I ended up sending B-2 bombers over Damascus!"

"You know you wanted to, sir."

"I suppose." The president studied the typed sheet of paper. "Now, Jonah, given this entrance you've given me, I'd like to know a bit more about the exit."

"You mean, what else I may request of you."

"Indeed."

"I'm not sure yet."

"So, I may be about to launch World War III?"

"Absolutely not. Just, perhaps, another Civil War."

"Somehow I believe you," the president said, rubbing his eyes. "The Polks were Scots, weren't they?"

"Originally, yes. Why?" I asked, surprised by the non sequitur.

"Those crazy Scots were all tied in with the Freemasons. You ever heard of the Knights of the Golden Circle?"

"It sounds vaguely familiar." I winked at him.

"So you have. I figured as much. I also figure I'm not the only one you've got roped into this."

"You are correct, sir."

"You recognize that certain things can't be run out of the White House. I suppose you'll need that Panamanian friend of yours?"

"Yes, sir. I'll keep you posted through Tigger, if you'd like."

"I wouldn't like, but I suppose like doesn't have much to do with it. Naw, you stay in touch with Tigger and she'll talk to Dexter." There was a fleeting surge in his pupils. So, he knew about them, too. "Now, let's me and you pray."

"For what, sir?"

"For the poor son of a bitch who's about to find himself on the receiving end of the plagues of Jonah Eastman."

PART FOUR

WHO IS POLK?

MAY–JUNE 1980

I do not think I have anywhere eaten fruit of such
delicious flavor as this tree produced.

—George Washington Polk, master of Rattle & Snap

PILLARS

"Matthew, Mark, Luke, and John . . ."

The horse trailer dropped me at the edge of Zion Road in Canaan, Tennessee, a demarcation on the map near Mount Pleasant. For security reasons, Mickey and Irv didn't want me to be dropped off right outside the gates of Rattle & Snap. I knew from a map that it was a few miles down, off of Route 43 South. I mounted Shpilkes from a nearby fence post and began riding him bareback. Every few hundred yards, I had to alternate hands between holding the reins and my canvas duffel bag.

The sun was on its slow descent, but it was still light and very hot outside. The housing was sparse. Most of the homes that I did see were ranches made of brick. I passed very little landscaping, but a huge amount of rolling land. A small, hand-painted sign read CHECKS CASHED—MOUNT PLEASANT–5 MILES. All kinds of surreal thoughts dominated my short ride.

This doesn't look like heaven.
Maybe this whole obsession has been in my head.
Maybe I have a mental illness.
Maybe Claudine isn't as beautiful as I remembered.
What if she has lost all her teeth?
Am I going to be lynched?
"The bride is too beautiful."
I am regretting this.
I have a gun.

I dismounted at first sight of the pillars. The house was planted a quarter mile from the road. Holy Moses, this house. *House?* No, *house* was a middle-class word for a residential dwelling. I could not identify the right word for what rose through the haze. So this is what Springsteen meant by "mansions of glory." Does one kneel at a sight like this, or dismiss it as a hallucination? Cross one's self? Await revelation? There were no seas for God to part, no bushes to burn, no arks to surf toward Claudine's Corinthian columns.

I pulled a sport jacket out of my duffel bag and slipped it over my shirt. This would make me look more regal for the Polks. Regal, the name of a Buick. *Schmuck.* I also wore a western-style belt with a thick silver buckle that Mickey had bought me on a trip to Nevada years ago. I must have looked like an orphan. Which I was. This duffel bag had seen better days—it had been to Cuba with Mickey.

I proceeded with awe to a low iron gate, which was closed. This was tricky. I had heard a lot about Southern hospitality and assumed that there might be some gate etiquette, so I stood pondering the metal for a few minutes. I noticed a Civil War–era cannon just beyond the gate. It was pointed toward me. Nice. Then I heard the queerest thing. I could have sworn that the Devo song "Working in the Coal Mine" was blasting from one of the mansion's windows. I had one of those netherworldly sensations of not being certain that I was, in fact, here.

Suddenly angry, I dropped my duffel bag against the brick post that supported the gate and turned Shpilkes around.

"We're goin' over," I told the horse.

"What, you can't wait two minutes for somebody to open the gate like a normal person?" I heard the horse say. *"Jumping bareback no less."*

"I came too far, beast. And so did you."

"Oy." From the horse.

I squinted at the gate, and kicked Shpilkes on, hard.

I should be institutionalized. This was my main thought as Shpilkes galloped toward the gate. I crouched down and wrapped my arms around her neck while holding onto the reins. Together, we flew over. Shpilkes's mane blew upward in the sudden breeze, and then down. I looked over my shoulder at the gate, tough-guy style, thinking, *Ain't nuthin' but a thing.*

Rattle & Snap was not the biggest residence that I had ever seen—Philadelphia's Main Line had its share—but it was the grandest. The façade was made of a buttery stucco. White trim, like frosting, had been neatly sculpted around the edges. Ten alabaster pillars supporting the structure appeared to be giant birthday candles. As I approached the front portico, I became hungry. I wanted to eat this place. The yellow ribbons tied around the pillars for our hostages punctured my appetite, and snapped me back to attention.

To the south of the mansion, humidity floated above the soil. An old black man stood by an even older stable, with his wrist balanced on the handle of a shovel. He wore a straw hat, not unlike the kind that other men of his generation wore on the Boardwalk in the summer. He slowly raised his hat in a gesture of respect and I waved at him. He pointed to the colonnade front of the mansion in an encouraging way, so I moved through another gate, this one open.

A handsome, coltish boy of about fourteen emerged from the front of the house. He set his hands on his hips and gazed at me studiously. I instinctively wiped my nose as if a giant green worm had been swinging from it.

"I know who you are," he said *Yeew are.* "I saw you take the gate." Good.

"Who am I?" I responded.

"You're that guy, Jonah, and that's a horse called Spilled Kiss," he said. He had elegant features similar to Claudine's.

"What's your name?" I asked.

"Guess."

"Robert E. Lee."

"Nuh-uh."

"Pete Rose."

"No way."

"Give me a hint, please."

"The Declaration of—blank."

"Independence."

"They call me Indy or Six. That's for Independence Polk the Sixth. You'll meet Indy Four soon enough." There was a number missing. The father.

I heard the sound of footsteps across a wooden floor and, from behind a pillar, Claudine bounced down the front steps, limbs flailing. She wore a gauzy, lime-green sundress that made her eyes roar with life. Dizzy, I dismounted—or fell. She didn't look at me until we were face-to-face. My stomach growled. She hugged me hard, eliciting eye rolls from Indy Six. I kissed her and got her ear. Suave. Claudine gave Shpilkes a kiss. The animal looked at me, human again: *"You're a dead man."* I responded with my eyes: *"But look at her!"*

Claudine had not lost her teeth. In fact, I wondered whether or not I should have been more heartsick all along, seeing her now. Pain was the only human response to her. But I was here, and being with her gave me something on which to drape the pain.

"I knew Spilled Kiss was coming, but I didn't know *you'd* bring her down."

"I kind of fibbed to your grandfather. He hired me as the stable boy."

"Stable boy. He said it was a guy named John."

"Like I said, I fibbed."

"I'm so glad you did. Six," Claudine said to the boy, "take Spilled Kiss to the stable." Six rolled his eyes, but obliged. "And turn down that Devo song!" Devo blasting from a plantation bedroom. Nothing made sense, but it had become a fun kind of confusion now, like when I had taken Claudine into the casino.

"I'm told I'll meet Four later."

"Why, ye-es." Claudine's eyes descended. "My father was Five. Indy Four is out camping on the grounds somewhere. He'll be back tomorrow. You look so tan."

"I live at the beach, remember?"

"Duh."

If any other eighteen-year-old woman said "Duh," it would have floated by me. This duh was evidence of brilliance, wit, grace.

I backed up a few feet to behold Claudine. In the sunlight—I had only seen her at night—her hair had a few light highlights. Her skin was a hue darker than I had remembered, perhaps from the sun, and her cheeks were flawless and flushed. *Was it humanly possible to be in love with someone's epidermis?* This wasn't love, it was psychosis, or some kind of poisoning that had to pass through me. Not content with simple worship, I wondered if it was somehow possible that her radiance was a mirage—that it was some kind of molecular convergence in my *mind* that had projected the collectivity of God's gifts onto an average creature.

Nah.

"C'mon inside and get some lemonade," Claudine said, grabbing my duffel bag and hauling it up the massive steps before I could stop her. "We'll set it here for a spell." *A spell.*

My eyes darted between Claudine and the columns.

"The columns were made in Cincinnati," Claudine explained. "They were delivered in pieces by rail to Nashville, then by oxen down here."

"Just like my columns," I said. Claudine flicked my shoulder.

The entryway was huge, with two smaller columns supporting it. Claudine explained that with the advent of modern plumbing, the Polks chose to run pipes through the columns rather than break through the walls, which were three bricks thick. The bricks had been fired here on the property by slaves during the construction of the mansion between 1842 and 1845.

A huge portrait of an imperious-looking Polk man glared down at us from the rear wall of the foyer. He wore a grand ring with an unfamiliar stone in the center.

"George Washington Polk," Claudine said. "He built Rattle & Snap."

"Where did he live before here?"

"In a cottage where the barn stands now. You'll see it out back later. The captain of the Union soldiers came inside the house with a torch. He saw this painting of George, which was hanging right here, and he noticed his Masonic ring. He ordered his soldiers to stand down. The captain went to the top man for the Union in the region, General Don Carlos Buell, who also happened to be a Freemason. General Buell was in Columbia not long after he took Nashville. He gave his captain orders not to destroy Rattle & Snap. He said, 'You are not to destroy the home of a Masonic brother.' All of the Polk plantations were spared."

We passed by a staircase to the right of the foyer and into a dining room, which was, get this, attached to another dining room. Two mammoth, carved pocket doors could be slid open and shut depending upon the number of guests. There was yet another staircase, even grander than the first, beyond the dining room. Beyond the second stairs there was a room that had no clear purpose, with small appliances, quilts, and photos scattered about, in a sense announcing, "This is what happens when you have so many rooms—some of them lose their way." Beyond this room, toward the rear of the house, was a large, modern kitchen.

Claudine retrieved a huge pitcher of lemonade from a humming Zero-King refrigerator and poured two glasses. She then tugged me up one of the staircases through a large living room that overlooked the front columns and into a bedroom where everything was puffy, even the photos. There wasn't a thing in this room you couldn't lie down on and fall right asleep. The huge four-poster was made of cherrywood.

"Polk girls have slept on this bed for centuries," Claudine explained. "And we all were taught the same prayer about these posts to say before bed. I say it every night."

"How does it go?"

She tilted her head to the side and blushed:

Matthew, Mark, Luke, and John,
Bless this bed that I lie on.

One is to see
Two is to pray
Three and four are to
Keep me from harm's way.

There was a silhouette of Claudine as a little girl near the door. I could tell by her turned-up nose. On a nearby table, there was a photo of Claudine at about six or seven. She was with her father, who was in uniform. She and Indy Six had his features, I decided. Claudine had been a coltish creature, I thought, and I knew that I would have fallen in love with her had I met her then. Other boys might not have noticed her—skinny, awkward, and quiet. But I would have seen what she would become.

There were four large bedrooms upstairs in the main part of the house. Claudine's was the fluffy-puffy one. Indy Six's bedroom furniture was a disparate collection of old desks, beds, and bureaus colliding with piles of vinyl albums from the likes of Devo, the Eagles, and REO Speedwagon. The whole room was an afterthought, a monument to male adolescence, in which furniture, like everything else, was a part of the adult conspiracy. Six emerged from the bathroom with a spot of shaving cream on his chin. I think he put it there on purpose.

"Hey, Jonah, wanna listen to some music?" he asked.

"Maybe later."

"Aw, c'mon, man."

"Six," Claudine asserted. "Jonah just got here, a-kay?"

Claudine explained that Indy Six had never known his father very well, and they both thought Indy Four was a nut. "Six will gravitate to you, Jonah, like the moon to the earth. You don't mind, do you?"

"Of course not."

Indy Four's bedroom in the rear of the house scared the wits out of me. There were glowering photos of Leonidas Polk, the "Fighting Bishop," and muskets along the wall. Leonidas was a Confederate general and the brother of George Washington Polk. There was a bronze bust of another scary-looking Polk glaring out at me. The bed was massive and unmade, as if Indy had been having a pillow fight with the Founding Fathers.

We breezed by the elusive Mrs. Polk's bedroom, which was sparse and neat, scarier in a way than Indy Four's. Ancient wallpaper with the Polk family crest aligned the walls. Claudine didn't concentrate on the room, and I wasn't inclined to go inside and look around.

Somehow, we ended back downstairs before a portrait of Andrew Jackson, a Polk family friend. Jackson's hair appeared flamelike. It was painted by George Washington Phillips, according to Claudine. I nodded at the name, as if I knew it, but I was just responding to how everybody around here seemed to be named after America's first president except for me. I felt like reintroducing myself as Benjamin Franklin Eastman and whipping up a Philly connection.

"All these dudes you've got on the walls looked pretty serious," I said.

"You bet they were," Claudine agreed.

I tugged at my shirt, and wondered why I was still sweating.

By the ghost of Jefferson Davis, there wasn't a vent, not a duct, not a humming window unit. All *this* and no AC. I needed air-conditioning. It was in the Talmud. I was raised in a casino. Noah's Ark had air-conditioning. God told Noah to bring two Westinghouse units, one for port, the other for starboard. Maybe the Freon imperative (along with the Kung-Pao-chicken-is-okay-for-Passover ethic) hadn't made it to the New Testament. Maybe the South wanted to compensate for slavery by saving the ozone. Heck with it. *Look at her.*

As the lemonade soothed my throat, a tall, fine-boned woman with light brown hair, in her early forties peered into the kitchen. I immediately put down my glass and wiped the chilly moisture from my palms against my khakis.

"You must be Mr. Eastman," she said.

"He *is*, Mother," Claudine added helpfully.

"Thank you for letting me visit, Mrs. Polk," I said, extending my hand. The thought flashed through me that I had once read that a man should not initiate a handshake with a woman. Had I blown it?

Mrs. Polk cautiously met my hand.

"I'm Petie Polk," she said. "What a nice handshake."

Petie Polk was dressed in a peach-colored cotton sundress and sandals. She had intense, attractive features, and shrewd laser eyes. Claudine and Indy Six did not look like her facially, but their builds were similar.

"We're very pleased you're here. Claudie says you know your way around stables."

Get to work, Yankee.

"I do. I've ridden horses since I was little and have worked at stables in the summer."

"At a racetrack," Petie said.

"Yes, that's right."

"My. My. Claudie, have you offered Jonah anything to eat?"

"Ooh, no, Mother."

"Why don't you. After all he's probably heard about Southern hospitality, he may not be terribly impressed."

Petie winked, wiggled her fingers, and made herself scarce somewhere on the continent of Rattle & Snap.

I waited, as instructed, in the formal dining room with my lemonade. I was afraid to put it down on the table with Martha Custis Washington snarling at me from atop a marble cutting board. *"What did I do, lady?"*

Within moments, a magical plate of chicken salad, fruit, and pumpkin bread drifted before me. Claudine sat down next to Martha Custis Washington, head balanced in her palms, and watched me eat bread that made me feel like a patriot.

IF YOU WANT TO KNOW THE TRUTH

"Faithful to every trust."

Claudine and I cleared the table, ditching Martha, and went out to the front portico. Claudine knocked on one of the pillars.

"See these, Jonah? They're hollow. During the Civil War, George Washington Polk hid his silverware and gold coins in the fourth pillar in case the Union soldiers looted the place. When the war was over, one of the young Polks was lowered into the pillars to retrieve it. Did you ever hear of such a strange place to hide money?"

"My grandfather hides his in Grand Cayman."

"Where's that?"

"It's an island in the Caribbean."

"How does he get it there?"

"The newspapers say he wires it."

"Wires?" *Wharrz.*

"I don't understand it myself. I just hope they don't have to lower me down someday to get it." A newspaper once wrote that Mickey was worth one hundred and fifty million dollars, but I knew this couldn't be true. When people can't see something, they assume there's a lot there when often there's nothing.

"Which one is the fourth pillar?" I asked.

"It depends on which way you look at the house. Only George knew."

"Did you ever look in there to see if there's any money left?"

Claudine shot me a silly look.

Bluish moonlight in our path, Claudine tugged me east of the mansion where an ancient brownstone church, St. John's Episcopal, rose before a cemetery. Several Polk plantations shared the church that the Fighting Bishop had built. Claudine said it was the oldest known plantation church in the country. It was a small and simple one-room affair with a single spire at its front. The Polks and their slaves had shared the church. They had all attended together and sat together. There had been no segregation—Claudine was adamant on this point. The church had been ransacked during the Civil War and had never been restored to its original form. In a change of plans, restoration was to be one of my main projects for the summer.

Behind the church there were dozens of graves belonging to Claudine's ancestors and Polk slaves. It was still light enough outside to identify the markers for George Washington Polk, Rattle & Snap's original master, and Sallie Hilliard Polk, his wife.

"We can trace back our ancestors to the Battle of Hastings in the year ten sixty-six," Claudine said. "The Polks were Scottish and Irish."

"Ten sixty-six," I repeated.

I noticed one grave that did not contain a Polk. It belonged to Colonel Robert Beckham.

"Who was he, Claudine?"

"Colonel Beckham invented the horse-drawn artillery wagon. He was close to my family. They were toughies. There was a Confederate general who said when he saw this cemetery that it was almost worth dying to be buried in such a place."

Another grave snared my attention. It bore the name "Mammy Sue." The stone read:

MAMMY SUE
Died January 1872
"Faithful to Every Trust"
The tender loving nurse of the eleven children of
George Washington and Sallie Hilliard Polk

In a far corner was a lonely obelisk bearing the name of Independence Polk the Fifth, Claudine's father. I took her hand sympathetically—I envisioned Pajamas crouching behind her father's grave marker—and said I was sorry, but she was stronger than I was.

"It's okay," she said. "See those headstones next to my father's? Those are for me, Indy Six, Indy Four, and my mother. Maybe even my children."

I let go of her hand and held her chin. "You know where you'll be, uh, where—"

"I'll be buried," Claudine answered. "Yes, I know. Right here. That unnerves you?"

"I've lost people before. My parents."

"Then death shouldn't be so exotic."

"That's not it. I mean, in a weird way I'm jealous."

"Of where I'll be buried?"

"No, that you know, that your life is so certain. I feel like I don't know what's going to happen in five minutes."

"Jonah, I don't know what will happen either, but I know what will happen eventually."

"Geez, I don't."

"Sure you do. Our destinies are the same. Our bodies will be in the earth, and our souls, if we are good Christians, will be in heaven."

Yeee. I flinched. Claudine noticed.

"What's wrong?" she asked.

"What if we're not good Christians?"

"You don't think you're a good Christian?"

Don't tell her yet, Jonah. Not the time. Never assume that others know. Your looks could be almost anything except for Swedish or Namibian. Waffle.

"I'm just not sure how it's defined, that's all."

"Oh, don't worry about it."

It wasn't going to heaven that unnerved me. It wasn't even hell. It was prehistoric Claudine and how she knew where the arc of her life would end. My history was fluid, wide open.

Claudine and I walked along the grass past a large pond to the site of the southernmost slave quarters, which had been torn down and rebuilt into little guest apartments in the style of motel rooms. This is where I would be staying. A blacksmith's shop had once been located nearby. A carriage house and a short structure built into the earth were only yards away. Claudine described the ground-level structure as the icehouse, which had been dug into the earth to preserve ice. The plant life around each structure was lush. Even under the moon, the colors were more vibrant than the neon in Atlantic City—perhaps because these colors were made by God, not fugitives.

"You're going to have a visitor to your room," Claudine told me.

I shuddered, fantasizing that this was a come-on, and felt deflated when she appeared to be stating a fact.

"His name is Elijah Polk. His family has lived here for hundreds of years. He's the last one. Elijah will be showing you your projects. He's responsible for the facilities."

"Elijah? Like the prophet?"

"I suppose."

"How's he related?"

"He's not related by blood, but he's family."

Claudine pushed open the door to the room.

It was laid out like a fifties-style motel room, with knotty pine paneling and old paintings of the plantation on the wall. There was an antique rolltop desk. The top shelf of the desk had a large photograph of a black family from yesteryear. Two twin beds were against the side wall separated by a wicker nightstand.

A soft creaking came from behind us. When we turned around, we saw a tall black man in late middle age. An elegant emblem of toil with reels of history whirring behind his eyes, he was the man who had waved to me when I rode up.

Claudine said, "Elijah, this is my friend Jonah Eastman."

"So he is," Elijah said sternly, shaking my hand, studying me.

"It's good to meet you, sir."

"Sir?" Elijah said, cracking a smile.

"Why not *sir*?"

"Why, son, I don't know," he laughed, incredulous.

* * *

Claudine left me to unpack, so I felt hollow. Elijah gestured to the twin bed farthest from the window. He clearly had something he wanted to say. He was a touch formal, like a teacher who had wandered for ages in search of a pupil.

"Claudine says your family has been at Rattle & Snap for hundreds of years," I said timidly, knowing full well what that meant.

"Don't have to walk on eggshells with me, son. I know my family was slaves here, if you want to know the truth. That's right, the Polks owned slaves, ninety-nine of them. They never bought, sold, or traded in slaves, though. The slave trade ended in eighteen-oh-eight; Rattle & Snap wasn't built till the eighteen forties. I live up in the mansion. There's rooms hidden there you'd never know. The house goes on and on. Sometimes I come out to this room to be with my thoughts.

"You must know a lot about this place." Duh.

"A lot? Pretty much everything. We farmed hemp here mostly. Don't get me wrong, I'm no fan of slavery. My grandfather said that in this life sometimes you don't get the best, you know, options. If he was going to be a slave, he once said, he was glad it was here.

"Never been a family like the Polks. Boggles the mind. People talk about the Kennedys. Those boys were just haircuts next to the Polks. President Jackson—he had no kids, you know—loved his niece, Mary Eastin, and wanted to walk her down the aisle when she got married to Will Polk's son, Lucius, so they had the wedding at the White House. The White House! President Jackson wanted to impress the Polks so much that he added a portico to the White House to be more formal. How about that?"

"Hmm."

"You ever heard of the Mecklenburg Resolves?"

"Something during the Revolution, right?"

"Started the Revolution, if you want to know the truth. Old Thomas Polk wrote up the Resolves. Know what they said, son?"

"No, sir."

"They declared King George's laws hooey," Elijah slapped his knee and howled. "The Polks told the king what he could do with his laws."

"Then what happened?"

"The Revolution happened. Polks financed a lot of the revolution. Now, say, you're from up near Philadelphia, Claudie said."

"Right. Jersey, actually."

"Well, Tom Polk's gang saved the Liberty Bell from the British. A group of his boys hid it out at a church, the Zion Reformed, up in Allentown."

"What did they think the British would do to it?"

"The British threatened to melt it down to make cannon balls."

Elijah pointed to my duffel bag, indicating that it was all right for me to unpack.

"I don't mind telling these stories as long as you don't mind listening."

I dropped a few shirts on the bed. "I love history. The more you can tell me about this place, the happier I'll be."

"Aw, you'll learn to love it."

"I already love it."

"Colonel Will Polk, you know, won Rattle & Snap from the governor of North Carolina. All of Tennessee once belonged to the Carolinas."

"How did he win it, in a war or something?"

"Why, gambling, son."

"Gambling?" I fell back onto the bed. "Is this the game rattle-and-snap?"

"You're all right, son. How'd you know that?"

"My grandfather told me about it. He's, uh . . . he had heard of the game."

Will Polk had led guerrilla bands during the revolution. He didn't hesitate to throw dice or use a musket. He had been shot in the face during one vicious battle, sparking the legend among the Redcoats that "the colonies had a man who caught bullets with his teeth." When his comrades approached him thinking he was dead, he just stood up cursing and ran after the British, shooting.

Will had divided the land between his four sons, Lucius, Leonidas, George, and Rufus. George had named his tract Rattle & Snap after the game his father had played to win the five thousand six hundred acres in 1792. This had caused of a scandal among the Polks, who didn't want to advertise the roguish manner in which the land had been acquired. The other brothers chose nobler names like Ashwood, Hamilton Place, and Belle Meade.

"Almost as soon as Rattle & Snap was built, the whole thing was over. After the meteor shower, everything came undone."

"What meteor shower?"

Elijah explained that many changes in a society were tied to God. God let men know about change through a warning shot. "Something natural-like," Elijah said. In 1856, a brilliant display of light spread across the Southern heavens, touching off widespread rumors of a slave rebellion. The plantation owners took the meteor shower as an omen of collapse, while many slaves saw it as a divine sprinkling of hope.

Elijah began a hearty guffaw: "You haven't met Indy Four yet, have you?"

"No, sir."

"You will. My Lord. My best friend. See, I told you about Old Tom Polk, Old Will Polk, but there's many more, that's why I get so holy. Indy Four's obsessed with them, if you want to know the truth. Harding Polk, Indy's uncle, for example, led the campaign against Pancho Villa. Did you ever have an uncle like that?"

"I had an uncle who led the campaign to bring whitefish to Bookbinder's," I answered. Bookbinder's was a legendary seafood restaurant in Philadelphia.

"Never heard of it, but I'm sure you're proud."

I half-smiled, like a bombing Borscht Belt comic.

"Indy's got the personality of a cyclone. You'll think he's crazy. Everybody does. He's not. See, he had these cousins who built America, but he never saw war himself and suspects he had it too easy, which he did. Hates himself for it, that old boy, spoiling for a war. Instilling it in his grandson. Goes out hunting with that child, plays cavalry, plots military strategy against varmints. . . . You're sweet on Claudine."

"Sweet? No, I don't think so. It's a disease."

"Ha-ha. She's sweet on you, too. Never seen her like she was when she came back from Atlantic City. Not with that J.T. either. She's been sailing around on a cloud till you got here. You're all right, son. You don't seem like a trivial man. Claudie's the prize that J.T. wants on his mantel."

I turned into a fountain of sweat. The room spun out from under me, and I fell back on my bed trying to appear as if I was sitting down by choice.

"My, my, my, I did it now," Elijah said. "You didn't know, didja?"

"Know what?" I gagged out.

"About J. T. Hilliard."

"No."

"Well, I'm sorry, son. You were gonna run into that boy sometime."

Everything is in the hands of its enemies.

STRIPPING THE CHURCH

"What are they buying?"

My turbocharged engine for longing is equipped with an exhaust system. Let's call it the Eastman Rage-o-matic. For all of my protests about my grandfather being a gangster and my having a warped childhood in casinos and hideouts, there is a beast inside of me capable of petty and vicious thoughts. I have long feared that this quality will someday turn me into Mickey, but, outside of becoming cold and distant, I've never lashed out at somebody innocent. The closest I've ever come to unleashing the beast has been a few schoolyard fights, where I won the reputation of being one of the smaller kids who would actually hit back even if, in the end, I lost the fight, which I almost always did. Some bullies didn't tangle with me, not because they weren't confident they could take me (they could), but because they knew there was a small chance that I would do something outrageous during the fight that would cause them to lose face.

Usually, the rages turned inward and pounded me down into a sluggish state, not unlike the way I had been feeling after I met Claudine. When I got depressed, I'd got scared too, scared that I'd do something completely crazy, either to myself or somebody else.

J.T.

I envisioned him as one of those Main Line guys I so feared Claudine falling for on the night I met her. I despised him in his unknown blondness and breezy command of his universe, but I despised Claudine worse for bringing me down to be tortured.

Having not slept at all, I rose early. Elijah had left a note for me on the door indicating that he would be at the church. He had beautiful handwriting.

The inside of the church was cool and damp. There were metal poles, not unlike for clotheslines, running horizontally above the pews and across the sanctuary that caught my eye.

"What are those poles for?" I asked Elijah.

"Those are supports for earthquakes."

"But they're so skinny. How could they help?"

"They can't. They just make white men feel like they've got control over something they don't."

Elijah cackled and left. I saw where he had begun stripping the paint off of the inside walls. I got to work, furiously. My anger resurfaced. I hated paint. What was paint but another scam to fake out people from knowing what something was made of? In the next half hour, I had scraped off the doors. My eyes were running like a schoolgirl's and I was sweating through my clothes.

Claudine approached on her broom. *With* a broom, actually, but I knew she could fly it if she wanted to. I glimpsed her face out of the corner of my eye and flinched. Whenever I saw her after even a brief period of separation, I was startled by her looks. A trick by a spiteful God.

"What are you doing up so early?" she warbled.

"Oh," I said casually, "Just starting my job."

"You don't have to start yet."

"Lots to do." I couldn't look at her.

This summer would be about work. Labor would be my sublimation. I would not confront Claudine about J.T. Then I'd seem like a eunuch. I could envision what Claudine would say already. It would be the "How dare you be angry that I date others" speech. I had no tolerance for this, and suspected that maybe Deedee was on to something when she said that women like Claudine want to want to be loved. Watching casino dramas unfold, I had grown to feel less sorry for the showgirls—Marilyn Monroe clones who wept volumes about looking for love when there seemed to be men everywhere that loved them. Maybe the Marilyns didn't want love, they wanted the passion of impossibility. If I had half a brain, I would be on the next train back to Philly and look up Jamie at the Golden Prospect, or Lisa and Deborah, who actually liked my poem about Claudine.

Claudine stood and watched me work for a few moments. "Elijah said you'd need something to sweep up with."

Yeah, I need to sweep up what remains of me.

"Great. Thanks." She was even prettier with a broom.

"Jonah, what's wrong?"

"I'm just a hard worker."

"No, really. Did Elijah say something?"

"We talked a while. Interesting guy. I learned a lot of neat stuff about this place, about Will Polk, J.T., and the Mecklenburg Resolves, the Liberty Bell, J.T., how good the Polks were to their slaves." I kept scraping. "What do you suppose is under all this paint? J.T. It's hard to get through, you know?"

"Jonah, get over here."

I dropped my scraper and proceeded to the pew where Claudine had pointed. She took my face in her hands, which reminded me that I hadn't kissed her since my arrival, and here I was sweating.

"J.T. and I have dated off and on for years. Our families are friends. We're off now."

"Now?"

"I went to the prom with him a few weeks ago, but all I've been thinking about since I met you has been you. He's going to Vanderbilt, too, this fall, just so you don't find out from someone else."

"I'd duel, you know."

"Are you insane?"

"You have no idea."

She threw her arms around me and kissed me. She didn't back off when a lone bead of sweat fell from my eyebrow onto her nose. The image made me think of a TV promo for ABC's *Wide World of Sports*, which featured a ski jumper hurtling down a stilted ramp, skiless. The voice-over said: "The agony of defeat."

I didn't know where the rage went, but it abandoned me. Had

there been a minister here, I would have married Claudine whatever her denomination.

"Elijah," she whispered, "doesn't like J.T. for beans. He thinks he's a good ole boy and has his father figured for Klan, which he's not."

"Hey, don't be too hard on the Klan. They burn a mean cross."

"Jonah!"

She kissed me again until I had the brilliance to blurt out a question: "What's Rattle & Snap's business now? How do you keep all of this, pay people like me?"

Claudine sighed. "Do you know how much five thousand six hundred acres is? A lot. Over the years we've sold off land. That's kept some money coming in. And we grew a ranching business, here and in Texas, that did all right."

"I'm not a business whiz like my grandfather, but it must take a fortune to live like this. I've met some pretty rich people in my life, but this—"

"Jonah, you mustn't say anything to anyone."

"I won't."

"We're running out. We don't own everything we live on. These businesses don't do so well anymore. We've still got land, but we've had to sell most of it. It's like water flooding around an island over time, making the island smaller and smaller."

"Who buys it?"

"Investors."

"I don't see a lot of building going on."

"No."

"Why would someone buy all this land? If farming isn't big money, and ranching and horses aren't that big, what are the investors buying?"

Claudine stammered, "I don't know," and then she pulled me toward her and kissed me, more, I thought, to change the subject than out of affection. I didn't care. She gripped the back of my head with her fingers fastened in my hair. Her grip was superhuman.

"This wasn't how it was done in the old days, courting," she said.

"How was it done?"

"Fans. If a girl liked a boy at a dance, she would hold her fan down away from her face. It was a signal to come on over. If she didn't want him to come on over, she'd hold her fan up over her face."

"Geez, that's nothing like what they do in Jersey. Where I'm from, if you like somebody, you go, 'Yo! Get over here'."

"What if you don't like somebody?" she asked.

"Then you go, 'Ey, ya mind?'" I performed this with the requisite ticked-off, De Niro expression.

"Ey, ya mind?" Claudine said.

"That was pretty good."

I pulled her upstairs to the choir loft. We kissed for an hour on an old bench.

"I feel heinous kissing in the church," Claudine said.

"Why?" I asked like a moron.

"It's a church, Jonah. What would your minister say?"

"I don't have one right now."

"Weren't you raised in a faith?"

"Yes, yes I was."

Showtime. Dodge, bob, and weave some more.

"Which one? Presbyterian? Methodist?"

"No."

"Catholic? Are you Catholic?"

"No."

"Disciples of Christ?"

"Uh, no."

"You're not a Christian Scientist, are you?"

"I'm an Indian," I said, tickling her.

She squinted. "Like 'How!' Indian? She held up her hand in the Indian greeting. The question evaporated in the humid morning kisses in the choir loft.

INDY FOUR

"Seek him out, don't wait for him to come to you."

"I've heard about Indy Four from Elijah. Will he be back soon?" I asked Claudine, as I scraped up linoleum in the mansion's kitchen.

"This morning."

"What does he actually do out there?"

"He's waiting for General Sherman to return. Or maybe he's digging for the gold some Confederate troops supposedly buried here. Jonah, a word about my grandfather. He's preoccupied with the Lost Cause, fighting for the Confederacy—minus slavery, of course."

"That makes no sense. How can—"

"I know. Sometimes he thinks he's George Washington."

"George Washington Polk?"

"No, the big guy. The first president. You'll be liable to think he's crazy."

"I thought he was obsessed with the Civil War, not the Revolution."

"He's not always specific. But, Jonah, just understand that he's only half-crazy. He's a smart, smart man and I love him dearly."

"Was he always half-crazy?"

"No. When my father was alive, he was completely crazy. He became half-sane after Vietnam, and he had to become a father to us."

A loud crash echoed through the mansion. It was a door slamming and ancient china shivering.

"Eastman!" a voice boomed. *East man.*

I instinctively took a step back. The ghost of Claudine's father coming to kill me. We had kissed a lot in a *church*.

"Don't be scared," Claudine said, taking my hand. "It's Indy Four. Seek him out. Don't wait for him to come to you."

I pushed the kitchen door open. Standing in the archway of the dining room was a giant with sunlight kicking in a chorus line around his head. He was shaking his right hand loosely, as if to relieve a cramp that had been caused by having just written the Bill of Rights. He held a riding crop in his other hand. Khaki pants were tucked into his tall boots. A white, short-sleeved cotton shirt was, in turn, tucked into his pants. Its flawless whiteness offset his tan face, which was deeply lined and divided by an immense handlebar mustache that had begun to yellow at the sides. Rimless glasses shielding screaming green eyes, and white hair parted in the middle further decorated the Mount Rushmore head of Independence Polk the Fourth.

I stepped toward him, sensing that with each step I was climbing higher, like "Jack and the Beanstalk." When I extended my hand, he shook it firmly, not letting go. Now I felt like a munchkin from the Lollipop Guild in *The Wizard of Oz.*

Indy Four, imperious and unsmiling, bent down toward me, still gripping my hand. He then grinned broadly, displaying imperfect Chiclet teeth with many gold fillings.

"Eastman," he thundered, "You sly dog! Six just told me all about your arrival. *You're* our stable boy? Hah!"

"I'm sorry I was less than honest with you."

"Less than honest? My whole life is made up, son! Did they tell you I was a few tulips short of a patch?"

"I have heard it said, sir."

Indy Four's eyes flashed wild.

"An honest one," he said to Claudine, who had since appeared in the dining room. He let go and put his hands on his hips. "Tell me, do you call bringing a horse down to a plantation to a woman you don't know to work for a family you've never met the act of a lucid man?"

"Not exactly."

"Then why did you do it?"

"Because of a girl."

He appeared to be touched. "Sounds crazy to me."

"Not to me, sire, eh, sir." *Dammit, Jonah.*

Indy Four put one eagle wing around me and another around Claudine.

"He believes in you, Claudine. If he has you, and if you have him, the world will be at peace. Ah, we believe what we believe when we are young. . . . You're from near Philadelphia." This was an accusation.

"I am."

"My old cousin, President Polk, had a vice president from Philadelphia. Mr. Dallas."

"Really?"

"Yes, sir. I even know the campaign slogan used by his opponents. They'd sing:

> Hurrah, hurrah, the country's risin',
> Henry Clay and Frelinghuysen.

"Catchy," I said.

"Boy, did they ever taunt James. The Whig party had a chant they'd yell at rallies: 'Who is Polk?' they'd say. One fine President, I'll tell you. Gave us the rest of the continent out to California. Taught the Mexicans and the Indians a thing or two. Gave us the Smithsonian, Annapolis. Started building the Washington Monument. 'Who is Polk?' This," Indy Four thundered through the mansion, holding his arms skyward, "is Polk!"

Suddenly, Indy Four took two steps out and plucked several grapes from a bowl. He stuffed them in his cheeks and tilted his head back.

"I never wanted this for you," he said aping Brando in *The Godfather.* "I wanted Senator Eastman. Governor Eastman. There just wasn't enough time."

God, he *was* crazy. Or he wasn't. He knew about Mickey, but how much? His name had been in the papers nationwide since the Kefauver hearings. Kefauver was from Tennessee.

"Well, what do you think?" he asked.

What could I say? So I said, "Luca Brasi sleeps with the fishes," another line from the film. He let out a gargoyle's roar, which I interpreted as a laugh, and disappeared into the afternoon shouting, "Henry Clay, my arse!"

Claudine said, "He's still upset about an insult he never witnessed a century and a half ago."

Feeling I could dodge the issue no longer, that evening I snuck upstairs and left a poem on Claudine's pillow that mimicked her bedtime prayer.

> Price, Eastman, Hilliard and Polk
> What we're doin', Claudie, ain't no joke
> My grandpop's a gangster—
> The rumors are true-ish
> By sunrise you'll know
> That your boyfriend is Jewish.

NIGHT ON FIRE

"The glowing dice of God's Revelation."

Little Tennessee aliens were chirping outside my window. In a half-sleepy haze, I thought they might be crickets with Southern accents. When I blinked myself awake and lucidity took hold, I concluded that crickets in Tennessee didn't have Southern accents any more than crickets in New Jersey confronted their woodland neighbors with *"Whatta you lookin' at?"*

I tried falling back asleep, but my most gnawing tendency kept me awake: the conviction that wiser humans were doing some authentic living while I was perpetrating a fraud with my time.

Claudine traverses the valleys in my brain. I know by sound the distance between her footsteps and the precise blade of grass that her soles will crush when her foot touches down. I know the wind path in which leaves will blow when she breezes by a tree. I can anticipate the moment she'll nibble at the inside of her lower lip (right side) during a pregnant pause in conversation, and how many milliseconds it will take to return to the unposed pout—borne either by a sequencing in her upper lip's genetic code, or God's decision to focus his full powers on torturing me. The scent of known flowers lingers long after she's out of my sight. The last thing Claudine says to me before a separation reverberates in my limbic system as if it's a command from Mount Sinai ("That grass down by the icehouse needs some mowin' . . .")

I could see from my window a light on in the mansion. I envisioned Indy conspiring with Patrick Henry to give somebody liberty or somebody death (probably me). The night whisperers outside my window continued to beckon. I slipped on a pair of cutoff shorts and my work boots, grabbed a flashlight, and left my quarters.

It occurred to me when I stumbled on a rock that this excursion might not be wise. I didn't see myself as an intrepid youth, certainly not the horror movie genius who inevitably came up with the suggestion "let's split up." Nevertheless, everything associated with Claudine Polk in my kindling brain promised wonder and awe, so I proceeded stupidly into exotic darkness.

Pacing to the west of the plantation, the high-pitched whine grew louder, and cultivated the rhythm of something man-made, perhaps hydraulic. My visceral reaction: fear. Nevertheless, I proceeded through a patch of woods. I saw a ridge in the distance ahead of me, and set it as my final destination. If the mysterious beast didn't reveal itself there, I'd beat it back to the safety of the old slaves' quarters.

The ridge began to swell beneath my feet. I figured I was about a mile from the mansion, unsure if I was even on Polk grounds anymore. When I reached the top, I peered into a valley and saw globs of lava dripping like tears from another planet onto the ground. *Urim and Thummim, I thought—the glowing dice of God's Revelation.* The lava, once on earth, oozed through a stream and vanished in a death hiss somewhere beyond my vision—and well out of sight of the slumbering Polks.

I considered the possibility that I might be the spirit of a Confederate soldier witnessing the final mile of Sherman's march. Perhaps I was the soul of a slain warrior about to greet a saint or even a Polk. Could I use the Polk name to advance my status in the next life? Maybe things here didn't work like a casino disco in Atlantic City.

I returned to modernity when a mosquito bit me close to my heart. Anybody who itched this badly couldn't be dead.

I studied the sky once more and concluded that the fireballs were being secreted from the heavens in syncopation with the sound I had originally attributed to crickets. My *Fantasia* sensibility collapsed when I saw the lights of a massive truck go on. The power of the lights revealed two human shapes, a slim wiry man and a squat, beefy one. They were no further than one hundred yards from me.

I heard my own breathing, and turned quickly around on the path.

This movement sent a handful of pebbles tumbling down the other side of the ridge. The silhouettes reacted to the infinitesimal shift in tundra. I began to run.

My feet were sliding in my work boots, which were making too much noise against the earth. A masculine voice echoed from the direction of the glowing sky, but I knew the voice did not belong to God. It had a foothills twang, the kind that is attached to rural places, Union or Confederate.

I thought about turning off my flashlight, but was afraid I'd careen into a tree. Glancing over my shoulder, I did not see the silhouettes. Throttling down to a brisk walk, I made it back to my quarters. Until the sun rose, I lay in bed staring at the fireballs waltzing across the ceiling and listening to the washing-machine swish of my heart.

RECEIVED

"I'm just not getting you at all."

Claudine knocked on my door. I was already dressed.

"I don't believe you," Claudine said, looking more like a Technicolor lithograph in an orange polo shirt and khaki shorts than a mere person.

"You don't believe me about what?"

"I read the note you left on my pillow."

"I didn't know how you would take it."

"I think it's neat, your religion."

I was exotic. This could be good. No, it couldn't. Claudine pulled me outside, and we sat on the grass.

"I was worried about what you would think," I said.

"Why would I think something? I'm Episcopalian. You don't think strangely of me."

"That's because you're not strange."

She thought for a few beats.

"I don't understand why you would be afraid to tell me."

"Claudine, it's the South. There's that whole 'Who killed Jesus?' thing."

"That has nothing to do with you."

"Claudine, who do you believe killed Jesus?"

"The Jews."

"*Aha!*"

"But this was God's will. It wouldn't have happened unless God had wanted it. It's not like some ongoing vendetta."

"I don't know, Claudine."

"Well, it's not what we think here. I don't even understand why people don't like Jews."

"Do you know any besides me?"

"I know one. I knew a girl from Nashville named Judith Altman. Someone said she was Jewish. What do you think hating Jewish people is all about?"

"There are different brands of hate, I think," I said.

"Brands? Like soap?"

"Exactly. Different reasons to hate appeal to different people. Some people hate the Jewish commie—the activist, protesting type. My grandfather goes nutty every time he sees some guy like Abbie Hoffman whining on TV. Mickey says, 'If you want to feel sorry for somebody,' he says, 'Feel sorry for the Indians!' He says that showing weakness makes people want to kill you, not defend you."

"That's terrible."

"Maybe. . . . Then there's the Chosen hate. There are the people who park illegally in certain spaces because they think they can, and push their way to the front of lines because they think that's what being Chosen means. They have big hair and wear gold."

"That sounds like Texas."

"Aren't there things about Southerners that make you be critical of your own."

"I guess. Feminists make fun of the Southern hostess, who just run around asking if you'd like some pie." Claudine pronounced pie loudly for effect—*pah!* "When I see certain types, like the bubbas, I get embarrassed—like everybody'll think we all support what they believe."

"See."

Claudine was on a roll. "Then there's the stupid but harmless hick, like Jethro in *The Beverly Hillbillies*. What about who you marry, Jonah?"

"If my parents were alive, they would want me to marry someone of my own faith."

"What do *you* want?"

"I don't know, Claudine. I think the world is different than it was when my parents got married. Jewish kids are brought up to want the whole world, and then parents get angry when they go out into that world and find things that aren't Jewish. You can't win. The Jewish guys I know all want to meet Christian girls and the Jewish girls view Jewish guys as . . . Motel the Tailor."

"Who?"

"The tailor Motel Kamzoil in *Fiddler on the Roof*. You saw the play at your school, right? This nice Jewish boy who you have to end up with because, in the village, Motel's a catch, remember? In a bar in Margate, he's depressing, he's a huge step back for a girl. He's evidence that she blew it in America."

"I'm sorry, Jonah, I'm just not getting you at all." *Gittin' ye-ew eh-tall.* "*Fiddler on the Roof* is a play, not a dating guide." I kissed Claudine because I had to. How could I not kiss a woman who said things like *gittin' ye-ew eh-tall*? There was no hope of resolving this existential debate. She was the answer to this question.

Claudine's voice grew husky as her lips left mine. "Know what I think?" she asked softly. "I think we take the things that we like and leave the rest behind. Like we've had to do at Rattle & Snap."

"But you can't have a successful slave-free plantation."

"We are trying, Jonah, we are trying so hard. What about you?"

"I'm a kid from the Jersey Shore. But I haven't found answers there. I've found answers here."

"Do Mickey and Deedee see you with me?"

"Deedee thinks you're going to break my heart."

"I see," Claudine said sadly. "Do you think I will break your heart?"

"Oh, absolutely."

What I could not tell her was that Heartbreak was how I defined her. Deedee and her sage insight, predicting things. Claudine was discontentment and impossibility wrapped in a sweet, wafer-thin confection of longing. I pushed her slowly back onto the hot, soft grass and kissed away my doubts.

"I saw something funny," I said eventually.

"In the mirror?" Claudine inquired, pleased with her mock.

"Well, there's that. But I couldn't sleep last night, so I took a walk. There was a chirping sound, a hissing or something."

Claudine scrunched up her nose. "I've never heard anything like that."

"Anyhow, I took a walk southwest of the plantation."

Claudine sat up. "In the middle of the night? Why would you do that?"

"Because I heard a strange noise."

"You shouldn't have done that."

"Why, is somebody going to mug me?"

"No, nothing like that. It's dark. You might have fallen."

Claudine hadn't struck me as a girl who sat around worrying about the fragility of men. "I had a flashlight."

She said okay, cautiously.

"When I got over a ridge, I saw the sky glowing. It was like drops of lava were falling."

"That sounds crazy," Claudine said. She began to kiss me assertively. It was not her style, but I didn't care for the moment. Usually when I kissed Claudine, I thought of nothing but her, the consummation of my hair-trigger romanticism saturating my senses. This time, I was thinking of the fire in the sky and the two men who stood by the snaking valley of lava. I sang to her a verse from "Volcano," a popular Jimmy Buffett song:

> Lava come down soft and hot
> You better love-a me now or love-a me not

She laughed at me, so I tickled her. After hours in the grass, we rose, our faces chapped with kiss tracks. Neither of us had left the issue of our origins.

"What kind of name is Price?" Claudine asked.

"It's made-up. Mickey changed his name when he was thirteen. He was born in Romania, but I think his name got mutilated on the boat over by a Polish officer. That happened to a lot of immigrants. By the way, how do you think of Jewish people?" I asked.

"Just as people looking for the Promised Land."

"And where is that, Claudine?"

"Israel, dummy," she answered.

"Mmhh."

"Mmhh what, Jonah?"

"Israel isn't my Promised Land."

"What is, Jonah?"

"Rattle & Snap."

Claudine rested her head against my collar. "Well, that changes things, doesn't it?"

FINE, MOTHER

"Yeah, I'd say she loves you. As best as she can."

On a punishing hot day in mid-June, I wrapped up my work inside the church early. During the past few weeks, I had cleared the sanctuary of debris and stripped away and stained the floor and pews. Elijah was impressed with my progress and hurried down to a hardware store to buy paint for the ceiling and walls.

"Didn't think you'd do all this so quick, with such passion. My, my."

I wandered toward the mansion to see if Claudine wanted to ride horses into the woods and have lunch. This was code, of course. While we had spent many hours during the evenings together, the Polks were never far away and I was very self-conscious about getting caught in any textile removal. Last night, as I rolled around in bed, hugging my pillow pretending it was Claudine, I made the decision to use any legal means necessary to get her somewhere far away where we couldn't be caught. The worst she could do was to wave me off, but I figured I'd be some sort of mutant if I didn't try. I thought the Valley of Lava might be a romantic overlook, but remembered how upset Claudine had become when I told her about my wandering. Now, here I was, semimolesting a pillow in a converted plantation slave house.

Claudine suddenly burst out of the kitchen onto the brick patio, crying. She shouted "Fine, Mother," as she slammed the door.

What to do. It was one of those times where I was afraid of getting decked if I tried to insert myself into the situation, but afraid of coming off like an insensitive ass if I just stood there.

"Claud?"

"I can't now, Jonah," she cried. She held up her hand the way a cop would.

Claudine stomped somewhere behind the mansion.

Unbeknownst to me, Indy Six was watching this from the back porch.

"Petie nailed your girlfriend with her six-shooter," Six said happily, as a little brother would. "Pow!"

"What was that about?"

Six bounded down the inside stairs in his bathing suit, holding a transistor radio grenade-style, and invited me to swim in the pond. Given that Operation Apparel Minimization had to be aborted for now, I got a pair of swim shorts and followed Six to the pond.

The water bubbling up from a natural spring was surprisingly cool. Six dived in. I swiped at the water from a gazebo with my toes, a maneuver I immediately regretted. Totally gay.

"Enough toeing the water, Jonah," Six said from midpond. "C'mon in."

I hopped in, went completely under, and shot up, mouth agape, like Mr. Bruno. The machine-gun piano prelude to Billy Joel's "Angry Young Man" was playing on Six's transistor.

"Too cold for ya, huh?" Six splashed.

I responded by swimming toward him and dunking him. He tried dunking me back, but I tripped him from beneath and crammed him down again. Seeing the mansion rising behind him, I felt like I was drowning history itself, so I let Six up for air.

"So, what was that about back there with your sister?" I asked.

"Claudine and Mother go at it now and again."

"What about?"

"I think this one was about J.T. stopping by for dinner tonight."

"Tonight?"

"Yeah, he called and talked to Petie. His girlfriend. She told him he could come by for dessert."

"Oh. What did Claudine say?" Casual interest masking clinical depression.

"Don't know. Can you be cool with this?"

"Can I behave? Yeah. Can I be cool with this? No way. I love her, Six."

Six stuck his neck out, ostrichlike, aghast.

"Why so much, though?"

"If I knew, maybe I could turn it off."

"Maybe you should try, Jonah."

"Why would you say something like that?" I asked, watching the sunlight reflect off of Six's hair.

"Because you've got all the odds against you."

"Does your mother hate me that much?"

"No, I don't think she hates you. You're just, I don't know, standing in the way of this big old train she's got coming down the tracks."

"What's the train exactly?" I wondered. "Claudine can't get married this young."

"I dunno, Jonah. It's like it's gonna be. Hilliard's a big name down here, like the Polks are. You saw that gravestone: Sallie Hilliard Polk. It ends up that way, I guess. J.T.'s father, Smoky Hilliard, is a big businessman."

"What does that have to do with Claudine?"

"What are you yelling at me for? I'm just telling you the way it is. Sorry to hurt you so utterly."

I laughed. "Utterly," I repeated.

"What's wrong with 'utterly'?"

"Oh, nothing. It's just a strange word. It makes me think of milking cows."

"Yeah?" Six asked. "You milk Claudine yet?"

"Six!"

"You oughta."

"Watch it, Six." I bit my lip and submerged. When I resurfaced, Six was still stuck on sex.

"I'm serious. If it was me, I would. Six put his hand on my shoulder. "You really love that dumb girl crazy, don't you?"

"I told you I do."

"I just don't see it. She's not made for it like you are."

"What's that supposed to mean?"

"You're like this gangster guy on the outside with your family and all—"

"Where'd you hear that?"

"C'mon, Jonah, we're Southern; we're not in a coma. But you're no gangster under the skin."

"Thanks, Six."

"Elijah and I were talking about it. Claudie thinks you're . . . I dunno, the outlaw Josie Wales or somebody. But we see how you are with Claudie, and you're like the guy you hope she'll marry."

"You say that like you're disappointed."

"Oh, I'm not. I'd take you over J.T. any day of the week. That guy thinks he owns her. Maybe where you come from, you've got what it takes to win the games you play, but down here's another story. I dunno, Jonah, maybe not every girl wants what you think she wants."

I wanted to drown. The kid had sliced me wide open.

"Hey, Six, does she love me?"

"Whoa . . ." He slipped under water for a while.

Six, soaking: "I don't know how you figure a thing like that, Jonah. All I know is that I've never seen her like this with anybody. I see her grinning like Raggedy Ann up in her room. Yeah, I'd say she loves you. As best she can."

THE ANTICHRIST SWINGS BY
FOR A LITTLE KEY LIME PIE

"Darwin requires that we find some feature in our sexual adversary to certify his lack of legitimacy."

Claudine told me before dinner that J.T. might come by later. I knew she had been having a rough time, so I told her that I understood and was behind her. I was impressed by my capacity to engage in my Supportive Boyfriend fraud at the same time I was trying to locate implements with which to impale myself. Claudine was, nevertheless, petulant throughout dinner.

Elijah wore a mask of sorrow. He said nothing throughout the meal. We all just made small talk about the weather. Indy Four asked me what I planned to study in college and I answered with something vague, mixing English, political science, and economics as if they were the same discipline. I heard words fall out of my mouth and roll around the table like marbles. I didn't even know what we were eating, other than it was being sliced on what Petie called a "ham table." Uncharacteristically, I took Petie's reference to the ham table as some sort of attack on my deep and abiding devotion to kosher rituals. Like eating bacon on Rosh Hashanah, which I had done at least six times I could remember. Murray's Delicatessen in Margate didn't have a ham table. I longed for home.

"Howdy!" a self-assured Southern voice boomed after a screen door audibly shut. The Antichrist.

"What a nice surprise," Petie said, blowing a kiss to J.T., which reminded me that I had a loaded thirty-eight-caliber Smith & Wesson in my duffel bag. The rage again. No, I could not kill J.T., not because murder was immoral, but I didn't want to martyr the bastard. Perhaps I'd shoot myself and say J.T. did it.

J.T. was tall, with sandy brown hair, built like a high-school athlete, and had a pronounced jaw. Was that his biggest flaw? Dunno, keep looking, Jonah. Build a catalogue of flaws. Darwin requires that we find some feature in our sexual adversary to certify his lack of legitimacy. No, the jaw wasn't that bad. His nose was a touch broad for his face. I decided to home in on that. No, he was a good-looking guy, but his looks were almost corny. He had toxic little eyes, but his movements were princely and fluid. The Polks—Elijah, too—appeared to shift back from the table as J.T. bored deeper into the house. The avoidances weren't deferential—the way someone would move aside for Indy Four—there was another reason for it that I couldn't process. It was as if a dozen pirates had preceded J.T. with severed heads dangling from their hands, reminding everyone what could happen if we all didn't pay homage.

I stood, shook his hand feeling like an engorged toad, and smiled as sincerely as I was able. He did the same. Indy Four and Six greeted him perfunctorily. Elijah didn't even look up from his platter. I loved the guy.

J.T. kissed Claudine on the cheek and she half-smiled, more smile than I had hoped for. Once J.T.'s eminently white rear end hit the seat, Key lime pie glided in from Petie's kitchen. Before I took a bite, I decided to fire a volley of diplomacy. "So, J.T., what are you doing this summer?"

"Thanks for asking, Jonah. I'm working at the family's business, Hilliard Valley Energy. We're mostly drilling for natural gas. With these shortages going on, that's where it's at." He said the name of the company like I'd know. Like everybody knew. Like he, J.T., had sucked the ground dry himself. The soft sons of self-made men always think they built the family fortune, only the Hilliards were Old Money. These types rarely bragged.

J.T. punctuated his comments with a broad grin. His appearance was suddenly less corny. His handsomeness was unequivocal. Crest-fallen, I could envision Claudine with him in a photograph that made sense on a mantel. My hate cycled all the way through and dissipated down a cosmic drain until all I could think about was how much I missed my mother.

A powerful revelation transmitted from Eros whispered at me from beneath the table: There was a sexual hierarchy—an objective one with rank and everything—and this schmuck was at the top of it.

And not me. Or maybe not me. I wasn't sure.

"So business must be good, with the gas crisis and all," I said.

"It's not a bad time at all. Senator Baker—he's an old friend of the family—thinks the Russians will calm down if Reagan gets elected. So we win either way."

I momentarily thought Marxist thoughts, a first for me. This guy was living in Xanadu when the rest of us were running scared. I wondered if he had even bothered to register for the draft as I had.

J.T. said, "I understand you're staying out where the old slave quarters were. For us, it's rich justice seeing a Yankee staying there." He laughed. No one else did, and I was glad. Elijah looked especially wounded, and Six offered up a bored expression. Despite the remark, however, even the mighty Independence Polk the Fourth, self-imagined conqueror, remained silent. Petie winced a little while Claudine curled her upper lip at J.T.

"I had to stay somewhere," I said, cursing myself for not coming up with anything witty.

This was a very unhappy moment for everyone in the room, for different reasons. Even J.T. appeared miserable. I suppose he was winning, but what had he actually won?

Suddenly, J.T. shifted in his chair and the legs dragged across the wooden floor, emitting a flatulent sound.

"Whoo!" I said, "You gotta cap that excess natural gas, J.T." It just came out. My quip, I mean.

Indy Four, Six, and Claudine almost spit out their iced tea. I heard

Elijah giggling from the kitchen where he had retreated after the slave quarters remark. Petie was not amused. J.T. used all of his hydraulic muscle to crank out a fake smile.

"A little third-grade humor, Jonah?"

Alive again, I said, "More like second grade, J.T. It's the level where I operate best."

J.T. complimented Petie on the Key lime pie. I had brought myself down with my immature remark, so he couldn't take me any lower. Self-deprecation wasn't bad after a left hook. I had seen Mickey do things like this when questioned by reporters. He would sell himself short by criticizing his minimal education or slight build. "Oh, sure," he told one reporter, "nations tremble with fear of a five-foot-three gambler from Romania who didn't graduate from high school."

Dessert ended with Indys Four and Six offering J.T. a few hearty slaps on the back, Petie giving him an awkward kiss on the cheek, Elijah giggling at me from behind J.T., and Claudine biting her lower lip, gradually happy again. We all walked J.T. out to his brand-new golden Camaro Z28. The sight of it brought J.T. back to life and deflated me. I had gone from being in my arena as a smart-aleck outsider at the dinner table to being a dishrag against the might of this graven, but turbocharged vessel. The car had a smashed headlight. J.T. described with a chuckle how he had rammed it into a pole "horsin' around," but the local cops just laughed "like a pack-a hyenas when they pulled up and saw who it was." I got the message: Recklessness is the ultimate status symbol. J.T. roared out toward the sunset while I returned to the slave house to change into my overalls and get some more labor out of the way.

EASTMAN DISCOVERS AMERICA

"Where did you stop in Delaware before we met?"

My mind was running half-crazy, half-analytical, but this was nothing new for me when it came to sexual matters. I was always posing legalistic questions trying to get at some empirical truth about sex, as if the Socratic method would resolve it.

When people say they're dating a few people, what does it mean they're doing with these few people? Figuring out what to do with one girl was hard enough.

How many girls was I supposed to have kissed by eighteen? The honest answer was three, including Claudine. Was this low or high? Probably low.

What was wrong with me that I didn't want to mess around with girls I didn't like?

If so many guys have and so many girls haven't, who are all the guys doing it with?

If, by doing it with me, Claudine liked it, would this incline her to try it with someone else, too? Would I be playing this more shrewdly, then, by abstaining? But what did that get me?

At what point does doing it with a lot of people go from being "natural," like Lex, the concierge at the Golden Prospect, had told me, to being gamy? Men or women who got around made me think: DISEASE.

Do any of the girls that I think about so much ever think about me? In that way?

How many guys had had their first encounter with a "cocktail waitress" dispatched by their gangster grandfather when they were fifteen? Did this mean that said guy didn't have what it took to get a girl on his own?

What if I was sterile?

* * *

In the weeks since my arrival, it had been unbearably hard to spend too much time alone with Claudine. I sensed she wasn't as frustrated as I was. Until tonight. Her mood after my dinnertime quip had been pure filly—snappy, strong, and sexed-up mean. It actually scared me a little. I slipped back to the carriage house to evaluate how I'd rip the old doors down.

Upon inspection, I give up quickly. I'm a good workhorse with this kind of thing, but Elijah was the brains of our plantation repair duo. There is nothing else to do at the church until all of the paint arrives in. I sit on a pile of hay and stare at the doors like a nitwit. Claudine appears in the glow of a fading sun.

"Hey, where ya been?" I asked her.

"Talking to Mother."

"On friendly terms again?"

"Oh, yes."

Claudine climbed up to the loft and sat beside me.

"You Confederates have an interesting approach to handling family conflict."

"And what's that, Dr. Joyce Brothers?" Claudine replied.

"Retreating to your tastefully-appointed private hells and shoving the decaying skunk carcass under the canopy bed."

Claudine's eyes flashed fury. Rebel defiance. Sexy.

"How does *your* family deal with all its problems?" she snapped.

"We blame everything on anti-Semitism then go out for Chinese food."

Warmth flooded back into Claudine's eyes. "Well, that's one approach."

"It's worked for five thousand years."

We collapse upon hay, my stomach growling. Claudine laughs as I fall against her. Self-conscious, I sing:

> Hurrah, hurrah, the country's risin',
> Henry Clay and Frelinghuysen.

We both laugh. A tangle of limbs. Snaps unsnapping, hooks un-hooking. Like a farmhand in a made-for-TV movie, I had worn no T-shirt beneath my overalls. I think she likes this. Jungle graceless-ness on both our parts. Relief at the identification of a horse blan-ket behind the swinging door. Because the hay hurts. Ravenous mouths retreat with stunned gasps above and below Mason-Dixon lines. *Is this happening?* Sweet struggle in the carriage house. A seminal reminder from Mickey about "condos." The grandson isn't stupid. Sometimes. Four wide eyes in the golden light the remain-ing sun throws. Claudine inhaling through her teeth. Me, not be-lieving I am here. Potential echoes through the little cabin; Claudine, aware of consequences, muffles with a bite against my collarbone. A nuclear-era Polk devours a Jersey Shore gangland spawn; Eastman discovers America, for seconds anticipating de-scendants: Leonidas Eastman—we'd call him Leon. A staccato laugh misinterpreted by the mistress as alpha-male joy. It is terror. My heart gradually slows. She traces her fingers along the outline of my lips.

"Claudine?"

"Yes?" *Ye-esss*, whispered.

"Where did you stop in Delaware before we met?"

"Fort Delaware."

"What was there?"

"It's where they held some of the Immortal Six Hundred. Confed-erate men like Independence Hilliard Polk. He was the youngest cap-tain in the Confederate Army. He was raised at Rattle & Snap by his parents, George and Sallie." I winced internally at the name Hilliard. "Sallie would wait on the porch night after night for him to return home from the war. The Immortal Six Hundred were singled out by the federals to be used as human shields. Some of them were placed around Union batteries so that when the Confederate army shelled back, Southern men would be killed."

"What happened?"

Claudine sprouted a wise-guy twinkle in her eye.

"The Confederate Army fired anyway. For weeks they fired. The Southern men didn't die, at least not at that battle."

"What about Independence? Did he return?"

"Yes, he did, Jonah. Opened a ranch in Texas. The sheriff of Laredo tried to rob him while he slept."

"What happened?"

"Indy shot him stone dead. He was Indy Four's grandfather. He told Indy that story when he was little. See what happens when you do something bad to a Polk?"

"Have I done anything bad?"

"Why you're just about the sweetest thing."

"I'd probably shoot a sheriff for you."

"You don't strike me as the shootin' type. . . . You know, back in Civil War times, it was considered promiscuous for a woman to show a man her ankle."

"Well, I don't think I saw your ankle tonight."

"You're clever with words and thoughts. That'll make your fortune someday."

"I love you, Claudine."

I felt her honey, iced-tea breath, perhaps from a gasp. She rested her head on my chest. "Oh, my."

Claudine and I, outside, dancing on the antebellum dirt path, spilling kisses. We float apart, she toward Corinthian columns, I back to the carriage house.

ERUPTION

"After it's done, the world looks different forever."

I awoke to the most extraordinary headline in the Nashville *Tennessean*:

MT. ST. HELENS ERUPTS IN WASHINGTON STATE
VOLCANO LEAVES 57 DEAD OR MISSING
Dormant 100 Years, Explosion 500 Times Stronger Than Hiroshima

On the way up to the mansion, I passed Elijah. "My God, Elijah, it took off the top third of the mountain."

"Somethin' else, son."

"I'll never understand what causes those explosions."

"Maybe it was that gammahoochin' you've been doing in that carriage house," Elijah snickered.

Mortified. "I mean volcanoes."

"Oh, I see, Jonah, I see."

"I just don't understand what causes them."

"Change, boy," Elijah said, gripping my wrist. "I read up on these things once, being as how I love the weather. See, one big plate that holds up the land collides with another plate that holds up the sea. Now one of these plates is gonna win, see. One goes under the other and there's a weakness, a fracture in the surface of the planet." Elijah now stood oddly close and whispered as if he were telling me something that no one else ever knew or could ever know.

"The fire underground, Jonah, has been building for billions of years. It senses that weakness in the earth and blows right through it.

It's angry, see, it's pent-up. One plate goes over the other and, after it's done, the world looks different forever."

I kept thinking, *We don't have volcanoes in 1980.*

I drove one of the Polks' pickup trucks into town, ostensibly to pick up supplies at a hardware store in Columbia. My real reason was that I wanted to call Irv the Curve. I called the number he gave me and identified myself to the waitress-sounding woman that answered. She asked me for the number of the pay phone and I gave it to her. Within two minutes, Irv called me back.

"Howdy, Slim," Irv said.

"Slim?"

"We can't call you by your name anymore. It has to be something folksy."

"Slim it is."

"What's with the girlie?"

"She's great, but there's a guy down here who's trouble."

"With a girl like that, there's always a guy like that."

I was in no mood to engage Irv about the laws of love, especially when I suspected that he might be right.

"His name is J. T. Hilliard and he doesn't like me. He's after Claudine."

"Sounds like he's got the inside track, *boychik.*"

"He's from this old Civil War family."

"What the hell does that mean, may I ask?"

"His name is J. T. Hilliard and he's from a big-time rich family."

"Where are these old Tennessee families getting all this money? I, for one, would like to know. Cotton money didn't last long. Were the Polks into tobacco? That would make sense."

"No cotton or tobacco. They grew hemp. For rope."

"You sure they're not growing it for some other purpose?"

"No way." I was offended as a Confederate, which I truly believed I had become in comparison to my gangster Union family.

"Just asking."

"The Hilliards are in gas or oil or something."

"They weren't drilling for it in the Civil War, Jonah."

"I don't know. He came last night in this souped-up golden Camaro, with racing stripes and all."

"A nice old-money car."

"Weird, huh?"

"Weird. Did you provoke him in any way?"

"Yeah, I'm with the girl he thinks is his wife. Then he insulted me at the dinner table and, when he moved in his chair, it made this noise like a fart, and I suggested he get his natural gas under control."

"Heh. But I imagine this silly kid feels like you cut him off at the hoo-hahs."

"So what's next?"

"Keep your head low. Avoid him. Keep that implement your grandfather gave you close by your bed, but avoid any situation that would require you to use it. We don't know the law down there. This means, of course, that the Hilliards are probably more adept at subverting it. Keep in mind that their subversion of justice, Jonah, should be viewed as being immoral."

"What about our subversion?"

"Justified. You read me?"

"Yes."

"Call me back if you get ants in your pants. I'll look into these Hilliards. In the meantime, make sure that girlie doesn't tie you up anywhere you can't escape."

"She doesn't tie me up."

"I must challenge you here, Jonah. You are tied up, but not beyond escape. Keep your eyes open."

ARCH OF THE HEAVENS

"Bless this hayloft that we're sharin'."

In the weeks that followed the eruption of Mount St. Helens, ash covered Rattle & Snap. At first, I thought it was pollen because it had a yellow-green tint, like pulverized tennis balls. It never occurred to me that one event could scatter residue so far, clouds and ash moving in hyperspeed from Washington State to central Tennessee. God wanted to remind us that his fingers reached forever.

Since our night in the carriage house, Claudine had pulled away from me. We held hands, took walks and kissed, but she was distant for a few weeks. I could tell that her eyes and her mind were somewhere foreign. Once, I tried to inquire about her mood, but it annoyed her. I began to feel a familiar emptiness that took me a few weeks to identify as being that orphaned feeling. It was the precise sentiment that I felt after my parents died. *You are alone, Jonah.*

"She's got the faraways, huh, boy?" Elijah said one night when I collapsed on the front steps of the mansion after a long day's work on the church.

"Yeah."

"She gets that. Has since she was little with her daddy and all, I suppose. Can't touch her during those spells."

"So it's not me?"

"Naw, it's not you. She's work, that one. You've got a heart the size of the Smoky Mountains, boy, don't you? Bless your heart. You're all right, son. And you've been doing great on that church, too. Mmm-mmh. You work at it like it was yours. That's where you pour what you've got inside. It goes into a craft of some kind. That's good. That's good."

"I'm glad I've been able to help."

"Aw, you have all right. I get to come in a bit early from the sun and take my notes in this diary here."

"It looks like you've had a lot to say lately, with all that ink."

"Yes. Yes. Sometimes I don't think things are a darned bit better, I swear. That J.T. and his slave-house talk—heh, heh, heh—did I ever write about that, and how you sassed him. Loved your gas talk there, did I ever. You're all right, son. Wrote that down the night you said it. A bright spot. Then there's things that aren't so bright. They evacuated seven hundred families from this Love Canal up in New York State. They said there's all kinds of poison people are eating and drinking. They shot a man name Vernon Jordan yesterday. You know him?"

"A civil rights guy, right?"

"National Urban League. Shot taking a walk. By a white man. He'll live, though."

"That's good."

"Yes. That's good."

"Unbelievable that it happens today."

"Not so unbelievable, son. It is what it is."

"I guess."

He read me pretty well and could tell I was down.

"Claudie, always Claudie, right, Jonah?"

"Right."

"You know, you're smart to focus on your work. You have to focus on a thing, a task, not what you feel about her. Do something, son."

Elijah was right, and it was a lesson I never forgot. Do a thing. Don't sit. Maybe that's why the Polks built up America—they had longed for someone they left behind in Scotland, so they bided their time by creating a nation. Activities were seldom about their stated purpose.

I returned to St. John's Church and admired what I had accomplished. The church would be used soon enough. I wondered if I would ever get to sit through a service.

I slipped behind the rear wall to a small room that overlooked the cemetery. I had been in this room before and vaguely remembered Elijah telling me that it was where the clergy used to change clothing and prepare the service. When I stood on a wooden plank against the back wall, the ground felt hollow. I tapped my foot on the floor and the plank loosened.

I retrieved my tool kit from the church's entryway and returned to the little room. The plank wasn't hard to dislocate, and I managed to kick up the one next to it with my work boot. I peered beneath the surface with a sawdust-covered flashlight and noticed a tin box. Had I dug up a grave? I shuddered and caught my breath. I ran the light against the box and saw that it was much too small to contain a body. Relieved, I reached down to grab it. My invasion startled a few gruesome little mice that actually spoke the word "eek!" as I withdrew my hands and shuddered for a second time.

I found a broom, the same one that Claudine had flown in on a few weeks ago, and used it to wedge the little box toward me. More eeks from the mice. Shut the hell up, I thought, and jammed them away with the broom. If they found me so terrifying, why did they insist on hanging around? Creatures bring so much upon themselves. Once the box was close enough, I lowered my legs into the hole and straddled the open ground with my palms lifting the box out with my feet. It jingled.

The box was about one and a half by two feet. It was entirely rusted over and creepy looking. It had a lock on the outside that wasn't hard to crack open with a screwdriver. Light from a decorative window shone through and stung my eyes. A mosquito flew into one of my eyes, and I said, "Dammit!" but then apologized to the folks out in the graveyard for talking like this in a church.

The first thing I saw inside the box was a blue velvety cloth. It was a bag, actually. Inside was . . . a book. It had no title. I opened the book, careful to keep it out of direct sunlight. The pages were a dark tan, which didn't offset the black writing terribly well, but well enough. The opening page read in beautiful script:

NOTES BY GEORGE WASHINGTON POLK

The Holy Grail, I thought. Every entry was dated, beginning with descriptions of the architectural planning process in the early 1840s. I sat for two hours alone, just God and Jonah, reading what the master of Rattle & Snap had written. Toward the middle of his diary, I honed in on the word "meteor." It popped out at me just like that mosquito had. The passage had been dated July 18, 1856, and read:

> The meteors blazed across that fair summer sky and in the minds of the superstitious portended dreadful calamities, and when we night after night never tired of viewing them, a feeling of awe and mystery enveloped us. The brilliance rained down from the heavens.

I gently placed the book back in the cloth, and heard the jingling again. Then I dumped out a handful of gold coins and ran crazy-fast west toward the mansion. From the gazebo, Six, who had E.L.O.'s "Don't Bring Me Down" blasting from his transistor radio, called, "What do you have there?"

"Follow me," I said. I must have looked like a mental patient running up the hills with this noisy rusty box. J.T.'s golden chariot was in the driveway. I burst into the mansion. Claudine was walking up the stairs. J.T. must have been lobbying Petie.

"Eew, what's that, Jonah?" she asked.

Out of breath, I pointed to George Washington Polk's portrait. "It's . . . his . . . diary."

Claudine's mouth fell open.

"His diary! Mother!"

Petie Polk and J.T. emerged from the great living room, the one with the portrait of Family Friend Andrew Jackson and Will "Scowly" Polk, who must have been talking about what a non-bullet-catching-in-his-teeth pansy I was. Indy Four came charging down the stairs.

"Mother!" Claudine shouted, "Jonah found G.W.'s diary!"

"Where, Jonah?" Petie asked from the living room.

"Under the church where I was working."

Now all of the Polks had gathered around, plus Sir Golden Jaw, J.T. Indy Four set the book down gently on the dining room table. His eyes filled up, the tears magnifying behind his lenses.

"My Lord, boy, what have you found? What have you found?"

After five minutes of feigning interest in Polk history—and perhaps his own—J.T. slipped out the front door when Indy poured the gold coins onto the table.

A long overdue return to the loft of the carriage house with my quilt-totin' Polk. This was why I lived. Claudine and I wrestled, occasionally flinching at the straw's abrasive edges. It was a contest to see who could pin the other first and get in the most kisses. I let Claudine win, although I think she liked it better when I didn't. I counted the vertebrae on her back with my fingers as she leaned far back above me. The arch of the heavens, I thought.

While she showered back in the mansion, I grabbed a piece of her stationery in the kitchen and I wrote a note in verse, sealed it in an envelope, and placed it beneath a pillow on her bed upstairs:

> Abraham, Isaac, Moses and Aaron
> Bless this hayloft that we're sharin'.
> These are the straws
> That scratch us and bind us
> So set down the quilt
> And pray Indy don't find us.

DIRTY LAUNDRY

"Why are you smiling, Jonah?"

Claudine and her mother had to audition a band in Nashville for a party they were planning for Rattle & Snap, so I was on my own on this midsummer Sunday. As I slid into the driver's side of the pickup truck, Six planted himself in the passenger seat. He was decked out in a sport jacket, tie, and khaki pants. His collar was aflutter, but there was something about his caste that conveyed neatness nonetheless.

"What about church, Six?" I inquired.

"*You're* not going, Jonah."

"I'm not Episcopalian."

"Well, I'm not going, either. Nobody'll care. Where are you headed?"

"Into Columbia to take a bunch of laundry to the cleaners. I found a seven-day-a-week place."

"Let's go."

We were in Columbia within minutes. Across the street from the cleaner's, two guys with slicked-back hair were reading a paper and smoking. They both wore off-white painter's outfits. A black family dressed in their Sunday best passed by the painters. I felt tingles of paranoia on my scalp. My pistol was strapped to my ankle. Six and I each carried a pile of laundry and a bunch of used wire hangers into the cleaner's. We deposited everything on the counter and I took the stubs.

In the mirror's reflection, I saw J.T. with two of his friends walking by on the opposite side of the street.

"Six," I said. "Don't turn around. Just look in the mirror and tell me if you see J.T. and two guys with him."

Six stiffened in the mirror. "Yeah, that's J.T. The big guy is Phil Tewkes. I don't know who the guy in the yellow is, but I've seen him around. They keep staring in here."

"I know they do." I slid the pile of wire hangers toward the woman behind the counter, but I held one of them back. I began to twist it loose.

"They're just waiting over there," Jonah.

"I know, Six. They're waiting for me. I think you should just stay in here."

"No, I'll go out with you."

I was transfixed by Six's big, soulful eyes. His face was all angles, angles that would have been seen as masculine in a Ralph Lauren advertisement for beachwear, but not on the Boardwalk. Six's angles were mild, the way mine were when I was nine or ten, but I had lost mine by the time I was his age.

"No. You shouldn't see this kind of thing."

"J.T. won't hurt me."

"That's right, he won't."

"He thinks he owns Claudie and all of us."

"I know he does. Look, just stay in here, Six."

"We can call the police."

"J.T. probably owns the police."

"Why are you smiling, Jonah?"

"I'm not."

Maybe I *was* smiling, the way Old Will Polk had when he caught that bullet in his teeth.

We both stepped back from the counter. I continued untwisting the hanger until it came undone. I held it by the hook and let the sharp edge of the twisted end stick out.

"You're grinning. Right there, I see it. You've fought like this before, haven't you?"

"Six—"

"What are you gonna do?"

"Use a weapon," I said.

"*That?*" Six asked, pointing to the hanger.

"What do you think J.T. and his friends expect will happen out there?"

"They expect to beat you up, Jonah. You said so yourself."

"Right. That's my weapon," I said, hopefully. "What they expect."

"I don't get it."

"Listen to me," I said, loosening my heavy silver belt buckle. "They're not going to hurt you. If you won't stay inside, do this: Pick up some gravel from near that tree. Bend down like you're tying your shoe. When I say, throw the rocks as hard as you can at the guy closest to you. Right in his face. Then run to the truck."

"What are you gonna do?"

I knelt down, making certain that my Indian belt was loose. I felt down my ankle to make sure that my gun was still there. It was. "My grandfather told me once that nothing shocks a man as much as the unexpected sight of his own blood. Who's the toughest of these three do you think?"

"Probably Phil. I don't know about the guy in yellow."

"Then you throw the rocks in Yellow's face when I say so, not before."

My heart galloped like Shpilkes herself was in my chest. It was more than just raw fear, although that was part of it. I felt my gums throbbing. I *wanted* to hurt these guys. I was glad they were here.

Six and I left the cleaner's. I held the hanger, folded, in my right hand so the boys couldn't see it from across the street. Six bent down, as instructed, and picked up a handful of gravel.

"Hey, it's Jonah the Prophet," J.T. shouted.

I did not answer. We kept walking toward the truck. J.T. and his gang crossed the street.

"What are you, deaf?" J.T. said. "I'm talking to you." The boys pursued. They were no more than fifteen feet away.

"Six," I said under my breath. "Stop when I do, but don't turn around until I do. As soon as I turn around, you hit Yellow with those rocks."

We stopped walking and waited until the footsteps were upon us. I bent open the hanger, turned around, and swung the sharp tip at Phil's face. I hit him somewhere near his eye. I swung at J.T. and hit him on his neck. He was stunned, but not badly hurt.

"Damn," Phil shouted.

Six winged his rocks on cue at Yellow's face. Yellow muttered something unintelligible, and drew his hands up around his eyes. I switched the hanger into my left hand. I whipped my belt off and swung the heavy buckle at Phil's head and hit him square on his lips. Phil staggered backward, registering pain. J.T.'s mouth fell open and he swung his head, confused, between Phil and Yellow. I swung the belt at J.T. and connected near his temple. I whipped Yellow with the belt twice in his head. The metallic thunks betrayed connections with bone. Six, bless his heart, then jumped on top of the woozy Yellow and began pummeling him.

Phil was crouched on the ground confirming that the moisture around his mouth was, in fact, blood. I kicked him as hard as I could in the nose with the heel of my boot. He fell back, groaning.

"You dirty—", J.T. started shouting, more narcissistically wounded than incapacitated. I whipped him hard with the belt buckle and he fell back against a parked car. I moved toward Yellow, who had pushed Six off of him. As Yellow tried to stand, I swung at him again, hitting him on the side of the head with the belt buckle. As he fell back, I kicked him hard in the mouth. He rolled into the street, spitting teeth. I kicked him in the crotch twice. My man Six jumped back on Yellow and got to work.

J.T. tried to stand, cursing. He was dazed and couldn't tell where I was. I cut behind him and kicked him in the ass. When he turned at the insult, I punched him in the nose. As soon as I saw his blood flow, I pounded him in the mouth. As he fell, I kicked him in the chest.

I should have run, since all of the men were down. I did not, an acute memory that haunts me.

I brought my right leg up and began to lift my cuff to go for the gun. I envisioned the expression that J.T. would have as he saw the bullet rocketing toward him. But I put my leg back down once I felt the cold metal. It was my fear of becoming my grandfather that did it, and what that stark reality would do to Claudine and me. I didn't want Mickey breaking us up.

Instead, I threw my belt around J.T.'s neck, beneath his hateful jaw, and began to tighten it. As I drew the belt tight, I envisioned this scene from above. I saw J.T. gasping, but I was not the strangler, at least not completely. It was Carvin' Marvin's face, but my hands. "I want you to just die," Marv's mouth told J.T. But it was my hands that stopped the moment I saw J.T.'s eyes soldered open. I opened my eyes wide and let J.T. fall to the street.

Townspeople had emerged onto the sidewalk. Six followed me, walking fast, but not running, to the truck. I was breathing heavily as I slipped my belt back through the loops of my jeans. The two painters who had been reading the paper across the street when we had entered the cleaner's were now standing near the wounded J.T. & Co. I could have sworn they sent approving smirks my way. It was chilling because I didn't know whose side they were on. They moved toward J.T., but they didn't help him. Then came the wacky smirks, but the painters didn't approach me. The churchgoing black family stepped aside, along with vague expressions that I did not know how to register.

On the ride back to Rattle & Snap, Six was giddy. "Like a mongoose," he kept saying to me, admiringly. I was scared. On the street I was fine; now I was scared. "Tell your grandfather what happened, but Claudine can't know, Six," I said.

"Why not?"

"I don't want sympathy. I don't want it from her, and I sure as hell don't want J.T. to get any."

"But he came after you!"

"I don't want her to know, Six!"

Before Claudine returned from her day in Nashville, I called Irv the Curve at Masada. I told him what had happened. Irv reminded me that I was not hurt. But I almost was, I explained. "You will not be hurt," Irv assured me like Obi Wan Kenobi. What did he know?

I told Indy Four what had happened myself. I apologized for taking Six with me, but he brushed away my repentance. The old man listened lucidly and then apologized to *me*. He complimented me, laughing a little, on my "intestinal fortitude." Then he angrily promised me, a quiver in his voice, "This is not *my* South." Indy Four then disappeared into his bedroom to conspire with ghosts.

In the evening, Indy Four explained to Claudine and Petie that there had been threats made against me. Claudine hugged me. Petie looked appalled.

"One final thing," Indy Four announced, rising, general-like. "I have invited Mr. Price to Rattle & Snap. He and Mrs. Price will arrive tomorrow."

PART FIVE

LOST CAUSE

2005

Men fight from sentiment. After the fight is over they invent some fanciful theory on which they imagine that they fought.

—Confederate leader John "the Gray Ghost" Mosby

MIDLIFE EFFICIENCY, APRIL 2005

"I felt like we weren't so much passing through the house
as we were haunting it."

There are different theories about when middle age begins. On the
evening before I left for Tennessee, I typed "midlife crisis" into an Internet search engine on a White House computer. The computer spit
out articles denoting ages ranging from thirty-five to fifty-five. The
male midlife crisis, according to the experts, comprised "depression,
marital disharmony, obsession with death, feelings of worthlessness,
trouble at work, intense attractions to younger women, and sexual
problems." All in all, Mardi Gras.

As the Panamanian and I boarded a Learjet used to carry out Air
Force Special Mission 14060, we overheard one maintenance engi-
neer ask another where the plane was headed. The other man responded, "What plane?"

The nonexistent aircraft took off from Andrews Air Force Base in
Suitland, Maryland, at nine o'clock EST in the morning and traveled
five hundred and twenty-seven nautical miles to land at Maury
County Airport, a small regional affair that accommodated small jets.
The land beneath the airport had once been a part of the Rattle &
Snap tract, and was about a mile from the mansion. This proximity
would prove to be very useful.

The manifest had listed the mission's call name as Operation Dixie
Knish. Very funny, Mr. President.

"Put on your getup, Jonah," the Panamanian reminded me before
we deplaned inside of a private hangar. It consisted of a ponytailed
blond wig and matching mustache. I looked like General Custer at a

NASCAR event. "And don't interact with anybody. Just go straight to the car." We drove a hunter green rented Chevrolet about a mile to Rattle & Snap.

The plantation's landscape was refreshingly the same as it was when I left in 1980, with the exception of several industrial buildings that sat low in a valley to the east of the mansion.

The house, bless its pillars, appeared to be precisely the same. The trees, perhaps, were thinner. I envisioned General Don Carlos Buell returning to Rattle & Snap and again giving it a reprieve from the torches of his men. It would not be George Washington Polk's Masonic ring that saved the place this time. My sense was that this burden would be falling to me.

I parked several hundred yards from the mansion when I saw a figure move in a first-floor window. "I'll have a look around the grounds," Marcus said.

"That would be best, given—"

"No need to justify, Jonah."

What does a man think about after all these years when he returns to visit his epic love? In my case, I was thinking about my hair. I removed my disguise, but could not shift my eyes away from the passenger-side mirror. What would Claudine see first, an aging fool (in pretty good shape for forty-three, I might add) or sunlight bouncing off my brow?

When I had last seen Claudine, my hair was thick, wavy, and black. I could work in the sun for hours and have no pink on my scalp to show for it. This was no longer so. A sizable patch of hair had decisively thinned out during my thirties. I had plenty of hair flecked with silver insurgents, except for this, this damned moon roof. I didn't kid myself: No one would confuse me with an eighteen-year-old knight-errant anymore.

As I opened the car door, I thought of Neil Armstrong. I had the notion that I was about to take a historic step. I studied the rocks on the driveway and tried to determine if there was anything lunar about them. I decided that the extraterrestrial quality of the plantation had more to do with the blur of time and space than anything that could be found in rock samples. Here I was, a living contradiction: a Man of Achievement who had fallen from an exalted place; a married father of two with an expectation of meeting a gorgeous eighteen-year-old girl; a hard-nosed realist with delusions of reversing God's orbit. But maybe it was possible: Wasn't the earth, after all, in the same approximate position in space right now it had been in on my first giant leap onto this soil in 1980?

Claudine stood, Corinthian, on the porch beside Rattle & Snap's other columns. Slender, taut, and chiseled by the spirits of her frontier, she took gazelle steps toward my Jeep. In middle age, Claudine had cropped her hair to an efficient shoulder length, her long hair having proven to be some sort of threat to the operation of a millennial plantation. Her smile was tight; she may have just been the wreck that I was. She brushed a renegade strand of hair from her temples, perhaps covering a few silver strands. Her discomfort cruelly served as a booster shot that gave me the juice to move closer.

Claudine was wearing khakis, a pink polo shirt, and paddock boots. The outfit was the natural evolution of what she had worn when we first met. She wore little makeup. I wore khaki pants, a gauzy white cotton shirt, and a light sport jacket that I bought from Brooks Brothers not long after I graduated from college.

I could see that Claudine's eyes still flashed green, but the untamed edge they once had had throttled down. She had made the precise metamorphosis that I had imagined, from a tearing beauty to an aging royal—like Jackie Kennedy had looked when her kids hit their teens. Maybe I was perverted, but I always thought Jackie was hotter in her forties than she was as first lady. Claudine was beautiful, but, finally, of a species resembling my own.

When nervous, Jonah, be a smart-ass.

"Sorry I'm late," I said. "The pilot said we'd be landing in nineteen eighty." *Ba-dum-dum.*

Claudine laughed. "Well, you know how it is with vectors, but at least you got here all right." Despite our earlier phone calls, I had forgotten how deep her accent was, all Confederate coins spilling into a wishing well. *Yew gawt he-yar owl rah-aht.* The accent defused the tension I was feeling, the compulsion to explode with the question: *"Who was that girl outside the White House?"*

I hugged her, wondering when adultery officially left the starting block. I feared that Claudine may have felt my tension (tension = not sexy). She hooked her arm in mine, and we climbed the seven steps toward the portico—I remembered that number, seven—and I felt like we weren't so much passing through the house as we were haunting it. I felt the loony impulse to creep from room to room shouting, "Boo!"

The place was eerily the same as it was when I left, which, I suppose, was the whole point of being a Polk. The great portrait of George Washington Polk still hung in the entryway. Colonel Polk, Sallie Hilliard, and Andrew Jackson still disapproved of me from the same walls.

Claudine took me into the kitchen and poured me lemonade. Our reunion ritual. I heard a creak from elsewhere in the house and turned around.

"J.T. and I have been separated for eight years, Jonah. He's not here."

I drank. "Separated, not divorced?"

"He won't grant me a divorce."

"Were you the one who wanted out?"

"We both wanted out, but certain things prevented it."

"Would one of those certain things be a child?"

Claudine set her lemonade down on the counter.

"Actually, Jonah, Sallie supports the divorce."

"Sallie?" I said. My voice cracked. I could stand before the national press corps and not flinch while announcing a missile strike on a foreign capital, but Claudine says the name Sallie and I almost faint.

"I understand you've met."

"She didn't tell me her name, Claud."

"She was nervous, I'm sure."

"Why would that be?"

Claudine sighed. "You're famous. She's heard so much about you."

My vanity was piqued. "Like what?"

"Oh, Jonah, our history."

"She has your bewitching quality."

"You're still charming," Claudine said, flipping back her hair. Her features remained classic. I suppose one could ask, Why wouldn't they? After all, a nose is a nose. Perhaps. Maybe something happens to a nose, perhaps subtly in the cells itself, in the mind of the outside observer who covets the nose, or in the invisible atmosphere between the two parties. I'm not sure which, but there was a practicality about her midlife good looks, a practicality, as opposed to the hot-fudge-sundae deliciousness that had once engulfed me.

"Tell me about her," I asked. I wanted to say "Sallie," but couldn't.

"She's a wonderful girl. She graduated from Vanderbilt. She works on Capitol Hill as a legislative aide."

"When did she graduate?" I asked.

Claudine hesitated.

"She got her degree in two thousand three."

I was terrible at math, so I took a slow sip of lemonade as I attempted to back out her birth year. I'm awful at dates, too. I honestly don't know which months have thirty days and which have thirty-one. There was a calendar tacked to a corkboard on the wall. My eyes caught the minuscule letters in the date boxes. It was Passover. There was cornbread on the counter. Total violation.

"So you and J.T. got married while you were still in college, huh?"

"Yes. Thanksgiving, nineteen eighty."

"Wow. Fast-a-mundo."

"Yes, I suppose. I got pregnant after you left."

"I left in early September. When was Sallie born?"

"May twenty-third, nineteen eighty-one."

"Are you sure? About when you got pregnant?" Slick, Jonah.

Claudine didn't respond. This could mean anything. The date of Sallie's birth could point to either J.T. or myself. My old girlfriend was the Sphinx.

"Tell me more, Claudine, about our reunion?"

Claudine walked me outside to the porch. She brought out the cornbread, perhaps to remind God that my stay in Eden should be limited. We sat across from each other. She took my hands. The obstacle in the divorce proceedings between Claudine and J.T. was Rattle & Snap. Through a legal trust mechanism that Claudine didn't understand, J.T. had the property switched into his name. He had slipped her the bombshell document among routine tax papers many years ago, when things between the two of them were better.

RED FLAG: *Claudine's too smart to have fallen for something like this.*

COUNTER: *Mickey was supposedly so smart he had hundreds of millions of dollars squirreled away in overseas accounts. My inheritance? A few acres of land in West Virginia.*

THE MORAL: *Smart people can do stupid things.*

"Have you looked at legal options?"

"Of course. My lawyer—after he throttled me—told me that it would be very hard to prove fraud."

"Even though it was fraud."

"I signed the documents, Jonah. It would be a mess to prove otherwise, especially since J.T. would argue—truthfully—that he had managed so many of my business affairs. I can't stand in front of a judge and say, 'Yes, Your Honor, I let him handle these ninety-nine things, but not this one hundredth matter.'"

"Does he want to live here?"

"No, he just doesn't want me to live here."

"What about Sallie? He'd throw her out, too?"

For the first time, the sunlight caught Claudine in a way that betrayed crow's-feet around her eyes. "I don't know. I don't think he'd see it that way."

"What's their relationship like?"

"It's never been good."

"And why is that, Claudine?" I asked. I felt a shiv in my own voice.

Claudine was exasperated. Exasperation had never been a Claudine attribute. This aging beauty had become a trapped she-wolf. "Chemistry, Jonah. Or whatever causes fissures between fathers and daughters."

Confront her directly, Jonah. No, don't, she'll lie. Play her game. Be patient. (Not your strong suit.)

"What is it you think I can do to help?"

"I don't know."

"Then why call me after all these years? What is my magic?"

"Rattle & Snap is my heritage, my history, my blood. I can't just throw up my arms and give it up. In a way, it's your history, too."

RED FLAG NO. *2: It's my history. In a way.*

"I spent a summer here, Claud. Are you telling me that this is part of my history, or are you telling me that it's part of my blood?"

"It is part of you."

"But is it in my *blood*? Do you see where I'm going? There's a difference. You may be mistaking what's good for you with what's a part of me."

"What did you see in Sallie, Jonah?"

"She had that forest fire in her eyes like you did. Furies whirling around in her pupils. Like I did. Like Deedee did. Like my daughter Lily does. Lily has auburn hair, too."

"I know she does. I saw you holding her once on TV."

Getting nowhere, Jonah. Throttle up: "I'm sorry to be so crude, but did you ever have blood tests done?"

"Let me ask you something, Jonah. If you were in my position, would you have had blood work done?"

"What *was* your position exactly?" I was shaking now. I took a piece of cornbread. It dissolved, unleavened, in my mouth.

Nuclear eyes from Claudine! My God, how had she interpreted this? A bawdy Shakespearean pun?

"My position was my position!" she said, breaking down, which set off my own catharsis. "My family didn't have a dime, Jonah. This great plantation, and nothing to back it up." We collapsed into each other, an evolutionary manifestation of our ancient, demented attraction.

"What was I supposed to do?" she asked, her voice muffling in my shirt. The second I felt her movement against me and smelled her hair, the promises of 1980 poured back—a fresh start—and I knew I was going to do it. Whatever "it" was. I had never gotten a straight answer from Claudine or a clean expression of sentiment, so why would this night be different from all other nights?

YOU ARE ALWAYS SO GOOD TO HER

"Where did we go?"

Claudine and J.T. had moved into Rattle & Snap after graduation from Vanderbilt. J.T. had rapidly lost interest in Claudine, and she had reason to suspect he had gotten himself involved with women who belonged to their country club, which, Claudine pointed out, she never visited.

How—how do you cheat on a woman like this, I wondered? I would have never done that. I was angry. I felt my eyeteeth growing. I thought of that lunatic that smashed the *Pietà* years ago. Why? Because some men are smashers, I guess. It was hard to let Claudine off the hook though. I had seen my share of beautiful women being treated this way by gorillas over the years. In fact, this pattern had been the norm. There was free will in all of this.

After attempts at a variety of different arrangements, Claudine had asked for a divorce. J.T. had said no.

"I understand," I said, not altogether sincerely. "What about the others in your family? I hate to ask."

"Indy's gone, of course. Elijah died a few months after him."

I nodded no, no, no, as if this should be a big surprise. "What about Six?"

"Six teaches Civil War history at Southern Methodist. He's writing a book about people in our family, our ancestors, Civil War legends . . . but he doesn't know what to do about these things."

"These things, meaning J.T. stealing your ancestral home?"

"He's an academic, Jonah. He doesn't fight guerrilla wars."

"But he teaches the Civil War."

"Correct."

I fingered my eyelashes. "We may need to reach out to him, Claudine."

"What would you have him do?"

"I don't know yet. What about Petie?"

Claudine looked down at my shoes.

"Petie has Alzheimer's, Jonah. It's in the early stages. She fades in and out, and I can't start this up with her, partly because she's not well, and partly because the side of her that is lucid knows that she played a role in all this."

"Claudie, but you played a role, too."

"I know that, Jonah." She was angry, but I wasn't sure at whom.

"Where is Petie? Is she in a special place?" I asked, like a reject from *Mister Rogers' Neighborhood*. *Sure, special friend, and why don't you cheat on your wife with Scarlett here, and then you can visit Petie in the nursing home. That would be special.*

Petie was in the garden. She was well enough to live at home, but a nurse had begun to live in the mansion. Deedee had gone through this. Mickey, however, had been sharp until he died at almost one hundred years of age.

At first, Deedee's situation hadn't been hard, and we got spoiled after her initial diagnosis, which they never gave us straight out. She had been a yahoo before Alzheimer's, so why wouldn't she be a yahoo with the disease?

I followed Claudine outside. "Don't be hurt if Petie doesn't remember you, Jonah," she said.

"It was strange with Deedee. She didn't recognize me after a while, but when I showed her pictures of myself when I was little, she'd say, 'Oh, that's Jonah,' and start telling me all about myself."

Petie's hair was cotton white, but her face was very much as it had been when I last saw her. She was holding a bouquet of flowers that she had picked from somewhere near the old trellis. A strawberry blond nature girl of about thirty stood beside Petie. I thought of a hauntingly gentle song by the British punk band the White Stripes called "I Want to Be the Boy to Warm Your Mother's Heart," and quietly sang a few lines to Claudine as we approached. She elbowed me.

The nature girl, who upon second glance was quite good-looking, identified herself as Pepper, a nurse. Good Lord. She helped Petie take a few steps back to seat herself in a heavy iron garden chair.

"You're somebody, aren't you?" Pepper asked me.

Claudine became uncomfortable and shushed Pepper.

"Why he's the stable boy," Petie said, holding the bouquet up to her nose. She removed a handkerchief from her pocket. I knelt at Petie's feet. Claudine and Pepper lingered a few steps back. She crinkled her eyes, and appeared to be happy.

"What a nice job you did," Petie said.

"A nice job?" I asked.

"On the church. What a nice job you did."

"Thank you, Petie. I tried." I liked her all of a sudden and felt, wrongly of course, that she had always liked me. Time makes old friends of everybody.

Petie waved me over closer and put her finger up to her mouth in a hush gesture. Then she whispered, "Where did we go?"

"We're right here, Petie."

She nodded her head shrewdly, no, no, no.

"We went away," she said, wiping her eyes. "We all went away."

"No, Petie."

"Yes, yes. We all went away. What a nice job you did on the church. Will I see you at church?"

"Maybe sometime," I said.

"Good. I prayed for thanks for the nice job you did. I prayed you would come back. You can stay in the house now. You don't need to stay out there anymore. You can stay and then we'll go to church. You are always so good to her."

"Okay, Petie."

Claudine tapped me on the shoulder again.

I kissed Petie on the cheek. I was angry with myself that I had ever seen her as my nemesis. I thought of her conspiring with J.T. and, for a second, a quick surge of frigid hate returned, but it went away again.

CATCHING UP
AMONG THE TOMBSTONES

"If you want to keep this place, you'll have to fight like
a rebel."

Claudine told me that she had read about my family in an online version of an article *The Washington Post* did upon my appointment as
press secretary.

I showed her a picture of Edie and the kids that I carried in my
wallet.

"Where did you meet Edie?"

"At Mickey's funeral. She was a klezmer musician. Still is, I guess."

"A nice Jewish girl, huh?"

"No, actually. Methodist. She's one-quarter Lenape Indian."

"Leave it to my Jonah to get his tribes mixed up. Tell me more
about Edie," Claudine asked.

For one thing, Edie tells me she loves me.

I didn't say this. I suddenly missed my wife. Actually, I had begun
missing Edie when she became pregnant.

"Edie is the last romantic."

"How do you define that?"

"Romantics marry men who have nothing, and carry their underwear up and down the steps to the laundry room year after year with
no tangible payoff. Lasting romances aren't very romantic."

"We do what we have to do."

"Yes, we do. If you want to keep this place, you'll have to fight like
a rebel."

"I know it."

I put my arm around her in a studied way—supportive, not amorous.

"You are either the most naïve woman in the world or the genius of geniuses. With you, I never particularly cared."

Claudine scowled like Colonel Will.

"It's not an insult, Claud. I wish I could have gone for as long without knowing such things."

Claudine stroked her eyes shut and opened them wide, blinking. When she blinked, she looked eighteen again.

"Is Smoky Hilliard still alive?"

"No."

"Hmm. That could make things trickier."

"Why?"

"Because he was smart, that's why."

We walked toward the Polk family graveyard. We passed a corral where a few dozen horses were grazing. Claudine said that three of them were Shpilkes's descendants. It hurt to look at them, so I didn't. Indy Four and Elijah rested beside one another in the Polk graveyard. I found two small stones, and placed them on their tombstones, explaining to Claudine that this was a Jewish tradition, a way of letting others know that the dead had not been forgotten.

We sat by the graves. I peppered Claudine with questions about Six. She became uncomfortable, sensing correctly that I had shifted into business mode. She wanted to protect him, which may have been the core pathology in the Polk family's current predicament. The more she told me, the more opportunities emerged in my professional brain, which had become molded over time into a template for dramatic narrative. I picked up a dandelion and held it up to Claudine's lips. She remained still until I said, "Go ahead," whereupon she let out a puff of air that turned the fluffy plant into a stalk.

"Do you have a cell phone number for J.T.?" I asked.

"Why, do you plan to call him?"

"Not exactly."

I handed Claudine a scrap of paper from my pocket and a pen. She wrote down J.T.'s phone number. "Would you add his full name and date of birth, please?" There was a what-did-I-get-myself-into fear in her eyes. Good.

I flipped the dandelion stalk into my mouth, cowboy style, and said, "Now, let's call your brother."

INTERROGATION PROFILE

"Everybody in detail is revolting."

The Panamanian sat on an iron chair on the brick patio outside of the kitchen. He had his laptop open, probably blowing up a cave in Pakistan. I handed him a piece of paper with J.T.'s full name and his cell phone number. He glanced at it. "The husband," he said.

"Right. Can you get an interrogation profile on him?"

"Would you like me to hook electrodes to his privates, too?"

"Sure, we'll do a whole barbecue."

"Looking for anything specific?"

"You know how it is, Marcus. Everybody in detail is revolting. Vulnerabilities. Psych workup. I'd also like to get a handle on the land around here. I know J.T. owns the mansion, but I remember Mickey telling me that his old man bought a lot of the other property around here."

"I'll look into it. Did you hatch a plan with your old flame yet?"

"Not yet. I've got a few ideas cooking."

"Like what?"

"I'm toying with doing something with her brother."

"Is he here?"

"No, we're trying to get ahold of him."

"Let me know when you do," Marcus said. I turned to go away, but Marcus stopped me. "Jonah, are you okay?"

"I know what you're asking, Marcus. Yeah, it's personal now."

Marcus closed his eyes. "Have you given any thought about how you're going to tell Edie, your kids?"

"For the time being, my approach is denial."

"How the hell do you find yourself in these situations?"

"The original Jonah asked God a similar question."

In the war on terror, we want to get the bad guys, but if we can't, we get what's gettable. Case in point: what I—a former high-ranking government official with serious access in the intelligence community—can do to find out about a dude I don't like. While I was on my phone arranging a focus group in Nashville, the Panamanian learned a lot.

Through J.T. Hilliard's name and date of birth, we get his driver's license number. From that, we obtain his digital photograph from the Tennessee Department of Motor Vehicles computer. We match it to the facial image that appears multiple times on a security camera in a Nashville condominium. J.T. enters this condo roughly four times a week, after work, and emerges, a little disheveled, before the eleven o'clock news.

Via Nashville public records, we determine that one of the residents of the condo is twenty-eight-year-old Patricia Evers, who runs an events planning firm, Hermitage Occasions, which has Hilliard Valley Energy as a client. We pull up the photo ID of Evers. *Sweet.* Electronic banking transactions indicate that Hilliard's company deposits $3,000 in Hermitage/Evers's corporate account each month, and just under $2,000 is debited from this account one day later by Evers's condo mortgage company.

J.T. is Patricia Evers's sugar daddy.

Through J.T.'s credit card, we learn he had purchased a zinc-based vitamin cocktail that promises greater sexual energy. He dines out a lot, usually at the same places. His tab during the past several years, however, has gone up. Closer examination of the credit card receipts, which are shared by a private data-collection firm in Arkansas that has a contract with the government under the PATRIOT Act, reveals that the "delta," or change, in the check amounts can be attributed to an increasing bar tab, versus food allotment.

J.T. drinks more than he used to.

The health-care records for Hilliard Valley Energy, which are housed in a database in Nebraska, betray that at the turn of the millennium, J.T. had been prescribed Claritin for allergies. He also had three prescriptions filled by a Columbia internist named Burns for Klonopin, an anxiety medication, Ambien to help him sleep, and Viagra, presumable for the delicious Miss Evers.

We can track J.T.'s movements through his mobile phone, which he uses often. In fact, the call volume is so extensive when compared to his home phone (in a large colonial in Columbia) that it appears he conducts most of his business while on the go.

Through a corporate debt database, we learned that Hilliard Valley Energy was indeed a successful company; however, like any commodities business—magnesium, phosphates, fertilizer ingredients, natural gas—it experienced downturns. The company had shifted its disbursements several months ago from a thirty-day cycle to a ninety-day cycle. The company also had recently extended its line of credit by $25 million, for which J.T. had signed personally.

Maury County records showed a gradual purchase of Rattle & Snap lands by different entities from the late 1970s to the present day. The transactions were handled by a law firm that had set up the purchases through various trust mechanisms. Marcus said he was still digging into this. The mansion, along with twenty acres immediately around it, hadn't transferred to J.T.'s personal ownership until 2003. Interestingly—and consistent with what Claudine had said—the mansion itself had gone from Claudine's family trust into J.T.'s name directly. He wanted there to be no ambiguity about who owned Rattle & Snap.

Along the Dulles Corridor outside of Washington, D.C., there is a nondescript cinderblock building that houses purchasing records for some of the nation's leading online retailers. It also uses cookies, or digital footprints, to monitor search-engine queries. We know from J.T.'s online book purchases that J.T.'s literary interests are limited to fiction and nonfiction dealing with the exploits of the Delta Force and other paramilitary he-men. The most frequent search-engine terms that turn up on our printouts from his home and office computer are

"Navy SEALs," "Delta Force," "Army Rangers," "Green Beret," "Mossad," "Special Forces," "sniper," "Jonah Eastman," "Mafia," and, of note, repeated "welcome back" greetings from the landing page of www.maximumbooty.com.

The Panamanian and I decided that for strategic purposes, it was important to inspect this last Web site, which featured women of Asian, Hispanic, and African descent with protuberant rear ends.

"When will we stop being amused by this stuff?" Marcus asked me.

"I don't know, Marcus, I still laugh at the word 'fiduciary.'"

"Precisely. Now, shall I click on 'the Incan Delinquent,' or this nice young lady in the cowboy hat, 'Butt Masterson'?"

"Why choose?"

"Oops," Marcus said, flicking his mouse. "Ms. Masterson requires a credit card. Adieu, sweet princess."

With the exception of two regressed middle-aged men ogling naked women, this other high-tech activity probably seems far-fetched. Good, keep thinking that. When we are alone, we *feel* alone, and this illusion of solitude trumps analysis. The fact is, every piece of data gathered on J. T. Hilliard was done without the mobilization of "human assets"—in other words, it all came from a massive data infra-structure that did not exist last time I was at Rattle & Snap. The challenge was determining whether any of this information could be exploited.

"What did your psych profiler say?" I asked the Panamanian.

"He said that psych profiling isn't an exact science."

"C'mon, Marcus, no equivocation. J.T.'s a threat to national security," I winked.

"My guy said that, in many respects, J.T.'s not so unusual. Lots of guys balance Conan the Barbarian artistic tastes with sexual insecurity. He clearly has a mistress, but J.T. and Claudine are estranged, so that's not a big shocker. His prescriptions and alcohol increase coincide with a downturn in his business commodities, so his business worries are genuine. Still, his company has huge assets, so he's got plenty of room to maneuver."

"And lots to lose."

"Sure."

"How do we play a guy like this?"

"I don't think we know enough yet to say for sure." An evil expression descended across the Panamanian's face.

"What? What is it?"

"I'd like you to have a meeting with J.T. at his offices. You'll have a camera in your lapel. While you're there, screw with his head, but don't emasculate him if you can avoid it. Get him seesawing between wondering if you're a nut, or if you could really hurt him. Give him something to work with on both ends of the spectrum. On one hand, build up his ego by letting him think you're a fraud who's in above his head, but then do something that'll make him wake up sweating. Keep looking for something that could destroy him, but even if you find it, leave him with an escape hatch."

"I can't back this guy off by dangling a Viagra prescription in front of *The New York Times*."

Marcus kicked a pebble. "Aw, shucks, the Jonah I know doesn't back losers. My Jonah bets on winners. Help me help you. Once I get a look at his office setup, I'll go in to see what else I can find."

"You seem confident you'll find more, Marcus."

"My Jonah wouldn't waste his time down here if he thought this guy was just looking at naughty Internet sites. What else do you know, Riptide?"

"I'm not sure I know anything?"

"But you've got memories."

"Yes, I've got memories."

"What are they, man? Help me help you."

"I need you to look into something else."

"Sallie's birth records?"

I nodded.

SLEEPWALKING

"They were going to make it like it was at the beginning."

That evening, I slept in Indy Four's old room. No, I didn't. I was cold all night, as if Indy's spirit had hopped into bed with me and hogged all the sheets. I got up once and flipped the light on, which displeased Leonidas, who told me to get back to bed and stay away from the Polk women. My actual thoughts were anything but lascivious. I was trying to imagine the life I might have led with my now grown daughter.

A Venn diagram was forming in my head, one circle containing Sallie, and the other Edie, Ricky, and Lily. I couldn't conceive of how to bring them together. I had options here, which ranged from keeping my mouth shut to total disclosure. After more than two decades in the black art of damage control, I had discovered that disclosure was overrated. Despite its benevolent halo, honesty could be a very cruel thing, and was usually met with the wrath of the truth's recipient.

I had wanted to sleep in the mansion since the spring of 1980, but now that I was here, I was a wreck. I heard footsteps outside my door. The Panamanian was assigned Six's old room, which was across the second-floor sitting area, so I thought he might be restless, too. Elijah? What if it was Claudine? Undressed, with only a blanket, like a Bond girl. I am such filth. No, Claudine was presumably asleep in an unknown tower being guarded by sentries. I threw on my khakis and polo shirt and went into the sitting area.

A chandelier above the staircase provided enough light for me to see. The door to the bedroom that Claudine occupied when she was young was open. I could see that the bed was empty, so I turned on a light. The bed was all softness. I pressed down on a pillow and saw my handprint briefly appear and then, like the Cheshire cat, disappear. A portrait was on the wall that I did not recognize. There were more contemporary photographs set in frames around a dresser below it— photos of Sallie in assorted stages of gorgeousness.

As for the painting above the dresser . . . it was Sallie, too. She appeared to be in her late teens. She was dressed in an old-fashioned frilly outfit. Sallie's eyes were following the line of the unmistakable nose she had inherited from Claudine off to the north of the mansion. I looked over there, too.

Footsteps again. My first instinct was to run, but I decided against it. I was tired of running. Petie Polk appeared at the door in her nightgown.

"Oh, it's not in here," she said.

"Hello, Petie," I said softly. "What are you doing up so late?"

"You're the new stable boy, aren't you?"

I nodded.

"You won't find it in here," she said. "I've already looked here."

"What's not in here, Petie?"

She whispered to me: "The gold."

"Oh," I said. "I wasn't looking for that."

"Everybody's looking for it, but it's not in the house. Not in the columns, either."

"Have you seen the treasure, Petie?"

She glanced around conspiratorially, and sat on the edge of Sallie's bed. "Not in a long time," she said. "Not since you found some of it— those coins, remember—beneath the church? They used to melt it down out in the valley."

"Who melted it down?" I said, sitting beside her.

"The army men," she said quietly. "They dug up what they buried, and then melted it down little by little. That way they could get it out without anybody seeing."

"What were they going to do with it?"

"They were going to make it like it was at the beginning."

I wanted to ask Petie what "they" were going to bring back, but I sensed she was getting confused, and didn't want to make things worse.

Petie pointed to the portrait of Sallie. "That was painted when she went to her debut in Nashville. Claudine was so proud. You weren't here. No, you were away, unfortunately."

"Do you remember where I was, Petie?"

Petie took my hand and guided me to an ornate sofa beneath the window.

"I'm not sure. Sometimes a baby can chase a man away. The mother puts all she has into the baby and forgets the man. Claudine fell madly in love with Sallie. I saw you on TV. You couldn't be everyplace, I suppose."

"I take it you don't think I was a very good father."

"You did such a nice job on the church," she said. "You were always so good to her. Did I tell you that?"

"Yes, you did. I appreciate that." A tad late, no?

"Are you going to fix the house some more?"

"I'm going to try, Petie."

There was creaking in the hallway. More ghosts. No, it was Pepper, Petie's nurse, in her nightgown. Freckles dotted her cleavage beneath her gold cross. "Petie," she said, "were you looking for the treasure again?"

"It's not in the house," Petie said.

"Well, honey," Pepper said, in a sleepy drawl, "we'll go looking for it tomorrow."

Pepper helped Petie stand. "Sometimes the stable boy is on TV," Petie told Pepper.

"Yes, I've seen him," Pepper said.

Pepper nodded, and took Petie back to her room. I returned to Indy Four's canopy bed, lay down fully clothed, and tried to navigate my thoughts of Pepper and the certification of my paternity by a sleepwalking Alzheimer's sufferer roaming antebellum shadows in search of Confederate treasure.

PROVOCATION

"So why are you back?"

The Panamanian slept with his eyes open. I waved my hand across his face. He did not blink. "Marcus," I said.

"Yes?" he responded with a blink (but no fear).

"I'm going to see J.T. this afternoon. Claudine said he'll be in his office."

Marcus sat up. "Are you ready?"

I shrugged.

"All we want now is to rattle him, and see what he does," Marcus said. "J.T.'s very impressed with who he is, his status. He'll go for a power maneuver."

"All right, I'll try to provoke him. Another thing: Can you find me an environmental guy? A metallurgist . . . I don't know, somebody who can test for, uh, metals."

"What are we looking for?"

"Buried treasure," I said.

"I didn't know they had pirates in these parts."

"Did they ever."

"Do you have a map?"

I tapped my forehead.

"By the way, have you seen the online edition of Southern Methodist's college newspaper?"

"Oh, fudge," I said sarcastically, "I must have forgotten to do my hourly log-on."

"Well, your buddy Six Polk has gone missing."

* * *

I called Joe Diamond, senior vice president for news at the Empire Broadcasting Service. EBS News was the last remaining broadcasting network known for breaking journalistic ground. While the others had become embroiled in scandal or watered themselves down into sugary oblivion, EBS News still prided itself on getting substantial scoops, especially interviews with world leaders. They had fouled up once, however, reporting inaccurately that President Truitt had bombed a Middle East nursery school instead of a terrorist camp. Rather than humiliating EBS for basing its report on an unreliable informant (as we normally would), I cauterized their error by accepting an on-air correction and allowing EBS's anchor to have an in-depth one-on-one interview with the president.

My message to Joe was simple: I was calling in my marker, so stand by.

The offices of Hilliard Valley Energy were housed in a three-story building in Columbia, which was attached to a series of boxy industrial structures. The main entrance was decorated in urban contemporary. Seated behind the receptionist's command post was a matronly woman with purple reading glasses and blond hair piled atop her head like a skyscraper. I made certain that my American flag lapel pin–camera was pointed straight at her so the Panamanian could fully appreciate her high-rise cranium.

"Good morning, I'm here to see Mr. Hilliard."

"Hmm. Now, aren't you somebody?" the receptionist asked, her eyes unblinking over her reading glasses, which had been trained on US Weekly. According to the magazine's cover, Jessica Simpson and her husband Nick Lachey had not been having sex five times a day in recent weeks. Well, kids, I thought, tragedy strikes all of us.

"Not anymore."

"Aw, c'mon. You're somebody in Washington."

"Well, I used to be somebody in Washington. Would you tell Mr. Hilliard that Supreme Court Justice Jonah Leonidas Eastman is here to see him?"

"I sure will," she said, now convinced I was deranged.

I was well aware that my appearance here was in direct conflict with the Panamanian's stealth imperative; however, we had agreed that there was no other way for me to get the intelligence we needed. It was more important that I not be linked to the Polkapalooza that was about to rain down on the nation in the next forty-eight hours. While I wouldn't deny being in Tennessee, I'd need deniability on the impending deeds.

When J.T. walked out, I said in the manner of a long-lost college buddy, "J. T. Hilliard? If that don't beat all. Is that really you?"

J.T.'s jaw was outthrust in a primate attack gesture. He wasn't quite as big as I had remembered. He was still a pretty good-looking guy—he had a full head of darkening sandy hair—but he was definitely thicker across the middle and, to some extent, across the cheeks. He reminded me of a congressman. A congressman on a golf course. If he still possessed a scar from our battle, it had blended in with his ruddy skin.

"You look different than you did a long time ago," J.T. said. His voice was as friendly as it had to be, but no friendlier. I may have disliked the man, but he was not inherently hateful. His ease with himself carried a certain charm. We were James Bond and Blofeld exchanging pleasantries before the overchoreographed slaughter, but who was who? I had another vain and competitive thought: Was it preferable to have thinning hair and be wearing the same clothes that you wore in college, or was it better to have thick hair and a spreading ass? I didn't know, and it bothered me.

J.T. did not shake my hand, and I did not reach out for his. He waved me back toward his suite of offices. High-rise Head, the receptionist, couldn't quite figure out what was going on.

"You look a lot like you used to," I said. "You did pretty well in the hair department."

"And you're in fine shape. Now, may I ask what you're doing here, what you want—my wife, for instance?"

"Why not? You don't want her."

"You're married, aren't you?"

"Yes, J.T. Happily." Be a little *more* defensive, Jonah.

We passed J.T.'s assistant and entered a large corner office over-looking a corporate garden and picnic area. I made no secret of my study of the room. One wall was a tribute to golfing leisure. J.T. golf-ing with a barely alive Bob Hope. J.T. with a few U.S. senators. J.T. with Warren Buffett. J.T. getting trophies. I felt a pang of jealousy, not because I wanted to golf, but because I envied his being in a position where he could sit atop this empire *and* golf. Even his computer screen featured a golf course.

J.T. had a few small photos on his credenza, but I couldn't quite make out their faces from this distance. Several of them appeared to be feminine, and I assumed them to be of Claudine and Sallie. I'd have the Panamanian zoom in and check. Across from his desk, there was a painting of Rattle & Snap. The rest of the office was generic power furniture that didn't betray much wear and tear. J.T.'s desk was covered with various paperweights and penholders, but only one file folder. Again, an ugly pulse of envy in my veins.

J.T. sat behind his desk and rocked back. I stood. Fine, all the better to film his office. "So why are you back? Are you going to whip off your belt and hit me with it?" J.T. chuckled. His arms were now crossed.

"No, J.T., I don't want to fight. I want to go home."

"Then why don't you?"

"Because Claudine wants to go home, too, and she can't because you won't let her. She wants her family's house."

"This isn't yours to negotiate, friend. It's between husband and wife."

"You can win."

"What the hell are you talking about, I can win?"

"It is completely within your power, not my own, to make your problems go away. Just give her the property, J.T."

"I'll tell you, friend, for a presidential spokesman—perhaps I should say *former*—you don't talk too clear, because I don't know what you're saying."

"What's at Rattle & Snap, J.T., that you need so badly? What makes it so enchanted? Is there a fountain of eternal life in a well somewhere? What is it?"

"You're the one who came back. You tell me."

This was a fair point, and I couldn't deflect it cleverly.

I held my palms out in a mock-timid gesture of surrender. "Just give her the house, J.T., then I'm out of your life forever."

"Out of my life? You've been in my life for twenty-five years."

Finally, a straight answer, even if it was from my bête noire. But I couldn't press J.T. too hard now, castrate him. *"Yes, Jonah, you're the father of the child I've been pretending is mine. You win. I lose." "Oh, and by the way, Claudine can have Rattle & Snap, and you can live together happily ever after."*

"What do you mean?"

"C'mon, living with that nagging suspicion that I'm some kind of rebound from your Summer of Love."

Take it slow here. It's business. Be cool. Like Mickey.

I sucked on my upper lip. "Fair enough," I said. "I'd be the same way. Actually, I'd be worse. Don't forget, J.T., she married you."

"Thanks for the compliment, Eastman."

Try it this way: "Did you ever think about how all of this impacts Sallie?"

"You don't seem to have given too much thought to Sallie, coming around here making threats."

"I always think about how things impact children," I said instead.

"Are you planning to send some of your gangster buddies down here?" J.T. asked, getting hot, "Because I'll tell you something, boy, there will be more troopers around here than your guinea friends can muster.

Damn it! He ducked it. Lightbulb number one: He's in denial. Lightbulb number two: Claudine never told him. She either told him that Sallie was his, or kept him in limbo, too—doubting himself, doubting her, doubting that the earth was round.

I clasped my hands together and took one step toward J.T., speaking softly, conspiratorially to him. "The more cops you can have around here, the better. That would be some maximum booty."

I thought I saw his eyelid twitch.

"Excuse me?"

"Just an old expression a friend of mine in the Special Forces used to use."

"Yeah, what branch?"

"Uh, Navy Seal Penguin Special Strike Force Delta Niner Black-hawk Down Foxtrot Green Berets. I served with him over in Bosnia Hertzkowitz."

"Lord, you're still a smart-ass."

"No, it was a secret mission we did. Trained up at Viagra Falls. Some bad memories, but it happens to most guys."

"You don't make a bit of sense, friend."

"I apologize. I've been anxious, having trouble sleeping. What do you take for something like that?"

"Look, I don't know what kind of stunt you're hatching, but keep in mind that I have options of my own. You're not the only cowpoke with political juice."

Fair point. One of the biggest mistakes men make is assuming that they're the only ones with friends.

"So, that's your answer. You keep the house; Claudine moves to a garden apartment. Well, I've clearly proven my skills as a negotiator."

"This isn't yours to negotiate."

With that, I left, giving his office one last visual sweep. My first instinct was to hate him for his lack of appreciation of Claudine. But, seeing him, something registered with me that hadn't before: He had spent his life with her; I hadn't. Perhaps he didn't find her quirks to be endearing. In fact, maybe he had good reason for his antipathy, and my medieval fascination was the true sign of the lunatic.

CERTIFICATION (OR NOT)

"Why would they want to hide something that they so blatantly coveted?"

I located the Panamanian, who was working on his laptop in a sitting room upstairs in the mansion.

"How'd it go?" he asked.

"I could be wrong, but I think he likes me."

"Good. It's prom season, you never know," he said.

I handed Marcus back his flag pin–camera.

"Were you watching while I was inside?" I asked.

"Off and on," he said.

"J.T. sure likes golf."

"Workhorse, huh? What about security, Jonah?"

"I was cleared in by a grandmother. I could probably kick her ass if I had to."

"You're not a man to trifle with," Marcus said.

"What have you learned about Hilliard's other security?" I asked.

"We've been scouting them at night. They've got watchmen. Average age: one hundred and four. The guy they have sitting at the main desk watches TV. We've got a little treat for him. Oh, and I know a bit more about the property ownership."

"Lay it on me," I said.

"The land around the mansion has been purchased in parcels by a trust that's administered by a law firm in New Orleans called Moscowitz & Forelli."

"MoFo!" I exclaimed.

"Huh?"

"MoFo. That's what Mickey used to call that firm. He used to laugh about it." I fixated on a cloud that resembled Carol Channing.

"What is it, Jonah?"

"Mickey didn't keep a lot of records, but I saw an envelope from MoFo years ago when I cleaned out his safe-deposit box. There was a bunch of legal stuff, bills and all."

"You don't seem too surprised by this intel."

"I knew the Hilliards subsidized the Polks. Mickey made that pretty clear when I left for college. I just thought it was a pretty straightforward thing, like the Kennedys and the Bouviers—the Hilliards brought the cash and the Polks brought the class. But why would they set it up in a trust through some mobbed-up law firm?"

"Maybe the Hilliards wanted to hide their ownership," Marcus said.

"Why would they want to hide something that they so blatantly coveted? The mansion and a few acres around it are in J.T.'s name."

"They'd want to hide ownership of property if they were up to no good on that property. Or if there was something valuable on that property," Marcus said.

"I don't know, Marcus. That doesn't quite work. First of all, Smoky was too cagey to swallow all that buried treasure talk. And even if he did, wouldn't he want the land in his own name, so that when he found it, it would belong to him?"

"I don't know. Maybe those buried treasure stories aren't so crazy. You've said yourself that some folks around here take that Lost Cause stuff seriously. What now?"

"I'll have to go back to Washington to look through my safe deposit box to see if I still have that MoFo envelope," I said.

The Panamanian nodded, frowned, and pulled a scrap of paper from his pocket. I unfolded it. The first thing I saw was a tiny footprint. *Omnia vestigia retrorsum*, I thought. It was a copy of Sallie Hilliard's birth certificate. May 23, 1981. No surprises. Claudine was listed as Sallie's mother, J.T. as her father. Birthplace: Nashville.

"Marcus, don't these things say anything about blood type?"

"No, Jonah, they don't," he said.

"I left Rattle & Snap in September of nineteen eighty," I said. "Or . . ." I envisioned Claudine and J.T. together in the hayloft right after I was booted out. Or, worse, maybe they "got together" while I was still here. My eyes felt heavy, and the muscles around my jaw stiffened. A wave of nausea passed through me.

"Can't we check . . . blood?" I asked.

"You want us to grab Sallie off the street and take a blood sample?"

"Of course not. I don't know. There aren't records or something?"

"No, Jonah. It doesn't work that way. To confirm paternity, you need to draw fresh blood. Preferably with the child's consent." The Panamanian smirked.

"Or, Marcus, I have to take Claudine's word."

"Sounds like you don't trust her."

"Obsession and trust are two very different concepts," I said.

POLLING CONFEDERATES

"It's symbolism is all."

The difference between polling for businesses and polling for politicians is time. When you design a poll for a corporation, they run it through a committee made up of people who like to say things like "Let's take a few steps back." In English, this translates into "Let's not do anything." In large corporations, only a few people think about gain; the remainder are content to contemplate how to avoid losing. The pathway to not losing is doing nothing.

In presidential politics, the rewards are huge, but failure is a probability. Everything, therefore, is done quickly and with minimal "strategic thinking," because there just isn't any time to do it any other way. So it was that when I called Sydney Crane, a brilliant Atlanta-based opinion researcher, she designed a focus group guide in thirty minutes and had a facility booked in Nashville for the following day.

In her early thirties, Sydney Crane had the scrubbed good looks that men associate with the-pretty-girl-who-was-nice-to-me-anyway in high school. Similarly, Sydney's wholesome appeal managed not to be threatening to women who would feel guilty about being mean to someone who was so, well, nice. Her approachable demeanor was a big asset in focus groups, which were designed to draw people out, get them talking with someone they trusted.

Today's group consisted of eight people who, loosely speaking, represented the population of central Tennessee. They were (as I designated them in my notes from my perch behind a one-way mirror) Soccer Mom, a thirtyish blond; an athletic professional man in his midforties I called Ralph Lauren; an impeccably dressed black housewife, Proud Mary; Miss Dixie, a grandmother with a silver powercoiffuer that could house a Super Bowl game; a voluptuous beauty queen type, Peach Pie; Preacher Bob, a grave and studious black man who wore an expression betraying disappointment in a civilization that had failed to hold itself to a higher standard; a sensitive, doe-eyed woman in her thirties I deemed Earth Mama; and Garth Brooks, a strapping agricultural products salesman hell-bent on using this group as his stepping-stone to the presidency.

Sydney began, "Thank you all for coming. My name is Sydney Crane, and this is what's called a focus group. I have a client that is interested in learning what consumers—you—think about certain issues. The way we learn is to spark discussions and listen to what people say. Behind the one-way mirror back there, there is a camera that records our session for analysis later."

"Are there people watching us?" Soccer Mom asked.

"Sometimes," Sydney said. My clients come and go as they please, but sometimes they watch the proceedings."

I observed some low-grade fidgeting on the part of Soccer Mom and Ralph Lauren.

"The subject today has to do with the state of our country, how things have evolved in the South since the Civil War," Sydney continued.

"Who is your client?" Ralph Lauren asked.

"I'm not at liberty to identify my client, because it may bias the group."

"Will you tell us at the end?"

"Unfortunately not, we have to keep this confidential."

"Why?" Ralph Lauren pursued.

"Clients often don't know how the research will be used, and prefer that people don't know that they're conducting research in the first place."

I sensed by the way Ralph Lauren adjusted himself in his seat that he was unappeased, but his gentlemanly nature and respect for decorum restrained him. The discussion began on vague territory: the political climate.

"Very divisive," Garth Brooks said.

"How so?" Sydney asked.

"Red states and blue states. We're all at each other's throats," Garth said with a confident bob of his head.

"It's a shame," said Earth Mama. "There's no reason we can't all just get along."

I was pretty sure that I saw Ralph Lauren roll his eyes. I was inclined to roll my own. *There's a good reason we can't all just get along,* I thought: *human nature.*

Fortunately, Proud Mary weighed in. "We've been divided from the beginning. There's nothing new in all of this, we just give it different names. North and South. Red state, blue state. It doesn't matter."

Sydney facilitated a debate to identify the fissures in our culture. Everyone had a theory.

Ralph Lauren: Black, brown, yellow, and red versus white.

Soccer Mom: Mason and Dixon.

Miss Dixie: Anarchy versus decorum.

Peach Pie: Feminists versus the beautiful (scoring a wince from Earth Mama).

Earth Mama: Tolerance versus insensitivity (a snort from Peach Pie).

Preacher Bob: NASCAR versus *The New York Times.*

Garth Brooks: Beer and hot dogs versus chablis and quiche.

Proud Mary: City versus country.

There were other mentions: Tobacco versus microchips. Democrats and Republicans. Wall Street and Main Street. Choice versus life. I scribbled these things down, suspecting every one of these people of being a little right and a little wrong. The discussion, as planned, got specific when Sydney brought up symbolic battlegrounds. Clinton and Lewinsky. Clarence Thomas and Anita Hill. Terry Schiavo. She concluded another round of spirited exchange by asking if anyone believed the South would ever gain cultural respect.

"Are you kidding?" Soccer Mom said. "Look at who's become president. LBJ. Carter. Clinton. Bush II. Truitt. Southerners. We're doing just fine, thank you very much."

Everyone chortled.

"I read that seventy percent of Americans attend a church of some kind," Proud Mary said. "We're a religious country."

"But the Confederate flag isn't flying over statehouses," Garth Brooks said. "And I don't think it should, by the way. Brings up bad memories." Earth Mama nodded, pleasantly surprised, having probably pegged Garth as the Imperial Wizard of the Ku Klux Klan.

The discussion shifted to the perception of the South as a hotbed of bigotry. Earth Mama cited an article from the 1930s that purported to explain why so many Jews played basketball. "The article said that basketball required cunning and deception, which is why Jews excelled at the sport. Isn't that incredible?"

Preacher Bob laughed: "Remember when Jimmy the Greek said that blacks couldn't swim because they're not as buoyant as whites?"

The group laughed.

Proud Mary said, "And now, so many African Americans play professional basketball, and I don't know of any Jewish players. When did my people get devious all of a sudden?"

Soccer Mom speculated archly, "Maybe while African Americans were getting devious, Jewish people were getting buoyant!"

Preacher Bob: "That must explain Mark Spitz!" Everyone howled. "He floated pretty well in Munich."

Sydney allowed the tangent to proceed unabated, which was smart. Tangents, provided that they're not totally off point, relax subjects and give them permission to be candid without retribution. When the chatter subsided, Sydney said, in a manner that seemed offhanded: "Speaking of divisive issues, there have been legends since the Civil War that Confederate militias hid gold in different locations throughout the South. Have you heard these stories?"

All but one of the people (Earth Mama) were familiar with the legends.

Miss Dixie and Ralph Lauren told stories about how they had first heard the legends as children. The gold was in an Arkansas mountain. The gold in Fort Knox *was* the Confederate gold, the U.S. government having stolen it. It's in the pillars of some old plantation between Nashville and the Georgia state line.

Ah.

"Let's say gold is discovered? Who does it belong to?"

"Whoever finds it," Proud Mary said to near unanimous acclaim.

Sydney: "I believe the law says that the U.S. Treasury can seize any gold once controlled by the Confederacy."

"See," Ralph Lauren said. "You can define the law any way you want. That's the problem. Every big institution is a protection racket. Business. The Vatican. The government. If you pay up, you're okay. If you don't, you're in trouble. I don't know if there's gold all over the South or not. If there's gold down here, be it one ingot or Fort Knox, the government will want it. It's not about the Union versus the Confederacy, it's about power and money."

"It's not about gold, it's about culture," Miss Dixie said. I was intrigued. "It may sound paranoid, but I think the government still likes to remind Southerners that the North won, that the way of life in New York is better than the way of life in Nashville. Washington doesn't need that gold, they want it as a tweak."

Sydney asked, "You believe this even though the president is a Southerner?"

"They're giving him what-for," Miss Dixie said, "But he can only do so much, especially with this Supreme Court fight. Judge Dewey's a fine man, but the folks on the Upper West Side of Central Park don't like him, so I think he's going to get hammered in those hearings coming up. These are the same folks on Wall Street investing in the companies that want to pave over Civil War battlefields to put up Wal-Marts."

"Wal-Mart's an Arkansas company," Ralph Lauren said.

"But they've got to go through Wall Street to get to Main Street," Peach Pie said.

"What does that mean to you, if the legends about Confederate gold were true?" Sydney asked the group.

Peach Pie said, "I think what we're trying to say is that it's not about who the gold belongs to, it's about how a lot of us feel, which is that we don't trust the government. We don't like being stepped on, whether it's for gold or Supreme Court justices or snide remarks about how President Truitt pronounces the word 'nuclear.' It's code, Miss Crane. It's code for 'I'm better than y'all.' "

This point was a catalyst for cross talk and shooting hands. Almost everybody had a comment.

Soccer Mom: "No sane person anymore thinks Southern values are about slavery. Our values are about God and family. Any way Hillary Clinton and her crowd can ridicule that, they will."

Preacher Bob: "Wherever that gold is found is where it ought to stay."

Proud Mary: "If there's money, it's dirty money, but that doesn't mean I trust the government's motives. It's symbolism is all: 'I have the power to do this to you.' "

Earth Mama: "I think the government has a right to take whatever plunder came from slavery."

Ralph Lauren: "It's all tribalism. One tribe thinks it's better than another tribe. It's just a matter of finding the right obscure law to justify it. Your tribe wants to pave over my tribe to build a Wal-Mart; my tribe wants to pave over your tribe to fly the rebel flag—and so on."

Garth Brooks: "Well, I don't want to fly that flag myself, but no matter how you shake it out, we're two countries."

"It's symbolism is all." That's what Proud Mary had said. People reacted to symbols of disrespect as opposed to engaging in prolonged analysis. Think about what happens whenever a white person speaks to a minority group using the phrase "you people." Not a bigoted statement per se, but the suggestion of a broader agenda.

The other simple concept that leapt out at me was derived from a word Miss Dixie used: Tweak. One didn't need to elaborate on a belief, one simply had to tweak it. The challenge then became locating the mechanism with which the tweak could be visited upon our target audience.

STRATEGIC EXCAVATIONS

"Can I keep it?"

Tommy Rawls had been retired from the Franklin Police Department for fifteen years. He had always been a night owl, but his proclivities had intensified since his wife of more than fifty years died last year. Rawls didn't need the money he made working security at Hilliard Valley Energy, but he enjoyed the spare change because it helped finance vacations with his grandchildren, not to mention the beginnings of a college education fund for them.

Rawls's nightly ritual at Hilliard began with the retrieval of the latest magazines from the reception area. He would sit here beginning now, 7:00 P.M., until the following morning. Next, he would get settled in his chair and flick on the twelve-inch television that was on the reception desktop. He used the remote to tune into Fox News, where he would watch *The O'Reilly Factor* for an hour before switching to ESPN to watch basketball.

All of these things were eminently observable by a combination of visual surveillance and heightened sensitivity to local gossip.

At 8:10, an odd thing happened on *The O'Reilly Factor*. O'Reilly was replaced by the moaning face of a peroxide blonde who, were it not for her shiny hair, would have been considered funny looking. Rawls shook his head as if trying to defuse an antihistamine buzz. The next thing he saw was the quivering upper lip of an Asian woman who was sharing a mutually beneficial encounter with the peroxide blonde.

Tommy Rawls craned his head around to confirm that he was alone. He was. So he kept watching the Spice Channel, which had been piped into the cable system of Hilliard Valley Energy courtesy of intelligence operatives underwritten by the American taxpayer.

While the two moaners lit up the screen, the Panamanian opened a rear door in the wing that housed J.T.'s office. A maintenance man had been kind enough to tape down the bolt of this particular door for one hundred dollars. Marcus was inside of J.T.'s office within forty-five seconds. First, he tapped J.T.'s computer mouse, which brought his screen alive. Marcus scrolled through J.T.'s e-mails and his list of logged calls. Then he played J.T.'s voice messages. Most were innocuous, but one stood out. The caller's name was Sam Platt. He worked at Boston Capital Holdings. He said they were "getting close."

Along with the rise of twenty-four-hour cable news there came a new strain of media personality: the Filler. The Filler's job was not to report news, it was to make news by "posing questions," an intellectual prophylactic device that freed him from factual obligation. If anyone impugned the Filler's journalistic credibility, he could simply remind the uptight prig that he was an entertainer. Lighten up, folks.

The leading on-air Filler of the moment was Enoch Squibbes of Global News Network. Squibbes was legendary for his helicopter jones. Publicists were known to commence their pitches to Squibbes by assuring him that the story would involve something to circle and land on. Most of his "stories" captured something from above, occasionally with a night-vision lens to make it look extra stealthy (even if it was a flock of geese unloading their bowels on an Oldsmobile). Of course, Squibbes himself would narrate the alleged action from his perch in the helicopter, which gave the whole thing a paramilitary whiff.

Today's filler involved a series of holes that had been found in the earth, often beside mountains, throughout the South. Of varying diameters, the man-made holes were large enough to fit a human being. Particularly interesting were the satellite photos that Squibbes displayed on a computerized screen. The most recent photos showed the excavations that Squibbes was tracking, while those taken of the same locations one month earlier displayed unblemished terrain.

The camera cut to a bearded man from Stone Mountain Agricultural College in Georgia who studied both the satellite images and photos that Squibbes had taken when surveying the excavations from a helicopter. Historian Ian Holloway Craven explained, "There have been legends since the final days of the Civil War about Confederate radicals stockpiling huge quantities of gold for an eventual reengagement with the Union. That gold was supposedly stored in mountain caves, accessible through man-made tunnels."

Squibbes pressed his subject: "How would stockpiling gold have helped the Confederacy resume the war?"

"The theories about how this might have happened have changed over the years. During the war and Reconstruction, the gold would have been used to finance militias, such as Nathan Bedford Forrest's band. In the twentieth century, a new theory emerged: The gold would be used to destabilize the U.S. monetary system, throw the economy into chaos. Economic terrorism."

"What kind of quantities of gold are we talking about?" Squibbes asked.

"No one knows for sure, but anecdotal reports have put estimates as high as several hundred tons."

"In other words, potentially billions of dollars' worth?"

"If we are to believe the legends," the professor qualified.

"Even if rebels had hidden billions of dollars in gold, the U.S. abandoned the gold standard in the early nineteen seventies," Squibbes said, self-satisfied (a risk taker *and* smart). "So, the whole conspiracy sounds rather far-fetched."

"That's true, sir. The conspiracy as initially conceived is utter foolishness. But you may be forgetting a much more practical question."

"And what is that, Professor?"

"Even if there's only a fraction of this gold cache out there, to whom does the gold belong?"

The GNN report triggered a round of on-air punditry. Gordon

Kinney of GraftNet had as his guest another historian, this one an expert on government policy during the Reconstruction era, from George Mason University. Kinney said, "Let me give you the question point-blank: If I dig up my backyard and I find Confederate gold, can I keep it?"

"I'm afraid not, Gordon. Any property that once belonged to the Confederacy now belongs to Uncle Sam."

"Even if it's in my own backyard?"

"If it was placed there by agents of the Confederacy, it can be seized by the federal government."

"Now, wait a minute. My backyard is my property, and anything I find—"

"Mr. Kinney, you are touching off the question that lies at the very foundation of America."

Kinney, outraged: "And what is that, sir?"

"Who owns what?"

The cable shows were ablaze with odd couplings, including property rights attorneys and Civil War experts.

Lee Woodruff, the sultry anchor of the network program *America Betrayed*, had snagged the cycle's big "get," Stone Mountain's Professor Craven. "The Civil War has been over for one hundred and forty years, Professor. Why all the fuss over it now? After all, nobody's finding gold in these excavations."

"Not yet, anyway."

"I understand, sir, but why the fuss *now*?"

"First, there are the satellite photos of the holes. Then there are other strange things kindling interest. For example, didn't you try to reach another historian to come on the program with me? Independence Polk?"

"We tried, I think," Woodruff said.

"Well, Lee, Indy Polk the Sixth—called Six by his friends and family—who has been tracking Confederate gold for decades, has turned up missing. Nobody can find him."

"Who is he exactly?"

"He is the only living scion of arguably the mightiest Confederate family America has ever known, the Polks of Tennessee. He has a sister, I believe, but Six Polk is the leading expert on Confederate gold. There's a legend that his family's mansion, Rattle & Snap, had gold hidden in its columns."

"But, as you said yourself, this could just be folklore."

"It probably is, Lee, but it would certainly give a young man who grew up in that mansion incentive to go looking, wouldn't it now?"

Professor Craven's final appearance that day came as Enoch Squibbes emerged from an excavation in the Ozarks holding a moldy slice of parchment with elaborate handwriting. There was no treasure in this crater, but there was an intriguing relic. Craven, having been read the text over the telephone, suggested an interpretation of the clue: When Union general William Tecumseh Sherman pillaged the South, Confederate gentry, afraid that their wealth would be seized, began hiding it. The possible location of key valuables could be imputed from the clue, along with a call to arms to retrieve it when the time was right. Squibbes again read into the camera the words written on the parchment, which had been encased in a small music box that had been buried long ago:

> Tecumseh thunders
> Fortunes sap
> Picks and shovels
> Rattle & Snap

HELL NIGHT

"It's incredible how we can mistake tiny movements for love."

It began to get weird. They came in the night, mostly in sport-utility vehicles. Some arrived in vans. There were a few campers. And then there were the motorcycles. I never would have made a connection between Confederate reenactors and motorcycles. As Deedee would have said, Who knew?

But they came. The media bitch goddess had stepped upon the live wire of Red State America—the unconscious notion that *they* were coming. *They* were a shadowy cabal on the precipice of seizing control. Who were *they*? Who knows, but whoever *they* (a.k.a. "them") were, it warranted protest. It warranted gun ownership. It warranted the freedom that our beloved motorized vehicles provided us, fossil fuel be damned. We wanted to be hair-trigger ready to haul ass from *them*. If you were a liberal, they were right-wing Christian fundamentalists; if you were a conservative, they were feminazi one-world pansies. It was wise to keep an eye open because you never were sure who *they* were—*they* had people everywhere. That was the secret that made America work: With all the talk about Civil War and culture conflict, we were a nation perpetually united against *they* and *them*.

I needed to step away from the gathering reenactors for a moment. The Panamanian caught me on my way to the icehouse.

"I've got good news and bad news," Marcus said.

"Bad news first."

"J.T.'s doing a little lobbying. His phone records tell me he's been in touch with Senator Hunter."

"Makes sense. Republican from Tennessee, supportive of the president in sensitive fights. J.T. gets the senator to rattle the president.

Prez gets cold feet, lets me twist in the wind. J.T. keeps all his winnings and gets to see me tossed out of the casino."

"That's the goal. J.T. has already hit the high notes with Hunter."

"Did you intercept?"

"Yeah. There's a voice mail from one of Hunter's aides who promised to check into it."

"Which could mean anything. These politicians are all full of crap. The senator isn't going to go barging into the Oval Office and chew out the president."

"Still, it's not easy to neutralize a United States senator, Jonah."

"Think small, Marcus. If we can't neutralize him, can we piss him off? I'm talking pedestrian, getting the short ball in the pocket. What's the good news?"

"Did you ever hear of Boston Capital Holdings?"

"Big holding company, right?"

"Yes. Looks like J.T.'s in talks with them to sell his company."

"Wants to play some more golf, huh?"

"Right. Would be a shame if something screwed the deal, you know?"

"Or *almost* screwed the deal," I corrected. "Sometimes the threat is more effective. I'm going to find myself a horse and think about it a bit."

I turned to go. "Jonah," Marcus said. "Costume, please."

I returned to the mansion. I advised Claudine to have a word with Pepper, who had recognized me. I affixed my General Custer mustache and hairpiece. Claudine loaned me a Confederate uniform— gray top with gold buttons running parallel from the shoulder blades to the waist. Then she handed me the cap, which I donned with considerable charm, grace, and panache. Rhett Putzler. Claudine laughed in a familiar way that made me wonder for a moment if we might not have made it together after all. It's incredible how we can mistake tiny movements for love.

I put my sunglasses on, mounted on impulse an old quarter horse roped to a tree, and trotted across the theater of battle to the icehouse. Pockets of Confederates dotted the landscape setting up tents and sleeping bags. The men (and a few women) were exuberant, greeting each other with embraces and unfamiliar battle cries. There was an odd diversity to the assembled—old, young, businesslike, hippie. There were also black Confederates, as there had been during the real Civil War. It was something I had never quite understood, but the political curveballs of America never ceased to keep me off balance. All in all, it was beginning to look like Woodstock.

I tied the rope to a post, climbed onto the low-slung roof of the icehouse, and scrolled through the songs in my little radio. As a rebel fired up a barbecue, my song piped into my earphones: Kinky Friedman's "Ride 'Em Jewboy."

I lay back, sunlight settling in on my cheeks. As Kinky twanged, I conjured up 1980, and how we all used to bake our skin "down the shore" without sunscreen. It was as if skin cancer had not existed until the new millennium. "They" didn't just invent the disease, did they? People must have gotten it back then. Not me, baby. I'd bring out that U-shaped piece of cardboard with tinfoil slapped on it, and prop it up against my face. I didn't want to miss one ultraviolet ray, lest Claudine sense something slightly unradiant about me.

> Ride, Ride, Ride. Ride 'em jewboy
> Ride 'em all around the old corral

I wondered how many people who owned these music machines stocked them up with the sound track of their lives. The narcissism of retreating to one's own planet with one's own score was staggering, but irresistible. I felt myself on Shpilkes jumping the gate.

> I'm—I'm with you boy
> If I've got to ride six million miles

I felt moisture beneath my eyes, perhaps effluent from squinting into the light. On the other hand, it could be straight grief for: one, a grown daughter I never knew; two, an old love lost in the hills of time; three, Edie, Ricky, and Lily, who were impossibly far away; four, ancestors who I sensed were searching for me; five, a career devoted to legerdemain.

> Now the smokes from camps are rising
> See the helpless creatures on their way

An image of myself carrying Sallie as an infant across Dartmouth's green to class. And where was Claudine in this image? At Vanderbilt? Did we swap her semester to semester? Were Claudine and I married? If not, what did I do during college about women? What does a pledge with a baby do at a frat house on Hell Night? I couldn't get out of my mental maze. What a mess! No wonder Claudine didn't tell me. I should be *thanking* her.

> Hey, old pal, ain't it surprising
> How far you can go before you stay

Despite my eyes being closed, I felt the sky grow dark. A cloud, I thought. But when I opened my eyes, I let out an unmanly gasp when I saw a giant looming above me in front of the sun. His hands were enormous, his mane of hair leonine. *All footsteps turn back upon themselves*, I thought, as the great ghost extended his hand, and citing Devo asked, "Are we not men?"

PART SIX

THE
BANDIT'S
VERSION

AUGUST 1980

Gambling's okay. I just don't want you people
to control it.

—Senator Estes Kefauver (D–Tennessee), Kefauver
Committee Hearings on Organized Crime, 1951

ON ICE IN THE TRUNK

"Every way of life has its enforcers, doll."

Petie yelled upstairs for Six to turn down his stereo. It was Lou Reed's Velvet Underground hammering "Waiting for the Man." I was disappointed when the volume dropped. The song made Rattle & Snap less imposing. I could envision Mickey and Indy connecting on the familiar challenge of raising teenagers. *What are you gonna do . . .*

"They're here," I hummed minutes later in a singsong way that would soon become associated with the little girl in the horror film *Poltergeist*.

"Waaahoooo!" Six shouted. I knew he wanted to meet a real gangster. *May it be everything you hoped for, kiddo*, I thought.

"Already?" Indy Four said, strolling from the living room in quasi-military khakis and a blazer with the Polk family crest. Claudine, divine in a white sundress, brought out a pitcher of iced tea. Petie followed cautiously with the glasses.

I was perspiring terribly, or at least I perceived that I was. I inspected myself for signs of injury from J.T.'s attempted putsch in Columbia. Outside of a few scrapes that I'd attribute to conventional labor, I looked all right. The royals and I awaited Bonnie and Clyde on the front portico beside the columns. I felt better next to my beloved columns. Forget the mansion, hold *me* up.

Mickey's Buick was furiously kicking up dust as it rolled toward the house against Lou Reed's angry beat. Once the wind blew away the dust, Mickey stepped from the passenger seat of the Buick. Carvin' Marvin had been driving. Mickey wore a seersucker suit with a crisp white shirt and a red, white, and blue bow tie, perfectly knotted. He was tan, which sharply offset his cotton hair. I was actually proud to show him off. He would have been pegged as an adorable old Good Humor Man peddling chocolate éclairs. Nowhere in his appearance was there a hint of what the newspapers said he was.

Now to Deedee. *Yaa*. Her red dress was simple enough, but it was hiked up far shorter than one might have expected from a woman in her midseventies. She could carry it off, though, in a Boris and Natasha kind of way. Her hair was a few shades less red than her dress and lipstick, and she wore a hat of a diameter upon which the Marines could have landed Chinook helicopters. Deedee's massive, black Jackie Onassis sunglasses slid down her nose as her eyes vacuumed the mansion. Petie Polk's eyes were frozen on Deedee's trademark legs.

"A lot like our first place in Ventnor, Moses," she said out of the side of her mouth.

Indy Four loved the comment, laughed like a madman. He trotted down the steps, took Deedee's hand and kissed it. "Mrs. Price, welcome to Rattle & Snap. I'm Indy Polk."

Deedee removed her sunglasses and gazed wide-eyed up at Indy. She smiled broadly. "Moses," she said to Mickey, "I've met someone." Deedee eyed his Masonic ring. "That monstrosity better not be my engagement ring. I'm into subtle."

Indy said, "When I tell you the whole history of this ring, I'm sure you'll wear it with pride." Indy took a Gulliver-sized leap toward Mickey and said, "Mr. Price, welcome. We can duel later."

Mickey shook Indy's dinosaur hand and pulled a white handkerchief from his pocket. "Mr. Polk, I surrender already. I know true love when I see it. Besides, it wouldn't be the first relative I've lost to a Polk this summer."

Indy said something about having arrived in time for the annual dance at Rattle & Snap. Good. A crowd equals camouflage. I hugged my grandparents as Carvin' Marvin unloaded the trunk of the car. I noticed an unfamiliar chest, but Carvin' Marvin closed the trunk before I could inspect further. Indy complimented Deedee on the luggage. "It's the nicest stuff we've got," she responded, "After all, we've had to use it enough." A dig at Mickey for a life on the lam.

"I'm glad you made it okay," I said.

"You hook a right at Canaan, and *badabing!* you're here!" Mickey said.

Even Petie appeared to be charmed by my grandparents, or perhaps they just validated her thesis that we were all mutants. Petie was somewhat taken aback, I thought, when I kissed Mickey. Claudine kissed Mickey and Deedee. Their familiarity thrilled me.

Deedee eyed Petie, impressed. "You've got some figure, sweetheart."

Petie pointed to herself, as if to inquire, "Me?"

"Oh, absolutely. Now I know where your daughter gets it."

"Well, thank you. . . . You really have lovely skin, Mrs. Price."

"It's all moisturizer and makeup, believe me. I *love* this new compact I got." Deedee removed her makeup from her purse and held it up. "It's called 'C'mere Rouge' or something."

Petie and my mouths fell open as if on cue.

"Khmer Rouge?" I asked.

"I'm not sure exactly what it's called, love," Deedee said, oblivious. "I know I heard that somewhere," she said, still holding out the compact, which Petie politely studied.

"Deed," I said, "The Khmer Rouge were Cambodian communists who killed like three million people."

"Look, sweet knees, I didn't ask the woman at Saks who made it!"

As we entered the mansion, Six reviewed the freak show the way one would expect a kid to review one—he gawked. Deedee handed Petie a giant tin of saltwater taffy and promised that there were more goodies "on ice in the trunk." Petie winced. Corpses perhaps? Mickey withdrew a suitcase, and gave Indy Four several volumes of Walt Whitman's poetry, explaining, "Whitman lived in Camden, where Jonah was born. He was a nurse during the Civil War who saw the horrors."

"I know he did, and I'm grateful for these." He held the books tight against his chest.

Mickey, still holding his suitcase, stopped cold at the portrait of George Washington Polk. He moved reverently toward it and put on his glasses. This image registered with me at a seminal and poetic level: Mickey in his seersucker and bow tie, carrying a suitcase—not a gun—and adjusting his glasses trying to figure out what the hell was standing before him. This *was* Mickey Price.

Claudine eagerly took Mickey's arm and explained the portrait to him.

"Union soldiers had been ordered to destroy all of the plantations they could," Claudine explained.

"Sherman, right?" Mickey said.

"He was the worst," Claudine said, "that's right. But another man, Buell, was in charge of Tennessee, who also happened to be a Mason. He gave his captain orders not to destroy Rattle & Snap. He said, 'You are not to destroy the home of a Mason brother.' All of the Polk plantations were spared."

"There were others?"

"Yes, Ashwood and Hamilton Place are nearby."

"That was one heck of a general, that Buell, huh, sweetheart?"

"He was criticized for being too soft overall and was relieved of his command soon after," Claudine explained.

"I'm sorry to hear that, honey, but I'm not surprised," Mickey said. "It's nice that some men believed in brotherhood. There's not much of that anymore."

I followed them to the scowling portrait of Colonel Will Polk, who had won the land for the plantation. "Colonel Polk was a toughie," Claudine said. "He was shot in the face when he was young and lived to be an old man."

"Every way of life has its enforcers, doll."

"I suppose that's true."

"My father was always talking about the gentry we Polks became,"

Indy Four said, having snuck up from behind. "I was always more interested in the highwaymen that got us here."

"Well, Indy," Mickey said, "then you'll get a bang outta me." Mickey glanced around the formal room. "This place would make a helluva casino."

Oooof.

Indy stroked his mustache, as if considering it.

We withdrew to the huge living room. Indy Four asked Mickey how he felt about the news.

"What, you mean the shah?"

"Yes."

"Dies in Egypt of all places, Mr. Polk. In the last few centuries, only a couple of Persians died at home in their own beds. Most died violently at the hands of their own people. Why should this one be any different?"

"Ah, leadership is overrated. You know what General Patton said—the reward for excellence is a little less punishment."

"That's about it."

I left the room for a moment to make certain Jimmy Hoffa wasn't lying on the floor of Mickey's car. A copy of the *Atlantic City Packet* was on the backseat. The headline asked: "Has Price Been Tagged?" According to the article, "Gambling czar Mickey Price has vanished." The reporter had virtually no other information, and compensated for this failure by rehashing everything that was known about the Bruno hit.

In the kitchen, Elijah was preparing a quickie dinner for Carvin' Marvin, who drank lemonade beneath the portrait of one of the vaguer Polks. Marv's eyes strained up at the painting. Elijah pointed to the portrait with a spoon and said, "Don't worry, Marvin, the old buzzard stares at Jonah and me, too."

"You'll get used to them, Marv," I promised.

Things were safe here. Okay then.

There had been no massacres back in the living room, either, so I paced the room a few times, feigning interest in the fireplace mantels. During a pregnant lull in conversation, I offered to take Deedee and Mickey to their rooms, my first foray into preventive damage control.

Mickey and Deedee's rooms were adjacent to mine. One for Carvin' Marvin was nearby. "Okay, Pop," I said, "how do you feel about sleeping where the old slave quarters were?"

"Marvelous. Gimme some time and I'll build a pyramid."

I slept well that night, all being comparatively well in my world, and dreamt of Claudine cantering on Spilled Kiss. I awakened to the sound of Elijah throwing *The Tennessean* against my door and twisting visions of men dressed like painters on the streets of Columbia.

GRITS AND CANNOLI

"He always provided."

"I slept like a hog," Mickey announced when he opened his door the following morning.

"Don't you mean a log?" I asked.

"Logs don't sleep, they just fall down in the woods. I slept."

I waved Mickey and Deedee to follow me down to the church. I wanted them to see all that I had done. Unfortunately, they had not seen what a mess it had been when I arrived, so they had no benchmark for my progress.

"My grandson the manual laborer," Deedee said. "In a church, no less." She made a swatting gesture toward the cemetery. She wasn't very interested in the church's history, but Mickey was. I gave him the same tour of the church and graveyard that Claudine had given me. Deedee tended to her makeup for a few minutes in the shade—I think the gravestones creeped her out—and she said she would head back to help prepare for brunch. My heart skipped a dozen beats as I imagined her in the same kitchen with Petie. Forget it, I thought, she was who she was. I quickly aborted my philosophical kiss-off: I was scared to death about what she might say, and hoped that Indy Four would be nearby to distract her.

I was proud of everything I showed Mickey, as if Rattle & Snap had been my own personal achievement. He was impressed by my ability to recall the details associated with those who were buried in the graveyard, ranging from George Washington Polk to Mammy Sue. Mickey was riveted by the tale of Colonel Beckham, the innovator in horse-drawn artillery.

"Why does everything come back to how well you can kill people? Do you ever wonder about that?" Mickey asked.

"Sure I do. How are things back home, Pop?" I asked in the shadow of Claudine's father's grave. "I saw that newspaper headline about you being missing."

"A guy doesn't show up for his morning bagel, this means he vanished? This is the same newspaper that said I'm a drug smuggler. Yeah, I smuggle Maalox. Ah, we've got some things going. It was good for me to get out of town. Just for a week. What happened with you and those gorillas was good timing. Your grandmother doesn't know. You're all right?"

"I'm fine."

"Still got the piece?"

"Yes."

"Indy called me aside. He apologized like the whole thing was his fault. He doesn't like that kid, J.T."

"Then why doesn't he stand up to him?"

"That Smoky Hilliard's no Mouseketeer. And the son, he's soft."

"Meaning what?"

"Meaning we deal with the father."

"You know, Pop, there's strange stuff going on around here. I went out for a walk one night when I couldn't sleep. I saw lava or something falling from the sky down in the valley behind the plantation."

Mickey's eyes hardened. "Listen, Magellan, leave the exploring to others. Do your job, be careful with that girl, and don't go looking for any more lava."

"I don't know what it could be."

"Well, neither do I, but save your curiosity for college, you hear me?"

I didn't want to give him the satisfaction of a direct response. "What else is going on back home?"

"What, we need something *else?*" Mickey flicked me away. "We've got heartache with Ange, that's the big thing now." Clever, Mick. Divert attention from one battlefront by raising a scarier one. I sensed I couldn't press him right now on the Hilliards, but they were sounding less and less like Ashley Wilkes every day.

"Do you know who killed Mr. Bruno, Pop?"

"Yeah, we know."

"Who was it?"

"Engelbert Humperdinck."

"So you're not telling me. Are they after Atlantic City?"

"These things don't always have one cause. Things come together and then *boom*, you know?"

"I know."

"No you don't. Are you being careful with this girl?"

"Yes."

"Do you know what you're doing with a girl like that?"

"Absolutely not."

"Heh-heh. Good, you're honest. Fifty years with your grandmother and I still don't know what the hell I'm doing. But a girl like Ava? The real deal."

"I can't figure her out. She runs hot and cold. I told her I loved her."

"Didja now?"

"Yeah, I did."

"And what did she say?"

"She seemed a little freaked out. I don't remember what she said."

"Did she say 'I love you' back? Do you remember that much, Warren Beatty?" Mickey slapped me on the forehead the way Moe always slapped Curly. I was fast getting the impression that my intellect wasn't universally admired.

"No, she didn't say it back."

"You recognize you're a world-class schmuck, don't you?"

"What exactly is the difference between a schmuck and a world-class schmuck?"

"See this place?" Mickey asked. He waved his hands mystically across the plantation's grounds. "This is a world-class place, which makes you a world-class schmuck. Do yourself a favor and don't tell your grandmother about this I-love-you business. She'll wipe out all of 'em, make the Civil War look like a pillow fight. . . . Ah, I've seen it before, though, but you're smarter than he was."

"Who's 'he'?"

"Ben Siegel. Yeah. This Virginia Hill he had, *kenahora*. She had him spending money, running some of it to Switzerland. God, it was a—" Mickey glanced heavenward for divine inspiration, and he found it. "Death ballet."

"Death ballet?"

"Yes. It's a death ballet with gamblers, alcoholics, addicts, the love-poisoned. It ends in destruction, but there's a beauty about it—the thing the mark goes through before it's over. I used to never understand people who go to theaters, ballets, because you know what's gonna happen. But as I got older, I understood." *Unnerstood.* "Even if you know how it ends, it keeps your eyes open because it's beautiful. Anyhow, we could all see it with Benny. Benny became the mark when he should have been the dealer. He borrows, he builds, he hits her, she hits him, he hits her harder, they collapse, she steals. Then they get up and do it all over again. What do they call the guy, the sissy, who arranges the dancing up on the stage?"

"Choreographer."

"Right. It's all very predictable and human and sad, but if you're an oddsmaker, you can bet on it every time if you can spot a mark with a circuit that works that way—that insane hope that keeps bringing you back to the thing that will kill you. An obsession is a transaction where the property acquires its owner with counterfeit bills forged to resemble love." Mickey laughed. "We pump that hope in through the vents."

"So, who killed Benny?"

Red snake eyes from Mickey. I wasn't trying to be a smart aleck, it just came out. "We did everything we could to save that kid. Everything! It couldn't be stopped. It was bigger than we were."

"Sorry, Pop." I stiffened. I had been stupid and I knew it. "Let's go up to the house and see what's going on."

"You should see what we brought in the icebox."

Holy Moses. "What did you bring in the icebox?" I asked like a prosecutor.

"Whitefish, Nova Scotia salmon, cannoli, pizelles. A smorgasbord. Wait until the Polks see it!"

Brunch. A synthetic word that means "the end of civilization." Here is what was on the brunch table in the dining room of Rattle & Snap: grits, Nova Scotia lox, pancakes, smoked whitefish, bread pudding, ham, cannoli, challah, biscuits, pizzelles, pickles, rice, pumpernickel bagels, egg bread, mint juleps, blintzes, stuffed bell peppers, sweet potato pie, and pumpkin bread. I was confident that at no time in the history of mankind had a meal like this ever been served. *The buffet heard round the world.*

Petie and Six surveyed the table as if Buddy Hackett had descended onto the stage of the Grand Ole Opry ("A rabbi goes into the cotillion with a pig . . ."). Indy Four and Claudine, however, were engaged by the sociological experiment. Elijah appeared confused, perhaps validating his suspicions that white people were psychotic. Carvin' Marvin shrugged philosophically.

Deedee strode proudly into the dining room with an apron around her waist, which obscured whatever she was wearing, thank God. She held her hand to her chest and pointed to Claudine, who was wearing shorts.

"*Legs!* She's got legs like a showgirl, that one," Deedee said, as if the Polks would want to merchandize this.

Mickey had on a polo shirt with the Golden Prospect logo, beneath which read his embroidered job title: "Moses—Bell Captain."

"You know, Mick," Indy boomed, "We used to have Kefauver parties here."

Oh, my gentle Jesus. He starts with *this?*

"Kefauver!" Mickey shouted, a hemorrhaging blintz on his fork. "You had Kefauver parties?"

I prayed that a character like Q in the James Bond films would emerge to give me some gadget with which I could propel myself into the carriage house with Claudine. But, alas, no.

"You bet. We used to get together and watch the hearings on TV. That's how I first heard about you."

"That man was the biggest hypocrite who ever lived. A degenerate gambler and womanizer!"

"You're not kidding!" Indy shouted gleefully. Mickey turned mauve. Indy Four seemed oblivious to the fact that Senator Estes Kefauver of Tennessee had been the first to brand Mickey a gangster (and his associates as "low-down rats"), which triggered law enforcement's obsession with him. Prior to Kefauver's hearings on organized crime, no one outside of gangland and the Delaware Valley had ever heard of Mickey Price. Anonymity had made Mickey's fortune; notoriety had stripped much of it away.

"I used to play cards with Kefauver," Indy continued. "He used to talk about you. He gambled at cards all the time."

"I know," Mickey said, "He just didn't want me dealing."

Indy cackled, still not understanding that for Mickey this era had not been amusing.

"Deedee," Indy Four asked, childlike, "what did you make of your husband's career?"

"He always provided," she answered. "I just could never stand the shooting in the early days. One day, you're dishing a guy some *kugel* and the next day he floats up in a barrel. I mean, honest to God."

"What are you gonna do?" Mickey said, calm again, jabbing at grits.

Petie's jaw was at its highest torque. Claudine took it all in like a Steel Pier freak show. Indy Four was living out a carnival fantasy. My inner organs heaved. Someday, I reasoned, all of this will be in the distant past. Six just said, "This is so cool!" and asked nobody in particular what Al Capone had been like. *Don't answer!*

"Oh, honey," Deedee answered, "like a big teddy bear."

REVELATION

"The big trouble came after my cousin, James, the president, annexed the whole West."

Indy Four and Mickey joined Claudine and me on a horseback riding trail. Indy led the way south on a quarter horse, Mickey on a small appaloosa. I became excited, thinking we were finally going to see in daylight what went on in that glowing valley, but when we neared its approximate area, Indy veered sharply in another direction.

"I like this horse, Mickey," Indy said. "He doesn't trot, he *shleps*."

Mickey threw his head back in one of the bigger bursts of laughter that I had ever heard from him. "Where'd you get that word, Indy?"

"I was on a charity board years ago with a guy named Rifkin who was in the music business in Nashville. I picked up a few words from him. . . . You know, Mickey, I'm aware from the papers that there's trouble up north."

"Like you wouldn't believe," Mickey said. "And not just in the gambling business. There's been talk in the legislature about turning Jersey into two states, North and South. You know all about that, don't you, Indy?"

"Studied it all my life. Know more about why we lost and why they won than anybody, I imagine."

"Maybe you could teach me something. All I know is why I think the war really started. Your war, the Civil." Mickey gestured, adamant. "Why would, say, a banker up in Philly really care about how you conducted your business down south? He may not like slavery, but is he going to give up his fortune to fight you for a moral reason?"

"'Course not. It was about money," Indy said. "In the South, we had slaves. Had ninety-nine of 'em right here. In the North, industry was booming. You had to rely on immigrants. You didn't pay 'em much, but you paid 'em, right?"

"Well, sure."

"We gave our slaves good treatment, but we didn't give them cash. My granddad, who grew up here, too, told me—and I believe him—that the North was worried about competition pure and simple. You know where the antislavery movement started? England. Yes, sir, they saw their riffraff—us—building a superpower. Then they started on the morality line."

"Well, to be honest, Indy, *slavery*—"

"I know, I know. The North didn't like it, but they didn't like blacks much, either. In New York, whites killed a hundred blacks in a riot. It's not like the South started slavery. It was the Spaniards. A half million slaves were brought over and they grew to four million by the Civil War just by, you know, populating."

I had never seen anyone cut Mickey off the way Indy had. Mickey came back, but with a concession.

"And the slave traders, weren't they Northerners?"

"Right. Now here's the point that nobody up North gets. With what you're going through with gambling, you answer this for me. How would you feel if Utah—okay, bad example—say, Vermont started telling you how to run your business in Atlantic City. You've been there how long?"

"Seventy years, my whole life almost."

"Right, and all of a sudden, Vermont's making all of this money with industry: Do this, do that. Now you know what the Civil War was really about. The North gets rich with its industry and starts with a swagger. The big trouble came after my cousin, James, the president, annexed the whole West."

"Oh, is that all," Mickey said. "I thought I rocked the boat when I sent a guy to scout out a desert town in Nevada for gambling."

Indy let out a guffaw. "You see, when the country moved west, the North said, 'Industry's the way of the future.' The South says,

'Nope, we're gonna farm it with slaves.' Do you have plans for gambling that go beyond Atlantic City?" Indy didn't look at Mickey when he said this, he just smirked, I don't know, like Al Capone. The teddy bear.

Mickey nodded. "Legalized gambling will be nationwide soon enough. Everybody'll be into it. Government. Fortune Five Hundred companies. Once they run the Italian and Jewish boys out, it'll be moral all of a sudden."

"Ah, slavery was a red herring, too," Indy declared. "It's what Lincoln used for moral cover, to get the Union upset enough to send their sons into battle for something other than machines and taxes. About sixty percent of America's exports were cotton. We had a way of life!"

"Indy, whether our ways were right or wrong, at least we had ways," Mickey said. "Now, there are no ways. Everything's okay. If you could go back in time, knowing what you know now, how would you have saved the South?"

Indy drew his horse closer to Mickey's and leaned over conspiratorially. Claudine and I advanced as the men approached a hill.

"We didn't need to win, Mickey, we just needed to keep the North out. There's a difference. We didn't want Pennsylvania! We just didn't want Pennsylvania *in* Tennessee. Slavery would have died itself within twenty years, wasn't a thing that could have been done about that, and shouldn't have. The problem was that we wanted to expand west and were in no position to take it. Sometimes you have to go with the best of your bad options."

"My people fought the Romans a long time ago," Mickey said. "Didn't do so hot. I figured, 'Why not cut 'em in this time,' so I did. Now it's 1980, and I'm still having trouble with the Romans. That's how clever I am."

Claudine trotted beside Mickey, which uncharacteristically emboldened him to talk. Beauty makes us all stupid.

"Such schemes we had, Claudine!" The Pine Barrens were perfect for making liquor, Mickey told the rapt Polks. The pines had had a population of ten people per square mile during Prohibition. Outside of the pines, the average in Jersey was about a thousand people per square mile.

"That's big trouble, my Polk friends."

Beneath the Pine Barrens was one of the biggest freshwater reservoirs in America. "Fresh water!" Mickey shouted, letting go of the reins. "Not saltwater like in the ocean. Not polluted water like in the Delaware. Perfect for quality liquor. Do you disapprove?"

"Heck, no," Indy said. "My daughter-in-law likes to talk about the Polk statesmen and generals, but she's not too keen on the gamblers and rogues that came before."

"The later generations find those facts inconvenient," Mickey said.

"Indeed they do. The Polks had duels. My grandfather killed a sheriff down in Texas. Will Polk, of course, gambled to win this property. Charlie Polk before him led night raids to kill Indians that were a threat to his property. Another Charlie Polk was a bit of a pirate. He sold bad hooch to Indians and scammed anybody they passed in the forests of Kentucky. Back then they were called 'Indian traders.' You know what they'd be called today?"

"Yeah, I do," Mickey said. "Mobsters, gangsters, Mafia. Everybody who makes it in America had to use a little muscle or a twist," Mickey volunteered. "We needed the Pine Barrens real bad. We needed to keep people away. We paid the pineys money to stay away from the stills, but sometimes a smart aleck would sneak on by. That's when we got this big monster costume from a friend who worked backstage at the 500 Club. It looked like a giant moose with a wolf's head. Two guys had to get in the costume, one on the other's back. We dragged dead deer carcasses around the still so it would stink to hell. We started telling stories about the mutant thirteenth son of an old woman in the forest named Leeds. Scared the crap out of the pineys."

"Pop," I said, "are you saying that you dreamed up the Jersey devil?"

"Dreamed up? We put him in business! But you can't make people believe something they don't already believe. Never forget that."

Indy, again: "You know, the real money the Polks made was made in hemp. Rope. The Polks used their friends in government to get all the contracts for the rope that the U.S. Navy bought. We supplied half the rope—*half*—that the whole navy used."

"Geez, what happened?" Mickey asked.

Indy Four squinted philosophically into the sun. When the Civil War came around, the Polks refused to sell hemp to the Union Navy. The South didn't have a navy so there was no business in the Confederate fight.

Indy sat straight up in his saddle. "We could have cut a deal, but we didn't. We were faithful to our way of life and we paid for it dearly. When my grandfather, one of the Immortal Six Hundred, returned to Rattle & Snap, he told terrible stories about Sherman's March. He was stunned to see our place still standing. Spent years digging around this property for gold that some of Nathan Bedford Forrest's troops supposedly buried around here for use in fighting the North." Thank God George had been in that Mason brotherhood."

Mickey began grousing. "The Pilgrims landed the *Mayflower* at Plymouth Rock. You know why? They ran out of beer. One of the guys kept a journal. There was about to be a mutiny over beer unless the captain pulled over. And what does the *Mayflower* crowd do a few hundred years later? Prohibition!"

"Hey, Mickey, you shouldn't complain. You did well by Prohibition."

"You know something, Indy, you're right. Tonight, we'll drink to hypocrisy." The old men, to Claudine's and my bewilderment, laughed for the remainder of the ride like two teenagers who had toilet-papered somebody's lawn.

When we returned to the mansion, Indy ceremoniously took us into his study and produced the diary of his cousin, General James H. Polk, who had been the first U.S. commander to hammer into Germany under Patton's command. General Polk had written:

The crime of this slave labor stinks up the whole world, this crime that the Germans can never pay enough for. You cannot conceive of how they have made beasts of people . . . I am bitter, bitter, bitter, tonight.

"When Jim, returned from World War II, the photos he showed me of the Nazi concentration camps sickened me. Those sights changed him forever. Jim liberated some of those camps."

I got goosebumps and shuddered.

"I, myself, was unable to serve in this war," Indy squeezed out a confession. "They said I didn't have the right vision." He tapped on his lenses. In addition to Claudine, I had fallen in love with her grandfather, brother, and groundskeeper. A spell indeed.

Mickey excused himself, holding a handkerchief over his face. When I saw him next, his eyes were red.

"The dust from that damned volcano" was all he said.

UPSIDE/DOWNSIDE

"There is much to lose, especially for those who have come so close."

At dusk, the straw-haired bandleader urged the crowd to clap their hands. He began singing a John Denver song called "Thank God I'm a Country Boy." While clapping her hands, Deedee (wearing a gold-sequined formal gown) turned to Petie and said, "Did you know that John Denver smoked the hemp plants that he grew in his own back-yard? *Marijuana*," she added helpfully.

"Why, no," Petie said.

"It's true," Deedee insisted. "He admitted it. Whoever heard of such a thing, growing hemp in your own backyard? You know, they turn it into reefer?"

Poor Petie nodded.

Tonight's event was an annual affair, held for no reason that anyone could remember. Hundreds from Maury County were invited to listen to music, dance, and sample local delicacies. Fortunately for the locals, Deedee had run out of lox.

As everyone clapped, a mammoth of a man with a burning red face, big nostrils, and a Marine jaw ambled through the revelers and kissed Petie on the cheek. She seemed happy to see the man, but he didn't strike me as the kind of person someone like Petie would like. As thick as he was across the middle, he had spindly little arms that sprung awkwardly from his short-sleeved Oxford cloth shirt. His legs were funny, too—twigs wrapped in a thin layer of khaki.

J.T. stood right behind the big man. J.T. wore a seersucker sport jacket. He looked like a swollen Kennedy. Ever the stateswoman, Petie made the introductions. The giant was Smoky Hilliard, J.T.'s father. J.T. stood back as his father slid his hand beside Mickey's and breathed down on him. A fresh cut wound was on J.T.'s cheek where I had struck him with the belt. Claudine, an appropriate but maddening expression of concern across her face, inquired about the injury. He attributed it to a football, judging from a throwing gesture. Mickey was polite, as was Deedee, who was still unaware of the attack on me. Indy Four shook Smoky's hand cautiously.

I had been warned. Indy Four had suggested that J.T. and I forge some kind of tolerable peace that would hold out for the summer. I wasn't happy about it, but saw no alternative. Mickey's arrival had been a bonus, of course, and Smoky Hilliard, through Indy Four, had requested a "word" with us.

Smoky squinted at Mickey as Mickey bobbed his head, too much like an immigrant tailor for my liking. Smoky's was a look of disappointment, not menace. *This* is Mickey Price, the squint said? I knew that Smoky knew who Mickey was. After what had happened on the street in Columbia, Smoky Hilliard probably did what we did—checked out his adversary. But *this* Lilliputian is the great bootlegger who once told Al Capone to stay west of the Alleghenies?

"Mr. Price," Smoky bellowed, "I'd appreciate nothing more than to spend a few moments with you when you are able."

"Fine," Mickey said. "In a few minutes, if that's all right."

"You betcha!"

The difference in the size of the men was outrageous, as if two different space civilizations had come to meet on a neutral planet in the *Star Wars* franchise. Smoky wistfully turned his head to take in the mansion, then plunged, hoglike, back into the crowd, where people greeted him in the same manner that they would greet a presidential fart—with a combination of awe and revulsion. J.T. followed his father, looking far less menacing than he had in our earlier encounters. There was something soft about him when he was next to Smoky. He was like a lot of the rich Main Line kids I used to see trailing their fathers into the casino. J.T. was just the sum of the quantifiable achievements and goodwill of his family. Youth fawned on guys like J.T. I hoped that adulthood would be less generous to him and vowed to chronicle his downfall.

Mickey watched the Hilliards walk off and took a hobbit stroll toward the band as soon as the song by the hemp-smoking John Denver was over. I followed out of curiosity.

"Here," Mickey told the bandleader, who reached out gently toward him. "I brought this music sheet. It's an old klezmer song called "A Tune from Meron." I carry these music sheets around and hum them when I'm on trips. Sometimes I find a band that knows klezmer."

"Why, I played a little klezmer down in N'awlins a long time ago," the bandleader said.

"Didja now?"

"Sure did. This'll be a hoot," he said taking the song sheet and sharing it with his band mates. "We'll look it over."

I took Mickey aside.

"Pop, what do you think Mr. Hilliard wants?" I asked, feeling dizzy.

"He wants what he wants. All I'll ask you is to keep your mouth shut when we talk. This little sit-down is no time for disunity. Do you understand me?"

"What if J.T. says something?"

"J.T. is not a man who knows what to say or what to ask."

I huffed.

"Jonah!" Mickey persisted.

"What are you going to say, Pop?"

"I'm going to play the downside, *boychik.*"

Before I could ask what this meant, Mickey started toward a picnic table beside the mansion where Smoky, a man identified as Smoky's brother, and J.T. waited. Irrationally, I expected the two smirking painters who stood nearby during the fight to emerge, but they didn't. I followed, feeling prepubescent.

Smoky Hilliard began. He had a deep, ambitious voice. His cadence was conscious, cautious. His eyes were cold and laser straight. Whatever bad things I felt about him viscerally, I sensed Smoky

Hilliard was intelligent—smart in the way that self-made men are smart. Smoky's strength made me hate J.T. all over again. Maybe I despised him so much for the same reason I loved Claudine so much: lack of availability. Underexposure provided the fertile opportunity for my imagination.

"Mr. Price," Smoky began, "I understand there's been some problems with my son and your grandson. I thought I might explain my position. Hopefully, we'll be able to avoid such unfortunate incidents as occurred not long ago."

"I would like nothing more."

"Swell, then. Just swell." Smoky took a deep breath and frowned at J.T., as if to say, "Now, this is how it's done, son." There was congestion in his lungs.

"These two," Smoky began, gesturing toward the land, "Claudine and my J.T. have been playin' around these fields since they were little kids. Whether or not it comes to anything else, only time will tell. You never know with these things.

"Now, when Jonah came to town, it set something off in my boy that was unwise, and I regret that it occurred. We have talked about it, believe me. But you know how boys are these days, heck, how they always have been. What J.T. did must be understood against the history down here. I certainly don't want trouble. None of us wants trouble, and I'm doing what I can to keep things calm from my end. But you must know, Mr. Price, that while your business may move the hills up where you are, it doesn't hold the same cachet down in these parts. We've got our share of Damon Runyon types around here, too. I beg you not to make the leap between what your influence means up north and what it means down south. I can't tell Jonah to leave. I can only tell you the hurt it has caused so it can be factored into what happened and what happens. If that is acceptable, I have no doubt that the remainder of this summer will be peaceful. That is all I have to say."

Out of the corner of my eye, I saw what I took to be a smirk on J.T.'s face. I felt an instinctive tightening in my lower back. Mickey had instructed me to keep calm. I hated him for it, but I would listen.

For now. All of my self-interest aside, I was afraid for Mickey, seeing him contrasted against this geological formation, Smoky Hilliard. I had never seen Mickey addressed like this in my life—I was used to moronic displays of obsequiousness, even among the cops. I wanted to protect Mickey, whose time had come and gone. I couldn't have raised a countersmirk if I had mobilized all of my muscles.

Smoky had not directly stated an action item, so I assumed that the message was ominous. People who have easily implementable suggestions just make them. Threats are made more subtly. I read the message as follows: *Beat it, ya rum-running little Heeb.*

Mickey nodded at Smoky Hilliard, again weakly, I thought. I felt ashamed and deflated. The little Wizard of Odds indeed was not much of a Wizard south of the Boardwalk. My existence suddenly felt like a factory error. *"Sorry, Mr. Eastman, this grandfather you got is a lemon."* All of a sudden, I wanted to reach out for Mickey and take care of him. I felt acutely aware of my roots. My parents' sad spirits slumped around me.

"Mr. Hicksen," Mickey began, softly but firmly.

Christ. *Hicksen?* Disaster.

"It's Hilliard, Pop," I reminded him very gently. I couldn't be completely silent, could I?

Mickey tapped his head and shook it to remind us that he was the oldest and feeblest one at the table. He was not angry with me for this interruption.

"Forgive me, Mr. Hilliard. I'm eighty years old," he said. Mickey's South Jersey accent and its associated fragments had evaporated. His voice was soft and ocean deep. Odd, but all of a sudden, Mickey seemed refined.

"I get that way myself sometimes," Smoky Hilliard volunteered, nostrils flaring.

"Yes, of course," Mickey said softly. "Mr. Hilliard, do you like to gamble?"

Smoky glanced at his brother and J.T. After a beat, he replied, "I enjoy a game of cards, yes. How about you, Mr. Price?"

"No, I don't like to gamble, I prefer a sure thing." Both men chuckled, Mickey more than Smoky. "I'd like my grandson's safety to be a sure thing. . . . It occurs to me that we have so much to lose. We're so close, so close to our dreams for our children. I appreciate your saying that it was your boy who attacked my grandson, but I think it's important that you do more than say it. It is important that you understand it. Your son not only took this action, he did so in a deliberate fashion. It was thoughtful. It was planned. An organized endeavor. The desired outcome was the destruction of my grandson, who is . . . my whole life."

A slight transfusion of energy crept into my blood. Had God breezed in at halftime?

"I certainly—," Smoky interjected.

"You spoke," Mickey parried, his face shining. "Now I speak." He held his hands to his heart.

Smoky held up his hands in apology. I stiffened my posture.

"There is nothing you can say that will make me feel better about what happened, nothing to cancel out my anger. Jonah's arrival here is about a boy falling for a girl, not about my desire to impose my way of life or my business on this community. I have nothing to do with Jonah's romances. If it were up to me, Claudine and Jonah would never have met, but they did. I'm dealing with that as you are dealing with the disruption this has caused to your plans.

"You have accomplished a lot in your life, and I would never try to judge a man for his dreams. But there was violence. Violence organized and executed by another gang, not by me, not by my grandson. I hate violence not because I am immune to it, but because it has become too easy. That frightens me for my grandson, especially because Jonah has no parents on this earth. I am, for better or for worse, his father, probably for worse. I won't live to see his promise come to light, but as long as I do, I will sacrifice everything I have to increase the odds of that promise coming true.

"My exploits unfortunately have been dragged through the press since Mr. Kefauver started his show business. Yours have not. Now we've got Love Canal and all kinds of things bubbling up. Captains of industry, criminals overnight.

"Jonah will go off to college far away from here after Labor Day. J.T. will go off to school. He will be with Claudine. What will happen will happen independent of me. *Entrances are wide, exits are narrow.* A saying. Things haunt us. Things are easy to break, but hard to clean up. There is much to lose, especially for those who have come so close."

The pizzicato beginning to "A Tune From Meron" began from the stage. Mickey rose. Color fell like a brick from Smoky's face. J.T. appeared to be confused. As was I.

"Your grandmother loves to dance to this song," Mickey said to me. "I can see that she is waiting for me. But first, Mr. Hilliard and I will have a few words alone." J.T. and I walked away, but not together.

More than at any time in my life, I loved my grandfather with violence because the aggregate of his goods and evils were aimed solely at my survival. I had never seen his fabled strength harnessed on my behalf before, even though I did not understand the action that would derive from what I had witnessed. The moonlight hit Mickey through the trees and gave him a ghostly strobelike movement. It actually made me think of him as Moses. I followed him as guests parted so that he could dance with Deedee, who waited like a teenager in the center of a circle. Light from dozens of yellow lanterns reflected from her eyes. With all the venom she tossed Mickey's way, she also adored him, and he did her. It would take me decades to understand this contradiction and its coexistence in a marriage. For now, I only understood the one dimension of Rattle & Snap love, which was at full throttle as I winked at Claudine across the blue lawn. She winked back, her surplus of sexuality downing the few moths that flitted between us.

We all watched Mickey and Deedee dance. Indy Four put his arm around Claudine, who kissed him on the cheek. Deedee was spinning, spinning toward no far-off place, but in the moment. I stood next to Petie, who surrendered this to me: "It's divine to see."

When the next klezmer song began, Claudine tugged me out to dance. It was a slow tune. I glanced around for the Hilliards, but didn't see them.

"Do you know this song?" Claudine asked. I felt her breath in my ear and I shivered.

"This one's called 'Miserlou.' It's about a princess who wandered through the desert to find her love."

" 'Miserlou'," she repeated, perhaps to make me shiver again.

The Polk and Price gangs said good night on the mansion's porch. The Hilliards briefly returned. Mickey and Smoky exchanged a few words, which seemed cordial enough. The way Smoky was bending forward to hear Mickey made me wonder why he didn't just pick Mickey up and put him in his breast pocket. After everyone left, Mickey and I remained.

"Smoky seemed scared when you called him the wrong name," I said.

"I get mixed up sometimes."

"No, you don't, Pop. What did you talk about when you were alone?"

"Small talk. Just two gamblers inspecting each other for tells."

"*Tells?*"

"Signs. Vulnerabilities. Things you pick up when you play cards."

"What was Smoky's tell?"

"When he's hiding something, he winks. Like he's holding a royal flush. He winks at the bluff. Right eye. When he's being humble, he doesn't wink, his face is calm. He's a smart man."

"Have you ever been wrong?"

"Certainly. With Castro. I thought we had a deal. I thought Castro was a smooth-talking punk until Che Guevara and his crew brought goats and pigs into my suite at the Sans Souci."

"If Smoky didn't have a royal flush, you must have had something."

"We'll talk when you're older."

The porch lantern in Mickey's eyes gave him an aura of supernatural brilliance. Yoda.

Without uttering a threat or raising his voice, Moses Price had given Smoky Hilliard a cold rendering of his destruction. He suggested that all of us had something to lose when, apparently, the Hilliards had more to lose than we did. *You are so close. The downside.*

During Mickey's brief sermon, Smoky envisioned TV news footage of his buffed son, the Hope, walking from the Columbia courthouse where he was being arraigned for a thuggish attack on a boy from out-of-state—a failed, ham-handed attack at that. A gangster's grandson? So what? Even better. The very whiff of scandal was a loss for Smoky and his clawing pursuit of genteel grandeur. If only I knew what Mickey was holding and what Smoky was hiding. Don't push him, Jonah.

"You were good, Pop," I said. "I was proud of you. But I'm not running away from Claudine. I'm going to marry her."

Mickey pinched my cheek. "You can marry her all you want. You can have a hundred kids. *After* you graduate from college."

"You don't think we'll end up married, do you?"

"I say she ends up with that bag-a-donuts, J.T."

"You don't know that."

"No, but it's the way to bet."

DERECHOS

"God's either asleep or very, very talky."

Early in the morning, as Claudine and I passed by the icehouse on our horses, we saw Mickey and Indy approaching on horseback from the southwest. As we drew closer, I saw that a caisson was attached to Indy's horse. I looked beyond them, in the direction of the Valley of Lava.

"Out protecting us from Sherman?" Claudine asked.

"Nah," Mickey said. "The Russians."

Mickey said to Indy, "Say what you will, they're something to look at."

Once they passed, I asked Claudine, "What do you think they were doing with that caisson?"

"Beats me. Indy sometimes uses it to carry camping stuff back and forth."

A half hour later, Claudine and I dismounted back at the house. It began to drizzle and I got depressed. Mickey and Deedee were leaving. A call had come from the Shore summoning Mickey back.

I felt like I had a soccer ball in my throat. We looked down at a newspaper, which had been set on one of the steps. The headline blared:

REAGAN IS NOMINATED AS VIOLENT STORMS
KNOCK OUT POWER AT CONVENTION

I picked up the paper. I read the opening paragraphs hurriedly. A line of rain and windstorms known as *derechos* had ripped through Detroit on the eve of Reagan's nomination by the Republicans for the presidency. For a time, the convention center had lost power. The energy had been restored in time for Reagan to deliver his acceptance speech and announce George Bush as his nominee for vice president.

Everybody said Reagan was a warmonger. Since I had registered for the still inoperative draft, I thought I was going to be eating sand by year-end. I handed over the paper to Indy Four, who said, "Mickey, God's either asleep or very, very talky."

"My bet is that, come this fall, it's going to be a whole different story," Mickey said, having since cleaned up from his mystery trail ride.

Indy Four hugged Mickey. "You know, Mickey, I think you're a gentleman."

"No, Indy," Mickey said, "I am not a gentleman, but my grandson will be. That Indian trader Polk, that colonel of yours—they weren't gentlemen. They couldn't be. You can. You are."

Indy took Deedee's hand and kissed it. She had on a tennis outfit. Not a warm-up suit, but an actual tennis skirt with white heels. She pushed her huge sunglasses down to the tip of her nose. Indy was speechless as he rose.

"Indy," Deedee said, giving the mansion one last visual sweep, "two words: *closet space*. It's a helluva house you've got, but to win me over, you're going to need more closet space."

"There will be a wrecking crew here by sundown," Indy vowed.

"Fine," she ruled. "I'll ditch these boys in Nashville and will be back by midafternoon. Jonah, give your grandmother, Olivia de Haviland, a kiss."

"You look more like Billie Jean King," I said.

"Bite your tongue with Billie Jean King. She looks like a prize-fighter."

"All right, Chrissy Evert," I switched.

"Better! Although she should have stayed with the other tennis player, with the temper. Connors. This thing with the British pretty boy won't take, *you watch*."

When Carvin' Marvin loaded the last suitcase into the trunk, I asked Mickey where the wooden chest was, the one I had seen upon his arrival. "Wooden chest? Who are you, Captain Kidd? There's no wooden chest." I considered the probability that I was insane. Mickey and Deedee shrunk into the car, and they rolled out the gates of Rattle & Snap. A heavy burgundy Lincoln emerged from behind a dogwood and tailed them back to the Jersey Shore.

That evening, after a full day of work cleaning out the stables, Claudine and I waited until everyone was asleep. I told her that I wanted to meet her at the gazebo by the pond.

"What for?" she asked.

"I have an idea."

We headed down to the pond at midnight using flashlights to see. I shed my overalls on the gazebo. I abandoned my body, and witnessed my audacity from above. I was not a guy who did things like this.

"Jonah!"

"Let's go."

Her eyes conveyed surprise, but she, too, undressed under the stars, which hung in the humid sky like mobiles.

"You know what's weird?" I said. "I have never actually seen you."

"Yes, you have."

"No, I haven't. I've been with you, but I've never seen you. It's been dark." She chose this moment to be shy and crouched beside one of the gazebo's wooden posts.

"Claudine, I want to see you. I go soon."

The moon caught her profile and I saw the dimple northwest of her mouth.

"Please, step out. You can close your eyes. Just let me look at you."

Claudine stepped toward me. Her eyes were closed. Mine, I thought. Look, God, mine. Within moments she turned away and descended the little knoll toward the pond and stepped in, drifting toward the silver-white reflection from the sky. I followed her in, oblivious to the temperature of the water.

"Have you ever done this before, swim with nothing on?" I asked her.

"No."

"Why did you choose to now?" I asked holding her up off the bottom of the pond.

" 'Cause I chose to, I suppose."

"That's true, you chose. I guess people like us can do pretty much anything."

"I guess we can. Anything at all."

I thought for a moment. "Maybe not anything at all. Just things within reason."

"No, anything at all," Claudine insisted, and tried to dunk me. She failed because I was stronger, so I dunked her. She bobbed up, surprised. Claudine tried to dunk me again, and again she failed.

"I'm stronger than you are," I said.

"Oh no you're not."

"Yes, I am," I insisted. Do you want to go to the carriage house?" I asked once she was against me.

"No, right over there near the geese. The grass is so soft."

SCHANDE

"You are in no position, boy, to assess my shame."

"Jonah, can I have a word?" Indy Four asked me on the mansion's porch one morning before Labor Day. His eyes were red and flat. He seemed preoccupied. "Upstairs, please."

He had never done this before. My breath felt short. There was no breeze.

I followed Indy up to his bedroom. He shut the door behind him and sat beneath the portrait of Leonidas Polk, the Fighting Bishop. I didn't know where to sit because there wasn't another chair, so I stood. I shivered visibly and thought I might wet my pants. Indy Four pulled his cheeks down with his palms.

"Jonah, ah, Jonah," he sighed and shook his head. "My ring is missing."

"George's Masonic ring?"

"Yes, Jonah." Indy glowered.

Do not lose bladder control in front of Leonidas. I fumbled a step back and leaned against the bedpost.

"Did you look for it?" I asked.

"Yes, Jonah, I did."

"Can I help you look more?"

"I'm sure you can, but I don't think we'd find much, do you?"

"Why not try?"

"Please don't make this harder for me than it already is," Indy said. "Jonah, that ring has been in this family for more than a century and a half. Not many variables have changed around here. Pretty much the same players."

Indy was being careful to stop short of a direct accusation, which angered me.

"Why would I take your ring?" I asked, doubting I was, in fact, here.

"I'm not a mind reader, Jonah. I'm just an old man without a ring."

From his perch along the wall, the Fighting Bishop began to amass his troops. The battle itself would fall to his descendent, the untested Independence Polk the Fourth.

Unbearable heat shot across my back. Every time I tried to speak, short, powerful frowns overtook my face.

"I didn't take your ring. There are pl—" I stopped myself before completing a sentence in which I would have said, "There are plenty of people who could have taken it." But there weren't. Who was I going to blame, Six? My embryonic political instincts told me that something larger was happening here.

"Indy, open your mind!" I said, immediately regretting my choice of words.

"Oh, now, Jonah, don't hold me hostage to my heritage," he snapped irrationally. "We deserve better, son. You can only ask people to open their minds so far before everything they have, everything they are, comes spilling out. Sure, we keep our doors and windows open at night at Rattle & Snap, but we have screens, boy, or it would all be chaos."

There was genuine anger in Indy's voice. The heaviness in his shoulders was so pronounced that I couldn't imagine that all of this anger was my doing.

"I didn't take it, Indy, I swear it."

He waved me off.

"Your people call it a *schande*, Jonah. A shame. A scandal. Something you don't recover from."

"*Schande*, yes. This is not a *schande*—"

"You are in no position, boy, to assess my shame."

"You have to believe me, Indy."

"Why, boy? Why do I *have* to believe you?"

"Because the truth is what matters."

"Would you care to tell me the truth about what goes on in that carriage house hayloft when the sun goes down?"

It was ninety-six degrees outside, but I was freezing. I did not avert my eyes from Indy. I decided that I hated my face even though I could not see it.

"Tell me, Jonah, what happens in your grandfather's business when something of value is taken? You're a man now, you know what goes on."

"Bad things happen—"

"Do you suppose," Indy asked, his voice hoarse and leaden, "that your grandfather gives out a lie detector test to every man who is suspected of something untoward?"

"Not a lie detector test, but . . . What were you doing riding out with Mickey with that caisson anyway?"

"*Jonah!*" Independence Polk IV thundered, rising beside Leonidas. I shuddered. I must have looked spastic, because the old man squinted at me curiously. His red eyes glistened through his glasses: "They do what they have to do for their way of life!" Indy's huge hands held my face as he whispered again loudly, perhaps to himself: "They do what they have to do for their way of life!"

I searched the mansion room by room for Claudine. Six was out somewhere. Petie was reading in the front parlor. She smiled unknowingly as I passed.

I found Claudine in the corral trotting Spilled Kiss. Witchy, she sensed my terror from fifty yards, because she dismounted and hurried toward me.

"What, Jonah, *what?*"

One side of my face felt light and springy while the other fell heavily, a cannonball inside my cheek.

"They know."

"They know what?"

"About the carriage house."

"How could they know?" Claudine asked truly skeptical. Two Machiavellis. *"You didn't!"*

My mind captures Deedee standing like the Jolly Green Giant behind Claudine. Deedee is in her combat fatigues: *The bride IS too beautiful.* Deedee's spirit exchanges knowing glances with Spilled Kiss and vanishes. Deedee is the prophet. My rage at Claudine is hot. She believes *them.*

"Of course I didn't!"

"Then how—"

"The Hilliards win, Claudie." I told her about the ring.

"You don't know it was the Hilliards."

"Then who was it? Who gains? Indy didn't mention the Hilliards, but I know what I have to know. They win."

"What do they win?"

"They win you, Rattle & Snap. Confederate gold in the columns."

"My God, Indy! Mother!"

"What did you think would happen?" I yelled at both of us. The terror in her pupils conveyed that Claudine Polk was not at all at home with the downside.

"What happened to 'people can do anything they want'?" I said, parroting back her skinny-dip speech.

"Stop it, Jonah!" She covered her ears. "Just stop it!" Her eyes were wet, broad, and wild. Her face was all angles, not gentle curves. She hated me.

"I'm leaving in the morning. I have to call home."

Claudine's nuclear eyes pointed without firing. I backed away from her to test her reaction. A flood of prayers encircled my skull. Please step toward me. I love you even though I despise you. Let's fight it out like we did the night Pajamas killed Mr. Bruno. It'll be a fun fight, Shakespearean banter. I kept backing away. She did not stop me.

Deedee answered the phone.

"I can't talk long, Deed, there's trouble—"

"My God, are you hurt?"

"No. Not that way."

"*Ava!* She did it to Sinatra, and now you!" Silence, and then a sudden calm and return to hypernormalcy from Deedee. "Okay, okay. You have to come home to pack for college. You have to pack, Jonah," Deedee said, adding, "I'm not Joan of Arc."

"What, was Joan of Arc a big packer or something?"

"I don't know, was she?"

"Deedee, you said that I have to pack. Then you said you're not Joan of Arc. What's the connection?"

"All I'm saying is that I'm not Joan of Arc. Why analyze it to death like an Ivy League know-it-all? I'll send a couple of gorillas down to pick you up first thing in the morning. I'm getting you out of there. Now you listen to me, Clark Gable—who I met, by the way. Just because you took a little voyage to the Valley of Goochie-Goo with Ava Gardner doesn't mean you know all about women!"

"I didn't say that I did—"

"Now, Jonah?"

"What?"

"Remember something. For later, when you'll understand it."

"What's that?"

I could hear her sigh.

"Those who marry for money end up earning it."

"Why are you telling me that?"

"Because, Jonah, I love you."

As I hung up the phone, my nightmare unfurled from the kitchen window. J.T. was speaking with Claudine. There was no overt affection between them, but their familiarity made me catch my breath. I balanced myself against the counter. Just two young, good-lookin' Confederates shootin' the breeze. J.T., appearing hangdog, was doing the talking, sweeping golden forelocks from his eyes, his head tilted to the side, greeting-card style. A conveyance from Darwin: The alpha brute can do more than sire children, he can nurture them. It was the precise scene that moved me to spar with Claudine on the night we met, when visions of Biff, Hoot, and Dirk cartwheeled in my sight.

From what I could see of his face, J.T. appeared to be stricken. Clever bastard. My summer window was slamming shut. I could strike a grizzly with my belt, but not a panda. J.T. walked off, as if he was hurting, too. Claudine watched him. Autumn dangled like a noose.

THE PHANTOM LIFE

"Your life, Jonah, is over those hills."

I stayed in my room for the remainder of the day, railing against my nature—that torrent pulling me toward my own core, which just happened to be within the breast of another human being. I was unable to envision a scenario in which I could continue living without being near Claudine. But I stayed in my room, Odysseus tied to the mast, while Claudine did damage control with the Houses of Polk and Hilliard.

"Now, would you listen to this sackload of information," Elijah said, reading *The Tennesseean* on the steps of the great house the following morning.

"A man flew upside down in a plane for four hours, nine minutes, and five seconds. A man flying upside down like a dumb-ass, and the newspaper prints it like it's an achievement. Is this what the future brings?"

"You're ornery today, Elijah."

"The best assistant I ever had is leaving me and I'm supposed to be singing 'The Battle Hymn of the Republic'?"

"You're starting to talk like my grandfather with your questions."

"He's not the worst man I ever met. Far from it."

I couldn't meet Elijah's eye.

"What did they tell you, Elijah?"

"Just that you had to be off today. Nothing more."

"If you hear anything bad about me, will you promise not to believe it?"

"Is this about you and Claudie getting all hot and bothered in the hay?"

"Did you tell anybody you thought that?"

"Who am I going to tell, son? Are you telling me nothing went on up there?" He pointed back toward the carriage house.

"What went on up there is what you think went on up there."

"Only the dumbest idiot in all the world couldn't figure that out."

"It's not that. You may hear that I stole something."

Elijah winced and swatted with his hand. "My Lord, you didn't steal nothing!"

"How do you know?"

"I know a lost cause when I see it. Of my two sons here, you're not the prodigal."

"I'm sorry. The prodigal?"

"The Bible story, son. The boy who goes away after he squanders his inheritance? From Luke?"

"Oh. New Testament."

"I see, you don't know that story. Well, you read up on that, you hear? But you're not the prodigal. Naw, you're a worker. You don't see that boy, Six, helping out fixing the church, do you?"

"That was my job."

"Yes, it was. And what was Six's job?"

"Being a kid."

"Tell me, son, when were you a kid? Don't answer. You just read old Luke. See about the prodigal. Go on, now."

After I said good-bye to a polite, but poker-faced Petie, Six met me outside of the church where I wanted to do one more walk-through. I explained away my departure with vague references to having to straighten out a housing issue at Dartmouth. I don't know if Six bought it. The church was pristine. I had completed the interior painting. The Polks would be worshipping here soon. Elijah said that they had considered air-conditioning, but decided against it because it would alter the aesthetics of the structure. For that reason, they would avoid using the church in the summer.

"This is all you," Six said.

"No, Elijah was the mastermind."

"Yeah, but you did it. You cleaned up history, fella."

Six put his arm around me. "You know, Jonah, I don't mean to sound like a homo or anything, but you're the closest thing to a brother I ever had in my whole life. Or a brother-in-law. I don't know."

"I don't know about a being a brother-in-law, but I was lucky you were here."

"I haven't said anything to Claudie about the fight with J.T."

"Thanks."

Six broke into an elementary school snicker. "But, man, I've never seen anybody fight like that in my whole life. I told my grandfather every detail."

I cringed. "What did he say?"

"He made me tell it to him three times!"

Six walked me up to the mansion and shook my hand. I hugged him. He probably thought it was weird, but I had to.

Indy appeared, faking jauntiness. He swatted Six in the behind and sent him off. Six bounced away as if I'd be back next week or something. Here I was, little Jonah Eastman of South Jersey, staring up at Indy Four, this mountain of history. He appeared to be only slightly less tortured than he had been yesterday, just more docile, resigned to his charge of the Polk legacy. I imagined it must have been the way a general felt after sending good men to their deaths: horror at the loss, but pride that a larger crusade was being served. If only I knew what that end was. If only someone else could be the one to pay the price.

"Indy," I said, "I am sorry that your ring disappeared. I did nothing wrong, but, still, I am grateful that you let me stay here. I know you disapprove of me."

A gemstone tear slid down Indy's cheeks. It was a point of honor for me not to cry.

"Now, Jonah. I don't dislike you," he said wiping beneath his glasses. "I admire your pluck, though I suspect you've put more than one thing over on me. You sure do have a conspiratorial imagination, seeing all kinds of goblins when there's nothing there, but, hell, boy, you are what we were."

"Why do you believe I would steal from you?"

Indy waved his hands around in front of him, and had a few false starts with a response. He finally settled on the following nonanswer: "Because, son, it's impossible. You two are children. You are special children, but children. Claudine is in love with the past, as we all are here. This happens to young girls who never get to know their fathers. They didn't bring my boy back from Khe Sanh, you know. Never found him. He's not even buried in our cemetery. It's just a marker. Claudine's life will be about restoration. She can't help it; it's in her blood. You stand square in the way of that. She'll do what she needs to do to keep Rattle & Snap alive. Not you, though."

Indy Four puffed out his chest as if he were a stage actor playing Indy Four. *What did any of this have to do with his stolen ring?* I thought of Deedee calling me "Jonah *Godol*," and considered what she might have been getting at. Which was this: As the 1970s—a decade where we were all marinated in our own specialness—receded, per-haps there were greater sands shifting in the universe than the ones between my toes at the Jersey Shore.

"Your life, Jonah, is over those hills. You'll bury your past the way we did, so lasses like Petie can celebrate those few generations that made the South, so that she can tell her sorority sisters what she mar-ried into. You're going to make your own plantation, once you forgive that old man of yours. Many great families got their start in some-thing unholy. I'm afraid Rattle & Snap will be your phantom life, the life you didn't lead. We've all got that phantom life that spooks us. It's the tax on having a romantic spirit."

I wanted to tell Indy that I knew very well the tax on a romantic spirit, but what exactly was the dividend? I was further tempted to bring up the unkosher Hilliards, but I had caused this giant to suffer, however unwittingly, so I kept silent. The circumstances surrounding the elusive arrangement between the two families probably distressed

Indy more than I would ever understand. The encroachment of the Hilliards was an intangible monument to what Indy must have regarded as his failure as a Polk—his "phantom life." Booting me out of Tennessee was the closest he'd come to making a strategic military decision.

I listened, unblinking, as Indy Four tugged at his fingers. He held my hand to keep it from shaking and bent down toward me. He began to speak quietly, his trademark pomp deflated.

"Claudie's father would have liked you, Jonah. He had one heck of a business mind, my son. Claudie has his kind of mind. I'm afraid I'm not much for business, and maybe that's what . . . hell, I don't know. I'm going to try to live long enough to watch your career. Dammit, I will try." I felt a quick rush of promise. "It just won't be here, son."

Indy turned and saluted me. Then he retreated inside his history.

I stood with Claudine on the front portico facing north. A black hole, the cosmic kind, bobbed through my stomach, sucking out vital energy that I needed. Neil Young whined "After the Gold Rush" from Six's window. Something about "Mother Nature on the run in the nineteen seventies." My delusion was that something biblical was happening, although I knew too little about the Bible to determine what. Claudine was quiet but tender toward me, as if some grotesque, pulsating creature creeping up on her had been vanquished. Or perhaps it was her confidence that this was so definitively The End. Everything that we shared had two poles, which made me think how I hadn't once looked at a map this summer in an attempt to see where I was.

The mansion's dual front doors were hooked wide open so that any curious Polks could have witnessed Claudine's unrepentant possession.

"As long as I live," she said, "I'll look out this way and see you riding up on Spilled Kiss the same way that Sallie Polk waited for James to come home from the war."

"I'm not going to war, Claudine," I said.

"But those men up there where you're from—"

"Mickey said it's safe."

"Not for us, Jonah."

"I love you, Claudine."

"Oh, Jonah, no."

Claudine kissed me and lightly bit my upper lip. She did it on purpose. To please the lover and punish the thief. She was angry, but not rabid enough to hurt me too badly. I felt a light whip of wind on the open wound.

The sky was a humidity-stricken, weak aqua. A brilliant streak of orange sun, perhaps the vestiges of a long-faded comet, had wedged itself between the foothills and the clouds. I read it as hope—hope that perhaps there was a life beyond Rattle & Snap, something that I found hard to imagine at this moment.

An autumnal breeze blew across the portico. It was strong enough to make the front doors creak against the hooks that bound them. A singular puffy cloud that looked like a bust of Elvis, pompadour and all, slid across the horizon. I felt a short blast of excitement at the second sight of the northerly foothills. The jackpot scent of ivy moved me north.

I climbed into Carvin' Marvin's Cadillac. He wasn't pleased to be back so soon. His ropelike hands, which could have been made from Polk hemp, assumed the ten and two o'clock position on the steering wheel. My Supertramp eight-track cassette "Breakfast in America" dribbled out of the mouth of the audio system. Deedee had probably made Marv bring it. My Eden disappeared along a treeline beneath the Elvis cloud. I became angry with my home state's balladeer, Bruce Springsteen. It was he, not Elvis, who should have been looking over me, strumming out The Ballad of Jonah and Claudine. I felt owed a ballad.

I remained composed throughout the ride back to the Shore, but I registered Mount St. Helens behind my eyes. I felt the abyss of loss, the sting of betrayal, and an aborted sense of wonder that I never found out what had been glowing in the night sky.

PART SEVEN

KNIGHTS IN DISTRESS AND DAMSELS IN SHINING ARMOR

2005

Feeling and longing are the motive forces behind all human endeavor and human creations.

—Albert Einstein

THE PRODIGAL

"They want something that doesn't belong to them."

"Are we not men?" the giant repeated, citing a popular New Wave song from when we were so much younger.

It took me a few moments to get my heart rate under control, stop the icehouse from spinning, and remind myself that a belief in the supernatural was more likely a reflection of whatever chemicals were coursing through my brain than actual events. Independence Polk VI, or Six, had grown up to precisely resemble his grandfather, Indy Four. The resemblance was almost spiteful, as if to remind the Upper West Side of Central Park that Dixie could rise in any millennium it pleased. Even Six's shoulder-length hair conveyed defiance.

Six helped me up, and I answered his lyrical question: "We are Devo." He bear-hugged me off the ground. He wasn't as monstrously tall as he had initially appeared against the backdrop of the sun. Maybe six two.

"You always bring the entertainment, don't you, gangster boy?"

"Special events are my thing."

"Well, let's kill the fatted calf, the prodigal son is back, baby!"

I backed up higher on the pitch of the roof in order to meet Six eye to eye. "Yes, but which one of us is he?"

Six and I sat on the roof.

"This is some crazy stuff," he said, taking in the swelling landscape of warriors and media.

"Well, Bud, you wanted to be a rebel. Time to be a rebel."

"Think I can command a division like this?"

"They're here," I said. "You don't have any choice."

Six scanned the battlefield.

"So what do you make of our reunion?" I asked. I was fishing. I wanted to hear that I was family. I wanted him to say that he knew about Claudine, Sallie, and me.

"The reenactors?"

"No. Uh, I haven't seen your sister in all these years—"

"Oh, yeah, that's great," he said. "Great."

"Sallie came to the White House," I prodded.

"Right, Claudine told me," Six said after a beat. His eyes dragged along the clouds. I thought I saw his Adam's apple quiver. Maybe not. I'd drop it. Too much too soon, perhaps. "Well, guess who just showed up since you've been lying around out here?" Six cackled. "The Tennessee National Guard."

The Maury County Airport had an average of seventy-nine landings per day. Today, the airport logged one hundred and forty-two landings. Many of the aircraft were owned or leased by media organizations, such as EBS News. Nashville-based helicopter-leasing services were experiencing an unprecedented boom in business. Both print and broadcast media were clamoring for aerial shots of what EBS's Liz Marsh referred to as a "Confederate Woodstock."

Fifty National Guardsmen were lined up at the outside gates of the plantation. Technically, they were not on Polk grounds. According to the "information officer" being interviewed by Marsh, the National Guard was called out as a response to a large "unscheduled assembly." It was a precaution. The Confederates weren't so sure, and began lining up on the other side of the fence facing the guardsmen. It was a peculiar display—the guardsmen in their dark, menacing gear and automatic weapons, and the Confederate reenactors in their antiquated costumes and toothpick-ish rifles. The scene appeared to depict storm troopers about to vaporize a local theater troupe.

EBS News had begun promoting short segments entitled "Rebel Voices," in which one of the Confederate reenactors would address Liz Marsh's seminal question. "What brings you to Rattle & Snap?"

Marsh asked a lanky reenactor of about thirty, as the "Rebel Voices" logo (which incorporated a black-and-white photo of an attractive woman in a Confederate uniform raising a fist) appeared, and the signature *pa-rum-pum* drumbeat sounded.

"Them," Lanky said, pointing to the National Guard. "They want something that doesn't belong to them."

"Do you actually think you can stop them?" Marsh asked.

"No, but we can get 'em thinking, now can't we?"

Marsh moved to a female Confederate. "What's your name and where are you from?"

"Kay Starr from Atlanta."

"What brings you here?"

"I started off wanting to do a reenactment," Starr said. "I didn't know I'd be fighting a real war."

"Help me out here, Kay," Marsh asked. "Is this a protest, or not?"

"You're darned right it's a protest."

"But what's at stake? Civil rights? Secession?"

"What's at stake is the freedom to be who we are."

"And who are you?"

"We're people who want to assemble."

"Nobody's stopping you."

"They are," Kay Starr said, pointing to the National Guard. "They'll probably shoot us down like at Kent State."

"Why would they do that?"

"I'm not a mind reader."

"They haven't set foot on the property."

"Then why are they here?"

"The government's got its own agenda," Starr saluted, walking away.

"And there we have it," Marsh said into the camera. "The fertile grounds of another Civil War, one not about slavery or secession. In the end, it may not be about gold as we initially heard, because no one has reported discovering any, at least not yet. The root of the conflict remains unclear. Nevertheless, it is a struggle that has an undefined passion at its core, plus the two necessary ingredients: Us . . . and them."

I saw in the monitor of a mobile EBS News crew the graphic box containing Marsh's talking head growing smaller, and being displaced on the screen by an ever-broadening fish-eye lens showing the ragtag band of reenactors fanning out across the hills to the horizon.

A QUESTION IN PRIME TIME

"I remember the legends told to me on muggy summer nights."

It felt good to be out of my Confederate uniform for the plane ride to Washington. I landed at Andrews Air Force Base in the middle of the day. A driver whose identity I did not probe drove me into town.

I kept a safe-deposit box at a bank on the corner of Pennsylvania Avenue and Seventeenth Street. I did not remember the last time I was here. I didn't like bank vaults. They smell like whatever comes before prison. I always feared that somebody would slam the huge door shut and leave me inside to suffocate. I told Mickey that once. He hated my worrying and other "crazy thoughts." If my thought was so irrational, then why would they have an emergency air supply canister on the wall? Whenever I would go into a vault with Mickey, it was to "snatch something" before we took off for a "long weekend."

I returned to Washington for the sole purpose of visiting the safe-deposit box. The bank clerk recognized me. I got a big smile. "Look how scruffy," she said of my unshaven face. "Not on TV today, I guess," she said. Perhaps never again, I thought. The woman couldn't do enough for me, inviting me to go through my box in one of the bank's "special rooms."

Entombed air belched out of the box when I opened it.

Mickey's passport. Deedee's passport. Their death certificates. What does one do with such things, frame them? *Mazel tov, you're dead!* A certificate of acquittal for a skimming case. The incorporation papers for Taste of the Shore Saltwater Taffy company. Ah, the legal papers. No wonder Mickey didn't leave me any money; he spent it all on lawyers. Stuart F. Cohn, Esq., known as the Cohn of Silence because hostile witnesses against his clients tended not to testify. Unger

& Miller. Flamperton, Putpharken & Schnell. F. Lee Bailey. (Cool) Moskowitz & Forelli—MoFo. I pulled this envelope out. Legal jabber, dates in the mid-1970s and early 1990s. Related to gambling. Nothing relevant to the current drama. A few dozen other meaningless legal papers. A note in Mickey's handwriting on a legal bill reading, *"Missed me again."* Nothing else. Nothing. Hope is abandoned. Almost.

As I excavated my way through this tomb of grift, Mickey's handwriting appeared on a plain letter-size envelope that must have once been white, but was now yellow. It read: "Jonah/Girl Mishegoss." I coughed up a laugh. *Mishegoss* is Yiddish for "insanity." I open the paper-clipped envelope, taken aback that my conduct with women warranted such a category, let alone a file. The envelope was scented and had a smudge of red nail polish on the edge. Inside: (1) a piece of paper containing telephone numbers in an unfamiliar area code; (2) a four-page dossier entitled "Elmer Hicksen/Hilliard Enterprises." Dated July 15, 1980; (3) a trust document on the stationery of the esteemed gentlemen of Moskowitz & Forelli. A signature, too.

There is a God, not to mention a worrywart criminal grandfather— and a meddling grandmother if the nail polish smear was any indication—who had gone to more trouble than I had ever imagined.

I was back at Rattle & Snap by prime time. The president's news conference came on at eight o'clock Central. Huddled around a television set in the mansion's first floor den were Claudine, Six, Marcus, and myself. I told them nothing about what to expect.

The president strode down the central aisle of the White House toward the East Room right on time. This part—the walking—always made me nervous. Too much time and space to trip and fall, and no podium for protection. Truitt still walked like a cop, as if he were maneuvering from his patrol car to the perp's VEE-hickle. There was a judgmental quality about his gait, which was off-putting. Once he was behind the podium, I felt better, because I knew he was going to tell America a story rather than give us a ticket.

President Truitt spoke for a few minutes about boring topics such as unemployment, the war against terrorism, his Supreme Court nominee, and the possible migration of an organ-melting disease from Indonesia. The media, rudely, followed up on these subjects for twenty minutes until EBS News's senior White House correspondent, Maddy Sherman, asked, "Mr. President, as a son of the South, what do you make of the activity around the Rattle & Snap plantation in Tennessee, and the rumors that billions of dollars in gold bullion may have been stored there by rebel leaders during the waning days of the Confederacy? Could the discovery of gold destabilize the economy in any way?"

The president brushed the top of the podium, one of his more endearing time-buying gestures. "Now, Maddy, don't go spreading undue anxiety about our rebounding economy," he drawled to titters. "We've been off the gold standard since you were in grade school, so I think finding buried treasure at an old plantation is the least of our worries. You know, come to think of it, I do recall hearing stories as a young boy about Confederate gold being stored inside Rattle & Snap's pillars. It was folklore, something you believe when you're a child, but let go of as you grow older. Even so, Maddy, if there is gold down there, I don't believe it would amount to billions now, do you?"

"I don't know, sir," Sherman said, "But folks are asking to whom the gold would belong if it were to be found. Would it belong to the Polks, who own the property, or the government, which is entitled to seize Confederate assets?"

"Aw, now, Maddy, you're getting into arcane aspects of the law, and I'm a touch rusty on that type of thing. It's a tricky affair. You've got a family that rightly owns a property, a family that had prominent Confederate leaders. Then maybe there's currency that belonged to rebel forces that may have been placed on that property, so you've got an issue that ends up in court."

"Are you saying, sir, that you think there *is* gold bullion at Rattle & Snap?"

"No, Maddy, I think you're saying that. All I'm saying is that I remember the legends told to me on muggy summer nights. Next question. Tom—"

A HOME ON SHORT NOTICE

"Our conduct is the prize and the badge of our heritage."

EBS News announced the return of Six Polk to his family's ancestral home. I wanted to keep Six in the shadows, allowing imaginations to run wild, so I prohibited him from giving interviews.

EBS ran with another installment of "Rebel Voices" (*pa-rum-pum*). The network had condensed the feature by removing Liz Marsh, and simply allowing the designated rebel to state his or her case concisely against the backdrop of milling Confederates.

The latest Confederate was a middle-aged black man, a school administrator from Kentucky: *"I've been going to reenactments for fifteen years—as a Confederate. Friends look at my skin, and they ask: 'You're a Confederate?' Look, I hate the idea of slavery as much as the black men who fought for the Confederacy in the real war did. But after a while, you find yourself fighting not for what the whole thing was about in the first place, but for your home. To keep the other guy out. Does that make any sense? Even if it doesn't make sense, it's how I feel. When I heard the government making noise about coming into this old house looking for gold— man, I felt it in my bones, it just stinks."*

It was late morning. The neo-Confederate Army was preparing the grounds for Claudine's press conference while Six and I discussed optical strategy. He had rigged up a sound system that piped out music that had been popular in 1980. It was a peculiar sensation, the kind one gets when taking cold medicine—I'm here, but I'm not here.

"Jonah, I'd like to stand beside Claudine, along with some of the troops," Six said.

"I'd prefer that she stand alone, Six. If there's too much ancient history beside her, it may give off the impression that she's a little loony. It's best if she looks like a lone woman standing her ground."

"But they all came out here to help us."

"I know, but there's a subtle difference between Claudine accommodating the rebels and her commanding them. There are some cultural nuances here."

"Is it that she's a woman?"

"Partially, yes. New York cameras don't flatter Southern white men."

Claudine wore a white cotton shirt, khaki pants, and paddock boots. An American flag was pinned to her collar. Her hair was around her shoulders. We brought in a makeup artist to prepare her for the intrusive media lights.

"Is this necessary?" she asked.

"Fact is, kiddo, you're great looking," I said. "We need to exploit that."

Linda Ronstadt spooked us from the brick patio:

> I like the way you dance, the way you spin
> And how do I make you, how do I make you
> How do I make you spin for me?

"The public won't support an ugly woman's right to her heritage?"

I held her chin. "No. Do you remember that cute kid a few years ago from Cuba, Elian Gonzalez?"

"Sure. Everybody was up in arms about sending him back to Havana."

"Right. Do you think everybody would have cared if he was an ugly kid?"

"That's horrible, Jonah."

"Yes, Claudine, it is."

Claudine sat in an ancient chair. The makeup artist, a ditz out of Nashville, blasted her with light, which made Claudine squint. "Oh, Jonah, go away, I must look horrid under this light."

I was glad that she cared.

"Do you remember this song?" I pointed toward the patio.

"Linda Ronstadt?"

"Right. It was playing when I first met you at the Atlantic City Racetrack."

Failing to detect an affirmation of this memory, I backed off, and sat on a sofa across the room where Claudine could not see me.

"What classic features," Ditzy said, studying Claudine's face. This stung me, provoking one of my "Did I blow it?" sentiments.

"Thank you," Claudine said softly.

"You don't need much, just enough to tamp out the glare. Did you ever do any acting?"

"Heavens, no."

"You've got the look," Ditzy said, getting to work with a small, triangular sponge.

"I don't even want to go out in front of these cameras," Claudine said. "I'm not good at things like this."

"Well, perhaps you can have your friend over on that sofa get you ready. I've seen him on TV. He's the secretary of defense or somebody."

"He's here as a friend. You won't tell anybody, will you?"

Ditzy zipped her lip. All Nashville would know I was here by the weekend. The key was to blow town fast. If my presence broke after the jig was up, the media would be on to the next spectacle. If it broke beforehand, I'd be the spectacle.

News helicopters circled to the north and east of the mansion. Microphones were set up on the front steps. Satellite trucks lined the quarter-mile driveway. Hundreds of rebel vehicles were parked in the fields beside tents. Cooking grills and sleeping bags rolled on to the horizon.

Dressed in Confederate gear, I supervised the press area, which was arranged using the White House format—chairs in front of a podium with a raised platform for camera crews at the rear from which to film Claudine against the backdrop of Rattle & Snap's pillars. We had erected a makeshift wall behind the podium where the portraits of Will, George, Sallie Hilliard Polk, Indy Four, Six, and Sallie Polk Hilliard were displayed. When the portrait of Sallie the younger was hung, I had to walk back into the mansion, find a couch, and rest my head on my knees. A terrible discussion in South Jersey loomed.

When I looked out the second-story window, every press seat was taken. Dozens of camera crews spilled over the rear platform and onto equipment trunks scattered nearby. Thousands of uniformed rebels created a perimeter beyond the press. I observed through a closed-circuit TV monitor.

As Claudine stepped from the side of the mansion to the podium, one hushed on-air personality speculated that she was going to deliver an ultimatum to the government, specifically its enforcers from the National Guard. Confederates lined the perimeter of the news conference but were not visible in Claudine's frame. The male reporters surveyed Claudine as men would—carefully, in order to mask any form of attraction that might be seen as less than journalistic. The female journalists had a slight edge to them as Claudine composed herself. On a raw, physical level, she was competition. She wasn't in her suicide-gorgeous prime, but it would have been difficult for a woman facing her not to feel a touch of envy at this emblem of American royalty, a status that wasn't supposed to exist, but, nevertheless, did. Modern American women were raised to rail against the very idea of princesses, but how much of this hatred was ideological, and how much was veiled disappointment that their own fairy tales hadn't come true?

Claudine's voice was inaudible at first. She was visibly nervous. This was good. It made her less threatening. The men would want to protect her. The women would lack the heart for resentment. A petty corner of my personality celebrated Claudine's tension. I wanted her to be bad at something that I was good at.

"Good morning. Welcome to Rattle & Snap," she began.

"You've heard of Southern hospitality. It's very real, but we're more hospitable when we know guests are coming. It's hard to feed thousands of people who make a pilgrimage to your doorstep overnight, but we're doing our best."

Perhaps I am biased by my misty affection for this region and its people, but there is no more alluring voice than a woman's Southern accent. To me, it's musical. It makes me want to go to sleep, not out of boredom or exhaustion, but because it's how I imagine that outside voices must sound to a baby in the womb. The baby rests in a warm fluid, passively confident in its security. There is no entertainment outside of the loving cadence of someone you cannot believe your good fortune to have adore you.

"I have never held a press conference before. I hope I never do again. I apologize up front if I don't seem very good at this, but my brother, Six, thought I should be the one to do it because I live here. You see, this house has been in my family for one hundred and sixty years. The land has belonged to my family for even longer. In all those years, there's never been a press conference.

"The Polks have been unusual for a very public family in that we've managed to be a private family, too. Our Polk presidents, statesmen, and generals were lucky enough to live in an age when they could fight for this country's independence, help establish our freedom, and even fight the Nazis, and then retreat into the shade when our time in the spotlight was over.

"My generation has been very blessed, and learned many things from our ancestors. One thing we didn't learn, however, was how to negotiate the spotlight. Ironically, that's why I've invited the press to Rattle & Snap.

"Several days ago, our home found itself at the center of a great American fault line. Rattle & Snap has triggered a debate about issues ranging from the appointment of Supreme Court justices to the true winners and losers of the Civil War. As I understand it, this interest arose from a legend that Confederate leaders buried a great amount of gold on this property. I certainly hope they did."

The audience chuckled.

"But after years of digging here and there, we've never found any gold. I guess we'll keep looking. I know the law says that the gold would belong to the federal government—"

A chorus of boos rose from thousands of Confederate voices. News cameras swung wildly to absorb the faces of these protestors. Claudine gave them thirty seconds to exhaust their cries, which were docile.

"I don't know much about the law. I can't even say what we would do with Confederate gold if we found it. My brother and I sure aren't strong enough to fight the government, nor would we want to."

A lone voice cried out, "We'll do it, Miss Polk!" The Confederates erupted in a spontaneous cheer.

The voice belonged to a roly-poly Confederate in his seventies. He wore a white Ernest Hemingway beard, wire-rimmed glasses and an immaculate uniform. He removed his hat and held it against his heart.

"Well, now," Claudine said, "We don't want anybody to get hurt. But I'm grateful for your commitment. I've never been to a reenactment. I understand that they're usually well planned, but I came to this one because it's happening at my home. Perhaps what it lacks in advance warning, it makes up for in soul.

"What I've gained from this reunion is not gold, but sometimes when we see something that glitters, even if it's not gold, it may remind us of something that's been lost. To me, it's the understanding that for all our sins and imperfections, this home still has a heart. You all felt as if you had a home on short notice. And you do. Part of having a home is that you can come back to a place where there was heartache in the past, and then make the future better. And just as our family has made this home grand again because of the love that so many have had for it, all I ask is that you help me to present our home and our South to the world in a way that we want to be embraced going forward.

"The Polks were once warriors and slave owners. These institutions had their day, and the sun set long ago on that day, as it should have.

We have since become many other things we can take pride in in a new millennium. Most of all, we still have a home. My one aim is to keep this home. It's not about gold or Supreme Court justices or how a person pronounces the terrible world 'nuclear.' It's about keeping this home, and most of all, keeping it using means that we can display before any camera that seeks to make this a judgment of history. It is more important to me during these days of awe that we demonstrate our capacity for growth as a civilization in a noble manner than it is to emerge with a prize. Our conduct is the prize and the badge of our heritage."

HEAVY METAL

"I saw some activity out here in this valley in 1980."

The crowd dispersed to warm news coverage of Claudine's performance. She was described as "hospitable" and "genteel." The phrase "steel magnolia" was sprinkled liberally throughout the reporting. Several reporters had expressed surprise at how calm and nonconfrontational the affair had been.

Our latest spectacle had been completed, and now it was time to dig again.

I had never met a metallurgist before, but if I had been asked what one looked like, I would have described Oliver Shackley. In his late twenties, with sandy blond hair and an impish grin, Shackley had evidently done work for the intelligence community before. He alluded to a prior trip with Marcus to Central America. One learns not to ask.

Alternatively guarded and insightful, Shackley drove Marcus and me to a valley deep within the plantation's grounds. It was a valley I had encountered—and run from—many years before, although I had not shared the details of my memory with either of them.

"Marcus tells me you were hoping to find buried Confederate gold," Shackley said with a wink below his Tilley field hat.

"Marcus exaggerates," I said.

"It's my job," Marcus said.

"Well, gents, sorry to disappoint you, but I didn't find any gold in the area I inspected."

"Did you find any other precious elements?" I asked.

"That's an interesting way to put it, Jonah," Shackley said. "I did find some other elements, but they weren't precious."

"Go on."

"Are you familiar with phosphate?"

"Honestly, no."

"It's a mineral used to make fertilizer. Phosphates are mined around here. Big industry, especially where agriculture is heavy."

"When you say around here, are you saying it's mined at Rattle & Snap?" I asked.

"No," Shackley said. "Phosphorus is processed in Tennessee. The problem is, it's highly toxic, and I'm finding huge readings down in this valley."

"What would explain that?"

"I had one of our satellites do some imaging of the grounds. The phosphorus contamination is pretty much concentrated in this particular area. In fact, the rest of the plantation is quite clear."

"Oliver," I said, "the Hilliards, who own this land, have a lucrative phosphate business."

"Marcus told me that."

"Why would there be high phosphorus readings here in the middle of a plantation. I mean, the Hilliards have factories."

"The best I could do, Jonah, is speculate."

"Fine."

"There were dirt roads at some point down in this valley. They haven't been traveled in years, but they were here. Somebody was moving cargo in this area. Phosphorus is a very serious chemical. Disposal is a heavily regulated process, it has been for years. It's also expensive."

"I saw some activity out here in this valley in nineteen eighty," I surrendered. "Late in the evening." I hadn't wanted to divulge this until I knew more. I knew more.

Shackley nodded. "Nineteen eighty, huh? Well, that was around the time of Love Canal, guys. Environmental regulation really took off around then. I'm thinking that if the Hilliards wanted to dispose of phosphorus waste on the cheap, they could have exported diluted, benign waste out of their plant for inspectors to see, but set up some kind of makeshift processing or transfer station out here where the rough stuff got done. If nobody was watching, they could cool the chemicals, transfer the nastiest waste, and sneak it out of here without being noticed. The Mafia used to provide services like these before the Feds cracked down. It's going on big time in Russia, other unregulated places now."

"Oliver, I don't know much about chemicals, so bear with me," I said. "If there was such an operation like that out here—cooling and transferring—what would it look like?"

"Man, if they were playing with phosphorus, you could see it, baby."

"But not if it was far away at night, down in this valley."

"The hell you couldn't. When phosphorous cools, Jonah, it glows."

THE GRIN OF THE DAMNED

"You have a business decision to make."

EBS News's next edition of "Rebel Voices" featured a thirtyish suburban Nashville dad reflecting on a recent family confrontation. *"I was visiting my brother and his family in Connecticut. We got to talking politics. Big mistake. I said I voted for Truitt. Well, my sister-in-law says she couldn't believe Truitt got elected. She said, 'I don't know anybody who voted for him.'*

"I said, 'Do you realize how insulting that is? There's a whole country outside of Connecticut!' No sale. She said Truitt was elected by a 'handful of religious nuts in Mississippi.'

"I'm here to protest prejudice of a different kind—to say that there's a whole country here of decent people who believe in God, but who aren't nuts, and who are proud of our heritage, but aren't racists."

The moment I heard Oliver Shackley utter the word "glow," I knew my move: Get J. T. Hilliard over here. Oliver gave me a quick course in chemistry. Phosphorus for Morons.

Claudine called J.T. the following afternoon. She told him there was a situation at the plantation. When he arrived, visibly disgusted by the burgeoning encampment, he confronted me beside the rear stairwell.

"Where's Claudine?"

"Tending to the wounded."

"Yeah, well, what do you got?" he asked, more characteristic of Jersey bluntness than Dixie charm.

"You're not a Hilliard at all. You're a Hicksen from Pulaski. You're no more Southern gentry than I am. Your clan came down from the hills just in time to escape the film crew for *Deliverance*. Your family bought off the Polks. Your old man kept buying their land, set up shop way out in the fields on private property, far away from the beady eyes of the Environmental Protection Agency. Love Canal, all that pesky scrutiny. Your father had officials sign off on the contents of your waste when it left Hilliard property. Then the Hilliards brought it out here to Rattle & Snap, boiled it down, or cooled it off, or whatever, and transferred it to the Marcellos in New Orleans, who took it away, and dumped it God knows where."

"First off, friend, that's all bullshit. It's true, I own the mansion, but the land around it is owned by a trust. I have nothing to do with it." Self-satisfaction suffused J.T.'s face. "Someone can only be held liable if they own the land, which I don't, Eastman."

I nodded mournfully, and let him rejoice in his flash of cleverness.

"But you do, J.T. Your father created the trust in the late 1970s through a mobbed-up law firm in New Orleans, Moscowitz & Forelli. Your father executed a document a long time ago granting the law firm authority to manage the lands bought from the Polks. It means your father directed a huge scheme for which you are the beneficiary."

"That kind of technicality won't hold up in court and you know it!" His face was burning orange.

"My guess is that you'd probably be acquitted in court after a long, nasty trial. But there's a law called Superfund that holds a company responsible for things that go back a century. Right now, there are conglomerates filing for bankruptcy because a squirrel got diarrhea on a parcel of land owned by a subsidiary they forgot they had during the Great Depression. Mammoth companies have teams of lawyers, technicians, consultants, and flacks who can spend millions of dollars over many years battling the government to a tie—at best—once they're targeted. If you boys did half of what I think you did, you could be bankrupted or go to prison. The E.P.A. is wading in the Duck River as we speak. They've got some questions about disturbing pH readings. Or, of course, they can just go home."

"You can't prove—"

"You don't know what I can prove. For one thing, I can attach you to property where we found toxic residue that any sane jury would believe came from your plant. There's not a civil jury in the world that won't give your many victims a blank check drawn on your account."

"What victims?"

"*What victims?* When this news gets out, everybody below the Mason-Dixon line who misses their beloved mama who died at the age of ninety-two will stand in line to get a piece of you. Science won't matter. You could bankrupt your company on legal fees alone just to prove you're an upstanding Southern gentleman."

"These stunts of yours, Eastman . . . don't you think they would make a hell of a story: Fired, mobbed-up White House mouthpiece gets big shots in Washington to bully an old rival for a girl? Talk about dirty tricks."

"It sounds far-fetched to me, J.T. A great story line, I'll grant you that, but it would take a lot of evidence to connect those dots. Could take months—if ever—to break it. It's the kind of story that gets editors fired, so they'd take their time on the research. Claudine, on the other hand, has the press camped out here today, right this very minute. What she's got on you can be all over the news in"—I glanced at my watch—"about ten minutes. Just in time for the E.P.A. to storm your offices and Boston Capital Holdings to change their underwear about that buyout you've been negotiating. I could be wrong, but I don't think they want Superfund on their docket. Yeah, we know about that, too."

J.T. affected one of those smiles Tom Wolfe writes about, the false, tight bureaucratic grin of the damned. I could see, however, that the arteries in his neck were filled to capacity. This was not a man accustomed to playing cool.

"I deal with the government and nervous partners all the time."

"C'mon, J.T., are you still an eighteen-year-old hothead? You're running a multi-billion-dollar company. This isn't about who's the bigger man, it's about business. You've got a business decision to make. An easy one, I might add. You sign over a property worth several million to save an empire worth billions. Your father wouldn't have needed a calculator."

"It's not about the money, Eastman."

"Then, what's it about? Love?"

"What it's about is none of your business." J.T. narrowed his eyes. "So, I leave, and you move in, is that the plan?"

I instinctively laughed, but it came out a snort. "Is that what you think? That this is checkmate from twenty-five years ago? No, J.T., this is not an assault on your rebel masculinity. If you sign those papers, I'm gone." I sat on one of the steps. I softened my tone, as I wanted him to feel strong, and stand above me. "Look, you've got a girlfriend. You're never here. I'm not a factor. What—"

"Since I was a little kid, I dreamed about living here with Claudine, Eastman. Those are a lot of memories."

His honesty disarmed me. I downshifted again, this time into a mode I was familiar with: punctured self-delusion.

"They weren't memories, J.T.," I said fraternally. "It was an obsession. An enzyme that got caught in your head. One your dad passed down to you. This house and that woman"—I pointed to a faraway place—"ordered your life. Mine, too, for a time. Maybe even now, a little, to be honest. You don't give a rat's ass about the Civil War, and you'd rather be with your girlfriend, or out on a golf course. I'd rather be with my family and teaching school, so I don't judge a man's time allocation. You don't want this Moby Dick of a house, J.T. Claudine and Six, though, it's all they know."

"It's my heritage, too, Eastman."

Be cool here, Jonah. This was no time to tweak Sallie's paternity, castrate him with it, imply that his home was now my heritage. Suddenly, the light caught J.T.'s face in a way that made him refract differently in my brain. I felt sorry for him. He was my nemesis, but also my Brother in Sorrow. Claudine Polk had been our Messiah, Rattle & Snap our Land of Milk and Honey. Only Claudine hadn't delivered us from torment, she *was* our torment.

"Rattle & Snap is your heritage like the White House is my heritage," I said, with regret lodged in my throat. "The White House is where I got to. Felt tables and bathtub gin are my heritage. The Hicksen heritage is chemicals, plastics, and phosphates. Maybe some bathtub gin, too. Take that heritage, call it Hilliard, and run with it. I know a lot of people, myself included, who'd take it anyday. My only advantage over you, J.T., is that I've been in the gutter before. You had diamonds on your crib. For me, falling is a part of life. For you, it's a novelty. You're too old for a novelty like that. Me? It's all I know."

"You're bluffing, friend."

"Bluffing? Tell me something, J.T., if the chances are a million to one that I am holding a full house, is it worth losing everything so you can tell your old frat brothers that you pimp-slapped your wife."

"You're extorting me—"

"I'm just extorting what you stole. Show me some professional courtesy—one hustler to another. You've got a lot on the line," I said.

"You want me to declare that I've learned my lesson, is that it?"

"People don't surrender because they learn lessons, they surrender because they are overwhelmed. The last thing you need is a government panty raid."

"And you could make that happen?"

"Seriously, J.T., listen." I pointed to my ear.

"Listen for what?"

"Let's go outside and listen there."

I pressed Tigger on the speed dial of my mobile phone.

"It's me," I said, standing on the steps, staring down on J.T. (Man, he had a lot of hair.) I inquired as to whether or not J.T.'s friend Senator Hunter had called the president ("Did Jethro reach out for Mr. Drysdale?")

"Negative."

"Then put the file in play."

"Are you sure, Wonderboy?" Tigger asked.

"Yes."

I motioned J.T. to follow me outside. He did. About twenty Confederates, including Six, were playing cards and horseshoes outside near their tents. J.T. shook his head in disgust.

"If I can bring this spectacle to Claudine's doorstep, I can bring it to yours."

"A handful of loonbird Confederate wannabes isn't much of a spectacle."

The call Tigger made did not come from the White House. It came from a Verizon pay phone outside of the McDonald's where Bill Clinton used to scarf down Egg McMuffins after a run. It was near the corner of Pennsylvania Avenue and Seventeenth Street. The recipient of Tigger's call was the Panamanian's assistant, Linda. Linda clacked something into her computer, which was transmitted to a satellite pirouetting above the Philippines. This satellite, in turn, relayed coordinates to a room deep within the National Geospatial-Intelligence Agency on Sangamore Road in Bethesda, Maryland. The function of the windowless colossus was to provide the U.S. military with the precise coordinates—and satellite photos—of a target anywhere around the world that the president of the United States in his own wisdom had decided to vaporize.

"Arnold, over," a voice in Bethesda said.

"This is Arnold."

Arnold is considered a milquetoast name. It conjures up an accountant doing a plumber's taxes at an H&R Block outlet in a strip mall in Secaucus.

Not this Arnold.

ATTITUDE, LATITUDE

"Senator Hunter's gonna hear about this, friend!"

The voice in Bethesda requested, "Coordinates."
   "Arnold is receiving."
   "Confirm please."
   "We have latitude at three five point five six two one seven."
   "Confirm next."
   "Longitude minus zero eight seven point one five five nine. Awaiting optics."
   NASA in Houston shares a satellite with the Pentagon, which is nice. This particular satellite is used to track the flight of the space shuttle as it returns to Earth. It can also take pictures. With a barely perceptible maneuver, the satellite adjusted its lens on the burial grounds of my teenage heart.
   "Optics received," the voice calling itself Arnold confirmed.
   The last word uttered at Arnold Air Force Base in Tullahoma, Tennessee, was "Engage."

Claudine was in the house. J.T. and I were standing beside his Mercedes. Six was still gambling with a few Confederates at a picnic table.
   The high-pitched whine fell short of being piercing. I felt a tickling sensation in my toes. I sensed J.T. felt something, too, because he looked down at his shoes. The trees rustled. Pebbles on the driveway danced like popcorn, betraying a greater force somewhere close by. We both craned our heads skyward—as did battalions of gray-capped heads. The whine climbed inside itself, a cirrus cloud slipping into a cumulus, as God slowly exhaled: Hhhaaaaaaaaaaa . . .

There were stars, but they were red. No, they were not stars. Too close. Too bright. Too fast. And way too low.

The signal lights of five F-15 Eagle fighter jets flying in formation winked down at us, letting us know they were in on the cosmic joke. Six rose from a picnic table and pronounced the word "Holy!" Whatever followed was rendered inaudible by the deafening thunder from above. J.T. fell to the ground, as did many of the reenactors. I remained standing despite the rattling of my brains like dice inside my skull.

"How's the mileage on this baby?" I asked J.T., tapping his Mercedes.

When the Eagles crossed the plantation's property line, the two to our left banked to the west; the two to the right banked to the east; and the one in the center kept its needle nose pointing toward the Union. Dust flew. The red lights melted from our vision within thirty seconds.

"Senator Hunter's gonna hear about this, friend!"

"No doubt."

ROUTINE EXERCISE

"This was a bullying act, a provocation."

A major Tennessee newspaper ran with the following headline and lead paragraphs the following morning:

U.S. WARPLANES STRAFE PLANTATION
Furor Over Confederate Gold,
Property Rights Escalates
By Stuart Eliot

Five F-15 Eagle fighter jets screamed over rural Mount Pleasant yesterday at sunset in what was described by the Pentagon as a "routine exercise." The low-flying planes roared over the Rattle & Snap plantation where Confederate Civil War reenactors had gathered to protest the looming encroachment by the Federal government on the historic Polk family lands.

The privately-owned property has been rumored in recent days to contain gold hidden by Southern battalions from the devastating Union march led by General William Tecumseh Sherman in 1864.

Eyewitnesses said that the powerful jets flew at an altitude no higher than two hundred feet, which experts say is highly unusual in inhabited regions.

"This was a bullying act, a provocation," said Claudine Polk Hilliard in a statement. Mrs. Hilliard, who was raised at Rattle & Snap, the land which has been in her family for more than two hundred years. "We thought they'd bomb us."

Air Force Colonel Henry Stuever dismissed Polk's claim.

"The Eagle is aerial combat equipment," said Stuever. "While they can get loud, it is preposterous to infer hostile intent to a handful of Civil War buffs."

The antebellum home has been thrust into the national spotlight, tearing open a historic debate about the role of the Federal government in seizing property that once belonged to the Confederacy. While there is no dispute that Rattle & Snap is private property, according to the Department of the Interior, any materials of value that can be demonstrated to have belonged to the Confederate army convey by law to the United States Treasury. While it is unclear whether the Polks lay claim to—or indeed possess—any gold on their property, the invocation of the 140-year-old law has set off furious debate in the media and on the Internet.

Particularly outraged have been the swelling number of Confederate Civil War reenactors who have initiated a pilgrimage to Rattle & Snap. Many of the reenactors are also believed to be Freemasons, Rattle & Snap having reportedly been spared by a Sherman subordinate who learned that its owner, George Washington Polk, was, like himself, a member of the secretive society.

Six blast e-mailed this story from his laptop to several hundred of his Confederate reenactors and Masonic brethren, one of whom was a National Press Newswire reporter in Atlanta. The story went out on the wire before the business day officially began in the central and western United States. A half-dozen cable news channels had news crews on the ground in Nashville by 11:00 A.M. By noon, our cyberspooks had counted eighteen million "click-thrus"—people who were actively monitoring the strafing incident online. By dinnertime more than three thousand Confederates were milling about old Will Polk's grounds and being segmented into color-coded divisions by his heirs.

ALL OVER AGAIN

"Well, sister, do you want pepperoni or mushrooms with your Civil War?"

I learned a valuable lesson last night: Twenty-first-century Confederates don't like to get buzzed by supersonic aircraft. As the Confederate crowd swelled to five thousand, the Tennessee National Guard increased its presence by two hundred.

Six and I watched the gathering from the second-floor living room, where multiple television receivers had been installed and linked to rooftop satellites. EBS News's latest installment of "Rebel Voices" featured a fine-boned woman holding up a photo: *"Do you see this picture? It's a Pizza Hut. You see them all the time, right? Wrong, because this one's in Franklin, Tennessee, not far from here on the grounds of a Civil War battlefield that left six Confederate generals dead. Now it's a Pizza Hut. Well, sister, do you want pepperoni or mushrooms with your Civil War? I hear the Polks don't even really own this land anymore. I hear it was sold to a Boston real estate company for development. That's right, check it out. I like pizza as much as the next guy, but I came to Rattle & Snap because I don't think history should come with a wide selection of toppings."*

"Are you ready?" I asked Six.

"I can't believe it's gone this far," he said.

"Can't call it off now."

"No. They know what to do."

Six activated his walkie-talkie. "All colors: Fort Sumter," was all he said.

From every corner of the plantation, the designated field captains received the call. The troops had been separated into divisions of roughly one hundred each. Four news helicopters were in perpetual circulation, trying to avoid crashing into each other. The Maury County Airport halted all flights in and out of Mount Pleasant because radar indicated that some of the choppers were crossing into the flight path. The ground-based camera crews began filming the concurrent assemblies from their positions on pickup and flatbed trucks.

The moment the Confederates picked up their rifles, reporters attempted to determine the cause of their actions from the field captains, who conceded nothing.

B-R-E-A-K-I-N-G N-E-W-S: Twelve letters designed to send a rush of bile through whatever bodily systems process bile. The combination of these words immediately after the rude interruption of scheduled programming signaled a promise that your life was about to change, and that you would always remember where you were when you heard the news. Presidential assassinations, wars, jilted prom dates on sniper rampages.

Global News Network shifted its programming status to Breaking News. The talent began, "We have a development here at the Rattle & Snap plantation in Mount Pleasant, Tennessee. As GNN was the first to report this morning, the Tennessee National Guard has increased its deployment significantly. This appears to have provoked the thousands of reenactors who have descended upon the plantation in the last several days in protest of the government's potential seizure of gold reserves that Confederate troops are said to have buried here toward the end of the Civil War."

EBS's Liz Marsh: "We are now seeing what appears to be a systematic advancement by Confederate Civil War reenactors on the National Guard who were dispatched for the purpose of keeping the peace here at the Rattle & Snap plantation, which has become the epicenter of a firestorm of debate about the two Americas. I remember as a little girl watching the television footage of the massacre of students at Kent State University in Ohio by National Guardsmen . . ."

Grainy footage of the Kent State shootings now enveloped screens across the nation. The black-and-white photo of the young woman with long, dark hair, wailing as she kneeled over the body of a friend, slid across screens like curtains being closed for the evening. The young woman's festive white scarf eerily underscored the unexpected nature of the horrors unfolding. Even more disturbing perhaps were the other students milling about in the photo as if the carnage were as routine as a lit class.

I flipped to another cable network, which was feeding aerial footage from one of the helicopters.

"I recognize the ludicrous nature of my observation," a Fox News reporter said, "but it appears as if Confederate troops are advancing on the National Guard. . . ."

"Approximately fifty armed battalions of Southern Civil War reenactors are advancing on U.S. troops," another reporter observed (incorrectly).

Universe News Channel displayed a computer graphic of Rattle & Snap, along with icons signifying plantation landmarks and dotted symbols depicting troop locations. A stack of frantic red arrows featured "troop movements" from the south, west, and east grounds of the property, sweeping north to where the National Guardsmen were aligned in formation.

"There is an ominous chaos in the air . . . ," another broadcaster began as a view from the clouds took in the migrating throng.

But, on the ground, there wasn't chaos. There was only gradual movement being reported as chaos. To be fair, the Confederates were bracing rifles against their shoulders, which lent a taste of menace; however, the antiquated weaponry—not to mention that they were being carried by men and women wearing comically ancient costumes—defused any promise of kingdom come.

No, the networks wanted a war, needed a war. At the moment, there were no other optical dramas playing out in the national theater. The cultural street fight over the president's Supreme Court nominee was weeks away. The press had exhausted funeral profiles of the poor souls who were killed in the recent terrorist attack in Philadelphia. The war against terrorism had become chronic—just another mind-numbing news filing from overseas—a grenade tossed into a cave in a hard-to-pronounce regime. Trashbagistan, Crapslapistan. No celebrities were on trial for driving naked and drunk through a kindergarten class. No expectant fathers raging against adulthood had opted to dispatch with their pregnant wives rather than grow the hell up. No fifth-grade girls had been snatched from jungle gyms by tattooed ex-cons. And no royal family members had been chased into tunnels by killer paparazzi.

In the age of news-as-profit-center, media conglomerates could not move equipment and personnel across the nation only to return with a goose egg: Nuthin' doin' here. Something had better been doin', or anybody who failed to produce would face budgetary and assignment repercussions.

Thus the rhetoric and imagery of war and protest. Computer maps with swooshing arrows and targets denoting rebel regiments with names like Purple and Double Red. Satellite views of the planet with frantic zooms and graphic call-outs to "Ground Zero." References to battalions, divisions, and personnel movements. Experts explaining the difference between tear gas and pepper spray, lethal and nonlethal ammunition. Personnel ratios. Grave Voices of God scattering comparisons to domestic and international flashpoints prefixed with "another": Another Kent State. Another Tiananmen Square. Another Chicago. Another Watts. Another Rodney King.

Occasionally the Grave Voices of God would shift from the prefix "another" to the suffix "all over again" (AoA). Antietam AoA. Gettysburg AoA. Sherman AoA. Richmond AoA.

Within fifteen minutes of Six's initial call to arms, the Confederates were only a few hundred yards from the front gates of the plantation. On one hand, their sheer number was menacing; however, they weren't marching toward the gates, they were simply walking. It was the helicopter views that lent the sense of doom—thousands of ragamuffin Grays quite literally facing one solid line of black-clad National Guardsmen with their medieval shields and weaponry readied for battle.

Choice Media commentary (Pulitzer Prize–inspiring sound bite for replay noted in **bold**):

HUSHED: **"Confederate troops are advancing on the National Guard.** I repeat: Confederate troops are advancing on the National Guard."

URGENT: "Government-dispatched troops are taking their positions creating a **wall of firepower** directly across from the Civil War soldiers."

CONSPIRATORIAL: (graphic accompaniment): "This is what I would refer to as a **classic flanking maneuver,**" said the retired general who consulted for the network. "The Confederate troops will attempt to draw fire from the National Guard over here, while reinforcements move in over here."

TRAGIC: "No one foresaw that it would come to this, and tragically, **no one can stop it now.** Given the sheer tactical might of government forces, this has the potential to be worse than Kent State."

REVOLUTIONARY: "There is a sense of outrage over the government's **mishandling** of the events of the past seventy-two hours. **A furious sense of overkill.**"

The Guardsmen were ordered to stand in the ready position. Shoulder-launched tear gas canisters were at the ready. Two Chinook gunships, their two rotors slicing the cool, moist air in cycles of Vietnam-era peril, banked from the southern end of the plantation.

After evaluating the coverage and the visible tensions outside the window, I gave Six an anemic salute. Six then gave the order to engage. Air horns echoed through the hills, and within seconds, thousands of antiquated firearms . . . dropped to the ground. In one protracted wave, five thousand Civil War reenactors of various genders, ages, religions, and colors . . . sat down. While the sight appeared haphazard from the mansion's window, from the aerial views, it looked like performance art—souls blowing over gently like grain before a storm.

Some of the Confederates from the Red group withdrew to play cards. One Asian reenactor from Double Orange played with a yo-yo. A middle-aged woman from Black began to play a harmonica. Groups within Green began to sing songs ranging from hymnals to Lynryd Skynryd. A few from Double Burgundy practiced tai chi. A portly black man from Aqua read a book. The only consistent sounds were those of helicopter rotors and laughter conveying a hearty toast to a fraternity pledge well hazed.

The National Guardsmen's faces were not visible behind their masks, but their stillness betrayed their likely mental state: They were stunned. Because they looked like jackasses on worldwide television—grown men clinging to elementary school Delta Force fantasies. Pathetic. Secret agent wannabes who had never been in a real firefight, so they declared war on a ragtag band of Civil War reenactors, hoping they'd be cross-burning, epithet-spitting racists. No, even better, the Feds had ordered these chuckleheads to duke it out with a handful of amicable history buffs who were just ticked off about an overzealous government.

The National Guard withdrew from their battle positions but remained outside the plantation's fence. The two Chinook gunships did one tortured swoop over the highway, and then eased away. The news helicopters remained, but the on-air correspondents vacillated between artificially sweetened melodrama and inarticulateness to summarize what they believed they had just seen.

"They, uh, heh. They . . . sat down. They just sat down."

"In a spectacular act of peaceful defiance worthy of Gandhi or Martin Luther King, thousands of Civil War reenactors laid down their arms in the face of overwhelming danger from Federal troops."

"Well, folks, what we seem to have here is an American Civil War that ends in . . . a sit-in."

As the cameras thirsted for a spark of conflict, the hills were at peace, as Elijah's ghost made his benediction of the pseudoevent. *My, my, my.*

CIVIL WAR BREAKS OUT AT THE
METAL DETECTOR AT DULLES AIRPORT

"Pay me out some of that psychic income."

There is a sophisticated computer analysis system based in Las Vegas. It is called NORA, an acronym for Non-Obvious Relationship Awareness. Among its capabilities is determining that a casino cheat sitting at the blackjack table has the dealer as his roommate. This was done by entering the name of the cheat into the NORA system and discovering that he had the same telephone number as the dealer. In other words, they were in the scam together. When I first heard about it, I knew it would have been something that Mickey would have marveled at. NORA wasn't only used by casinos, of course. It had been employed since 9/11 by the federal government to catch terrorists.

According to NORA, William Elkins Hunter had traveled four times to Saudi Arabia during the past three years using an airplane that had recently been chartered by one Ibrahim al-Fawazzi, a Yemeni banker with ties to the bin Laden family. Hunter had also received thousands of telephone calls at his office from Saudis. His office received periodicals that dealt with weaponry. Photographs had been unearthed showing him entering chemical and munitions plants in the United States and abroad.

Of course, virtually all of these things were perfectly benign for a United States senator. But NORA had other plans.

Today, Senator Hunter was scheduled to fly from Washington's Dulles Airport to Nashville at the urgent invitation of his good friend, J. T. Hilliard. It was not to be an easy trip, however, because the highlights of the information NORA gleaned had found their way into the Federal Aviation Administration's security alert—the one that is updated at the nation's airports hourly, putting people suspected of having terrorist ties on the dreaded no-fly list.

Hunter was detained and escorted out of the security maze just before he was to proceed through the metal detector. That William Elkins Hunter was a United States senator was of no matter to Shirley Latrelle, the security official on duty at the Dulles security line, where Hunter was standing with an aide. In fact, his stature made inconveniencing Senator Hunter all the more fulfilling to Shirley Latrelle, of Hyattsville, Maryland, who had spent fifty-two years on the receiving end of the self-important proclamations of the white Washington power elite.

Senator Hunter and his young aide, who appeared to have an aircraft carrier lodged up his kazoo, let forth a litany of threats. The angrier Hunter and his aide became, the more orgasmic Shirley Latrelle grew. Detaining these men wasn't the highlight of her day, it was the highlight of her career. She waved over a few colleagues. Their faces remained stoic, their words, by the book. But their eyes spoke four hundred years of history: "C'mon, boys, seethe a little more. Pay me out some of that psychic income. Threaten to get my ass fired, ruined. C'mon, gents, fire on old Fort Sumter, let's have ourselves a Civil War. Who do you think is going to win once those cameras get rolling and the Reverend Jesse Jackson shows up with a gospel choir?"

Hallelujah!

After the crowd swelled and the supervisor was dutifully called, Senator Hunter and his aide knew that this Civil War was a draw. The senator wins inside the Capitol, but Shirley Latrelle wins out on the street. It all depends on where you're standing when the deal goes down, isn't that right?

The senator remained cool. He smiled the tense smile of the flack who has just been mau-maued. Get me back to my turf, into the privacy of my car, he thought, where I can let loose unfettered by the gentle obligations of my caste.

Which he does, and the tape recorder the Panamanian's rapscallions placed under the seat picks up everything. The searing epithets, the mimicking of Shirley Latrelle's inner-city cadence: *Uh-uh, baby.* The kind of statements even decent people make when they're off-the-grid angry. The kind of thing you wouldn't want "out there."

Hunter personally called J. T. Hilliard to tell him he wouldn't be making it to Nashville. The senator apologized profusely, but did not disclose the reason for his aborted trip. He fobbed it off onto a breaking national security issue. As he spoke, the Panamanian's crew retrieved the senator's telephone number.

J.T. controlled his rage as the senator assured him that he was sending his "best man" to the White House to investigate Hilliard's claim of presidential skullduggery. Truth be told, senators didn't lightly undertake investigations of sitting U.S. presidents in their own party. J.T. may have been a big contributor and "good friend" of Hunter's, but he was also a blowhard. Still, the senator was obliged to "look into" the matter when he returned to his office.

The Panamanian activated his digital geeks, who quickly determined that the aide's Jeep Cherokee was equipped with the "Galaxy Locator" package, which provided communications and security support for travelers. The Panamanian's assistant telephoned Galaxy's toll-free emergency number and reported the vehicle stolen. Ten minutes later, a satellite spit out coded whispers that mated with a computer chip that the manufacturer had installed behind the Jeep's dashboard in a "revolutionary partnership in security with Galaxy." These codes neutralized the electrical signal that passed from the control panel to the engine.

The Jeep's engine conked out on the Dulles toll road as the engine was castrated from outer space. The senator attempted to call for assistance as his aide frantically tried to restart the vehicle on the shoulder. Hunter couldn't get a dial tone because its service had been discontinued due to its reported theft. He wouldn't be helping his constituents today.

AWAKENED BY GRACE

"Jonah is passionate; he overreacts."

I sometimes communicated with National Security Advisor Dexter Cane through Tigger's personal instant messenger account. Cane, of course, didn't do the typing, and all correspondence, if it was ever to surface, would be utterly deniable. The I.M. name we had set up to communicate with Cane was "Faulkner"; mine was "Roth," for New Jersey's bard, Philip.

The following exchange with Dexter/Tigger took place on the evening that I sabotaged Senator Hunter's trip to Nashville:

ROTH: Just need one final public word and we're done.
FAULKNER: What's that?
ROTH: "The government has no issue with the House of P."
FAULKNER: The law states clearly that if Dixie glitter is found, it belongs to government. No flexibility on that.
ROTH: It won't be found. Please withdraw personnel.
FAULKNER: R U trying to involve us in a heist?
ROTH: No. Columns are empty. No glitter.
FAULKNER: Figured as much. What about elsewhere on lands?
ROTH: Nothing here but ghosts.
FAULKNER: I'll be damned.

J.T. signed over Rattle & Snap to Claudine the following day. I got out of their way while the two of them reached an accord in the contemporary kitchen. The only thing I did hear Claudine say after I heard J.T.'s voice utter the words "freaking air force" was "Jonah is passionate; he overreacts."

At the noon White House briefing the following day, my successor addressed the government's position on the confiscation of Confederate gold at Rattle & Snap. She said, "The government has no issue with the Polks. The Department of the Interior has studied the matter. The government does not believe any gold on the Polk lands was placed there by Confederate forces and it does not, therefore, belong in government coffers. As soon as the Confederate reenactors disperse and public safety is assured, the National Guard will go home."

Claudine went to her attorney's office. Six and I toasted the Polks' victory with lemonade.

"I really appreciate all you did for us."

"I was happy to help," I fibbed. Happiness had nothing to do with it.

"It's great you care so much about us after all this time."

This struck me as being odd. How could I not care? Then I considered possible flaws in my logic. Was it possible that he didn't know what I knew? Could Claudine not have told him about where Sallie came from? She hadn't told me directly, so maybe all the Polks ducked straight talk. Episcopalians, I thought. But young Six had been very direct long ago. My usual tactics weren't working.

"Well, it gave me a chance to get back at J.T.," I said.

"For what?"

"Getting me tossed out of here."

"What do you mean?"

"You know. The whole mess with your grandfather's ring being stolen."

"You think J.T. was behind that?"

"Well, J.T. or his family."

Six shook his head. "You gotta sit my sister down for a nice, long talk, brother."

I became nauseous. It was the kind of nausea that possessed acute elements. Pain, not free-floating imbalance.

"What do I ask her, Six?"

"Have her tell you the story about Indy's ring."

"You got it back?"

"Well, yeah. Pretty fast, too. Jonah, you're a smart man, but when it comes to my sister, you still stack things up in your mind to make everything match up with your mental monologue."

Things clicking—actually making clicking noises and echoing in my skull.

"Did you ever talk to Claudine about Sallie?" I asked.

"Sure, here and there." Straightforward. Oblivious.

"Did you ever talk with her about why she married J.T. so fast?"

"It wasn't one of those things you talk about. She got pregnant, man."

"Yes, she did. In September of nineteen eighty."

"Right."

I test-drove my "tombstone eyes," a killer look that one of Mickey's men had taught me. Get a reaction. Nothing from Six. Nothing. Because I knew. I heard the voice of my grandmother: "Look at Mr. Ivy League Knows Everything . . ." Then I heard Six's own words just moments ago about my "mental monologue." These didn't sound like Six's words; they sounded like one of my own rants about human perception.

I was suddenly overcome with exhaustion. It was a dense exhaustion, the kind that bypassed drowsiness and graduated right to sleep. Even though it was midafternoon, I went up to my/Indy's bedroom, put my music player's earphones on, and fell asleep for twenty minutes. The sleep was unlike any other I had ever experienced, because I remembered every moment. I was on my back, falling.

I dreamed that my mother was holding my hand. I was very young, maybe six. We were emerging from a huge, dark cube. It may have been a movie theater. We blinked into the daylight. My high school English teacher, Mr. Hicks, was outside in the parking lot. "You did well on the test," he said. "Only one vocabulary question wrong."

"What did Jonah get wrong?" my mother asked.

"Peripetia," Mr. Hicks said.

My mother scrunched up her nose, unfamiliar with the word.

Mickey's voice echoed from the theater, but we could not see him. "It's from Greek tragedy. It's the moment when the hero realizes he's the mark."

I was awakened by a memory of Grace Slick's voice, a huge headache, and a simple realization: There is nothing cowardly about avoiding certain people, especially those whose greatest strength feeds from your greatest weakness. In my head, as the puzzle fell together, Slick was singing "White Rabbit": *"If you go chasing rabbits and you know you're going to fall . . ."* I took an analgesic, packed my clothing, and took my bags downstairs. I left my Confederate uniform on the bed.

EXODUS

"Mother Hen has called her chickens home."

I sat on the mansion's front steps. This would be my O.K. Corral. I was cool. We'd get into this slowly.

I heard Claudine speaking with Six inside before she came out. She shook her head in amazement at the events of the last week. "Is it really that easy to abuse power?" she asked.

"When there's a smokin' hot woman involved, certainly."

"Scary."

"For the other guy. I was just thinking, Claud, do you know what Sallie said to me when we met? She told me I didn't look like a thief."

"Of course you don't. You are some odd things, but you are not a thief."

"How would Sallie know that? When I left, I left as a thief."

"Because I told her about the cloud you left under." Claudine reached into her pocket and withdrew George Polk's Masonic ring, the one I had been accused of stealing.

My resignation quietly converting to stoicism, I quietly asked, "When did you get it back?"

"It never went very far."

Indy Four had told Claudine the whole story after Sallie was born and she was safely married. With lots to lose.

"Who stole the ring, Claudine?"

Claudine kissed my cheek. She said, "And God said to Moses, 'Send men that will spy out the land of Canaan, which I give to the children of Israel; of every tribe of their fathers shall you send a man, every one a prince among them.'"

I shuddered. "My grandfather used to traffic in that passage," I said.

"Those men you saw in the town that day J.T. attacked you. They were dressed like workmen, painters or something. They were his spies."

They were his spies. I thought about what Sallie had said to me at the White House that had confused me: *They worry, spaz.* Her Southern accent congealing with the traffic . . . As she walked away from me she was saying, "They were his spies."

"It was Deedee's idea," Claudine said. "The day after you left she had the ring returned with a note to Indy." Claudine went back into the house and returned carrying a wooden chest. It was the one I had seen in the back of Mickey's car. She opened it up. There was a letter inside on Golden Prospect Hotel & Casino stationery. It contained Deedee's loopy handwriting, that melodramatic slant, the exaggerated capital letters.

"Your grandparents left the trunk here," Claudine said. "Indy didn't tell me until years later. I figured that somebody would have said something if you missed it."

Deedee's letter read:

Dear Indy:

Now listen to me, sweetheart. By now you have your fancy ring back. It's a little garish for my taste, but to each his own. As you know, my husband had a few of his choir boys in Dixie this summer in case things got touchy with the Hope of America (my grandson). I had never seen Jonah so out of sorts as he was with Claudine, not even when his parents died. She's a lovely girl, but Jonah can't spend his life being her standing ovation.

I gave "Moses" a piece of my mind so he allowed me to give his Boys a special assignment. They pinched that ring of yours. You blamed Jonah (don't kid me, honey) as I knew you would. You had your reasons. My husband told me all about who pays the bills at your place. We do what we have to do, right? Just remember this: Those who marry for money end up earning it.

Mother Hen has called her chickens home.

When I told my husband my idea, he said no. "Indy will think we're crooks," he said. "We ARE crooks!" I told him. All I ask is that you don't think Jonah is some kind of gangster. He's a fine boy even if he does have a tendency to go too far where your granddaughter is concerned. (That one will be just fine!)

I am grateful that you took Jonah in this summer. I apologize for the stunt with the ring, but I would rather risk losing your affection than my grandson's future. You lost a son, I lost a daughter, so neither of us have a kind word to say about loss.

Maybe the whole affair was none of my business and I should have left matters in God's hands. The thing is whenever I leave matters in God hands someone I care about slips through His fingers. Enough already! Anyhow, my noble friend, another slave has been freed from that gorgeous prison of yours. I'll meet you by the gazebo.

Love,

Deedee

Mickey and Deedee had their own reasons for me to leave Rattle & Snap sooner than later. They had been terrified that Claudine had bewitched me sufficiently for me to abort my college career and whatever future budded beyond Dartmouth. Mickey's deal with Smoky was that J.T. would be kept at bay but that I had to leave.

The catalyst for my departure had to be severe, beyond debate. The lack of proof would be irrelevant. The aim, rather, was to make things so uncomfortable—and possibly unsafe—that a quick exit would be the only option.

As Claudine spoke, I began knocking on all the doors of my conscience in search of outrage. I thought of something Elijah had told me—the women always leave Rattle & Snap in tears. Well, brother, so do the men.

Surrender was my mode, not outrage. Me, tired: "What about Sallie?"

Claudine put her sunglasses on. "What about her?"

"I think we ought to have a blood test done."

Claudine shook her head. "What good could that possibly do, Jonah? What good could possibly come from it?"

"Perhaps no good at all, but I need to know what's mine in this world."

"And then what? Then what? Do we battle J.T. again?"

"I'm not sure."

"Well, think it through, Jonah! You have a wonderful wife, children you adore. And J.T. won't give her anything if he thinks she's yours."

"Then we won't provoke him; we won't show him the results."

"I can't have more sleight of hand in my life. I can't take it the way you can."

My grandparents were liberated within me. I saw Mickey's frown and Deedee's script: *That one will be just fine.* Claudine cannot have more sleight of hand in her life, yet she invites me back here to pull the most audacious stunt of my life, to abandon my family, to deceive on a massive scale, to break unfathomable laws.

I felt lava coursing down my brow. My head was boiling, but my arms were cold. I felt stalagmites in my fingertips and toes. My lower lip felt huge and absurd, like it belonged to a marionette—tugging downward. Then the vertigo, a storm in my heart, and my rush to balance myself—but not on Claudine, so I moved against the mansion's front wall. Silence, but for a bird pecking in futility at a Corinthian column. Utter clarity, a fleeting biblical thought about the Passover plagues. No, one plague: The slaying of the firstborn. My dizziness fell away. Because I was certain.

I had been the mark.

"You led me to believe Sallie was mine as soon as you needed muscle. I thought your indirection was due to a fear of having a child with gangster blood."

"Oh, for God's sake, Jonah, we all have gangster blood, so don't drag Al Capone into this. I wanted to keep my home and let you get on with your life."

"How long have you known about the Hicksens?"

"Hicksens?"

"Smoky Hicksen bought the name Hilliard."

"When did you know this?"

"Mickey told me when he was here. He checked them out because he thought I was in danger."

"Why didn't you tell me?"

"You were in no position to have believed me then, any more than you wanted to see close up what went on in that valley. Out of sight. I thought you would have investigated J.T. by now. You're good with all that lineage stuff."

"Investigated?" Claudine seemed perplexed. "Heavens, no."

Claudine wasn't so good with lineage she didn't want traced. It was of no use. She had known what she needed to know in order to do what had to be done.

"What does Sallie know?" I asked.

"Everything."

"How long?"

"Around the time Truitt took office. We were watching television, and you were doing one of your briefings. I told her about us. Sallie said, 'You should have married him, not Dad.' I just broke down. I thought she was right."

"We all want to replace our ancestry, don't we?"

"Not me," she said. "I went to Pea Patch Island in Delaware right before I first met you, where the Union held my ancestors as human shields. Maybe there was another way I could have done it."

This was the closest thing to an apology that I'd get from her. Still, I was complicit, as is everyone who is spun.

"No, Claud, there wasn't," I said. I frowned the way Mickey had. "It was the right move because you won more than you lost, but you paid a price."

"There've been times I thought we could have worked."

"Never," I said. "I would have failed you, and you never would have forgiven me for that. With me, you wouldn't have had Rattle & Snap. Someone else would have been living here. Probably J.T. and a mannequin with a fraction of your passion. And you'd be looking at my underwear in the hamper in our little studio apartment with screaming kids thinking, *Some deal I made.* It would all turn to hate. I'd be the gangster's grandson who cost you your home. You won, Claud."

"Jonah. I'm sorry that my purpose in your life has been to destroy your sense of wonder."

"You destroy my sense of romance, Claudine, not my sense of wonder. There's probably a reason for that. Anyhow, I'm glad I came. I couldn't let Rattle & Snap fall into the hands of thieves."

The Panamanian pulled up to the mansion in the government's sexless car. I kissed Claudine good-bye on her cheek. "Well, Claudie," I said inflecting Deedee, "if something comes up, you'll let me know."

DESIGNATED OPPRESSOR

"Weasels don't fare well in sunlight."

The small plane took off to the east from Maury County Airport and flew over Rattle & Snap so quickly that I was unable to reconcile the landscape with my mental image of the place. Sitting on the right side of the plane, I craned my head against the window and watched the north face of the mansion shrink like a Monopoly hotel. I was struck by how small it looked, and how pregnant the region had become with new homes.

The Panamanian fired up his ever-present laptop in a seat across from me as I tried to take in every last bit of Wonderland. Once the fields below became a vague quilt, I felt Marcus's eyes on me. I told him about my discussions with Six, Claudine, and how Grace Slick had awakened me.

"I've finally nailed your vice, Jonah," was the Panamanian's response.

"What are you talking about?"

"Remember when we were younger, the Reagan days, the guys would go out for happy hour after work? Not you. You didn't drink. Some of us would get drunk, troll around, take some girl home we'd never see again. Not you. No drugs. You were afraid of gambling, too. We used to sit around talking about you. What's Jonah's vice? What's his weakness, his kryptonite? We used to wonder if you went skydiving when nobody was around, maybe secretly defying death was your thrill. That wasn't it.

"I know what your jones is now: desire. Romantic passion, not sex even. It's sentiment. That's what Claudine played. A boy without parents or siblings, who lived with gypsy grandparents, either always moving around or fearing it.

"I did an undercover thing years ago. Ran into heroin addicts. I asked one guy who had a needle in his arm what he was thinking about as the heroin went in. He said, 'The next fix.'

"Claudine played that addiction, didn't she, Jonah? That possibility of fairy-tale life on a plantation. Horses and all. Camelot. That's your white rabbit: Arthur and Guinevere. You'll follow that furry little bastard anywhere. She even threw in a new kid, a consolation prize—a family with a lineage. You love your own wife and kids, but you've still got that black hole in there, and that white rabbit keeps burrowing down in there, no?"

I felt the impulse to argue, to deny. That's primal, too. What did Adam and Eve do when they were caught? They covered up, denied.

The alpha and omega were upon me. I was too tired. "Well, Marcus, at least I know it. That's a start, isn't it? I built a real life, didn't I?"

"Yes, Jonah. Despite your handicap, you did."

I closed my eyes to the rasp of Grace Slick admonishing: *"And if you go chasing rabbits, and you know you're going to fall . . ."*

The whole campaign had been about a divorce settlement, no more, no less. If I had to give my debrief a title, it would be *Rattle & Snap: How I Started Another Civil War to Impress My Old Girlfriend.*

To pull it off, I needed to do two things: Exploit a preexisting mind-set—validate the things that people insist upon believing—and leverage a lethal weakness of my adversary.

Modern American history is written by injured parties. Northeasterners harbor a bias that frames Southerners as bullies because of slavery. Nevertheless, there was something I was shocked to learn as an enraptured Southerner in 1980: Much of the South to this day sees itself as an injured party.

Contemporary Southerners did not, of course, support slavery, but they didn't like losing the Civil War either. As the generations passed, any hope of restoring the Lost Cause receded, but something else remained, coursing beneath the surface of the proud society: The specter of arrogant Yankees laughing at them, judging them, inflicting their progressive thoughts on them. As far as Southern life had come since Reconstruction, one sound bite of ridicule by a frizzy-haired Mount Holyoke professor (who just might adopt a Southern accent for her audience's amusement) could push a lot of folks back fifty years—not out of ideological regression, but outrage. There is a twitch in the human chromosome, a visceral antipathy that requires that we unite against a common enemy, fill our villain void, designate an oppressor even if one's differences amounted to *them* just not being *us*. The idea was to offend those who offended us and call it protest. The Confederacy was deader than Jeff Davis, but the politics of humiliation was thriving and in perpetual search of a designated oppressor.

This reservoir of outrage is directed now, as much of it was a century ago, against the federal government. My job: tap it.

The challenge was that I couldn't make it about any of the old Civil War issues—slavery, states' rights—per se. As I learned in the Nashville focus groups, I'd have to make it a coded, thematic, cultural snub: Us versus Them; people we like versus people we don't; tradition over fashion; honorable private citizens versus a rapacious government; relativism versus certitude; fashion versus values; atheism versus God; anarchy versus order; satyrism versus family; Hollywood versus Sunday school; quiche versus cornbread; chablis versus Jack Daniels; Volvos versus Chevy Blazers; "moving on" versus sticking with it; Sodom and Gomorrah versus Johnny Cash and Hank Williams.

There is something in the American psyche that demands just enough disrespect to get us revolting. Nothing will do that quicker than the ancient battle over property rights, who owns what. I remembered from my stay at Rattle & Snap the legends of hidden Confederate gold. What I had not realized was the hold that this folklore had over the huge community of Civil War buffs and reenactors. When I learned of Six Polk's expertise, I knew I had found my flashpoint. Together we would fan the folklore and mobilize enough neo-Confederates to create a media spectacle around Rattle & Snap that would make one J. T. Hilliard very uneasy.

Claudine called Six in Texas, told him to vanish, but bring his cell phone and laptop. It was time for him to stop futzing around about the Civil War and actually ignite one.

Our stunt with the mountainside excavations: We used government satellites to identify mountains in the South that happened to have holes beside them. There were plenty. We then shared these particular computer-generated photos with Global News Network's Enoch Squibbes and other media, claiming this was a significant development. When the media inspected the sites for themselves, they indeed found them to match the satellite images, thereby verifying the pedigree of the information they were getting. We also provided these same reporters with computer-generated photos that purportedly featured the mountainsides one month earlier. These images—doctored, of course—showed that the ground had recently been intact, thereby lending plausibility to the notion that something funky was up. In one of those holes we allowed Squibbes to find the "Tecumseh Thunders" battle cry, which I wrote.

The Civil War historians featured in the news were Six's fellow travelers, who were eager to promulgate their worldviews, not to mention appear on TV.

Once the Confederates had been mobilized, I needed to ratchet up the stakes. We needed to provoke the rebels in order to validate that there was a real conflict brewing, not just nostalgia.

The U.S. government had no more interest in lost Confederate gold than they did launching an invasion of Epcot. Nevertheless, once antigovernment protests had swelled for news helicopters, the government needed to address in some way the grievances at hand, not to mention ensure public safety.

First came the arrival of the Tennessee National Guard. Then came the air force flyover, which had been a twofer. One objective was to incite the neo-Confederates. The ultimate purpose was to frighten J.T., to demonstrate to him that I could summon a greater power and place his coveted—and stolen—crown jewel squarely in the media and government crosshairs. Everything about the Hicksens/Hilliards was corrupt. From the way J.T. had swindled Rattle & Snap to how the family had made its money and fabricated its origins. As I had learned from Mickey years before, weasels don't fare well in sunlight.

Clever, yes, I know. I'm very clever, but not the cleverest, now am I? In the end, the great spinner had been spun: Claudine was slick enough to know that a man in my position—forty something, fatuously sentimental, professionally fallen—would be receptive to believing what I needed to believe. I was treading in that midlife desperation, waltzing with my limitations, where one has to fall back on the surrender of "Well, at least I've got my health." Claudine had schemed out a fresh and mysterious new beginning, all linked to my proven kryptonite: A beauty who arrives in springtime—in this case a femme fatale who might be my own daughter.

The stinging reality was that Rattle & Snap was not my heritage but a daydream I once had; my grandfather was an old crook, not a wise man; my moment at the top of the great American mantel of Displayed Achievement was fleeting, and now over; and Sallie Polk Hilliard had dissolved into just another gorgeous twenty-five-year-old who would not be in my life.

Claudine and I were both romantics, but she, for all her brilliance, wasn't the type to beam it onto another person. Had I been her Last Hurrah before she boarded the bogus U.S.S. *Hilliard*, tied to the dock by her own hemp? Had I been a desperate adolescent strike against Petie? Or had Claudine loved me, as Six had told me in the pond, "as best she could?"

As the plane kissed West Virginia, I decided that the answer to Claudine Polk lay a short swim from South Jersey in the middle of the Delaware River on Pea Patch Island, where some of the South's Immortal 600 had been held before being deployed as human shields in the Civil War's final battles. The Immortals are very much alive in Claudine, and they hold her back from the mortals like me.

The spring and summer of 1980 was a time in my life I think of as Rattle & Snap, that delirious house and its inhabitants serving as a tidy agglomeration of optimism and operatic passion. My reenchantment with the South was the dream of renewal, of rising from ruins, reinventing my own history, playing up the pillared houses, and playing down the pilling green felt of Mickey's casino.

But for Claudine, Rattle & Snap *was* her history, her future, and her true love. Love is your history, that's all. I didn't know whether the antebellum South was the magical place Claudine thought it was, but after a lifetime, one's mental narrative becomes one's operational reality: the glorious Confederacy, its agriculture robust, and its slaves beaming at their good fortune to have been civilized by Christians. And, of course, all that hidden gold Out There to underwrite the Lost Cause. In the death struggle between what might have been and what is, what might have been maintains the perpetual edge.

Perspective marinated by time has a way of dulling some senses and sharpening others. The cast of characters in one's life tends to shift in their placement in that little theater we all have behind our eyes. The narrative of Rattle & Snap has only grown richer. It remains a love story, but the love object is my grandmother. Deedee had called everything right. She was a tactical romantic who stuck by her *gonif* husband and borrowed his methods when she needed to ensure the future of what she loved most in the world—me.

Imagine being loved like that.

Of course, this is the kind of love that goes unappreciated until time has stolen the actors. At some level, human beings are like crows: We dive for whatever shines up at us. The earth tones within our reach have a way of only gaining notice once we know what we're looking for, which is hard when there are a lot of shiny things out there.

Mr. Bruno's murder was the push that initiated my swift slide into the millennium. I think of him sitting lifeless in the front seat of his Chevy, his mouth wide open and dripping blood. He was mocking my generation for growing old in an age of electric gossip, knowing that he wouldn't see it. *My ride stops here, suckers.*

Against the backdrop of volcanoes, ayatollahs, and yellow ribbons, the hot months of 1980 were the spark of America's midlife crisis, which is why I went back looking for direction from Her. It was the emergence of the Sony Walkman, the music device that allowed us to withdraw into our own amphitheaters. When the planet cooled, I read that eighty-two-year-old Ginevra King—the enchantress who once drove F. Scott Fitzgerald to madness but inspired masterpieces—jilted this life without fanfare or confession. And now, midlife: an unprovoked eruption, a sense of running out of gas, nonexistent lovers, taunts, ghosts, the impulse of gunplay—all set against the night sweats of record heat and Devo's "Jocko Homo" pulsing the question, *"Are we not men?"*

PROMENADE

"Old promises get caught up in a dance that seems random."

In the study to the west of the Oval Office, the president eased back onto the sofa. "I must tell you, Jonah, that thing you did to Senator Hunter—"

I recoiled on my end of the sofa, afraid of what was coming next.

"—was the high point of my presidency. Him hopping up and down in that airport security line. I wish I could pull that kind of stuff all day long."

"Say the word, sir."

"Aw, go on! So, when did you know there wasn't any gold?"

"When I read this in nineteen eighty. I made a photocopy of a page in George Washington Polk's diary I thought you'd like." I handed it to him. The president read it aloud:

What rests here in this earth—a few nuggets of History and even fewer of gold—is the sum total of my Trust. If this chest is unearthed, I pray that the intrepid explorer neither digs nor dissembles further in search of treasure that exists only in souls. The silverware that for a time found its home in our columns is with my sensible son Independence, who will use it to eat not to dig. The columns serve the practical purpose for holding up the roof. I accept General Buell's word as a Freemason brother that the pillage is complete. The future of these lands will fall to the Destiny of men much like the Colonel who snapped those withered beans to such smiling Fortune so long ago.

The president set the page down as if it were out of the Dead Sea Scrolls. "Well, well. Despite all this texture, was your old girlfriend impressed?"

"I'm not sure. She's not easy to impress, sir. But she has her home back." I thought of President Carter's words describing the botched attempt to rescue our hostages in Iran: "Incomplete success."

"W. H. Auden said, 'Weeping Eros is the builder of lost cities.' Now your descendants will get to bask in its history."

"I'm afraid not, sir. Sallie is not my daughter. Turns out, my only connection to Rattle & Snap is mental."

The president held the fabric of the window curtain between two fingers. "But Claudine led you to believe that your bond might be something greater?"

"Yes, sir. She did. But I appreciate everything that you did. You were very accommodating. My demands weren't exactly reasonable."

The president rubbed his eyes, "Claudie was always bewitching. Bewitched her father, too," he said, light from the South Lawn lending him a ghostly glow.

I shivered. "Excuse me?"

"Her father, Jonah. Captain Polk." The president let the curtain fall against the window. The natural light receded making him appear human again. "Take a look over there on that table," the great man gestured. "You see my platoon? Khe Sanh Valley. Vietnam. The handsome gent to my right. That's Captain Polk, Claudine's father. Right next to old Dexter. Indy Polk and I had a certain bond. Yes, we did. We were the only two Southerners in that ornery crew. Both Freemasons, too. Talked about all those stories from the Civil War. The gold. General Buell saving his family's home—that whole Freemasons code. We lost Indy, as you surely know, in Khe Sanh. Never found his body to bring him back home. Always haunted me, having that covenant hanging over me. You know, the promises you make when your nerves are raw, the ones you never think you'll have to keep. I always felt it was a sacrilege to even talk about him."

I felt cold pinpricks against my scalp. "Hearing this, sir, is enough to make a guy think this whole drama was put in play by someone more powerful than an aging debutante with liquidity problems."

"Now, don't get too thinky on me, Jonah. As you once said yourself, 'You can only spin a man who wants to be spun.' "

"You needed me on the outside to work this—"

"No, son. See, you're thinking too complex. Complex things never work in a world where human beings are in charge. Only simple things work. Things converge. Old promises get caught up in a dance that seems random. A man finds himself in an elbow-swing with a wobbly Supreme Court nominee and a public that could use a little kick in the overalls from a segment of the population that feels unappreciated—maybe rattle a senator or two into thinking twice about launching a Holy War. Then there's a do-si-do with your partner, an allemande left with an old ghost, and finally a big old promenade with a disciple and whoever he can rustle for one of his miracles, once the good Lord puts him in play. Yessiree, I could go a thousand presidencies without such a convergence."

I searched the president's eyes for a betrayal of cunning, the blueprint of a master plan. I tried to work out the timeline, the exigencies. *He hadn't forced me to make that idiotic remark that put me in the soup.* "It seems like nonsense—"

"Of course it's nonsense, Jonah. The way things come together or fall apart in life. It's nonsense to mortals like you and me, that is. But it's not nonsense if you believe in a larger order that makes the nonsense happen at a given place and time. In which case, it's not nonsense."

"Sir, if I may ask, who is your emissary to that larger order?"

"Aw, son, we've all got prophets who whisper to us in some form or another. This time of year, the Hebrews leave their doors open for Elijah. I can only assume that when Jesus had his Last Supper—some say it was a Passover seder—a door was left open. Who knows who might walk in? A prophet, the devil, God himself, or a spy for the children of Israel—the lovely young granddaughter of my beloved comrade—

just outside these gates no less? Why don't you go on home, son, and pawn the whole thing off on Elijah?"

"As my grandmother used to say, 'Enough already.'"

A soft cackle left the president's throat. "Or, as others say, '*Dayenu*'"

Special Air Mission 14100 departed Andrews Air Force Base in Maryland thirty minutes later and touched down at a private airport in Salem County, New Jersey, twenty-six minutes after that. As I stepped off the plane, I had asked the copilot the call name of the mission. He checked his manifest and curled his lip in a manner reflective of Elvis. He showed me the clipboard. I laughed through my nose.

The rowdy spirits of the Polk boys trailed President Truitt's lonely footsteps along the White House colonnade as he ambled toward the grand but temporary residence. The upright lawman from Oxford, Mississippi, enjoyed a rare snicker celebrating covenants upheld and secrets kept upon being told by the military aide who was his perpetual shadow that Operation Enough Already had been safely completed at longitude 75.37630, latitude 39.66050 in Southern New Jersey. Riptide was home.

MISERLOU

"What's so bad about a beautiful bride?"

A familiar surrender onto a worn couch. The urgent union uncovers bodies lean from training, not youth. These are not the bodies of colts anymore, but aging workhorses that have done all right by time. I feel a hint of panic. *How'm I doin'?* In olden times, there was no tabulation, just feral senses in gyroscopic motion. She feels less illicit than she did once, perhaps because life had since grown from this act, whereas it had once been mischief and sanctuary. The bride is too beautiful, I think, this time in a good way. What's so bad about a beautiful bride?

As horses grind grass between their teeth outside, what happens inside confirms for me that I love her. I know she wonders as she falls onto me, *How'd I do?* She did fine, better than I did. I'm still alive, Pajamas! I worship her after she falls momentarily asleep.

"Oh, you again," I say to my wife when she opens her eyes.

We awake to an unfamiliar whinny. It is a higher-pitched sound than the ones our quarter horses made. I run outside. A dapple gray filly bobs her head wildly in the corral. Yes, yes, yes. I know this animal, don't I? Whoever had dropped off the horse was gone. I approach her slowly and stroke her nose. The sunlight catches a gold plate around her neck. I read it, taking a few moments afterward to collect myself.

My family comes out and marvels at the horse. I disclose our benefactor. Claudine means nothing to the kids, but Edie nods, keeping her protests buried down deep, perhaps with all that Confederate gold.

Ricky sits down on the porch to read his ever-present almanac with

Edie. His profile is his mother's. Lily spins wildly in a tire swing with a neighbor's boy. She is wearing a cowgirl getup: short shorts, a white hat, a yellow-gold vest, an Indian belt holding two toy guns that she made out of Legos—and a pair of slick, white Western boots with nasty heels. Her auburn hair flies up around the brim of her hat as she shouts something at the recoiling boy.

"I don't know where she comes from," Edie says, bewildered.

I do.

Lily will make you bleed if you cross her, but no one bleeds more than she does when she's at war. Lily and the boy are spinning and spinning in the moment as Deedee did so long ago at the dance at Rattle & Snap. She is unaware that someday when she is grown the arc of this boy's life may enrapture her, not because they are destined for each other, but because they are a part of each other.

I turn back to the new horse, and take the gold plate around her neck and see that it reads "Miserlou," the name of the klezmer song we once danced to. On the flip side, there was an engraved verse:

Jonah, Ricky, Lily, Edie
Saddle up, I entreaty
We gamble, spill a kiss
Mark Xs on the map
Spies and haylofts
Rattle and snap.

PART EIGHT

BIG GREEN

SEPTEMBER 1980

An era is said to end when its basic illusions are exhausted.

—Arthur Miller

MATRICULATION

"What I don't teach you, life will."

The gangland war over Atlantic City took fifteen years and two dozen deaths to play out before Angelo Bruno's once mighty Cosa Nostra was reduced to a handful of street-corner hotheads. The leading theory is that Tony Bananas killed Mr. Bruno because he was told he'd be installed as boss by his benefactors in New York in exchange for a greater percentage of the Golden Prospect "skim." An informant later testified that a New York boss called Nunzi had stroked Bananas' vanity, leading him to believe he'd replace Mr. Bruno, only to deny having given the order before the ruling Cosa Nostra commission. The double cross yielded Nunzi Bananas' lucrative New Jersey rackets upon his car-bomb assassination, which left him in pieces. It was a ludicrous gambit, and, if true, meant that the most brutal mob war since prohibition was sparked by a terrible delusion.

The hit on Tony Bananas occurred the day I drove up to Dartmouth with my grandparents in a tan Chevrolet station wagon. As I later determined, Mickey's accompaniment was more than familial support for my matriculation: I was his alibi. We were being shadowed by a nondescript van containing a heavily armed Carvin' Marvin and Fuzzy Marino.

"Just in case" was all Mickey said when I saw them looming in the rearview mirror when we pulled out of the Golden Prospect.

The leaves reddened as we cruised through Vermont. I had a queer thought that the redness may have been due to the planet's embarrassment, but dismissed it, concluding that I was not capable of rational thought by the time we crossed the Connecticut River into Hanover, New Hampshire, and Dartmouth College (longitude 74.63883, latitude 43.70337).

I was so distracted by all of the activity on campus that I drove right by the Hanover Inn. Looping back, the one-way streets brought us face-to-face with the columned façade of Webster Hall. "Again with the pillars," Deedee snapped. Later, walking up Main Street with my grandmother (who was *not*-impressed-with-the-shopping-here-*let-me-tell-you*), we engaged in our final dialectic about Claudine. "I don't know, Deed, I'd always worry that whenever she was out of my sight she'd be cheating on me."

"I have news for you, kiddo, with a girl that pretty, there's always cheating. Either she cheats because she's got all these options, or the man she ends up with cheats because abandonment is the only thing she respects. Knowing you, you'd love her, and she'd never forgive you for it. What I don't teach you, life will."

I nodded as if I understood.

Mickey awaited us on the porch of the Hanover Inn wearing a T-shirt that read BIG GREEN, Dartmouth's incomprehensible "mascot" ever since they kayoed the Indian in the 1970s because of concerns about racism. Seeing this gutter goblin proudly displaying his collegiate shirt struck me as being poetic, a nuanced irony that most people would miss, but would have registered with F. Scott Fitzgerald or another channeler enamored of the American saga.

"Jonah, why is this school so hung up on green?" Deedee asked, shaking her head ruefully at her husband. "It's an awful color for a woman, honest to God."

"Dartmouth only let women in a few years ago," I explained. "Maybe as the place gets more women, they'll change the color."

"What color does that Princeton place have?" she asked.

Mickey got annoyed: "Orange and black. You'd look like a pumpkin."

"What, do I look fat?" To Deedee, fat was on a par with leprosy.

"No," Mickey argued. "Orange and black are colors for Halloween."

"But I'm not getting fat, am I?"

"No. So you wouldn't look like a pumpkin, you'd look like a witch."

"A *witch* I can be. When you're asleep, I'm going to throw you in a-a-a pot and boil you. I already turned you into a bat. Look at you, all wrinkled." Deedee turned to me. "Jonah, I always thought I should have ended up with Peter Lawford. Who I knew, by the way."

A tall girl, hair the shade of autumn, the lingering kiss of windburn on her cheekbones from a late summer sail, walks up holding two unwieldy floor lamps. My heart flutters, and I read it as a betrayal of Claudine. Were my erotic obsessions so cheaply transferable? Was it possible that I was not a romantic at all, but a flake who had bought into his own adolescent histrionics, love sanctified by nothing more than neon? I replayed the wonder in Claudine's eyes when we rode up the Golden Prospect's elevator to meet the Wizard of Odds last spring. I mourned the possibility that Claudine had swooned for the casino's bells, with its Rat Pack patina, and I had been collateral to her core infatuation. It was the first time since I left Tennessee that I began to entertain the possibility of my own survival.

"*You*, with the eyes!" Deedee shouted to the tall girl. With the eyes.

Me?

Kill me now.

"Yes, you," Deedee said. "C'mere. You should be a lighthouse up on a beach with those eyes. This is my grandson, Jonah, and that's Moses. You know Mount Sinai?"

The stunned girl reluctantly said yes.

"Well, honey," Deedee snapped, "He thinks that was him. You should know my grandson."

The poor girl set down her lamps and identified herself as a freshman named Diana.

"*Those* are what you call *eyes*. Gorgeous eyes!" Deedee emphasized adding, "I'm really shallow that way, honey. Now, Jonah, help this beautiful girl with the lights. And be good."

Deedee walked into the Hanover Inn. I buried my face in my palms. When I looked up, I promised Diana I would help her as soon as I finished up with Mickey. She started across Wheelock Street.

"Jonah, of all the things my enemies have tried to do to me over the years—bombs, Castro, tommy guns, poison—she, your grandmother, was the lowest trick in the book!"

"We've both taken shots from women this summer," I said.

"Well, *boychik*, I can't stop you from thinking about your little friend down there. We all think about somebody, I suppose. But you don't want a girl like that. You need to pick a girl you can do business with."

"Do you think you can do business with Deedee?"

"It's been a good deal, actually. In a good deal, it's a draw. With Claudine Polk, you were the mark."

That one burned.

"What did you have on old Smoky, Pop?"

"You remember Mel Sletsky from back home?"

"A little."

"When he sold his sporting goods store and moved from Atlantic City to Stone Harbor, he changed his name to Sinclair. Sinclair, *mein tuchus*. Twenty-five years ago, Smoky Hilliard was Elmer Hicksen from Pulaski. The sticks. J.T. may not know this. The Polks probably don't; they're not the kind of people that go digging. Not anymore anyway. Those old Polks—did you see the eyes on Old Will in that painting? Shot in the face and kept swinging. If Will had lived a few hundred more years, there'd be blackjack tables all over that plantation. Anyhow, Smoky still is who he was. He wants to go back to Pulaski with the other cross burners like Joe Kennedy wanted to go back to running hooch after he had tea with Churchill.

"These investors you told Irv were buying up this plantation—it's Smoky Hilliard. He's got the Polks by the short hairs. He wants this place, preferably with your girlfriend in the boxed set. He's also got some kind of disposal arrangement for chemicals with my friends in New Orleans, too. Works with a law firm down there that does a lot of work for, uh, you know, guys like me. Waste from his plant that should be carted far away is dealt with some other way. Who knows? I just tweaked it. Like me, Jonah, he did what he had to do to get what he's got. He wants Love Canal on his docket like I want Kefauver to come back from the dead. That's what I got from his tell."

I could not think of anything to say, at least not anything intelligent. I just made a pensive face. "Are you going to grab something to eat?"

"Nah, I recently had a banana split," Mickey said, flicking a bug off his wrist. It took years for his pun to register with me. "Now, go help that nice, fancy girl with all the lights."

I cross Wheelock Street glancing backward. The campus green is a whirling panorama of pillars. *"Look!"* Mickey admonishes from the front steps of the Hanover Inn, pointing someplace unspecific out in front of me. This is the abbreviated version of Mickey's patented "pay attention" lecture. The tall parents of other freshmen give Mickey the novelty mien of a cartoon magician. If they only knew, I think.

On the corner of Main and Wheelock, the Dartmouth Aires, the school's a cappela vocal group, are welcoming one thousand men and women to the college of their choice with a riff on Skynyrd's rock anthem, "Free Bird." Mickey takes a cigarette out of a dull gold case and flips it into his mouth. He frisks himself for a lighter. No luck for the Mad Hatter. Carvin' Marvin emerges like a thundercloud from behind a white post to light the cigarette for him. Twenty years since the surgeon general declared tobacco a killer, and this old killer isn't scared. The Arieses' incarnation of Skynyrd echoes against pavement: *"And this bird you cannot change."* Mickey's demeanor hardens as the cigarette begins to ignite orange like the afterburner of a fighter jet. As smoke whispers from his teeth, Marvin, having done his duty, retreats back to the cool shadows, where gangsters and jackrabbits live. My grandfather winks at me as if he knows where treasure is buried.

As Mickey's ash falls to the pavement, my phantom youth goes on the lam.

I'm in play.

ACKNOWLEDGMENTS

Amon Carter Evans, who owned Rattle & Snap for more than a quarter century, was generous with his time and insight. Deane Hendrix, curator of the plantation during the Evans era, was a valuable source of historical information. I also gleaned lots of data from history books such as William R. Polk's *Polk's Folly*. Author Charlotte Hays set me straight on how things work below the Mason-Dixon.

Chris Myers and his Mississippi Mafia have provided a strong foothold for my literary efforts in the Deep South (I'm not talking about South Jersey).

My heartfelt thanks go to old friends in Tennessee who shall remain nameless because their warmth and hospitality so long ago should not be met with unwarranted speculation because of the daydreams of an obsessive adolescent. They may embrace or deny me privately as they wish.

My editor, Sean Desmond, has championed *Spinning Dixie* since well before he was in a position to publish it. Every writer should be so lucky. My new editor, Erin Brown, brilliantly shepherded the book to market. Kris Dahl at ICM gave me permission to shift into a new writing genre, allowing a youthful fantasy to become an actual book. Bob Stein felt the book's sentimental pull in the days when a book contract was just a delusion.

My wife, Donna, and children, Stuart and Eliza, are always my guiding lights. My equestrian partner Eliza was especially helpful with horse knowledge.